SMOKE
on the
WIND

OTHER TITLES BY KELLI ESTES

The Girl Who Wrote in Silk

Today We Go Home

SMOKE on the WIND

A NOVEL

KELLI ESTES

LAKE UNION
PUBLISHING

This is a work of fiction. Names, characters, organizations, places, events, and incidents are either products of the author's imagination or are used fictitiously.

Text copyright © 2025 by Kelli Estes
All rights reserved.

No part of this book may be reproduced, or stored in a retrieval system, or transmitted in any form or by any means, electronic, mechanical, photocopying, recording, or otherwise, without express written permission of the publisher.

Published by Lake Union Publishing, Seattle

www.apub.com

Amazon, the Amazon logo, and Lake Union Publishing are trademarks of Amazon.com, Inc., or its affiliates.

EU product safety contact:
Amazon Media EU S. à r.l.
38, avenue John F. Kennedy, L-1855 Luxembourg
amazonpublishing-gpsr@amazon.com

ISBN-13: 9781662528095 (paperback)
ISBN-13: 9781662528088 (digital)

Cover design by Kathleen Lynch/Black Kat Design
Cover image: © Elena Smirnova, © Westend61, © kampee patisena / Getty;
© Abigail Miles / Arcangel

Printed in the United States of America

For my sons.

*For Riley, who walked the West Highland Way
with me and
who is always up for going on an adventure.
I look forward to our next one!*

*For Rowan, who shares with me a love of stories and a
knack for seeing what others miss.
I am, and will always be, your biggest fan.*

*My boys, as you leave my nest and fly into
the world on your own,
remember that I will always be here as a soft
place to land. I can't
wait to see all the amazing things you are
going to do in life.
I love you both, so much.*

MAP OF SCOTLAND

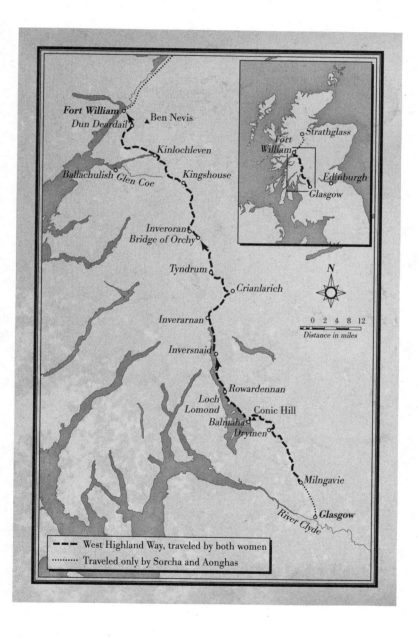

CHAPTER ONE

Sorcha

Whitsunday, 24 May 1801; Srath Ghlais (Strathglass), Scotland

A cry of alarm drifted faintly to Sorcha Chisholm's ears as she pushed to her feet and slapped the cow's rump to move her along after milking. But when she looked down at the village in the strath, she saw nothing amiss.

She told herself it was only children playing, running off their energy before being expected to sit quietly through the Sunday sermon. Sorcha glanced toward the kirk a short distance away. The service would begin soon, but first she needed to carry the milk home, slip into her good church shoes, and collect her son. She hoped he'd remembered to dress in his best trousers and jacket or she'd have to wait while he changed. If they had time, they'd gather wild daisies on the way to the kirk to leave on her other children's graves.

She left the pail on the ground and leaned backward to stretch her aching muscles as she wiped her hands on her apron. Then, indulging in one quiet moment more before facing the day, she pulled her wool *plaide* tighter around her body and let her gaze drift over the greening fields below and the thatched stone cottages that were the homes of her dear friends and neighbors. The gray sky above silvered the Abhainn Ghlais river as it meandered across the wide valley bottom on its way to the North Sea. Her heart felt heavy with love for this place she'd called home since her wedding day twenty-five years past.

When her husband, her sweet Tàm, had brought her to this strath so many years ago, the community had welcomed her as one of their own. Even with Tàm gone now, she never wanted to leave. The valley, its people—even the firs, bracken, heather, and stones—were as much a part of her as her bones and flesh.

A promising ray of sunshine burned through the early-morning cloud cover and warmed the white mutch she wore over her hair. She lifted her face to the sky and let come the memories that were never far but only indulged in during quiet moments such as this. In her mind's eye, she could see Tàm swinging one of their babies high in the air, the babe's squeals underscored by his deep laughter. She saw Tàm and their two boys working side by side, threshing bere in August or telling stories as they cut peat in May. She saw Tàm and their oldest, Dòmhnall, marching off with the Inverness-shire Fencibles to fight in Ireland, neither of them to return but both looking so strong and proud that all she could do was smile.

Another cry of alarm—louder this time, and so unexpected on this blessed morning—caused her eyes to fly open and her breath to catch in her throat.

In the valley below, to the north, a knot of men on horseback was making its way toward a cluster of cottages, including her own, causing an oily coldness to wash over her. She squinted to see them better.

One man, dressed all in black from the rounded hat on the top of his head down to his boots, led the pack of what must be a dozen others. He held the reins in his left hand and carried a club in his right. Why would he have a club?

She took a step forward down the hill and turned her gaze upon the other men in the pack. She stopped breathing. They *all* carried clubs.

A flash of light snapped her attention back to the leader. That was a pistol at his hip, glinting in the sun. Fear slammed through her body like a blow.

And then she saw the smoke.

Every single cottage in the valley behind the men was on fire.

Her own cottage lay directly in their path, and inside was her only living child, her only remaining family.

"Aonghas!"

She shouted his name, although he couldn't possibly hear her from this distance, and started to run, not caring if she drew the men's attention to her. She would welcome their attention if it saved her boy from harm. She focused singularly on her cottage, searching for Aonghas, hoping he'd snuck off with his friends somewhere even though he was supposed to be doing chores.

Running as quickly as the terrain and her bare feet allowed, she flew down the hillside, her gaze searching for him. *Please don't be in the house!*

Pain shot through her foot and up her leg as her bare toes caught on a rock, tripping her. Her legs tangled in her long skirt, and before she knew it, she was on her hands and knees, her palms scraped and bloody.

Cursing her clumsiness, she ignored the pain and raced onward.

There! There was Aonghas, coming from their kale yard at the back of the cottage. He disappeared through the open cottage door and didn't seem to be in any hurry. He must not yet have seen the men who were now in the process of carrying her neighbor Màiri's rocking chair from her cottage and throwing it in her yard as her husband hurried behind, carrying a large chest. Màiri huddled in the yard, holding her children tightly to her side as she screamed at the men to leave them be. The closer Sorcha ran, the more smoke she could smell and the more cries she could hear coming from other homes. She could even taste the burning thatch now, its acrid flavor mixing with the terror already on her tongue.

No matter how fast she ran across the bere and oat fields, it wasn't fast enough. She shouldn't have dawdled on the hillside. She should have finished milking the cow and returned straight home, where she would have been with Aonghas long before the men showed up. She would be there now, keeping him safe.

Keeping Aonghas safe was her reason for living. She would do anything she had to do to see her only remaining child grow to adulthood. His need of her was the only thing that had pulled her from her bed after his brother Dòmhnall's death. It was the only thing that still got her up every morning. She would not fail him.

She was still a full field away when she saw one of the men enter her cottage.

Hot tears dripped down her face, but she didn't bother to wipe them away. She lifted her skirt higher so she could run faster. "Aonghas!" Desperation ripped his name from her throat.

Finally, finally she reached her cottage and rushed inside through the attached byre, calling her son's name yet again.

The sudden darkness of the interior blinded her, and it took a moment before she saw the scene in front of her. Another moment to understand it.

Aonghas stood near the fire, which always burned on the earthen floor in the center of their one-room home. His head was bent down as he stared at the man lying on the ground, unmoving, unconscious, a pool of dark-red blood under his head, his skin gray and waxy.

"Aonghas?"

Her boy lifted his tearstained face to her, and at the expression of horror and guilt she saw there, she decided not to ask him any questions about what had happened. What mattered now was gathering what they could carry and then leaving before the rest of the men arrived.

It was probably best if she didn't know, anyway.

A shout came from the yard outside, and they both jerked as though struck. As Sorcha and her son stared at each other in horror, a voice called out in her native Gaelic, "Cummings, if you're still in there, get out! We're lighting it up!"

And then, to her further horror, Sorcha heard the crackling sound of dry grasses bursting into flame over her head. She tore her gaze away from Aonghas to the pitched ceiling above, where sparks were already drifting down through the thatching and roof timbers. Hens roosting in the rafters squawked in panic and beat their wings frantically as they escaped to the ground, trailing feathers and straw after them.

She didn't spare another glance at the man lying on the floor. "Go!" she yelled to Aonghas. "I'll be right behind you."

Without waiting to see if he obeyed, Sorcha jumped over the man's prone legs and dashed to the box bed in the corner of the room, where she kept her most prized possessions. She wouldn't have time to gather any food, but she wasn't going to leave here without her coin purse. She had a feeling they were going to need every last pence.

With purse in hand, she turned toward the door and found, to her admiration and horror, Aonghas struggling to drag the man's body out. Sparks were falling now, singeing hair and clothing. "Aonghas, go!"

Just then, a loud groan sounded overhead. She looked up in time to see fire race along the roof beams. Every twig of thatching seemed to be aglow. "Run!"

She jumped over the man's body and pushed Aonghas toward the rectangle of light that was the door.

They made it out just as the roof fell with the loudest noise Sorcha had ever heard. Her throat, nose, and eyes burning, and with tears running down her face, she fell to her knees in the yard, coughing. Aonghas dropped beside her.

For several long moments all she could do was cough and fight to draw breath into her smoke-burnt lungs. But then she heard the screams of children. The anguished howls of women. The furious shouts of men. The terror-filled bleats and bellows of goats, sheep, and cows.

Blinking to clear her streaming eyes, she brought into focus her surroundings and wondered if she'd died and gone to hell.

Fire engulfed every house in the strath. Dark-gray smoke rolled into dark-gray clouds, indistinguishable from one another. People and animals rushed about in panic as men on horseback rode past, laughing.

She was unable to move as she took it all in: Her next-door neighbor sitting expressionless and stunned amid a meager pile of belongings; her infant daughter flailing on her lap; her older children clinging to her, crying. Another neighbor gesturing wildly and shouting at Alasdair Macrath, the chief's factor. Factor Macrath resting a hand on the butt of his pistol and sneering back with contempt.

Sorcha blindly reached for Aonghas and pulled him against her side as she watched a man laugh as he slit a goat's throat and left it to bleed out in the mud before spitting insults at the distraught woman who owned the animal. Yet another neighbor clenched her cow's lead tightly and begged the man pulling it away to give it back. "You cannot take our beast! We'll starve without her!"

Starve. The word hit Sorcha like a blade in the chest. It was the truth. They were going to starve without their cows or access to their kale yards, or to the grain growing in the runrig fields. It had been six months since Factor Macrath had served Sorcha and all the villagers a Summons of Removal, signed by their clan chief, An Siosal—the Chisholm. None had believed it would come to this. Their rents were not in arrears. They had the hereditary right to live on this land that they and their ancestors had worked for generations to make productive. The people had nowhere else to go. No money to start over elsewhere. No family in other parts of the country with room or provisions enough to take them in. No industrious skills other than farming.

Sorcha and her neighbors had convinced themselves that An Siosal would never allow matters to come to this. They had believed that *dùthchas*—the hereditary right of occupation rooted by ancient lineage to a particular place that is held by all the people of the clan—would stay An Siosal's hand in his eviction threats. The land belonged to all the people equally, not to An Siosal or his family. They'd thought the chief understood this.

They'd been so wrong.

She must have made a noise, because, suddenly, one of the factor's men stopped in front of her and Aonghas. Sorcha's eyes were drawn to the wooden club he tapped against his leg, and she tasted blood. Dozens of iron nails protruded from the club, and snagged on one was a clump of human hair. "You can remove yourselves from An Siosal's land this minute or I can remove you for him. Your choice."

Sorcha heard more than felt the moan that slipped from her lips. Keeping her eyes on the club, she dragged Aonghas to his feet with her and backed away from the man.

Then, holding tightly to Aonghas's hand, she turned and ran.

CHAPTER TWO

Keaka

Present day; Glasgow, Scotland

The hardest part of being a parent is letting go. For the past two days my son and I have ticked items off his to-do list to settle him in his new university, city, and country. Each tick has turned the vise squeezing my heart a little bit tighter. Colin is starting his exciting adult life, and it's going to be half a world away from me. Getting on that airplane and flying home to Oregon without him seems absolutely impossible right now.

At least we have our hike together first.

Our only commitment today is Colin's meeting with his adviser at the university later this afternoon. Until then, he's dragging me all over the city, playing tourist, and we're both loving it. Even though he's not a Glasgow resident quite yet, he's loved Scotland from a young age, compliments of his father, and is well versed in the country and her people.

We're strolling along the south bank of the River Clyde when Colin announces, "We should pop into the train station and buy our tickets for the morning. I don't know how busy the early trains will be, and I don't want to risk having a late start to our hike."

We take the next bridge across the river, but just as we're halfway across, I spot a carving in the stone side rail, down low near the sidewalk. It's crudely done, but something about it intrigues me and I must stop to run my fingers over the four-petaled flower and the looping four-cornered knot carved behind it.

The moment my fingers touch the rough stone, I feel an intense surge of emotion, and suddenly I'm crying, which I hide from Colin.

But then I feel him looming over me, so I snatch my hand away and force a laugh. "Don't mind me, I'm just being silly." My voice catches in my throat, and it cracks open a truth I didn't plan to say aloud: "I cannot let you go!"

I stand to pull Colin in for a hug, but in doing so, I awkwardly bump into a woman passing on the sidewalk. A wave of dizziness tilts my vision, catching me off guard, and I blindly grab for Colin to steady myself.

"*Gabhaibh mo leisgeul!*" I call to the woman's back as she walks away, though I catch only a glimpse of a dingy gray cap, dark-colored tartan shawl, and long blue skirt swishing with each step before it disappears behind a couple of kids on scooters.

I finally get Colin into my arms for a hug and he allows it, which I'm grateful for, as it eases the confusing jumble of emotions inside me. With one final squeeze, I step back and wipe my eyes. "I promise I won't be this ridiculous all week."

Colin laughs and we resume our walk. "What was that you said back there?"

I look at him to see if he's making a joke. His face shows only mild curiosity. "To that woman? I said, 'Excuse me.'"

He shakes his head. "No, you didn't. You said something in Gaelic. It sounded like '*Gavuhv moh leeshgul.*'"

I can tell by his voice that he isn't pulling my leg. "You must have heard me wrong, with all this road and train noise. All I said was 'Excuse me.'"

He makes an exasperated sound in his throat. "I know what I heard, Mom."

I don't want to fight, so I say the only thing I can think of to smooth things over. "Well, then, I must have heard it somewhere. Or maybe Dad taught me the words and they've been floating around in my subconscious ever since." My deceased husband, Adam, had taken a few Scottish Gaelic language classes, and so it's plausible I'd picked it up from him years ago. Although, why I'd drag it out now is beyond me.

The mystery is soon forgotten as we buy our train tickets, have lunch, and make our way to the University of Glasgow for his meeting.

"Are you sure you don't want me to come in and wait for you?" The building gives me gothic vibes with its multicolored stones in shades from black to beige and numerous arched and mullioned windows. I imagine shadows moving behind the glass.

"No, Mom. I've got this." Colin grasps the strap of the bright-blue backpack hanging from one shoulder. "I expect my meeting to take an hour or so. Why don't you go to the museum or something and I'll call you when I'm done?"

He's so eager to start his new life here that I think he would be fine if I flew home to Portland right now. "Okay, but text or call if you need me, and I'll come right back."

Colin lifts the cell phone we bought yesterday and checks the time. "I've got to go or I'll be late." He starts walking backward away from me. "Have fun exploring!"

I watch him disappear into the old building, and I feel the same as I did the day he started kindergarten. The space around me feels too empty, too quiet. I hate it.

I shake my head and turn back to the main road heading toward the Kelvingrove Museum, which we'd passed on the way here. I don't know what kinds of exhibits the museum holds, but it's as good a way to kill the time as any. Plus, it will keep my mind off Colin's new university life, or my nerves for the coming week.

We are about to set off on a journey that Colin had planned to do with his dad, but then, ten months ago, Adam died, and I had, in a moment of insanity, offered to take my husband's place. I have no idea why I thought I was capable of walking nearly a hundred miles across the Scottish countryside, but in those weeks after Adam's death, when Colin had been utterly gutted from the loss, I didn't want him to also lose the hike that he and his dad had spent years planning and dreaming about. So I'd offered to join him. We start tomorrow morning, walking the West Highland Way from the Glasgow suburb of Milngavie northward. In seven days, we'll arrive in Fort William, where we'll hop on a train to return to Glasgow.

I might be dreading the hike, but it's what comes afterward that I dread the most—when I will hug my boy goodbye and then leave him here. How the hell am I going to get through that if I'm already struggling to be parted from him as he meets with his adviser?

A black-and-white bird with a long tail hops across the paved walkway in front of me; its sudden appearance pulls me from my depressing thoughts. Just ahead I see the massive red sandstone building that is the Kelvingrove Museum, and I make my way inside.

I wander through the varied exhibits on the first floor, then climb the stairs to the second, where I turn into a room that seems to be devoted to Scottish paintings. Several landscapes are displayed on one wall, each looking moody and using a preponderance of brown and gray. I hope the actual Scottish landscape where we'll be hiking in the coming days will be a little greener.

When I see a large painting showing a group of dejected-looking people standing around an old man on a white horse, I stop to inspect it. Both the man and the horse are downcast, their heads lowered and shoulders slumped. A girl standing beside the man has her face buried in her hands as though she's crying. Several of the others have their hands pressed to their chests in obvious sorrow and pain. Their emotions match my own today.

Intrigued, I step closer to the information card on the wall beside the painting and read the title: THE LAST OF THE CLAN, 1865. The artist is Thomas Faed. The card goes on to explain that the painting depicts a family that is homeless and destitute, saying goodbye to family members departing overseas, after being forcibly evicted as part of the Highland Clearances. I snap a photo to show Colin later. He'll be studying history at the university, and I know he'll like this painting.

I move on to the next canvas and am struck by a sudden punch of desperation. The woman in the painting—brown hair streaked with silver peeking out from under a white cap that is tied under her chin, a brown-and-green wool blanket around her shoulders—is looking straight at me as though she's about to step from the painting. Behind her, a building is on fire. Flames leap from the thatched roof high into the sky. To the sides of the small cottage, other homes are also on fire and people are racing about, pulling animals and children away from the flames, dragging heavy chests to safety, kneeling in the dirt, crying. But the woman. The woman captivates me entirely. She's not moving. Her shoulders are drooped; her hands hang limp and empty at her sides. Unlike the dejected Highlanders in the last painting, this woman has her chin lifted as though readying for a fight. And yet the emotion pouring from her is of pain and loneliness. And total claw-at-your-throat desperation.

I can't look away.

A voice speaking from right beside me makes me jump. "*Sorcha Chisholm: Mother, Widow, Innocent.*"

I turn to see a twentysomething man reading the information card posted on the wall. When he sees me looking at him, he smiles wide and points to the card. "That's the name of this painting. *Sorcha Chisholm: Mother, Widow, Innocent.*" The way the Scot says her name, it sounds like *sorduhkuh*. He squints back at the canvas. "Do you think she started the fires?"

I look again at the woman and shake my head. "No, definitely not. She's too sad to be the one who started it."

"Then what is she innocent of?"

I stare at Sorcha Chisholm's face. Her gray eyes, though full of emotion, don't reveal any information. I shrug. "I don't know."

"Well, whatever it is, whoever she is, this painting is fabulous." The young man wanders away, and I stay for a moment longer, trying to discern the woman's secrets.

A text notification buzzes, and I grab my phone from my pocket. It's Colin, ready to meet me. I quickly reply and then, before I head to the exit, I snap a photo of the painting to show him.

An hour later, I've forgotten all about the painting as I follow Colin on a self-guided tour of the city's murals. The incredibly detailed one of Saint Mungo may be the most famous, but I love the one titled *Fellow Glasgow Residents* the best. It depicts a multitude of animals and a pair of feet wearing hiking boots—the perfect emblem for our coming hike.

Later, at dinner, Colin shocks me by ordering a Tennent's Lager. He sees my surprise and explains with a grin, "The drinking age here is eighteen, Mom."

That's going to take some getting used to. I've never before seen my son drink alcohol. "Well, then, make it two. We might as well toast to our adventure."

As we eat, Colin tells me what he can remember of Scotland's history in the areas where we'll be walking. This is my first visit to the country, but Colin was here five years ago with Adam.

Adam's grandmother had been Scottish and had filled his head with stories and his heart with affection for anything and everything having to do with her homeland. Adam had then done the same with Colin. It's why Colin chose to attend university here, and why Colin and Adam had hatched a plan to walk the West Highland Way together before he started classes.

But then Adam's heart gave out. And here I am, in his place.

Colin's thoughts must have been running parallel to mine, because he suddenly sits back in his chair and lets out a long sigh. "I wish Dad was here to see all this with us."

My heart breaks all over again, as it does every time Colin says something about his dad. I squeeze his hand. "I know, sweetie. Me too. He'd be so proud of you, starting college in a couple weeks, doing exactly what you always said you were going to do."

"Thanks, Mom." He returns the squeeze and then pulls away to reach for his pint glass. After drinking deeply, he clears his throat, then lifts his glass higher in a toast. "Anyway, here's to the West Highland Way, and to my mom for walking it with me."

I click my glass against his and drink, hoping to wash down the emotion and bitterness stuck in my throat. Damn Adam for dying. Damn him for leaving our sweet boy to do all this without him.

The beers hit us both hard and cause our fatigue and jet lag to catch up with us. We're back in the hotel and in bed by nine.

Convoluted images and sounds come to me in my dreams. I see Adam and his mistress kissing each other. I see Colin and his backpack walking away from me. The old man on the horse in the painting at the museum lifts his head, and I see tears pooling in his eyes. I toss and turn and, finally, slip into a deeper sleep late in the night.

Fire. I stand in an unfamiliar house with fire eating at the walls and heather-thatched roof. I hear screaming, and I rush outside to find what looks like dozens of similar homes in various stages of burning. Smoke clogs my lungs, and I choke. Terror like nothing I've ever felt before rolls through me, and I fall onto my hands and knees, dry heaving. People are everywhere, screaming, crying, pleading with the men on horseback and on foot, all scowling, shouting, and cursing at me, at my neighbors, like we are nothing more than pigs. "Go!" one of them shouts at me. "Get off my land!"

As I sit amid this horror, a man dressed all in black suddenly jerks his head toward me. His black eyes bore straight into mine with such contempt, such evil, I am certain I am looking at the devil himself. The man stalks toward me, raising his right fist enclosed in a leather glove and brings it down with all his strength, right for my head.

I awake with a jerk a millisecond before the blow hits. It takes a long moment to remember where I am—in Scotland, in a hotel, with

Colin in the next bed. I'm okay. It was only a dream. My heart still pounds loudly in my ears, and my pajamas are damp with sweat.

Water. I need a glass of water.

Moving quietly so I don't wake Colin, I slide my legs off the side of the bed and sit up. But then I see something that terrifies me even more than my dream.

There's a shadow standing in the corner at the other side of Colin's bed, leaning over him. As I stare, the shadow solidifies into the shape of a woman wearing a long skirt and a blanket wrapped around her shoulders. Her features become so crisp in the dark room that I can see she's crying. Waves of pain and longing pour from her. Her long, silver-streaked hair is falling out of a messy braid that hangs over her shoulder. She looks ancient, wrinkled and stooped from a hard life.

I'm frozen in place, no longer scared but confused. Am I still dreaming?

As I watch, the woman reaches out and looks like she's about to embrace Colin, but then she stops and pulls back. After wringing her hands and continuing to cry, she tentatively reaches out again. This time one hand lightly brushes a lock of hair off Colin's forehead.

Colin lets out a deep sigh, as though the touch comforts him in his sleep. I gasp, realizing he feels her touch. Realizing she must be real.

The woman's head snaps up, and as she looks directly at me, I feel like I should know her, have always known her.

Then, suddenly, she disappears. There one moment, gone the next.

I stare at the dark corner where the woman was just a second ago. All I see are the shadows of the window drapes against the dark wall. I blink, hard. When I open my eyes, the shadows have not changed. They are only drapes. I must have still been dreaming.

Water forgotten, I lie back down and close my eyes.

My mind is racing, and so, a minute later, I open my eyes again and stare at the spot where the woman had been standing. No one is there, of course. No one was likely ever there. I *must* have been dreaming.

But I feel wide awake. As awake as I'd been when I saw her.

Deciding I still need that glass of water, I grab my phone from the charger on the nightstand and tiptoe into the bathroom. There, with the light shining bright and confirming that yes, indeed, I am very much awake, I check the time. Four o'clock. Three hours before my alarm is set to go off.

Knowing I won't get any more sleep tonight, I chug a glass of water from the tap, then turn on the shower. Might as well start the day early.

The water washes all thoughts of the ghostly woman away, and in their place come the doubts that have been plaguing me for months: *What if I can't hike that far? Adam should be here like he was supposed to be. But no, he was a master of broken promises. What if I can't do this and I let Colin down?*

My lungs constrict and I open my mouth to take in gulps of air, and choke on water in the process. I'm not even supposed to be here. I was supposed to fly over and meet Adam and Colin in Glasgow after they returned from the hike, and help Colin settle into student housing.

But I'm here now, and I'm doing this hike. And, for Colin's sake, I'm going to like it.

CHAPTER THREE

Sorcha

Five days after eviction; somewhere near An Gearasdan (Fort William)

Terror pushed Sorcha and Aonghas through the first days of walking, for every time she closed her eyes, all she saw was bloodied clubs and raging flames. But then, as fatigue and hunger grew stronger and her body grew weaker with the pain of walking, a new kind of fear pushed Sorcha forward. With no place to call home now, where were they walking to?

All they had were the clothes on their backs, the coin purse she'd managed to grab, and—perhaps most important of all—the clumps of soil and grass she'd pulled from the graveyard that first, terrible day and had stuffed into the tie-on pockets she wore under her skirt. The clumps had no monetary value, of course, but they meant everything to her. No matter what happened to her or where she ended up, with these bits of soil, she'd have a physical connection to three of the children she'd lost.

She didn't even have shoes. Those had burned along with everything else. But, with it being summer, she wouldn't need to worry about cold and ice for several months.

For these past five days, she and Aonghas had followed An Gleann Mòr, the Great Glen, toward the setting sun, knowing that it would take them away from the dangers at home in Srath Ghlais. The journey gave Sorcha time to think and talk over their options with Aonghas and the handful of strangers who'd offered them tea and a place to rest.

One man, a MacDonell living on Loch Garadh whose wife had offered Sorcha and Aonghas a bed in their cottage that first night of their walk, had listened patiently as Sorcha talked of returning to Srath Ghlais. He then had removed his pipe from his lips and bluntly told her, "You cannot go back. That's why the chief's men burned everything—to keep you and all the others from rebuilding. They'd only drive you off the land again. I've seen it happen before and we'll see it again, mark my words."

Sorcha hadn't wanted to believe it, but she knew it was true, knew their only option was to continue. That was exactly what they'd been doing, but they couldn't keep walking like this forever, with no idea where they were walking to.

"We could go to the islands and catch fish for our supper." Aonghas's shoulders slumped with hunger and fatigue even as his eyes sparkled with the dreams he was weaving for their new, unknown future. "Da taught me how to catch trout from the loch. I'm sure the sea wouldn't be much different."

Sorcha smiled at her boy's confidence. "Do you know anyone in the islands who would offer us a home? Or a boat?"

His face scrunched as he considered, then shook his head. A moment later, a wide grin showed his teeth. "Well, then, we can go to North America. They say land is free there for anyone willing to work for it. We know how to work hard, don't we, Ma?"

"That we do, son. That we do." She tugged Aonghas off the side of the narrow path to allow an oncoming cart and pony to pass.

"Feasgar math," the driver called down to them with a friendly tip of his cap.

"Good afternoon," Sorcha replied in kind, wondering if the man had any food in the bags and boxes loaded in the cart. "Can you tell us where this road leads?"

With obvious reluctance, he signaled the pony to stop, and then he leaned one elbow on his knee to peer down at her. "Just around that bend is An Gearasdan—or Fort William, as the troops refer to it. Next to it, the town of Maryburgh. Where're you heading?"

Sorcha exchanged a look with Aonghas. They didn't know where they were heading; that was the problem. She looked back at the man and had to squint as a blast of wind sent tree pollen into her eyes. Since she had no answer to his question, she asked another of her own. "Are there very many troops in An Gearasdan?"

His eyes slid from her to Aonghas and back before he answered, "There are less than there were a few years ago, but the town is still red, if that's what you're asking."

Like all Highlanders, Sorcha had a healthy fear and dislike of the Redcoats and would avoid them if possible. Deciding she'd used enough of this man's time, she wished him a safe journey.

He nodded in reply and clicked the pony's reins. Sorcha waited until he'd disappeared around a bend in the road before nudging Aonghas to resume their walk. "We will avoid An Gearasdan. I don't trust the English."

A short distance down the road, Sorcha remembered their earlier conversation. "I wish I could take you to North America, *a ghràidh*, but we don't have enough to pay for passage."

He nodded and kicked hard at a rock on the path, sending it skittering into the bracken, his disappointment palpable.

She bumped his shoulder with her own. "But we can save up and maybe someday we can go to Alba Nuadh. Would you like that?"

"How do we earn the money?"

She'd been thinking about that. The Highlands offered few opportunities for paid work. Over the years, she'd known several young people who traveled south each year to work on farms or in mills in the Lowlands. At forty-two years old, she might be too old to be hired for many of the jobs, but surely Aonghas could find work, and she could take in laundry or sewing.

"We go to Dùn Èideann," she answered, doing her best to sound excited by the plan. "It's the biggest city in our country. There must be jobs to be had there." She watched his eyes light up even as she squashed down her own misgivings. So many people lived in Edinburgh that they say folks didn't even smile at each other when passing on the street. It was where thieves, murderers, and ladies of the night lived side by side with surgeons, solicitors, and members of the peerage. It sounded like a terrifying, soulless place, but it was the best place to find work.

Just then, Sorcha heard a woman's laugh coming through the trees ahead of them, across the road leading to An Gearasdan. She didn't think anything of it until the strangest sight stopped her feet. Emerging from the trees, laughing, was a dark-haired woman wearing men's trousers alongside a younger man who was much too old for the short trousers he wore. On their backs were bundles like nothing she'd ever seen, in colors brighter than any fabric she'd ever imagined, with straps around their shoulders and waists, with yet another across their chests. The strap clasps looked nothing like the brooch holding her own *plaide* to her chest.

Sorcha stood transfixed as the pair walked toward her.

"Are you sure you don't want to go back and climb Ben Nevis?" the woman asked in a voice so flat and strange, Sorcha knew she was a foreigner. Even more strange, the pair weren't speaking Gaelic, the only language Sorcha had, and yet she understood their words.

"Naw, it's okay, Mom," the young man replied as they passed right by Sorcha and Aonghas without so much as a glance. "I can come up some weekend and climb it."

The pair turned in the direction of An Gearasdan and disappeared into the lengthening shadows.

"That was odd," Sorcha said to Aonghas, who was poking in the vegetation beside the road.

"What was?"

"Those two. The man and woman." At Aonghas's blank face, she asked, "Didn't you see the strange pair?"

He stepped toward her and carefully asked, "What strange pair?"

His confusion made her question her own mind. Had she imagined the encounter? The stress of the past five days, and not having enough to eat, could possibly cause her to see and hear things that weren't there.

And then something fell into place in her memory. The woman had mentioned Beinn Nibheis. They must be near that well-known mountain. Her husband, Tàm, had once told her of a man he'd befriended in the Fencibles who came from the glen at the base of the huge mountain. A Cameron, he was. He'd told Tàm so many stories of his home glen that Tàm had mentioned it to Sorcha. One of the only things she remembered him saying was that the glen was isolated. It sounded like the perfect place for them to spend the night and avoid the English in An Gearasdan.

"Come, we'll go this way." Sorcha crossed the road and entered the trees right where the strange pair had emerged. Only now did she see a footpath leading deeper into the darkening glen.

"How do you know which way to go? I did not see a path here at all."

Sorcha couldn't explain it, even to herself, so she answered vaguely. "This is Gleann Nibheis. Your da once knew a man who lived here. I'm certain we'll be safe."

They followed the path alongside a river much smaller than the one they'd followed through An Gleann Mòr. A short distance later, they came upon a huge round boulder that brought to Sorcha's mind a jumble of memories that made her long for their home in Srath Ghlais.

She laid her palm on the rough, cold surface of the stone and closed her eyes, picturing another stone, miles away, on the hillside above their cottage. In her mind she could see the smiling face of her beloved Tàmhas, her Tàm, as he crouched by that stone on the day of their wedding and carved a symbol into it next to the one his father had carved on his own wedding day.

Suddenly, it was all too much: the horror of their burning cottage, the pain in her legs and feet, the weight of the soil taken from graves of children she'll never see again.

Tears stung her eyes, then spilled over to run down her face. She let them fall unchecked.

"Ma? What is it?"

She had to swallow several times before she could get the words out. "They had no right!" The fury in her voice shocked even herself, and she had to take several deep breaths before she could say again, softer, "They had no right to destroy our home like that."

But then, before the anger could grow stronger and overwhelm her, she pushed it back, took another deep breath, and focused her attention on the rough stone beneath her palm. It felt smooth from years of wind and rain, yet rough where knots of lichen grew, and colder than the air around it. She thought again of the stone back home with Tàm's carving.

"Aonghas, do you have your *sgian-dubh*?" She kept her eyes on the stone and held her hand out for the knife. Aonghas gave her the short one-sided blade that he always kept tucked into his waistband, and she walked around to the other side of the stone so that she was looking back the way they'd come, toward home. There, she crouched low, feeling as though Tàm were right beside her, and set to work.

"What are you doing, Ma?"

She ignored him until she finished, and then she asked, "Remember the family stone at home, on the slope of Càrn na Beinne Bige, where your da and gran-da carved their promises to us?" He nodded.

"Remember the carving Da made?" Before he could reply, she decided to show him so that he'd never forget.

She grabbed his arm and tugged him a short distance away from the stone and then down into a crouch. With her hands, she cleared away old leaves and pebbles until a clear patch of soil remained. With the point of Aonghas's knife, she carefully drew the design in the ground. "Your grandfather carved something like this, a bow and arrow, into the stone as a promise to your grandmother that he would keep her, and all their children to come, fed and safe. He kept that promise until his dying day."

She looked at Aonghas to make sure he was paying attention, then she swiped her hand across the design to erase it and set to work again. "And right beside that carving, your da carved his own promise on the day I became his wife. This knot, with no beginning and no end, shows us his eternal love and his promise to wrap our family in his protection until his dying day." She felt a lump in her throat and had to take a moment before she could go on. "He carved this center circle inside the knot on the day your brother Dòmhnall was born; this flower petal on the right, the morning of your sister, Catrìona's, birth."

"And death." Aonghas had heard this story many times and knew of the sister who'd only lived a few short hours.

Even after all these years, Sorcha felt her heart catch when thinking of her lost baby girl. She traced the pointed oval a second time. "Yes, and her death."

Aonghas took the knife from her and drew the remaining petals sunwise in the dirt. "And this one was for Marcail, this one for Calum, and this one for me."

With the memories of her lost children, she couldn't help but wrap her arms around Aonghas and hug him tight. He allowed this for only a moment before pulling away and tucking the knife back into his waistband. "I know all of this, Ma. Why are you saying it now?"

Sorcha pushed to her feet and put her hands against her lower back to stretch the aching muscles. "Your father kept his promise until he was taken from us in battle. I've been upholding that promise in his stead ever since, and I'm promising you again, right now, that I'll continue to do so, even if we never return to the strath that is our home."

She slung her arm across his shoulders and squeezed, knowing she was straining his short tolerance for physical affection, then gently turned him back toward the boulder and the newly carved flower petal low on its side. "This flower petal matches your father's carvings. But look closely—the point of this petal aligns with the direction from which we just came. I'll carve these along our path, wherever we might travel, so that we can follow them back here when it is safe to return home. When we do return, we'll have to remember that this was our first marking. After this, we must follow An Gleann Mòr and our memories to find home. Do you think you can do that?"

Aonghas shrugged. "You can remind me if I forget."

She grabbed his arm. "You must remember. I might not be with you." That was one thing life had taught her: no one was guaranteed tomorrow. She'd birthed five babies, but only one still lived. She and Tàm had made a home in the same cottage where generations of his family had lived, and yet five days ago they'd been tossed out as though that history meant nothing. She needed to be certain Aonghas could find his own way if something happened to her. "Promise me you'll remember."

He pulled out of her grasp and scowled. "I'll remember."

Knowing she'd have to be satisfied with that answer, she turned back to the river. "I know it's growing dark, but let's go a bit further from the road."

They walked deeper into the glen as the light faded and took the warmth of the day with it. Sorcha yearned for a fire and the comfort of a heather-stuffed mattress, but with no cottages nearby to provide hospitality, they faced another night on the cold, hard ground, one ear open for danger.

Her bare feet ached from miles of scraping against sharp stones and stepping on gorse thorns. Her ankles were swollen from midge bites, despite the bog myrtle she'd crushed and spread on her skin to repel them. Her knees and hips ached from constant movement and sleeping on hard ground. Her whole body hurt, but the pain was nothing compared to the agony in her heart and in her soul.

Her sweet boy had been plagued by nightmares of fire and ghostly spirits and angry men grabbing hold of him. He slept plastered to her side every night in the warmth of her *plaide*.

She couldn't find the words to comfort him, for she was struggling to find peace herself.

The Highlands were all they knew, all she ever wanted to know. They were woven into her body and into her soul as tightly as the weave of her *plaide*, and now they were being forced to leave in order to survive. Who would she become without the mountains, lochs, rivers, and glens? Who was she without her people, her history, her traditions? Three of her children were buried in the kirkyard in Srath Ghlais, and visiting their graves was as important to her as visiting her neighbors and attending Sunday sermon.

She slipped a hand into her pocket to feel the three grass clumps there and told herself this was enough. She'd never been able to visit her husband's or her eldest son's final resting places. They'd both died in different battles in Ireland, fighting with the Inverness-shire Fencibles to suppress the Irish rebellion. Their graves were only imaginary images in her mind, but she often thought that they were lying beneath a field of wildflowers, where she'd one day go, lie down amid the blooms, and finally be able to talk to her dear Tàmhas and sweet Dòmhnall. In the three years since they'd been killed, Sorcha had found a measure of peace with their passing. But she'd never once imagined she wouldn't be buried next to Catrìona, Marcail, and Calum when it was her time.

Holding the grass clumps soothed her. Her children were still with her.

The only way leaving the Highlands, the only way any of this, could be made tolerable was to hope that she and Aonghas would one day return to Srath Ghlais. But the farther Sorcha traveled away from home, the more she was starting to worry that she'd never find her way back. Never be allowed to go back.

Srath Ghlais was all she'd ever wanted. She'd loved the wide, fertile valley cut through by a wandering river. She'd loved the steep hills, green with towering fir trees in some places and, in others, gold as the sunset, dotted with massive gray stones in areas that turned purple with heather in the summer and white with snow in winter. She'd loved watching smoke drift from the stone and thatched cottages that always seemed to have children, dogs, and chickens running freely between them. She'd even loved the runrig fields where she cultivated bere, oats, and potatoes.

Her very favorite moments were in the evenings, when the sun had disappeared behind Creag a' Choire Dhuibh and the valley turned a purple-blue color and someone nearby played pipes or a fiddle. No matter what chore she was in the middle of doing, she'd always stop in these moments, go outside, and take in the blessings of her life.

"*Och*, Ma, do not worry so." Aonghas gave her a one-arm squeeze, and only then did Sorcha realize she was crying again. "We'll figure it out. I'll find us food and a safe place to sleep. Leave it to me."

She smiled to hide the fact that his words broke her heart even more. Aonghas was only fourteen years old. A man, sure, and used to being the man of the house since his father and brother went off to war, but he was still young and shouldn't be burdened this way. He should be caring for their cow in the summer pasture while he flirted with Eilidh, who lived up Gleann Canaich. He should have more years to be young before having to shoulder these big responsibilities.

But even as her heart broke for all that her son had lost, it swelled with pride and love for her boy. He was her joy, and she would stop at nothing to protect him.

Aonghas let go of her and stepped off the path to pull up a bitter vetch root, which he handed to her to chew on to ease her hunger. Sorcha watched him pull up a second one for himself, and she made a silent vow: No matter what they did or where they went from here, they'd go together. She would not be parted from him. Ever.

The glen was being squeezed between two massive mountains, and night was dropping fast. Aonghas handed her a wilting handful of docken to eat, and she was grateful for the nourishment.

When she spied a dark, hulking shape through the trees, she stopped. "Is that a wall?"

It was, indeed, an old drystone wall with a heavy canopy of oak trees overhead. As they rounded one end, they found themselves in an old burial ground with stones standing at odd angles, a testament to the long years since they'd been placed. Sorcha moved toward the upper corner. "Those trees will give us shelter, and the wall will block the wind. We'll sleep there."

Sorcha unfastened the silver brooch pinning her *plaide* at her chest and pulled the blanket free of her belt so she could gather it around both her and Aonghas as they huddled together against the stone wall. The brooch had been a betrothal gift from Tàm, and she was so grateful she'd put it on Whitsunday morning or else it would be burned and buried in the ruins of her home right now.

The brooch was her last remaining connection with her husband, and she dared not risk losing it. She carefully pinned it to her skirt, then she took great care in tucking her bare feet into the warm fabric to protect them from the cold night.

As she drifted to sleep, Sorcha had no idea what tomorrow would bring or whether they'd make it south to Dùn Èideann safely. All she knew was that she'd make certain that wherever they went, she and Aonghas went together.

He cried out in his sleep, and his body jerked. The nightmares were plaguing him again. She wrapped her arm around his shoulders and pulled him close. "*Ist, a ghràidh.* I've got you. You're safe now." It was a promise she felt to the deepest part of her soul. She'd keep Aonghas safe. No matter what it took and no matter how many days she had to walk to find it, she'd find a safe place to make a life for Aonghas. A place that could never again be taken from them.

CHAPTER FOUR

Keaka

Day one; Milngavie

The gray granite obelisk marking the start of the West Highland Way stands proudly in the middle of the walkway, surrounded by a dozen hikers taking pictures and adjusting their packs. Every single one of them looks at least a decade younger than me, and again, I wonder if I'm making a mistake.

We've left our shared suitcase in the lobby of a nearby hotel, where a luggage transport company will pick it up and deliver it to the B and B where we'll sleep tonight. We have everything we might need in day packs on our backs. There's nothing left to do now but walk. I still don't feel ready.

Next to me, Colin is buzzing with excitement as he reads from the dog-eared West Highland Way guidebook he and his dad had used to plan the trek. Despite my fears, his mood is contagious. There was a reason, after all, why my husband and son had dreamed for years of doing this walk and why they both loved Scotland so much. Maybe it'll grow on me this week. I never admitted it to them, but to me, Scotland looks desolate and barren. Coming from the Pacific Northwest, where the mountains are cloaked in conifer forests, the treeless, brown Scottish mountains I've seen in photos look so . . . empty.

I'd always preferred spending vacations at my grandparents' place on the Big Island of Hawaii: swimming in the ocean; shopping at farmers' markets; and sitting under the stars at night, listening to Tutu tell stories of the old ways. Adam had spent vacations in Scotland. I can't even remember now when or why he and I stopped traveling together.

I stand off to the side and watch as Colin safely stows his treasured guidebook in a Ziploc bag and stuffs it into a side pocket of his pack before taking a photo for a group of Belgian men posing around the obelisk.

We take a turn posing for our own photo, and then Colin tucks his fingers around his backpack straps and bounces on the balls of his feet. "Ready?"

"As I'll ever be." I follow Colin under a wide sign emblazoned with the words WEST HIGHLAND WAY and down the sloping sidewalk, past panels of artfully rusted metal showing highlights of the trail—Conic Hill, Rob Roy's Cave, Glen Falloch. Soon we are walking beside a stream that fills the morning air with the trickling sound of water that, combined with the abundant birdsong from the trees all around us, lifts my spirits.

I barely notice when the pavement gives way to crushed gravel and then packed dirt. Several people pass us going the opposite direction, dressed for work or with their dogs, and I assume they are locals. I know we must be passing homes and businesses, but the trees, stream, and all kinds of shrubs and ferns make it feel like we're already in the countryside. Today's forecast calls for overcast skies and rain, but for now, September sunshine is breaking through the clouds and warming the vegetation. I greedily inhale the heady scents. If all of Scotland is like this, I'll be fine.

A small pond appears on my left, and I consider stopping to enjoy the tranquil scene, but Colin is charging ahead—and besides, we've only just started and have about a dozen miles to go today. If I stop at every pretty spot along the way, we'll never reach Fort William.

And I would never have to say goodbye to Colin, says a tiny voice inside me.

I push the traitorous thought away and keep going. But then, at a junction with a side trail, I glance down and see something that stops me in my tracks.

On a boulder, low to the ground, is a carving that reminds me of the one I saw on the bridge in Glasgow yesterday.

I step closer and squat down to get a better look.

It isn't a flower like the one on the bridge, nor does this carving have a Celtic knot of any sort, but it's a single flower petal exactly like the petals of the bridge flower. Its pointed end is upward, toward the top of the rock. Or maybe it's pointing up the trail as a way of telling walkers to go that direction, as much of a way marker as the thistle symbols marking the West Highland Way.

I reach out to touch the carving and feel the cold, rough stone worn smooth by years of rain, wind, and probably other fingers. A sudden and intense surge of urgency fills me, as though I need to go—now. I jerk my hand away and stand up.

What was that?

"Mom, you coming?"

Colin's voice snaps me back to the present, and I hurry to where he's waiting for me a short distance up the trail. The sense of urgency fades as I walk away from the rock, and I decide that it must have been my imagination. I was only feeling Colin's excitement and my own anxiety about the hike.

I catch up to where Colin waits, drinking from his water bottle. "Sorry. I saw a rock carving that reminded me of the one we saw on the bridge yesterday."

"What carving on the bridge?"

Surprised, I look at his face but find Colin with only a mild expression of interest and confusion. "You didn't see that carving on the bridge right before we went to the train station? A flower and four-cornered knot?"

He shakes his head and returns his water bottle to his backpack side pocket. "Nope. Nothing but smooth cement. Was that when you magically knew Gaelic?"

I look back toward the pond and see that a turn of the trail has hidden the rock from view. I don't understand what that whole Gaelic thing was yesterday, and was hoping Colin had forgotten about it. Apparently not. I regret saying anything about the carving. "Never mind. Let's keep going."

Soon we come to a deserted road that the way markers tell us to follow for a short jaunt before the trail picks up again on the other side. Now we have woods on our right and a wide, grassy meadow on our left, and I know for certain that we're finally in the countryside. To my delight, blue lilies, white daisies, and red crocosmia are blooming throughout the meadow. I breathe deeply and, again, feel like this is going to be an enjoyable experience after all. I was worried for nothing.

We pass a lovely lake a short distance from the trail and soon come upon a quirky house with a sign proclaiming it to be THE SHIRE. Colin, a big J.R.R. Tolkien fan, poses for a photo.

Farther on, we reach a set of squeaking gates at the top of a small hill. I feel weird about opening gates and walking through onto what seems to be private property. This kind of thing could get a person shot in the States, where farmers don't take kindly to strangers stepping foot on their land.

I mention this to Colin as he opens the first of the double gates, and his answer is surprising. "There's this thing called the Scottish Outdoor Access Code. It basically allows the public the right to cross private land and fields as long as we don't disturb livestock or cause any damage."

I'm impressed. "Wow. I wish we had that back home."

I open the second gate and wait for him to pass through before closing it behind us. When I turn and see the view spread before me, I gasp.

From where we stand, the trail snakes down into a wide, green valley and disappears behind a steeply rounded, tree-covered hill that surely must have been an ancient place of pagan worship, or maybe the site of a castle for kings of old. Far to the north, I can see looming purple mountains that must be the famous Scottish Highlands.

Nearly everything I look at is either green or purple—purple thistle, purple heather, purple verbena, green grass, green trees, green moss. As we quietly take it all in, I hear sheep bleating in the distance.

If I doubted it before, I would now know for sure that I'm in Scotland. To my delight, it is so much more than bare, empty mountains.

"See that white building with the steam coming from the top?" Colin asks a short while later and points to the base of the mountain to our right. "That's the only whisky distillery we're going to pass the entire way. I think we should stop."

The detour is a short one. I nod. "When in Scotland, right?"

We take the branch trail that leads to the distillery, cross the road, and find the visitors' center, where we decide to partake in a tasting. An hour later, I can't stop giggling as we step over piles of sheep poop in the field we have to cross to return to the trail. "Sorry I embarrassed you back there by asking for a Coke."

Colin groans, but then he, too, is laughing. "Now we know that it's blasphemous to mix whisky with anything but a couple drops of water."

"We should have lunch soon, though." I open the gate for Colin, then close it behind us as we step back onto the official trail. "My stomach is on fire from all that alcohol."

"There's a place just up here that Dad's guidebook recommends."

True to his word, we soon come upon a cute stop that seems to be a combination of a small farm, picnic area, and restaurant. Other walkers are lounging beside their backpacks on picnic tables scattered across the grass.

After ordering at the counter, we find a table just outside, where we happily drop our packs on the ground and sink onto benches. It's not until I'm sitting that I notice how stiff and sore my hips and feet have already become. I can't hold in a sigh. "I don't think I've ever appreciated a seat more than I do now."

A man at the next table laughs at my words, and he leans toward us conspiratorially. "I know what you mean. And we've still got at least five more miles to go today." His accent forces me to listen very carefully in order to understand him. "Unless you're stopping somewhere other than Drymen, of course." His eyes drop to my pack.

I see the two teenage girls with him whose light-blond hair matches his own, and decide he must be a father traveling with his daughters.

"We'll be in a bed-and-breakfast in Drymen," I tell him, then, glancing at his huge pack, ask, "And you? Are you camping?"

"My younger daughter, Terese, wished to stay in hotels, but my oldest here insisted we camp." His laughter is warm. "Ask me in a couple days if that was a good idea or not."

I laugh along with him and notice with interest that the older daughter and Colin have struck up their own conversation. I catch the girl saying something about Copenhagen. "Are you from Denmark?"

The arrival of our food keeps him from answering, and he sips his coffee as he waits. When the server moves away, he says, "We live in Copenhagen. What about you and . . . ?"

"This is my son, Colin." Hearing his name, Colin gives the man a quick smile and wave before turning back to the girl. "I'm Keaka. We're from the US."

"I have never heard your name before." Then, as though worried he is being rude, he quickly adds, "It is beautiful."

"Thank you. I'm of Japanese and Hawaiian descent. My name means *person of shadows*. I think my parents thought it sounded dramatic." I laugh to cover my sudden embarrassment; I feel like I'm talking about myself too much.

"I am Jorgen, and these are my daughters, Kirsten and Terese. I don't know what any of our names mean." A gleam in his eye tells me he is teasing, and I find myself warming to him. We continue chatting as I eat, and, I notice, he and his daughters seem in no hurry to leave even though their own food is long gone.

"Mom, you've gotta try this haggis," Colin tells me during a break in the conversation. "It's some of the best I've had."

I wave him away. "No thanks. I appreciate the cultural aspect of it, but if I ever go back to eating meat, it's certainly not going to include entrails."

He backs down. "Fine. Then try this soda. It's called IRN-BRU, and it sells better than Coke over here."

I sip the orange-colored drink, expecting an orange flavor, so I'm surprised to find it tastes like bubble gum. "Oh, wow, that is good. Super sweet but good."

As the conversation continues with Jorgen and his daughters, we learn this is the second long-distance hike they've done together. "My wife, before she passed, did not enjoy hiking, so we never went as a family. Kirsten convinced us to walk the Camino Ingles in Spain last year, and we were all surprised to find that we loved it, so here we are on a trail again. Terese chose the West Highland Way."

"I'm sorry to hear you lost your wife." I swallow and shoot a glance at Colin. "My husband died last autumn."

Jorgen puts his hand on my arm but quickly yanks it back, as though realizing he might have gone too far. "My sympathies."

The conversation turns to castles in Scotland, and since I haven't seen any of them, my mind wanders. With my stomach full of roasted vegetable sandwich, I'm content and could happily be finished walking for the day. Maybe even take a nap.

An image of the woman standing over Colin's bed last night comes to mind, and I inwardly shudder. What was that? I know it wasn't a dream. Was the woman a ghost? Or simply a trick of my imagination due to jet lag and stress?

Whatever it was, I hope she stays far away from me and Colin tonight. I need sleep if I expect to survive this hike.

I realize Colin is piling our empty dishes on a tray and the Danish family is shrugging on their backpacks. Before Colin can grab my glass, I pick it up and finish off the last of the water. Then I get to my feet, ignoring my aching muscles, and pull on my pack.

Together, with Jorgen and his girls, we return to the trail and turn northward.

Something has shifted in me, and the joy I found in walking this morning has disappeared. My feet hurt, my back aches, my hips protest each step. Each mile feels like ten, and all I want is to get to our bed-and-breakfast and take off my heavy boots. Maybe take a bath. Definitely take a nap.

It takes all my energy to keep up my side of the conversation. After a few miles of farmland, we find ourselves walking on a paved road, which causes my feet to throb with each step as though bruises have formed on the pads.

Right now, I'm hating my boots, hating my backpack, and hating my husband for dying and not being here instead. I hate that I have to pretend we had a good marriage, and I hate that I felt only relief when he died.

My fingers are swollen from swinging at my sides all day, and my wedding band feels tight on my finger, reminding me of its presence and mocking my sham of a marriage. I should have removed it after Adam died, but I didn't want Colin to become suspicious. So I kept it on and never found the right time to remove it without it being a *thing*.

Except now I wish I'd taken it off this morning, before this blasted hike.

Colin is walking with Kirsten and Terese up ahead, which leaves me with Jorgen. All three kids look like they could keep walking for another twelve miles. They practically skip with each step, and their chatter and laughter fills the air like birdsong.

Jorgen and I, however, have fallen into a companionable silence, which I'm grateful for. Fatigue is making me feel like I'm walking through mud, and it certainly isn't helping my emotions any. If we don't get to Drymen soon, I might not make it.

"Girls," Jorgen suddenly calls out, making me jump. "This is our campsite." He points to a fenced yard behind a farm building with a sign on the side announcing the fee to pitch a tent. It's much cheaper than the cost of the B and B we'll be staying in, and I can't decide if I'm smart for booking comfortable accommodation or foolish for spending so much money.

Colin and I bid them goodbye, and Jorgen says he hopes to see us again tomorrow. They wave and step through a swing gate into the yard, where I see other tents already set up and people lounging on the grass.

As Colin and I walk our final mile into town side by side, I do my best to hide my cranky mood from him. "They're nice."

Colin shoots me a wide grin. "Yes, they are. Jorgen sure seemed happy to spend the afternoon with you."

At first I think he is making a crack at my surly attitude, and I open my mouth to explain, but then I see he is chuckling. "What are you saying?"

"You seriously don't know?" Colin stops walking to turn and face me. "Mom, the guy likes you. He was flirting with you."

I wave my hand to brush off the suggestion and keep walking. "No, he wasn't." To change the subject, I tease, "Not like you were flirting with Kirsten."

Colin blushes, which makes me laugh and lightens my mood. I sling my arm around his shoulders. "Come on, there's a bed somewhere calling my name."

Colin suddenly freezes. "Mom, look! That's Loch Lomond!"

I look to where he's pointing, and sure enough, there in the distance, I can just make out a body of water shining in the late-afternoon sun. The water gleams like silver, and I realize I am looking forward to tomorrow, when we'll walk along its famous banks.

I know Colin has been eager to reach the loch since we first touched down in Glasgow. He and his dad stayed a night on the loch, in the town of Luss, during their vacation here five years ago. "Wow, Colin. We're really here, aren't we?"

"I didn't think we'd see it until tomorrow, from Conic Hill." His whole face is alight with joy, but then his smile falls and a shadow crosses his features. His eyes meet mine, and I see tears welling against the chocolate brown. "I really wish Dad was here."

Feeling a sting in my own throat, I rub his shoulder in comfort. "Yeah. He would've loved this hike with you."

"Do you miss him, Mom? You don't talk about him much."

I don't know how to answer, so I resume walking as I think it through. As far as Colin knows, Adam had died in love with his wife. His cheating had been a secret we both kept from our son. I swallow, then nod. "I do, sweetheart. Every day. I guess I'm still just getting used to him being gone." None of that is, technically, a lie. I do miss the Adam I knew and loved years ago, and I still forget that he's not a phone call away.

Colin stops in the middle of the road and pulls me to him for a hug. Our packs make it awkward, but I relish the moment. I hate lying to my kid, but I will to protect him from the truth. Besides, there's no reason to hurt him now. Adam is gone, and Colin need never know that his father was capable of betraying and deserting his family.

I hold on to Colin, imprinting the feel of his body in my arms, knowing I will call on this memory when we are separated by half a world.

When we break apart, I swipe at the tears in my eyes.

"It's okay, Mom." Colin pats my shoulder. "He lived a good life."

I nod, move my feet forward, and let my son think I'm crying over my dead husband.

CHAPTER FIVE

Sorcha

Six days since leaving Srath Ghlais; somewhere beyond Gleann Nibheis

For over an hour they trudged upward through the damp, misty forest, and Sorcha wondered if they'd ever reach the top. Her legs and lungs felt strained to their limits. Another route may have been better, but this path led away from An Gearasdan and to the south, toward Dùn Èideann.

Aonghas had gone on ahead. She was starting to worry about him when she heard him shout, "Ma! I can see for miles up here!"

When she finally broke free from the trees and caught up to Aonghas on a rocky knoll, she could barely believe her own eyes. The early-morning rain had burned away with the rising sun, and now steam rose in curls from the boulders. Far below lay the deep green and far-stretching cut that was Gleann Nibheis. At the very bottom of the mountain upon which she stood wound a thread of brown river cutting through the green—the same river they'd followed yesterday evening. Almost immediately on the other side of the river, steep slopes climbed up and didn't stop until they towered over her head across the valley in the form of Beinn Nibheis, so close and yet enormous and out of reach. A gust of wind started her heart pounding even harder than it already was from the climb. If she wasn't careful, the wind might blow her right off the edge.

Clouds hugged the top of Beinn Nibheis, obscuring it from view, but it was the northern view that clutched at her throat. She could see An Gleann Mòr, where the river they'd followed flowed southward into the great loch that bordered An Gearasdan and the town of Maryburgh.

Beyond it lay mountains, gray in the mist. Somewhere beyond that, farther than her eyes could see, was home. The home she'd been brutally driven from and told to never return to. The home where pieces of her heart lay buried in the cemetery. The home where she'd expected to one day see Aonghas marry a sweet girl and raise babies of their own.

Memories flooded her mind of all the days and nights she'd spent there—laughing, planting, crying, milking, dyeing, spinning, hoping, praying . . . She knew she could not return, at least not now, so why was Srath Ghlais calling to her, tugging on her across all these miles, pulling her back? Why couldn't it let her go?

Aonghas placed his arm around her shoulders and squeezed. She couldn't look at him or she'd break down. If she started crying, she might not stop.

After forcing a breath into her lungs, she swallowed and then cleared her throat. Giving voice to one last hope, she said, "Maybe we can go back. They said they wanted us gone to make room for sheep, but surely even sheep need tending. You could work for the shepherd and I could work for the family up at the castle. If we could make them understand—"

"They don't want us," Aonghas interrupted. "They would only force us away again."

"But we paid our rents and were never late. We were making them money."

Aonghas, looking much older than his years and reminding her so much of his father, shook his head. "No, not the amount of money that sheep will bring."

"But it is our home! Since when are people worth less than farm animals? Tell me that."

Aonghas only frowned, his gaze on the valley in the distance. Sorcha's gaze, too, was drawn back northward. They stood in silence for several minutes with only the sound of the wind whipping around them.

Remembering the plan she'd devised last evening, she gently slipped Aonghas's knife from his belt and left him to his thoughts as she hunkered down beside a large stone. An Siosal might not want them now, but one day they might be able to return to Srath Ghlais, and Sorcha was going to make sure they found their way. The soft limestone yielded quickly to the blade, and soon a flower petal emerged, pointing to the path down the mountain. When it was finished, she rubbed her hand over it, wiping away the last of the dust and feeling the rough edges catching on her calloused palms. She was not as skilled at carving as her Tàm had been, but anyone could clearly see it was a flower petal if they knew what to look for. The only people who needed to know were herself and Aonghas. If others discovered her carvings, let them wonder.

She pushed stiffly to her feet. Movement far in the distance, at the opening to Gleann Nibheis, caught her attention and she paused, squinted. She knew there were no wolves or bears left in Scotland, but that didn't mean she shouldn't be alert to other dangers.

As she watched, a man dressed all in black and riding a horse of the same color, so that she couldn't discern where the man's body stopped and the horse's began, emerged from behind a grove of trees. Another man on a chestnut-colored horse followed him toward An Gearasdan.

Something about them appeared sinister, or maybe that was only her imagination. They were, after all, too far away for her to see details. But, whatever caused it, a shiver went down her back, and she tucked

Aonghas's knife into her own belt before pulling her *plaide* tighter around her shoulders. "Come, son. We must go."

She turned her back on her last view toward home and walked away, every inch of her body screaming that this was wrong, she was going in the wrong direction. She ignored it and kept walking over the top of the hill and into another forest.

Her blood ran with Highland water. Her heart beat with the skirl of the pipes. Her bones were lichen-covered stone, her skin the hides of stags on the moor. With all this stripped from her, how would she keep from withering away to nothing?

CHAPTER SIX

Keaka

Day one, evening: Drymen

By the time we reach the village of Drymen, my emotions are all over the place. I'm fighting back irrational tears that aren't from the pain in my feet and hips, although that is intense. The tears are solely from my thoughts. I hadn't realized this hike would involve all this thinking time, and I'm unprepared for it. I hadn't prepared my body enough—daily walks in my neighborhood clearly hadn't been sufficient—but it's my thoughts that are doing me in right now.

I feel like I'm losing my son at the end of this week. I'm losing my identity at the end of this week.

I once had dreams of a glamorous career that would take me all over the world, but I got married right out of college, and after two miscarriages, Colin's arrival turned my life upside down in the most joyous, all-encompassing way. I loved being a mom. Loved volunteering in his classrooms, running the PTA, organizing sports banquets. I loved sending him out the door in the morning with a healthy packed lunch and greeting him at the end of the day with a warm dinner. I never resented the late nights, the worries, the demands on my time, because I was so happy being his mom. It's who I am.

All that is ending.

What am I going to do with myself now? I've been working part-time at the boutique, but I've always known it was temporary and I'd find something else when Colin goes off to college. I still have no idea what that will be, but it needs to pay more than the boutique if I hope to support myself. Adam had arranged for Colin's college fund, but little else.

The fact was, Adam had spent all our savings on a new house for him and his girlfriend, putting it only in the girlfriend's name, as though he somehow knew a heart attack would strike him down before he could divorce me.

I have a small amount coming from Adam's 401k and life insurance, but it's not enough to support me for the rest of my life. I should probably sell our house and get a smaller place since I'll be living alone now. I definitely need to find a full-time job. Soon.

But who is going to hire someone who spent the last two decades being a mother? No one, that's who. Society does not value motherhood as a marketable skill, even though mothers utilize a whole grab bag of skills that would make any company successful.

With absolutely nothing left in my tank, I'm dragging behind Colin along the sidewalk. I thought we'd be there by now. "Where's our B and B?"

I don't mean for my words to sound so grumpy, but Colin, bless him, ignores my tone. "I'm not entirely sure, but they said it's close to the center of the village. Hang on, we're almost there."

By the time we find the B and B, we're both starving. We drop our bags and go right back out for dinner at a local pub. Afterward, back in our room, we each shower, and then I leave Colin writing in his journal and go outside to the garden for some fresh air and room to think. My body feels lighter without my backpack, my feet pampered by the sneakers I'm wearing. I'm hopeful that after a good night's rest, I'll be ready for tomorrow's miles.

As I close the front door behind me, I see that the sky is dark with cloud cover. The forecasted rain will fall soon; I can smell it. A cold breeze shakes the rowan trees in the yard, and I'm grateful for the fleece jacket I threw on. The yard is tiny but filled with ferns, hydrangeas, and laurel. The moist evening air and the rich scent of fecund earth remind me of home, which comforts me.

What a day this has been. I drop onto a stone bench set under the trees and think through the roller coaster of emotions I'd felt. Tomorrow, I'll do better. I won't allow myself to get into my head so much. I won't think about leaving Colin at the university, and I definitely won't think about Adam. No, tomorrow—and every day for the rest of my time with Colin—I'll stay present in the moment and build lasting memories with him.

I lean against the backrest and close my eyes, trying to control the emotions raging through me.

Without warning, a wave of dizziness swamps me, and a loud roaring sound fills my brain. Alarmed, I open my eyes to steady myself. The scent of roasting meat dances on the breeze, and I wonder if our host is cooking dinner.

The peaceful garden is working its magic, and I settle heavier against the cold stone bench. I should probably head upstairs and call it a night, but I want to enjoy this moment a little longer. I close my eyes again.

The dizziness roars back in full force. Shaken, I open my eyes.

But this time the garden is gone, and I am suddenly inside a burning building. Smoke claws at my throat and stings my eyes.

Fear like none I've ever felt in my life slams through me. I'm going to die here. I know it. Flames crawl along the heavy wooden beams holding up the smoldering ceiling. A man is lying on the ground. I don't know who he is, but I feel afraid of him, even though he's unconscious. A loud creaking sound fills my ears, and I know I have only seconds before the burning timbers fall on top of me, trapping me, killing me.

But I can't leave yet. There's something I need. Some treasured possession, although I can't think of what it is. I hurry to a wooden cupboard in the corner and pull open the doors. The bed inside surprises me.

"Ma!"

The call curdles my blood. Colin is here? When I turn to tell him to run, I'm shocked to see that it isn't Colin at all, but a younger boy wearing old-fashioned clothes, his face streaked with dirt and tears. "Go! Run!" I choke on the smoke.

But it's too late. The roof is fully engulfed in flames and the timbers are falling. I run toward the boy who is not Colin. I don't have time to worry about the unconscious man. I leap over him, grab the boy's arm, and tug him through the side room toward the bright patch of sunlight that is the door. As we draw near, the sound of evil laughter fills my ears, and I'm terrified of what awaits us outside. But I have no choice. We must escape the flames.

The very second I rush into the sunlight, my brain explodes in pain and I fall to my knees on the ground, cradling my head in both arms.

The quiet penetrates my aching brain, and I drop my arms, open my eyes. It is dark, not light.

I look around in shock. I'm not outside a burning building with some evil spirit laughing at me. I'm crouched on the ground in the front yard of my B and B in Drymen, Scotland.

What just happened? Is my emotional state so fragile over the idea of leaving my son here that I've lost all sense of reality?

A burning in my lungs and throat sets off a coughing fit that brings tears to my eyes and leaves me fighting for breath. My throat feels seared, as though I really have just emerged from a burning building.

I slide back onto the bench and wrap my arms around my middle. I must have imagined it. It's been a long day, and I haven't had good sleep the last three nights, so of course I'm not feeling my best.

Something about that burning cottage niggles at me, and I suddenly realize why that is. The painting. The painting of the woman, at the Kelvingrove Museum.

My hands shake as I take my phone from my pocket and pull up the photo I snapped. There is the woman, standing in front of the burning cottages, emotion pouring off her.

I know that cottage behind her. I was in it just moments ago.

And I know this woman. I *was* her.

I swipe right and then left, looking for a photo of the title card that had been tacked on the wall next to the painting. I want to read the title again, and the name of the artist, and see when it was painted.

But I don't have the photo. I remember now that Colin texted me and I was in a rush to meet him. I must have forgotten to take a picture of the card.

But the young man in the museum had read the title aloud to me. What was it?

I search the woman's face, and suddenly it comes to me: *Sorcha Chisholm: Mother, Widow, Innocent.*

And then something else clicks into place in my aching head. This is the same woman I saw standing over Colin's bed last night. Without a doubt, I know it is her.

Did the painting affect me so deeply that it seeped into my subconscious to torment me with lucid dreams and visions?

Or is something else going on?

Is Sorcha Chisholm haunting me?

An owl hoots in the nearby trees, making me jump. Once I realize it's only an owl and not a ghost, I relax and then notice that I'm shivering in the damp night air. Feeling ridiculous and hoping no one has seen me out here acting like a madwoman, I rub my palms over my face, and then, with my entire body aching as though I've been in a wrestling match, I push to my feet.

I limp into the building and up the stairs to the room I share with Colin, and a thought blooms in my mind. Maybe I could talk Colin into renting a car tomorrow and driving through the Highlands instead of walking all week. We would still be spending quality time together, but in a way that would allow for more rest.

Because right now, I'm losing my grip on my sanity.

CHAPTER SEVEN

Sorcha

On the pass between Gleann Nibheis and Loch Lìobhann (Loch Leven)

Late in the day, Sorcha knew they needed to stop soon to rest, but there was no shelter in sight. The military road on which they walked led them through a wide pass between mountains, all of it entirely bare of trees.

Military roads such as this one had been built to suppress the Highland people after the last Jacobite uprising failed at Culloden fifty-five years ago, in 1746. Many atrocities had been committed against Highlanders over the last half century, and Sorcha was fully aware of the cruelties practiced by those the government put in positions of power. Even though she and Aonghas were not causing trouble of any sort, Sorcha was still nervous to be out in the open like this, where English troops, or others equally untrustworthy, might happen upon them.

To add to her strain, they were hungry. Early this morning they'd come upon several shielings, where one of the women tending cattle had given Sorcha a block of cheese, which she and Aonghas ate immediately.

Now, hours later, there was nothing to ease their hunger, not even wild leaves, for all had been nibbled to the ground. Cold wind blew through the pass and cut right through their clothing. If they stopped for the night here, she was afraid they'd freeze to death. Her toes had gone numb hours ago.

They continued walking as shadows climbed from the valley bottom to the tops of the mountains. She was so tired, cold, and hungry that it took several moments before she realized she was hearing a new, but familiar, sound.

They came over the top of a rise and saw, clumped in a mass beside the river, at least a hundred black cattle. Surrounding them, and clearly keeping watch for reivers, were four rough-looking men, each wearing a blue bonnet and some version of wool trousers and coat with a *plaide* across their shoulders held fast by the belts at their waists. One of the drovers whistled a command, and a black-and-white collie raced to maneuver a straying cow back into the herd.

Sorcha patted her head to make sure her mutch was tied in place. As she and Aonghas drew nearer to the herd, she noticed, with a stab of fear, that the drover closest to them had what looked to be a long, pointed dagger and a pistol stuck into his belt. In his hand he held a long crook. She couldn't remember the drovers who passed through Srath Ghlais wearing pistols, and she wondered if it reflected the danger in these parts, or the danger of these particular men.

She looped her arm through Aonghas's and quickened her steps.

The drover with the pistol touched his fingers to the flat brim of his cap and asked, *"Ciamar a tha sibh?"*

"We are well, thank you," she replied. "Where are you taking your herd?"

The man whistled for his dog, who came trotting up beside him with his tongue hanging out, looking like he had a big grin to match his master's. As the drover scratched the dog's neck, he said, "Craoibh with this lot, but we've come as far as we can for the day." He motioned toward his mate, who was bent over what looked to be an injured hoof of one of the larger cows. "You're welcome to make camp with us for the night. The beasts provide a lot of warmth, if you can stand their stink."

Animal smells had never bothered Sorcha, and the promise of warmth sounded very appealing. But it would be highly inappropriate for a woman to spend the night in the company of four strange men. "Thank you, truly, but we'll continue on our way."

"Ma." The way he said her name told her that Aonghas wanted to stay. She ignored him.

The drover was staring hard at her face, and Sorcha looked away, uncomfortable under his scrutiny. She tightened her hold on Aonghas's arm, which the drover clearly took note of. "If it's safety that has you concerned, I can promise you, missus, that you'll be safer with my men and me than out there on your own." He scratched the dog's neck. "And if it's us that's causing you worry, let me tell you that we each have a wife at home who'd skin our hides for leaving a woman and young man to fend for themselves on a cold night such as this one."

His straightforward manner and concern for their well-being won her over, and she soon found herself warming at a fire next to the river, a good distance from the road. The drover, who introduced himself as Seòras, pulled some spring onions and oats from his sporran and went about forming black pudding cakes using a bit of blood he took from the neck of one of the cows. He fried it up while the other drovers kept watch over the herd.

When he generously handed her one and she bit into it, Sorcha could've wept. It was the finest food she'd eaten in days, and she wanted to savor every morsel. With each bite, she felt her strength returning.

She was halfway finished with her portion when she saw that Aonghas was finished with his and was hungrily eyeing the remaining pieces in the pan over the fire. Without a second thought, she held what was left of hers out to her son. "I'm near to bursting! Will you finish this?"

It was gone in seconds, as were the remaining portions as the other drovers came to the fire for their suppers. Two of the men sat down at the fire with them, while the third took his pudding, nodded silently in greeting to Sorcha and Aonghas, and melted back into the darkness. It reassured her to know someone would be on watch throughout the night.

Each man was friendly and respectful and even seemed to enjoy her company, as they missed the wives, daughters, and mothers waiting for them at home. Long into the evening, as the waning moon rose and stars appeared through gaps in the clouds, Sorcha and Aonghas enjoyed the stories and songs the men shared. It felt—for a short time, at least—just like all the nights back home in Srath Ghlais. Sorcha shared some stories of her own. She told of the time her eldest son shot his first stag, but it wasn't a clean shot and the beast managed to limp across three mountain peaks before he caught up to it, and how Tàm and Dòmhnall had struggled together to carry the carcass home through the snowstorm that blew in. Aonghas told of the time his mate had dared him to swim across Loch Afraig and back to impress a girl he was keen on, and when he reached the shore, his mates had taken his clothes and disappeared, leaving the blushing girl alone to greet him.

Sorcha had not heard this story before, and promised herself she'd question Aonghas about what happened next, but later, when they were away from the men. Until now, she'd thought she had plenty of time to talk to him about the ways between men and women, but she might be too late. The idea worried her, and made her miss her Tàm all over again. Her husband would've known what to say to their son.

The moon was high in the sky by the time she and Aonghas lay down side by side near the fire and pulled her *plaide* over both their bodies. Seòras poked a stick at the fire as his companion, whose name she'd already forgotten, snored on the ground next to him. The other two were somewhere out in the darkness, awaiting their turns for sleep.

She was just drifting off when she heard a voice coming from what sounded like the direction of the road. "Ho there! I'm looking for a woman and boy traveling this way. Have you seen them?"

Sorcha recognized the voice instantly and felt panic slam through her body. It was one of the men from the day they were evicted. The one who'd slit the throat of a goat while yelling about it belonging to An Siosal and not to "Scottish filth."

Before she had time to react, Seòras got to his feet and, in one swift motion, dropped his own *plaide* over her and Aonghas's heads so they were hidden from sight. Under the smelly blanket, she heard Seòras walk to the road and greet the man. The drover who'd already fallen asleep stirred awake and followed his boss away from the fire.

"Ma?" The whisper told her Aonghas was awake and as terrified as she was.

She squeezed his shoulder. "*Ist.* Don't move."

Sorcha hardly breathed as she strained her ears to hear what was said, and wondered why the man's appearance frightened her so deeply.

"No, I can't say that we've seen folks of that description." Seòras's voice. "Have you, Niall?"

"No," came the gruff reply. "Nobody around these parts except you."

They were hiding them! But why? Sorcha squeezed Aonghas's shoulder even tighter.

"Are you certain?" The sound of a harness jingling told Sorcha the man was on horseback. "They killed a man up north. Murderers, they are. They were last seen heading this direction. We can't be far behind them."

Murderers?

And then she remembered. The cottage burning. The man lying prone on her floor, blood pooling behind his head. The roof timbers crashing down just as they escaped, burying the man in fire.

The black pudding revolted in her stomach, and she had to swallow several times to keep it down. With her forehead pressed against Aonghas's shoulder, she breathed in and tried not to move a muscle. It had been an accident. But, the good Lord help her, a man's life had been lost in her home.

Were the drovers going to turn them in? Were they at this very minute pointing to her and Aonghas?

"Well, if they passed this way, we sure did not see them." Seòras again. "Did we, men?"

Sounds of agreement came from the other drovers.

"What about that man over by the fire? He see anything?"

Sorcha clenched her fists under the blanket.

"I doubt it," Seòras answered, sounding like he was talking about nothing more important than the weather. "Pàdraig there has been asleep since sundown, which is a good thing after all that's left his gut today—from both ends, if you catch my meaning."

Despite her fear, Sorcha relaxed her hands and even smiled into the darkness. That was clever of Seòras, making their pursuer think there was a sick man lying under this blanket.

"Look here at their likenesses."

There was a rustle of movement, but Sorcha had no idea what was happening until she heard Seòras say, "Are you certain they're guilty? This drawing makes them appear no more threatening than my own wife and son."

"Oh, they're guilty, all right. Burned a man to death in their cottage."

"What man? Her husband?" Seòras's voice held a note of alarm.

"Not her husband, but worse. A man hired by the chief to evict tenants from his land. A cousin to the good Lady Chisholm. Burned him alive in retaliation and then escaped into the night, they did."

One of the men muttered something that Sorcha couldn't hear, and then she again heard Seòras speak. "We'll watch for the pair; you can count on that."

"Many thanks. If you see them on your journey, send word to the magistrate of the next town. And take care if you do see them. They're dangerous and need to pay for their crime."

"Might I ask who you are?"

"My name's Coghill. Lachlann Coghill. This here's Baltair."

There were two of them! The realization made Sorcha bite her lip until she tasted blood.

"We're asking everyone we encounter to be on the lookout and would be grateful if you'd do the same. Tell folks that if they do see the murderers, to take great care for their personal safety, and then, as soon as possible, to send word to Alasdair Macrath, factor to An Siosal, clan chief of Srath Ghlais. He'll know where to find us."

There was a pause in the conversation after Coghill's directive where the only sound Sorcha could hear was the popping of dying flames. When Seòras responded, he sounded bored with the conversation. "We'll be sure to send word if we find your murderers."

"Thank you. Might you be keen on sharing your fire? We've been traveling all day."

"No, sorry, mate. We don't allow strangers to hang around the beasts longer than necessary. Gets them agitated and likely to stampede. I hear them starting to rustle around already. You'd best get moving."

That Seòras was clever indeed! Sorcha felt her body relax into the ground.

"Oh, well, yes—of course. Good night, then."

The noise of two horses clopping over the rough stones of the military road sounded clearly now, and Sorcha wondered how they had not heard them as they approached. She listened, unmoving, until long after the sounds faded away.

Seòras settled onto the rock beside the fire. "You can come out now. They're gone."

Cautiously, Sorcha drew the blanket down below their chins. And then, with no idea what to do next, she sat up and wrapped her arms around her knees. For a long moment she could think of nothing to say, and then, finally: "Thank you."

Seòras tilted his head to one side and looked at her. His face glowed red from the fire, and his lips were pinched so tight she could not see them through his beard. Unease swept over Sorcha, and she stiffened.

Her gaze darted to the drover's weapons still hanging from his waist, and she wondered if he was going to use them on her. Or Aonghas.

She shifted to put herself in front of Aonghas. If Seòras intended to attack them, he'd find a fight on his hands. Biting her lip, she waited for him to speak, knowing their fate rested upon his next words.

He only blinked, and seemed to come to a decision of sorts, because he spat into the fire, then leveled her with expressionless eyes. "I reckon I'd be tempted to burn alive anyone trying to evict my family from our home, too."

"It was an acc—"

Seòras put up a hand to stop her protest. "I don't need to know." He got up to lay another log on the fire before settling back down and pinning her with a hooded gaze. "You can stay the rest of the night, and we will keep you safe. But you'd best be on your own way in the morning. Take care to avoid that . . . man."

She could tell he wanted to use a more descriptive word for Coghill, but his manners kept him from it. She bit her lip again and nodded, seeing Aonghas do the same out of the corner of her eye. Before she had a chance to say anything more, Seòras got to his feet and disappeared into the darkness, his dog trotting after him.

Sorcha turned to Aonghas and found him staring at the flames, his mouth open and his chest rising and falling as he fought to catch his breath. She reached for his arm, and the moment she made contact, he flinched and rounded on her, his eyes red-rimmed and filled with horror. "We killed him. *I* killed him!"

Urgently, she shifted to her knees in front of him so he was forced to meet her gaze and not miss a word of what she was about to say. "No, you did not kill him. We're not murderers, no matter what those men said. It was an accident." She put a finger under his chin and looked hard into his green eyes. "Do you hear me? An accident. He tripped and hit his head on that rock. He was gone before the fire claimed his body."

Aonghas gripped her hands, hard, his fingernails biting into her skin. "Let's go back. We can explain what happened—"

"That would be a mistake, if you ask me."

They both jerked at hearing the voice and turned as one toward another drover, Niall, who dropped onto the rock Seòras had been using as a seat. His eyes looked black in the flickering firelight, but his tone was kind. "The dead man was kin to your chief's wife. They'll be looking for someone to punish, and you can rest assured they'll never believe it was an accident." He took a swig from the flask he kept in his pocket. "When has a member of the landed gentry ever bothered with the innocence of a person they accuse? They want justice. And only they get to decide what that looks like."

She knew exactly what Niall meant. She'd seen children accused of stealing a bannock sent to jail. She'd seen men whipped for asking questions of their employers. She'd known women beaten and abused by men come from England for a hunting holiday, and leaving with naught to show for their sins. People of her class were always treated unfairly, were always bullied by superiors. The landed gentry took what they wanted, when they wanted it, without care for the innocent people who were hurt along the way.

The Chisholms wanted her and Aonghas to pay for the death of their man.

Sorcha's sick stomach turned over again. She dropped her chin to her chest and reached blindly for Aonghas's hand, which she clenched tightly as she thought about what to do.

They couldn't go back to Srath Ghlais and profess their innocence. The man was dead, and either her son had killed him in whatever altercation had caused him to be bleeding on the ground, or they'd both killed him by leaving him to burn with the house. Whatever the cause, it had been an accident, but they would still be made to pay.

Stars danced on the edges of her vision, and her entire body shook as she realized what was going to happen when they were caught by those men—Coghill and Baltair. Murderers swung on the gallows. Or, at best, they were sent to the penal colony of Botany Bay for the rest of their lives, to pay for their sin with hard physical labor.

Either outcome would mean she'd lose Aonghas forever.

༄

The drovers and cattle were gone when Sorcha woke, which saved her from having to face Seòras in the light of day. As was becoming her habit, before she did anything else, she touched her fingers to the clumps of earth in her pocket to reassure herself that she still had this connection to her lost children, and to her home.

She still felt in shock that those two men wanted to arrest them for what had been an accident. Aonghas was unusually quiet this morning, and she wondered if he, too, was grappling with the news. As they walked with empty stomachs through spitting rain, she quietly explained to Aonghas the urgency they must now have to reach Dùn Èideann. In the city, they could disappear into the crowds, anonymous and unseen. He nodded his understanding, but said nothing in response.

So they walked, as fast as her cold and sore feet allowed. With her *plaide* wrapped around her and over her head, Sorcha felt warm enough, and as hidden as she could possibly be. She eyed the locks of auburn hair that continued to blow into Aonghas's face every time he swiped them away and wished that he, too, had a *plaide* or even a hat to hide his identity.

As they came over a small rise, she spotted a mass of beasts far down the pass and knew that would be their previous companions. Her feelings toward them were mixed. Uppermost, she felt gratitude for the way the men had protected her and Aonghas, and shared with them their food, fire, and companionship. But she also felt fear now that the drovers knew she and Aonghas were wanted for murder. So far, they'd not turned them in—but would that last?

Deciding it best to keep her distance from the drovers, Sorcha slowed her steps and made Aonghas do the same. "Keep watch for signs of factor Macrath's men, Coghill and Baltair." She kept her own gaze moving over the dips and hollows of the landscape, searching for signs of the two men. "If they find us, you must run. Escape. Even if that means I am captured."

He scowled at her. "I won't leave you behind."

She arched her eyebrows at him. "You'll do as I say and run. Is that understood?"

His chin dropped to his chest, and he kicked angrily at a stone. "Yes."

They went only a short distance farther when an idea came to her. "We shouldn't make it easier for Coghill to find us by being on this road. We'll follow the river. See how it disappears behind that knoll?"

Aonghas agreed, and soon they were making their way over the rough and boggy ground along the water. Unfortunately, the river did not part from the road as much as she'd expected, and she could easily see the track only a short distance away. Still, being near the river might save them a few moments' time before Coghill spotted them, and those few moments might be enough to escape.

After an hour, Aonghas's continued silence was worrying her. "How are you, Aonghas? Are you afraid of what will happen if they capture us?"

He shrugged. "I don't think they'll capture us. We just need to make it to Dùn Èideann."

Sorcha was not so sure, but she didn't say so aloud. "What has you so quiet, then? Are you sad we cannot return home?"

Aonghas dipped his head like he'd been caught sneaking an extra bannock. Curiously, a smile tugged at the corners of his mouth, and then it spread all the way across. "To be honest, I'm excited." He skipped ahead and turned to face her, walking backward and nearly tripping over bog grass. "I'm sad, to be sure, and I'll miss the strath fiercely, but I've never been away from home. Da and Dòmhnall got to see other places before they were killed in war—and, well, I always wanted to go, too."

"But surely not to war."

His smile dropped. "Oh no, of course not."

Something in his expression told her he was saying what he thought she wanted to hear rather than the truth. The very idea of her only remaining child becoming a soldier made her skin feel like a million midges were crawling over it.

Aonghas turned to walk beside her again. "It's just that I'd like to see more of the world, and that's what we're doing now. Imagine it. Dùn Èideann. Our capital city." He jumped from one rock to another, as agile as a squirrel. "We're going to see more people than I've known in my entire life, and see things we never knew existed. Did you know that officials in Dùn Èideann are constructing an earthen mound where once there was a loch? It's so people can walk from old town to new town."

Despite her fears and her shock at learning how he felt, Sorcha felt a smile spread across her own face at his enthusiasm. "I've heard the castle there stands upon an old volcano, and that the nephew of Robert the Bruce once scaled the rocks and overtook the English when they were asleep in their beds."

This got Aonghas even more excited, and Sorcha felt some of her worry ease. She'd been thinking only of what they'd lost, but Aonghas was reminding her that new adventures could bring joy, too.

A sound on the wind caught her attention and she froze. Aonghas opened his mouth to say something, but Sorcha held up her hand. "*Ist!* Listen."

They both stopped moving, tilted an ear forward, and waited. The wind had risen and was now whistling over the hills and through the valley; the river gurgled, and the sound of a cow lowing echoed toward them. And then another sound filtered into the rest. Was it a child crying? People shouting?

They exchanged worried looks before silently moving forward to investigate. Sorcha could taste the fear in her mouth, acidic and slick.

Who was there? Was it Coghill and Baltair? Was it some other danger they wouldn't be able to avoid?

Slowly, they crept toward the sound, staying low and out of sight. The noises seemed to be coming from over the rise, in the direction where the military road disappeared. As though they were stalking deer, she and Aonghas silently got onto their bellies and scooted forward to peek over the hill.

In the valley below lay what looked to be the remains of two small farms, one on each side of a river draining into what appeared to be a long arm of the sea tucked between towering tree- and mist-covered mountains. This must be the loch Seòras had mentioned last night as being Loch Lìobhan.

On the far side of the valley, a mass of black cattle was threading up the mountain with the drovers and dog urging them along. Sorcha knew this would likely be the last time she saw them, and she whispered a quick prayer for their safety. And a second prayer that the drovers would keep her secret.

Returning her attention to the valley floor, she saw that the buildings at both farms were blackened, their roofs burned away, and she knew exactly what had happened here. Just as An Siosal had done in Srath Ghlais, the owner of this land had evicted people to make room for sheep.

The surprising part of the sight wasn't the burned-out buildings, but the group of people who seemed to be living beside the river in shelters made of wool *plaideachan* and old furniture. Two women cooked over a fire while an old man dozed under a tree. Three teenage boys played shinty in the meadow nearby. Their shouts echoed up the hillside, and explained the noises Sorcha had heard.

But then she saw them. Coghill and Baltair. They were mounting their horses a short distance from the cooking women and seemed to be saying goodbye to the three men standing with them. A shudder slid through her body as she recalled the contempt she'd seen in Coghill's eyes on the day of her eviction.

He wore a black beaver hat over long, graying black hair that hung to his shoulders. Even from this distance, she could see neatly trimmed facial hair and sharp cheekbones jutting over hollows that made him look as hungry as she felt. His companion, Baltair, also wore all-black clothing, but his face was clean-shaven. Or maybe he was young, nearly as young as Aonghas. He still had a youth's whip-lean build and a rich luster to his long, brown hair that most men lost by middle age.

Baltair's head swiveled in her direction.

Panic shot through her, and Sorcha ducked her head as her fingers dug into Aonghas's arm. He gasped in response, or maybe it was in reaction to the sight below, but he didn't pull away.

She waited a beat and then peered over the rise yet again, as though keeping her eyes on the men would pin them in place, far away from her and Aonghas.

The men sat on their horses and seemed to be bidding farewell to the families who had clearly given them hospitality during the night. Coghill's weathered face creased into a smile that made Sorcha hate him even more. It was so different from the expression he'd worn as he stood over the goat he'd slaughtered and shouted insults at the villagers. As the horse danced sideways, Coghill's eyes stayed shadowed under the brim of his hat, but Sorcha knew his smile wouldn't reach there.

Then she saw the knife and club attached to his belt.

A quick glance confirmed that Baltair wore similar weapons. Weapons they intended to use against her and Aonghas.

"Ma, calm yourself. They don't know we're here."

Only now did Sorcha realize her entire body was shaking. Terror gripped her firmly, and all she could do was lie on the heather, unmoving, as though waiting for the men to discover her and take her away. She pulled air into her lungs and forced herself to back away from the rise until the men and the rest of the people below were out of sight. Then she dropped her head onto her crossed arms. Aonghas was right: The men didn't know they were up here. They were safe for the moment.

But what about tomorrow? Or the day after that?

How were they going to make it to Dùn Èideann?

CHAPTER EIGHT

Keaka

Day two, morning; Drymen

The alarm wakes me far earlier than I'd like after another night of little sleep. Inevitably, every time I started to doze off, images of the burning house filled my mind and had me snapping my eyes open to ward them off. But being awake wasn't much better with my thoughts spiraling around and around: talk Colin into giving up the hike, tough it out for his sake, suggest he walk it alone and I'll meet him in a rental car at the end of each day. And on and on.

At least there were no spooky ghost women lurking around the room.

But now, as I lie for another much-needed moment with my eyes closed, the truth becomes clear: there's no way I'm going to ruin this hike for Colin. He planned it for years, first with his father and then with me. It was always the big adventure he was going to have with a parent before starting his new life in Scotland. It's my last chance to spend quality time with my boy before he's launched into adulthood.

So the long miles hurt. Big deal. So it is mentally more challenging than I ever imagined. Big deal. So I am imagining ghosts and house fires. Again, big deal. Nothing is as important as Colin and my last week with him.

The hike is making Colin feel close to his dad, which is a good thing. No matter how lousy he was as a husband those last few years, Adam had always been the greatest dad I could've ever dreamed of for my kid. Adam gave Colin his love of Scotland and his love of hiking. Of course Colin is feeling close to him this week. I should encourage Colin to talk about Adam instead of getting wrapped up in my own issues with him. I will try to do better at that today.

"Mom, are you awake?"

I open my eyes and find Colin already dressed and rearranging the contents of his backpack. I didn't even realize he was up.

"Mom, get moving. We have Conic Hill and Loch Lomond today!"

I take a moment to reach my arms over my head and point my toes toward the end of the bed in a full-body stretch. Every muscle protests. After a noisy yawn, I smile at my boy. "Give me thirty minutes. I can meet you down in the breakfast room if you don't want to wait."

True to my word, thirty minutes later I pad downstairs in my stocking feet for a quick breakfast of potato scones with sauteed mushrooms and roasted tomatoes. Then, after leaving our shared suitcase in the front parlor for the baggage carrier to pick up and transport to tonight's destination, we say goodbye to our host and carry our boots to the front steps. As I lace mine up, my wedding ring catches my eye, and I remember how my fingers swelled yesterday. As Colin is distracted with his own boots, I quietly slip the ring off my now normal-size finger and deposit it into my pocket. If Colin notices and asks, I'll tell him I removed it because of finger swelling. But really, I have no plan to ever put it back on.

"Ready?" Colin's smile lights up his face, and his energy is palpable.

I can't help but smile back, just as wide. "Ready."

I waddle the first few steps, and my feet feel like I am walking on spikes, though I know it's only nerves protesting after yesterday's long walk. Eventually, though, my muscles warm up and the pain subsides.

The trail for the first mile or so out of Drymen goes through the town and then onto a path that skirts a wide pasture, where brown cows graze. On the other side of the path is a dark patch of forest, where I spy two tents, their inhabitants sitting in the doorways in front of camp stoves with tiny flames heating attached pots.

The flames remind me of my vision—or whatever it was—in the garden last night, and in response my throat feels scratchy. I pull my water bottle out to take a long swig and decide to ask Colin about it. "So," I start, busying myself with stowing my water bottle back in its pocket, "you know a lot about history." I sling on my pack and keep my eyes on the trail ahead. "What do you know about people being burned out of their homes here in Scotland? Small one- or two-room houses with thatched roofs being burned down, sometimes with people still inside."

I glance at him and see sunlight glinting off his brown hair, highlighting the red strands he inherited from his dad. A breeze blows a lock into his eyes, and he swats it away before he answers. "Well, it happened at the Glencoe Massacre of 1692, and during the persecution of the Highlanders during and after the Jacobite uprisings. But the greatest concentration of occurrences was probably during the Clearances." I can tell by the tone of his voice that he loves talking about this, probably because it reminds him of all the conversations he used to have with Adam. "They didn't all involve burning houses down, but it was an effective way to keep people from staying."

"You're going to have to start at the beginning. I've heard of the Clearances, of course. But what exactly were they?" The path we're following ends at a gravel forest road, and the West Highland Way trail marker guides us left to follow the road up a slight incline and through a recently planted forest.

"They happened in the eighteenth and nineteenth centuries when, basically, landowners decided to turn their property over to Cheviot and Blackface sheep to bring in more profit than they were getting from human occupants paying rent. With a startling lack of loyalty or empathy for their clan's people, they evicted everyone."

"That's awful." My feet are starting to ache, but I determinedly ignore them. "But wasn't that their right as landowners?"

He shrugs. "Yes, of course—but be careful not to apply your American beliefs of land ownership to this situation. For centuries, it was the clan itself that owned the land, not the chief. His was a position of responsibility more than entitlement. The relationship between the chief and the people was a mutual one, where the chief would keep life running smoothly and, in exchange, the people would willingly step up when called to battle threatening forces. The Clearances felt so shocking and personal to the people evicted, because they were not simply renting the land their homes and farms were on; they'd paid for it with their own blood and that of their loved ones and ancestors. The roots of their souls were buried deep in the land."

I think about all this as we walk and am only half-aware that the newly planted trees to our left have given way to an older, much taller forest. "Then how could they force people out of their homes like that?"

Colin waves his hand in the air to shoo away a swarm of tiny flies. "That's where it is complicated. In most cases, they gave tenants several months'—or even years'—notice. The people, however, either didn't believe they would really be evicted, or they literally had nowhere else to go."

I can see that Colin is only half registering the flies and that his mind is on what he's explaining to me. I wonder if he's forgetting to notice the scenery. Looming ahead is a hill that seems to be growing taller the closer we get, and I'm growing increasingly worried we're going to have to climb it. I turn my attention away from the hill and back to the conversation, and as I do, I remember the painting at the Kelvingrove Museum depicting distraught Highlanders. "Is that why so many people ended up immigrating to North America and Australia?"

Colin suddenly stops and pulls out his phone to snap a photo, and only now do I see through a break in the trees a stunning view of Loch

Lomond sparkling in the morning sunshine. It doesn't deter him from our discussion, though, and I love hearing his passion for the subject. "Yes, although in the early years, the government actively discouraged emigration by making it outrageously expensive. They needed soldiers for the Irish Rebellion and Napoleonic Wars."

He slips his phone back in his pocket, and we resume walking. "But that changed once the wars ended. A few landowners—a small few—paid for their people to emigrate. Most, though, just shoved the people off their land without a care for what happened to them, or with the misguided pretense that they could find a new way of life on the coasts in the kelp or fishing industries."

Everything Colin is telling me feels like it matches my vision of the burning house, right along with the arrogant hatred on the unknown man's face. "Who did the actual evicting?"

He shoots me a confused look as though he's wondering why I have this sudden interest in the subject but, bless him, he doesn't ask. "The factors—the managers in charge of the day-to-day running of the estates—were usually the ones to evict, and they got either the local police or forces from Glasgow or Edinburgh, and sometimes military soldiers from Fort George, to assist."

I feel conflicted by all that Colin is telling me. On the one hand, I understand the landowners' need to stay profitable. But on the other, it should never be done in ways that force people out of their homes with nowhere else to go and put their lives at risk.

We continue to discuss the Clearances as we walk through the forest, occasionally passing or being passed by other walkers. Each time we encounter someone, we exchange greetings and small talk, but always we return to just the two of us walking. I'm loving every minute of talking with my boy and feel, acutely, the ticking clock that is the time I have left to delve into Colin's head like this.

I stop myself from letting that thought cascade. Today I will stay positive. I will stay in the moment and not worry about next week.

Colin suddenly stops and points ahead. "Look! That's Conic Hill!"

I look to where he is pointing and feel a sense of dread settle in my stomach. The hill that I noticed earlier has now grown into a mountain. "Do we have to climb it?"

"Yep." He sounds thrilled by the prospect. As though eager to reach the mountain, he slips both thumbs under his backpack straps and sets off at a fast clip. "Come on!"

I hurry to keep up with him, but I don't feel even a fraction of his anticipation. "Why is it called a *hill* when it is clearly a mountain?"

"Oh, come on, it won't be that bad. It's only a little over a thousand feet. That's less elevation gain than Silver Star Mountain."

Silver Star Mountain was one of the few hikes I'd gone on with him back home in Portland to train for this trip. Remembering that day, I make a face at him. "I barely made it to the top."

"Nah, you did great. Conic Hill will be no big deal, you'll see."

I don't believe him, but knowing the hill stands between us and our lunch stop, I march on.

When the forest ends and we pass through a gate and onto a moorland—our first of the entire hike—I can't help but feel excited for the vast moors Colin tells me we will cross in the days ahead. There is a special beauty to the moor, with blooming heather giving a purple wash to the meadow as it slopes downward to where leafy trees just starting to turn color mark a river flowing at the base of Conic Hill. A short distance from us, up the slope from the trail, stand two woolly sheep, one with black horns curling toward its face. They ignore us and continue munching the grass.

Seeing the sheep, I remember my vision last night, and how it felt to be burned out of my home. The evicted people must have hated the sight of sheep.

After following Colin across a narrow footbridge, I see that the trail immediately starts to climb the mountain, and there's not a single tree on the entire path up. "I need to put on sunscreen. You go ahead and I'll catch up."

As Colin heads up the hill, I dig through my pack to find my SPF 30. I'm slathering it on my arms when I feel the sharp bites of midges on my legs and realize they are the tiny insects that have been swarming around us all morning. I bat them away and accidentally catch the strap of my backpack, sending it tumbling to the ground.

Shaking my head at my clumsiness, I squat down and start shoving everything back into the pack.

And then I see it.

A rock carving. A perfect flower petal pointing north, toward the top of Loch Lomond.

I can't help myself—I reach out and lay my fingers on the stone, expecting . . . something.

I don't know exactly what I expected, but I get nothing. No vision, no strange emotions, no ghost woman suddenly appearing.

And yet I know with absolute certainty that these carvings I keep finding are connected to the woman who was crying over Colin two nights ago, and to the vision I had in the garden last night. I know they are connected to the woman in the painting. Sorcha Chisholm. Maybe it was even Sorcha who carved them.

A thrill snakes up my spine to the top of my head. I don't know how, but I feel as though I'm supposed to find or learn something. Why else would these weird things keep happening to me when I've never experienced anything like this in all my life?

In the bright light of morning, it no longer feels like I'm losing my sanity. It feels like an opportunity. I'll keep looking for the flower petals, and I'll keep an eye out for signs of the woman. For Sorcha Chisholm.

I place my palm flat against the flower petal in a silent promise. I then finish slathering on the sunscreen, stuff everything into my pack, and hoist it onto my back.

And I start to climb.

I can't see Colin, he is so far ahead of me. I focus on each step because if I think about having to climb all the way up this mountain, I'll be overwhelmed and will feel like quitting.

My heart pounds loudly in my ears, and I am grateful when a soft breeze blows across my skin and keeps me from overheating.

One step. My thighs are burning. Another step. My lungs are on fire. Left foot, right foot, left foot. At one point I have to stop at the side of the trail with my hands propped on my thighs as I struggle to breathe. I can't imagine having to do this with the weight of a full camping pack on my back, as the Danish family we met yesterday and so many others are doing.

When I finally lift my gaze to the view, all I can say is, "Wow." I'm not to the top yet, but already I can see Loch Lomond spreading into the distance to my right. Islands dot the blue expanse here and there, and I wonder what stories lay hidden on them. Who lived there? Have battles been fought there? Did someone need to take refuge on that island from a storm or a human threat? Colin would probably know.

I start hiking again, eager to catch up to him and learn what he can tell me about the loch.

I find Colin sitting on the ground to the side of the trail as it reaches its crest. The only problem, I realize, is that this isn't actually the top of the mountain. If we want the full view, we will have to take a side trail up a steeper climb.

"Should we do it?" Colin asks me the moment I stop beside him.

I look at the breathtaking view of the loch, then up the spur trail, then at Colin's face. His hopeful eyes give me the only correct answer: "Of course we should. Lead the way."

At one point, I find myself using my hands as much as my feet to scramble up the path, but it isn't long, and soon we're on the rounded summit of Conic Hill. Wind blows my hair around my face, so I gather it in one hand.

Colin keeps walking, and I follow him across the top of the mountain a short distance until we are standing on the edge of the highest knob. The mountain falls steeply down in front of us, and I see several people picking their way up across loose stones. One man is even carrying a bicycle up the scree.

Colin drops his pack onto the grass and pulls out his phone. I follow suit, then carefully toe aside some old sheep droppings to find a clear place to sit. I hug my knees and feel every muscle in my back stretch painfully.

I take in the stunning view. We got lucky with the weather again today. Sun is poking through the clouds and lighting the entire loch, making it look enchanted. In the distance to the north, big purple and blue mountains disappear into dark clouds, all of which look as equally enchanting as the loch. To the south, patchwork farmland and rolling green and forested hills stretch into the sunny distance. Scotland is already so much more than I expected.

"Mom, you are currently sitting on the Highland Boundary Fault. To our left is the Lowlands, and everything to the right is the Highlands." Colin points out the islands that line up across the lake and tells me they are also part of the fault line.

I'm impressed by his knowledge. As he tells me of the nuns who once lived on the closest of those islands, and the female saint who founded the church there, I watch his face. My heart swells with pride. When he is finished with his stories, I smile at him. "You're going to thrive at Glasgow. I can just see it."

Colin smiles even as his face reddens, and he ducks his head. "Yeah, I think I'm going to like living here."

A sharp pain in my chest makes me gasp. One of the invisible cords tethering me and my son together since before he was born has just snapped like a rubber band. It is as it should be, I remind myself, but it still hurts. Even more, I must pretend it doesn't. I must smile and encourage him to spread his wings and fly away from me.

To distract myself from my pain, I urge Colin to tell me more of what he knows about the area. As he launches into tales of Rob Roy MacGregor, I listen and take in more of the view. For the first time, I finally understand what my husband meant when he told me that there was something magical about Scotland that pulls at your soul and makes you hunger for more. I feel this pull. I feel it coming from the north, as though the Highlands are calling to me, beckoning me farther into their depths where they can wrap me in the embrace of their mountains, moors, waterfalls, and people.

For years I resented that Colin shared a love of Scotland with Adam and only a passing interest in my side of his ancestry. But now, standing on this mountain and looking at this beautiful land, I'm starting to understand. I'm actually feeling a new eagerness growing inside of me to listen to the call of the Highlands. I want to walk north into those mountains and connect with the spirit of the land, not solely for Colin anymore but for me, too.

When Colin stands up and straps on his backpack, I follow his lead. But when he starts his careful descent down the scree, I hesitate and look one last time upon the loch below. I follow it with my eyes as it stretches north, toward the misty purple mountains.

I say the words before I even know they are in my mind. *"An till mise chaoidh gu Gàidhealtachd mo rùin, far an cluinnte a' Ghàidhlig air bilean a daoin'? Le seallaidhean bòidheach a-nis ri mi dhrùim, gum bris e mo chridhe."*

Only when my words hit my own ears do I realize I have not spoken in English, but in a language I somehow know to be Scottish Gaelic. Not only that, but I understand the words and their meaning: *Will I ever return to my beloved Highlands, where Gaelic can be heard on the lips of its people? With beautiful views now at my back, it breaks my heart.*

I've only heard Scottish Gaelic a few times in my life, and I certainly don't speak it. Yet here I am, lamenting my leaving the Highlands when I am actually entering them. It makes no sense.

First the Gaelic on the Glasgow bridge, then the ghost woman, then the fire vision, and now I'm speaking in full sentences in a language I don't even know.

What is happening to me?

Going down Conic Hill proves to be worse than going up with all the steep steps. I descend on wobbly legs. But, finally, we reach the little town of Balmaha at the base, and even the hard pavement doesn't bother me. It is flat, and it leads to rest.

I see the Oak Tree Inn across the road, and my mouth is salivating in anticipation of lunch when I hear our names being called. Surprised, I turn and see Jorgen and his daughters coming our way on the shaded sidewalk.

"We wondered if we'd see you today." Jorgen's smile is warm, and I remember Colin telling me that the man was flirting with me yesterday. It makes me feel awkward and uncertain how to act around him now.

Colin saves me from having to reply. "Have you had lunch? We're heading there now and would love for you to join us." He motions toward the inn, but his eyes are firmly on the oldest girl, Kirsten.

The family has already eaten, but we make plans to meet up for drinks later this evening since we'll all be ending the day at Rowardennan. As they continue on their way, Colin and I head to the inn to order our much-needed food on their outdoor patio.

The little town feels like a summer tourist destination, with visitors lingering over lunch or a cold drink at the coffee shop, or licking ice-cream cones as they perch on rock walls in the park. Others are boarding boats for cruises of the loch or resting against backpacks in the shade. I recognize many faces from the last two days on the trail.

After lunch, I stand up and discover that my muscles have stiffened. My legs feel fatigued from the Conic Hill climb this morning, and I'm starting to worry that I won't make it through the afternoon. I keep on going, and eventually, I'm back in the groove. I'm determined to do this.

We're emerging from a wooded hill onto a wide sandy beach when I start to feel an inexplicable but overwhelming sense of fear. It's visceral. I can taste metal on my tongue and my stomach is quaking, yet I don't see anything around me that could be causing such an intense reaction.

I ignore it as best I can and keep following Colin toward what looks to be a parking lot. I'm sweating now, and I know it's not from the sun or exertion.

"Oh, good, there's a public restroom here. Need to go?" Colin is already heading toward the small stone building at the edge of the pavement. I follow him and use the toilet, then splash cold water on my face. Still, the weird emotions are clinging to me. I feel panicked, and I really want to get away from here, or hide.

When I come out of the restroom I spot Colin on the beach, taking a picture of a solitary tree near the water's edge. Instead of going to him, however, I feel an undeniable pull in the opposite direction, toward the road and the oakwood forest beyond it. I'm hoping that my fear will ease with each step, but it doesn't.

I pause just long enough to make sure no cars are coming, then I cross the road and step into the woods. I have to push leafy bushes aside to get through, and as I do so, I see in a flash the image of another woman's hand pushing branches out of her way.

I stop and look around. What am I doing? Colin's going to wonder where I am, and I have no reason to be out in these woods. I shake my head and take a deep breath, hoping both will clear the tumble of emotions in my gut. Just as I'm turning to go back to the beach, a man's voice sounds as clearly as though he's talking into my ear: "I will not lose you again, bitch."

I gasp and spin around, but there is no one there. I turn in circles, looking for the threatening man with contempt dripping from his voice, but I see nothing but trees.

Still, I need to get away from him. I need to escape.

I run as fast as I can, deeper into the woods, and I hear curses following me. The man is close. I have to get away. My son needs me.

I dart around trees, never slowing, never looking back. I don't need to look back because I know the man is there. I can feel him like a hot iron against the back of my neck.

"Mom!"

Oh no, Colin is here. I can't let the man get to him.

Up ahead, the trees are thinning, and I smell peat smoke. A house. I can run there for protection. No Highlander would turn away a person in need.

But would they help *me*?

"Mom, what are you doing? Where are you going? The trail is back this way."

I feel a touch on my arm and I jerk away from it, which causes me to stumble on a tree root, but I catch my balance and spin away to keep running.

"Mom, what's wrong?"

I blink. My feet slow to a stop, and I blink again. What *is* wrong?

I look around and see that I'm deep in the woods now, but close by I can see a clearing that looks to be a field with grazing sheep. Colin is looking at me like I've lost my mind. Maybe I have.

"You two need some help?" A voice suddenly asks from behind Colin, startling us both.

I look past Colin and find a middle-aged woman dressed in work pants and a button-up shirt with sleeves rolled to her elbows. She's carrying a crook and has a sheep dog panting beside her. A wide-brimmed hat shades her face, but I can still see the kindness in her eyes. Before either of us can reply, she offers, "I saw ye run past a moment ago, and ye seem to be in distress."

Colin turns back to me with a look that says he's also wondering what is causing my distress.

"Bees." It's the best thing my brain can come up with, and even as I hear myself say the word, I cringe. "Bees," I say again, doubling down. "There was a swarm of them, and all I could think to do to get away from them was to run. I must have looked like a madwoman." I laugh, hoping they believe my lame excuse.

Colin gets a crease between his eyebrows like he doesn't believe me, but he laughs with me and seems willing to let it go.

"Well, the beasties seem to have gone now," the woman says, looking around. "Ye look like you could use a break and a cuppa. Ma house is just down that track there, if ye'd care to join me? I was just about to head in for tea myself."

"Oh, no," I immediately reply. "We don't want to bother you. That's very kind of you, though."

"No, really. I insist." She gives a low whistle, and the dog starts trotting beside her toward the dirt road she pointed to. "Walking the Way, are ye? Heading to Rowardennan for the night, I bet?"

She's walking away from us, and the only way to answer her questions is to keep up with her. Colin and I exchange a look. He just smiles and shrugs, so I smile back and jerk my head to the side to indicate we should follow.

We both hustle to catch up to her. Colin reaches her first. "Yeah, we're coming from Drymen last night and going to Rowardennan tonight. How much further is it, would you say?"

I follow behind the two and absently listen to them talk, but really my mind is on the buzz of fear I still feel under my skin. It's lessened considerably, but still, as I walk I turn my head to look to each side and even behind me, searching the forest for the threatening man.

I know that I'd imagined him, otherwise Colin or the woman would have seen him. But, he had sounded so real. My fear had been real. I still feel it lingering in my stomach and throat.

We walk past a handful of farm buildings to a small two-story house, where the woman lets us through the kitchen door. The room is warm and homey, and even though I just ate lunch, the smell of something baking makes my mouth water.

An old woman is filling the electric teakettle with water when we enter, and she turns to greet us as though we were expected. "Good day to ye."

Our host motions us toward the table. "Can ye serve our guests tea, Granny? I'm going to go change. I'll just be a moment." She starts to leave the room but suddenly stops and turns back, shaking her head.

"Look at me, forgetting ma manners. I'm Rachel. This is ma granny, Morag. Please, sit and have a cuppa."

I realize I've been awkwardly hovering just inside the door, but at her invitation I ease my pack off and set it on the floor, out of the way. "My name is Keaka, and this is my son, Colin."

Rachel disappears through a door, and Morag bustles about collecting mugs, a tin of tea, sugar, and cream, which she places on the table. Colin is still standing on the rug by the door, and Morag gives him a stern look. "Never ye mind yer clarty boots; these floors have seen much worse. Ma Rachel tracks in all sorts of muck from the fields."

Colin drops his pack beside mine, and we both sit at the round table, gratefully accepting the mugs Morag hands us. "It's so kind of you to let strangers into your home like this. We really appreciate it."

Morag waves her hand in dismissal. "I enjoy the company. 'Tis only maself and Rachel living here the noo, and she's off working at the clinic—she's a nurse, ya know—or she's out in the fields with this one." She pats the dog's head fondly before motioning him toward the woodstove to lie down. "With no one else around, I seem to have developed a bad habit of talking to maself, and I've heard all ma stories twice over." She winks at Colin.

We laugh and I find myself relaxing. Soon, despite saying she's bored of her stories, Morag has launched into a tale of the time her own son was fishing on the loch and nearly drowned.

Rachel hurries back into the room wearing jeans and is tying her hair back into a bun. "*Och*, Granny, you're always going on about things no one cares about."

I feel the need to defend the sweet woman. "Oh, no, really. I love stories. Colin too. He's going to be studying history at Glasgow uni." I feel so British using the word *uni*. "We're hiking the West Highland Way as our last adventure together before I leave him here and fly back to Oregon."

"Yer going ta love Glasgow, Colin. If ye can stand all the people and fankle. I find there's plenty of excitement happening here by the loch to keep me entertained." Morag gets to her feet in one smooth motion, defying her advanced age, and grabs a cloth, which she uses to pull a hot pan from the oven. "Noo, who would like a hot scone?"

As Rachel sets butter, cream, and jam on the table, Morag places a scone on a plate in front of each of us, all the while entertaining us with anecdotes from the area. We hear about the pyroligneous acid works that used to be in Balmaha; how the area along this side of the loch was active for many years in the charcoal production industry; how the surveyors who created the West Highland Way route in the 1970s sat in this very kitchen, drinking tea with her and her daughter-in-law; and many more stories. "Ma family has lived in this verra house for generations, since the time of Rob Roy MacGregor." She presses her fork to her plate to catch the last crumbs.

Colin is soaking up all of Morag's stories. He shovels in the last bite of scone, swallows almost immediately, and asks, "Do you have any photos of the area through the years? I'd love to see them."

"*Och*, now you've done it," Rachel warns in a teasing voice, her hands wrapped around her mug. "Now Granny will never be quiet. I'm afraid yer trapped here for the rest of the day, ye are."

Colin and I just smile in reply as Morag leaves the room. I glance out the windows to gauge the time and see that the sun is still high in the sky. It is midafternoon, at the latest.

When Morag returns, she is carrying a big black leather-covered scrapbook, which she places on the table between me and Colin. She flips it open to reveal a sepia-toned photograph of a family staring, unsmiling, into the camera. Behind them is a house that I can tell is this one, but the flowering bushes around it are newly planted. They now half cover the windows. "This was ma mother, father, ma three younger brothers, and that is me." For several pages, we see old photos of a family at various weddings and other occasions. We see an article clipped from a newspaper about her son's accident on the loch and several other articles of local fishing derbies and steamship mishaps.

And then she turns the page again, and I'm suddenly looking at the face I've come to know well over the last few days.

Sorcha Chisholm stares out from the brown-stained, fragile-looking paper. It is a sketch, and though Sorcha is drawn to look angry in the depiction, I recognize her instantly.

I am not at all surprised to read her name under the drawing, although it also gives her middle—or maiden—name: Macdonell. But then I see the words written at the top of the page and am shocked. OUTLAWS. WANTED FOR MURDER.

"What is this?" I ask, trying my best to sound no more interested than I've been in all the rest. Sorcha. Of course it was Sorcha that brought me here. The voice. The fear. It was all Sorcha.

Morag, who has returned to her seat across the table, leans over to see what it is I'm looking at. She shakes her head. "*Och*, now that's a sad story. I dinna ken why ma mother chose to put that in our family scrapbook."

"On with ye, Granny. Ye know yer dying to tell it." Rachel takes a big bite of her scone and nods at her grandmother.

Morag settles back against her chair and rests her fingers lightly on the table. "Well, ye see, ma three times great-grandmother was but a wee lass at the time. Six years old, she was, and prone to 'flights of fancy,' as they called them. So when she told her parents that she saw a woman in the woods being attacked by a bad man and the woman killed the bad man, I'm afraid no one believed her. Even a few days later, when her father was given that flyer in town and he brought it home, his daughter told him the woman was who she'd seen in the woods, and still no one believed her. She never changed her story, though, and insisted that a bad man had been killed in their woods. Nae body was ever found, and it was all forgotten."

I will not lose you again, bitch. The words I'd heard in the woods echo in my mind, and I'm starting to suspect they were said by the very man this little girl had seen. I rub at the goose bumps prickling my arms.

Morag sips her tea and seems to be choosing her next words carefully, although I'm suspicious that she's simply relishing having an audience for a change. None of us make a sound.

"But then—in the eighties, it was—ma husband, rest his soul, cleared some land to make way for a new barn. The verra one you see standing oot there. And that's when we found the bones."

I can't help but gasp. I really did not expect there to be an actual murder. And if it had been Sorcha, why? "How did he die?"

Morag shakes her head. "The authorities could not determine cause of death, nor even the man's identity. The body had been in the soil for an estimated two hundred years, and there was no physical evidence left to tell us the story. Even though I told the authorities what ma three times great-granny had witnessed, they closed the case. We ken the truth, though, dinnae we, Rachel? We kent the man was murdered by that fleysome woman and her son."

I blink and turn back to the flyer and, for the first time, see the drawing next to Sorcha's. Her son. The very boy I had pulled from the burning house in my vision. The name under the drawing reads *Aonghas Chisholm*.

"So she wasn't innocent after all, was she?"

Rachel frowns. "How do ye mean?"

I realize now that I should have stayed silent, and wished I had. "It's just . . ." I swallow and try to measure my words so I don't reveal anything that will make me sound like a crazy person. "It's a painting I saw the other day in the Kelvingrove Museum. I think it was of this woman. Sorcha Chisholm." I pull out my phone and open my photos, swiping through until I get to the right one. I hand the phone to Morag. "I failed to get a picture of the card that showed the title, but I remember it as being *Sorcha Chisholm: Widow, Mother, Innocent*. What do you think? Is that the same person?"

Morag squints at the phone, then silently hands it to Rachel, who also inspects the photo and even pinches at the screen to zoom in. I can tell they are both shocked by this discovery.

"Why didn't you show me this earlier?" Colin holds his hand out toward Rachel, and she reluctantly hands the phone over to him. He inspects the photo and then leans forward to see the flyer again. "Well, it's definitely the same name, if you're remembering it correctly. And the woman in the painting does look like the woman in the drawing. I say it's her." He hands me the phone.

"I kent she was right all along!" Morag slaps her palms on the table, startling us all. "I kent my three times great-grandmother was not making up stories. I kent it when we found the body. Oh, I wish she was here the noo to learn this."

"This doesna really prove anything, Granny." Rachel gets to her feet and refills the teakettle. "All we ken is that a body was found of a man who'd died about the same time as when yer three times great-granny lived here and claims she saw this Sorcha Chisholm murder a man. And now we ken that someone painted her picture."

Morag presses her lips together and shakes her head at her granddaughter. "Sorcha murdered the man and she got away with it. I ken it in ma bones."

A thought comes to me. "Wait. If no one discovered the body during her lifetime, why was she wanted for murder?"

Morag's eyebrows lift into her curly gray hairline. "*Och*, didna I tell ye that part of the story?"

I shake my head and look at Colin to make sure I hadn't simply missed it. He also shakes his head.

"Well, ye see . . ." Morag is back in her storytelling element. "The story goes that Sorcha and Aonghas were evicted from their home up in Strathglass, and during all the commotion, the man doing the evicting was killed in their home. Some claimed he was burned alive."

The burning cottage from the painting. The burning cottage from my vision. The man in my vision, lying on the floor.

I feel sick and take a tiny sip of tea to try to settle my stomach.

"I have so many questions." Colin's eyes are dancing as he leans his elbows on the table. "Where is Strathglass? Did anyone consider self-defense in the evicting man's murder? Why was her son also wanted? And what does it mean to be 'put to the horn'?"

"'Put to the horn'?" I'm confused by his last question.

Colin just points at the flyer in response and turns back to Morag for answers. I look at where he points on the Wanted poster and read **Sorcha Macdonell Chisholm and her son Aonghas Chisholm have been put to the horn at the Cross of Edinburgh and are wanted outlaws.**

The words make no sense to me, so I, too, look at Morag.

"It means they failed to appear in court for trial, and so they were declared to be outlaws by the blowing of three blasts of a horn at the Market Cross in Edinburgh. If a person accused of a crime didna appear in court to defend themselves, they were convicted of that offense. To be outlawed meant they lost all legal protection and anyone was legally empowered to persecute or kill them."

Colin turns to me with a wide smile; his eyes are glittering with delight. "Oh, man, I can't wait to study this stuff!"

Morag goes on to answer Colin's other questions, explaining that she doesn't know what became of Sorcha and Aonghas. Then she has Rachel retrieve a map of Scotland from the other room, and she points out where Strathglass is located, northwest of Loch Ness.

After that, I realize we've been here for two hours already, and I know we are overstaying our welcome. "Colin, we should be going. Morag and Rachel, thank you so much for your hospitality and your stories. I'm quite grateful to that swarm of bees for leading us to you."

Rachel laughs as she gets to her feet along with us. "After your dash through the woods, be sure to check yerselves for ticks before ye go to bed tonight."

"Ew, really?"

All three laugh at my obvious disgust as Rachel confirms that we do, indeed, need to be on the lookout for ticks. "Do ye want a ride to Rowardennan? I've got my car out front, and it would be no bother."

"No, but thank you. I don't want to miss any part of this hike." Colin pulls on his pack.

Accepting his decision, I reach for my own pack. "I don't know how to thank you both for everything. I know you had better things to do with your day."

Rachel waves me away and reaches for the door handle. Morag is cleaning up our mugs and plates. "Consider it Highland hospitality. I enjoyed oor time together. Best wishes at uni, Colin!"

We make our way down the driveway, cross the road, and return to the trail. I can't help but scan the woods the entire time, waiting for a voice, or an emotion to overwhelm me. Nothing happens.

The late-afternoon sun is bright as it bounces off the lake and through the trees where we walk. It is beautiful, and I try to enjoy the scenery.

But really, my mind is on all that we've learned from Morag. If it's true, then Sorcha Chisholm was a murderer, and for some reason, I'm connected to her in some way. Why else would I keep seeing visions of her?

Why is a murderer haunting me?

CHAPTER NINE

Sorcha

Near Loch Lìobhann (Loch Leven)

Sorcha and Aonghas took turns resting and foraging for food while the other kept watch on the glen below. Their pursuers had ridden across the river and along a path that followed the far side of Loch Lìobhann until they disappeared to the south.

Sorcha had planned to follow the loch, but now she knew they would be going in any direction but that one.

It was Aonghas who declared they should follow Seòras and the cattle. From her vantage point over the valley, Sorcha's gaze traced the faint path that ran upstream along the river before turning upward to climb over the mountain and continue south. It would lead them toward Dùn Èideann and away from Coghill. It would do.

Coghill and his helper had been gone for hours before Sorcha felt brave enough to move on.

They picked their way across the top of the hillside in order to avoid the settlement below. Now that they were on the move again, Sorcha wanted nothing more than to quickly cross the valley and disappear into the fog enshrouding the huge mountain opposite.

"Angus!"

Sorcha snapped her head around upon hearing an Englishwoman's voice calling her son's name in fright. Just as she did, she saw Aonghas's foot slip off the rock he was balancing upon . . . and then he disappeared.

Now it was her turn to call his name in panic. She rushed to him, terrified she was going to find his body bloodied and broken at the bottom of a gorge.

She carefully peered over the edge to what was, indeed, a deep ravine with a waterfall pounding into a small pool. No Aonghas.

"Ma! Help me!"

A sob burst out of her as she fell to her knees. "Where are you?"

"Here!"

He sounded close. She lowered onto her belly and edged forward as far as she dared on the slick moss. There. Aonghas was there, not far down the side of the gorge, clinging to roots that had kept him from sliding all the way to the bottom. "I see you. Can you climb up?"

"Not by myself," he said, his voice quavering.

She needed to do something fast, before Aonghas fell the rest of the way to the rocks below. A sturdy tree branch would help. There was a grove of birch a short distance down the hill, but that would take time.

Her belt. It was long enough to reach him, and it was strong. She'd fashioned it herself from the leather she'd received in barter from the traveling people many years ago during their annual visit to the strath. It would take her son's weight as long as they could maintain hold of either end as she pulled him up. She quickly sat up and unlatched the belt, taking care to set her *plaide* and brooch safely to the side. Gripping the buckle end tightly, she threw the opposite end down to Aonghas and then dug her heels firmly into the earth to give herself leverage as she pulled. "Grab the belt. Hold tight!"

She couldn't see him from this angle, but judging by how long it took before she felt his tug on the belt, she knew he must be afraid to let go of the roots. "You can do it, Aonghas. Just grab hold, then climb. I won't let you fall."

Once she felt his weight, she gripped the belt tightly in both hands. Slowly, she scooted her bottom back and brought her heels up to the edge of the rock to get an even firmer hold. His weight grew heavier, and she knew he now held the belt with both hands and was starting to climb. She leaned backward, wishing she was strong enough to pull him all the way up.

The leather dug into her palms, but she only held tighter and willed her son up the climb.

When his head popped over the edge, she said his name in great relief but didn't slacken her grip on the belt until she felt him release it entirely and drop next to her on the rock. She pulled him into her arms and held tightly for several long minutes, noting that he held just as tightly to her. "Don't do that again! You scared me! I cannot lose you."

His laugh sounded forced. "I am good, Ma. You worry too much."

When he did pull away, she was sad to let him go. The only place where she could truly keep him safe was by her side, and even that wouldn't always be enough. She'd learned that years ago, when she'd lost one infant at birth and two toddlers, one right after the other, to fever. She'd held each of her cherished children all through the long nights, praying constantly, and it hadn't been enough to save their lives. But a mother's arms were made for holding her children, and that was what she would do for as long as Aonghas let her.

Aonghas flopped back on the rock and looked up at the sky. She lay beside him, needing the rest, and felt the ache drain from her hands, wondered if the ache would ever drain from her heart. Such was the curse of motherhood.

"I heard you call my name as my foot slipped. You sounded scared, like you knew it was going to happen before it did."

Remembering the woman's voice, Sorcha shot up and looked around. She got to her feet and scanned as far as she could see. There was no other soul in sight. Confused, she sat back down. "It was not me who called your name, Aonghas. But I heard it, too. It made me turn back just in time to see you fall." She thought for a moment and then asked, "Did she not sound like an Englishwoman? She said your name as only the English say it, with that hard throat sound in the middle." His name in the Gaelic was longer than the English said it, and rolled from the tongue like water down a hillside burn—*Uh-noo-iss*. Not the harsh-sounding English way—*Ang-gus*.

With furrowed brows, Aonghas surveyed their surroundings. "We're far from An Siosal, and Coghill has Gaelic. Who else here knows my name?"

With no answer, Sorcha only shook her head. Then another explanation came to her, and she froze. "Was it one of the Other Folk?" Everyone knew the Good People weren't to be trusted.

Aonghas's eyes grew round before his head snapped to the left, then to the right as though in search of the underground dwellers.

An even more alarming explanation came to Sorcha. "Or maybe it was the sight?"

"Like the time you saw Da and knew he was killed?"

Sorcha's heart clenched at the words. Even now, three years later, her husband's death felt raw. She nodded. "It was but two months since we received word of your brother's death at Tara Hill. You were out tending the crops; I was alone in the cottage, making supper. Suddenly, there was your da sitting at the fire and letting out a huge sigh like he'd just come in from a long day working the fields. I couldn't move, nor say a word. I was so surprised to see him, and yet, at the same time, I knew it was not really him."

She turned toward the opposite mountain, but all she saw was her husband's dear face. "He smiled at me and gave me that look that always made me know he loved me more than anything in the world." She paused and swallowed. "And then he disappeared. That's when I knew it was your da's specter that had visited and that he was gone."

After a moment, Aonghas broke the silence. "Did you know you had second sight before that night?"

She shook her head. "I still don't know if I have the sight. That was the only time it has ever happened. Until today, if that's what the voice was. But that wasn't using sight at all, was it? second hearing?"

Aonghas's stomach rumbled, and they both laughed at the absurdity of it amid talk of specters and death. "Let's go," she told him, pushing to her feet. "I'd like to put this settlement well behind us before nightfall." She pulled him up and tried not to fret over his hunger.

She brushed dirt and moss from the back of her skirt and then set her *plaide* to rights with her belt fastened securely around her waist. As she watched Aonghas brush dirt off his backside, his hand brushed against his knife, and she remembered the stones. She hadn't carved a mark in several miles! Moving quickly, before Aonghas could start thinking of his empty belly again, she took his knife, dropped to her knees right there, and made her mark on the stone where they'd been resting. A few minutes later, she sat back and surveyed her work. Good enough.

Aonghas helped her back to her feet, and then they were on their way.

They continued down the hill to the valley floor a good distance upriver from the settlement and were relieved to find no other signs of people between them and the river.

Although she'd watched Coghill ride his horse across the water with no problem, when they arrived on its bank, they found it was much deeper and swifter flowing than she'd realized.

With no bridge, and no other option, they walked upriver, looking for a safe place to cross.

And then, suddenly, there was a boy standing barefoot in their path.

Sorcha gasped and reared backward, stepping on Aonghas's foot in the process. After having just been discussing the Good People, she half expected this boy to be one of them. "I didn't see you there!"

The boy's laughter mixed musically with the sound of the river, and Sorcha found herself relaxing and smiling in response. Freckles dotted the bridge of his nose, and his fair hair needed a trim.

"Where are you off to this lovely day?" the boy asked, sounding years older than he appeared.

She glanced up at the heavy gray sky and raised a questioning eyebrow at his description of the day.

"We're heading to—"

Sorcha shoved her elbow into Aonghas's side. "South," she quickly interjected. "We're heading south." She shot Aonghas a warning look.

"My family is just down the way," the boy offered, motioning downriver. "You're welcome to share a meal."

Her own aching belly made her want to accept, but knowing Coghill had just spent a night with them, Sorcha thought it best to decline. Before Aonghas could speak, she shook her head. "Thank you, but we must keep moving."

"Do you need a guide?" The boy seemed extremely eager to be of help, and Sorcha was starting to grow suspicious. But then the boy grimaced and went on. "Unless, of course, you're traveling to Baile a' Chaolais? I don't want to go there. My da says that my brothers and I will find work at the quarry, but hammering stones all day sounds terrible. Are you going to Baile a' Chaolais?"

Sorcha couldn't help but be charmed by the scamp. She had a feeling he and Aonghas would get along well.

Knowing they needed to be wary of whom they trusted, Sorcha evaded his question. "A fine guide you would be, I'm certain, but we know where we're going. Thank you . . ."

"Iain," he offered. "My name's Iain Ramsay. Who are you?"

"Ao—"

"Archie," Sorcha quickly interrupted before Aonghas gave his true name. "This is my son, Archie, and I am Mrs. Macdonald." They were the first names that came to her. They dared not give anyone their true names, especially since Coghill had already been through here, but now that the false name was past her lips, Sorcha worried that it was too similar to her birth surname of Macdonell.

"Iain!" a man's voice called through the trees, making Sorcha freeze in panic. "Iain, it's time to go. Where are you, boy?"

Iain's open, eager face shuttered, and he scowled. "I've got to go."

"It was nice to meet you, Iain. I wish you well at . . ." She paused, realizing the boy wouldn't welcome a reminder of the quarry. ". . . Finding work."

Despite his father waiting for him, Iain took his time. When Sorcha last glimpsed him, he was walking downriver, slashing at the air with a stick he wielded like a claymore.

Sorcha nudged Aonghas's arm, and they moved away at a quick pace. She wanted to be well away from here before the boy told his family of the mother and son he'd met.

Before long they came to a wide section of the river with gravel banks scattered like stepping stones. At the other side, despite being in a rush, Sorcha quickly chose another stone and made her mark so that it pointed across the river and up to the mountain pass.

When that was done, they began the long ascent through the forest that blanketed the mountainside. Words were impossible, as they struggled to breathe on the steep climb through the mist.

When they finally emerged from the last of the trees, Sorcha was delighted to find an open moorland, where sun broke through in patches to light their way across a handful of rolling hills. She felt lighter up here, she realized. With not another soul in sight, along with the knowledge that their pursuers were many miles away in the opposite direction, she felt safe for the first time all day. She considered lingering here, but Aonghas's growling stomach pushed them onward.

The farther they walked, the colder the day turned. The sun disappeared, and heavy gray clouds pressed over them.

Soon they found themselves on the lip of the mountain, where the trail dropped down in switchbacks into a lush green valley. Across the glen, silver torrents of water flowed down the gullies of a towering mountain, its top obscured in clouds. She stopped to take it all in, even though rain started to pelt her exposed face. Quickly drawing her *plaide* over her head and adjusting the silver brooch at her chest to hold it in place, she looked down the long green glen where clouds swirled between mountains and danced across the grass, moss, and stones. Something stirred inside her, and she couldn't tell if it was fear or excitement. Maybe both.

She didn't know this glen, but she knew it held magic. She could feel it. And secrets. And promises. The people who lived here—if there were any—must have been born of the mountains and the mists themselves, for no mere human was worthy of its power.

"Ma? Are you coming?" Aonghas's words snapped her out of her reverie. He was already far below, on the second switchback, and was looking at her with impatience. "I think I see a cottage at the bottom."

The reminder of their need for shelter and sustenance scattered her fanciful thoughts and sent her feet forward. With the rain now falling steadily, she huddled beneath her *plaide* and focused on nothing more than finding secure footing on the path that had itself become a small waterfall. Her bare feet were freezing, and several times she slipped. Her falls, though cushioned by her drugget skirt and shift, sent spears of pain through her body.

By the time they reached the bottom, the glen had lost its magic. Sorcha was muddy, drenched, and miserable, and thinking only of finding warm shelter and a warm meal.

The path widened into a road big enough for a wagon. Sorcha wordlessly followed Aonghas as he set off in the direction away from the dramatic glen, which confused her. Wouldn't there be a greater chance of finding shelter in the glen rather than out on what looked to be another vast, empty moor?

As though he could hear her thoughts, Aonghas muttered, "That way leads to Coghill."

Surprised, Sorcha looked back down the glen and saw no signs of their pursuers, nor could she figure out how Aonghas knew that was where Coghill would be. But, she reminded herself, the boy had been taught by his father how to read the mountains and the glens and know where they connected, and so, if he said that direction led to Coghill, she'd believe him.

Knowing this would be an important turning point on the trail when they made their way back home, Sorcha drew the knife from her belt and set to work making her carving on the nearest stone.

As she worked, the freezing rain made her tuck her chin and huddle inside her *plaide*, but the water did aid in washing away the carving dust and made the gouges stand out. Satisfied with her work, she stood up and turned to tell Aonghas they could go, when she realized he was no longer with her. In fact, nothing surrounded her but the mists that had silently slipped down the mountains to envelop her as she carved.

Suddenly, old stories came to mind of the *glaistig*, who lured travelers to their deaths. The spirit favored wild places just like this one, Sorcha knew, and would appear as a beautiful woman.

Alarmed, she started running as fast as her aching and numb feet allowed. She knew Aonghas had gone toward the moor, so she ran in that direction, praying he'd not come to harm.

At one point, she heard what sounded like a woman singing through the mist, but she could only make out a few words. Something about the sky, or maybe it was the Isle of Skye. Whatever it was, Sorcha knew not to slow down or look for the source. Besides, it sounded like the the voice came from all around, even from the mist itself. The *glaistig* was close. Choking on a sob, she ran faster.

Sharp stones cut into her toes, but she ignored the pain and kept running. Rain clouded her vision, and it was her ears that found Aonghas before her eyes could. He was singing, not the song she'd heard through the mist, but a mouth-music tune about a boy spreading manure. *"Tha Fionnlagh ag innearadh, the Fionnlagh ag innearadh, tha Fionnlagh leis a' bhriogais odhar."*

"Aonghas, I was so worried!" She couldn't stop the reprimand from slipping out when she caught up to him.

He made a face at her. "Why?"

She just shook her head and focused forward. They needed to get off this isolated stretch of road. There must be somewhere they could find shelter.

"Look!"

She looked to where Aonghas pointed through the driving rain and was relieved to see shadows in the shape of buildings. As they walked closer, she saw a large square building made up of blue slate. It sat in the middle of the wide moor, and she wondered how the fierce wind screaming up the glen didn't blow the building apart.

It seemed to be an inn, judging by the number of horses tied outside or being led into a large barn. It crossed her mind to find a quiet corner in one of the outbuildings away from people, but she could not see any that did not have someone lurking about, tending to horses or guarding possessions stacked in wagons. The main door to the inn opened, letting out a burst of noise from the voices inside. Maybe there were enough people in there that no one would take notice of the two of them.

She and Aonghas desperately needed to get out of this weather, and she could see that Aonghas was weak with fatigue. He needed food if she expected him to be able to continue the journey. "We'll go inside, but only until the rain lets up. Understand? And don't talk to anyone."

Her heart raced as she pushed open the heavy wooden door of the public house. She felt like Daniel from the story Father Tormod had read to them from his Bible and then translated to the *Gàidhlig*. She and Aonghas were entering the lion's den and were about to be eaten— the lions, of course, being Coghill, his helper Baltair, and anyone they might meet who would eagerly turn them over to answer for their accused crime.

The first things she noticed were the blessed heat and the offensive stench of the large room, which was packed with men—drovers, travelers, horsemen, hunters. How had so many come to be out here in the middle of a seemingly empty moor?

The next thing she noticed—and this was because she made a point to look—was that Coghill wasn't among the lot. She felt her body relax, which brought with it a fatigue so great she wondered if she'd fall asleep on her feet before she found a chair. Or better yet, a bed upon which to rest.

The only other woman on the premises besides herself, that she could see, bustled past them carrying a large tray of empty pint glasses. She shot Sorcha a harried look. "Welcome to the Gleann Comhann King's House. Find a seat wherever you can."

The King's House? Sorcha knew all about king's houses. They were scattered across the Highlands, built or commandeered by English troops after the failed '45 uprising along with roads, bridges, garrisons, and barracks. All were used for one purpose only: to house the troops who worked to suppress the Highland people and their culture. The English had even made efforts to take away the *Gàidhlig* language and force the King's English onto the tongues of Highlanders. They were still working toward that goal.

Was it safe to be here? The military had long ago abandoned the king's houses, and many were now used as inns for travelers, but might Coghill arrive? Or might someone else recognize her and Aonghas from Coghill's description and apprehend them?

And, even more, she recognized the name of the glen, Gleann Comhann. It was the site of a brutal massacre over a century past, but knowing it happened nearby set her on edge.

While all this was racing through her mind, Aonghas had elbowed his way through the steaming crowd to two vacant stools near the fire. Sorcha followed and hesitantly sat down, still not certain they should be here at all.

The longer she sat, however, the more she relaxed. And the warmer she became. She removed her *plaide* from her head and shoulders and tucked it around her waist. Her linen mutch was soaked through and hot on her head, but she dared not remove it in the company of all these strange men.

The serving woman arrived with bowls of lukewarm barley soup, which she shoved into their hands, not caring that they spilled. Neither she nor Aonghas cared, either, and hungrily drank the broth without spoons, for none had been offered. The hunk of bread atop each bowl was also gone within seconds.

A trio of men sitting at a long table near them seemed to be making friends with every soul in the room, Aonghas among them, despite Sorcha's warning not to speak to anyone. Sorcha watched with concern as her son scooted his stool closer to the men and seemed to hang on their every word.

The poor lad hadn't had menfolk around for the past three years—excepting, of course, their friends and neighbors in the village, but that wasn't the same as living with a father or brother. Sorcha's heart ached anew for all that her son had lost.

Figuring it could do little harm, she left him to their tales of daring on the high seas and mountaintops and scooted her stool against the wall near the fireplace to rest a spell.

With her head against the wall and her arms crossed over her middle, she was surprisingly comfortable. In a sleepy state, she watched the other patrons and marveled that this was where life had brought her. It was midafternoon. She should be tending her small plot of potatoes and kale or her runrig field of oats and bere. Or, possibly, she would be sitting in the warm sunshine with her mending, or plaiting heather into ropes to replace the ones her goat constantly chewed through. Her entire body ached in a way that had nothing to do with her physical hardships and everything to do with missing her friends and her home.

She shouldn't be in this dirty, reeking, rough place in the middle of a rainstorm, hiding from men who would see them put to the noose.

The sound of a bow being drawn slowly across strings alerted her to the musicians in the opposite corner tuning up for some entertainment. The first strains of "Crodh-laoigh nam Bodach" filled the air, and Sorcha closed her eyes to listen. Her Tàm had loved this song. When the neighbors gathered for *cèilidh*, it was Tàm's baritone that had always led the singing. Oh, how she would give anything to hear him now.

"Ma! Wake up!" Aonghas shoved at her shoulder, and she forced her eyes open. "I've found us passage on a ship to Glaschu. But we must leave now!"

Sorcha blinked, confused by the noise and commotion around her when, in her dreams, she'd just been walking through the fields of Srath Ghlais. "Why would we want to go to Glaschu?"

Aonghas sighed and shoved a hand through his hair. Leaning closer to her, he hissed, "It's closer to Dùn Èideann, and we wouldn't have to worry about running into Coghill along the way."

The boy had a point. She was finally awake enough to push herself off the wall and glance at the group of men, who were busy dropping coins on the table and getting to their feet. "Tell me about this ship."

"It's a two-masted brigantine loaded with slate from the Baile a' Chaolais quarry—remember Iain telling us he and his father and brother were going to work there?" He paused until she nodded. "Anyway, they're carrying the slate to Glaschu, and they have room for any passengers who can pay the fare. But we must go now. They sail with the morning tide."

Sorcha's attention had caught on one detail. "What's the fare?"

Aonghas's grin did not slip. In fact, it widened. "That's the best part. If we don't require food, then it will only cost us a half groat each."

They had the money, thanks to the coin purse Sorcha had grabbed from her hiding place in her box bed just before escaping the flames.

Aonghas was on his feet now, trying to pull her up from her stool. When she looked past him, she saw the reason for his urgency, as the men were already heading for the door. "Ma, come on. We'll spend less buying our passage than we will buying food along the way if we walk. But we must go now. They are leaving!"

She couldn't argue with Aonghas's logic, so she allowed him to pull her to her feet, and after she handed him the coins for their fare, he dashed outside to secure their passage with the men. Sorcha paid for their supper and followed her son back out into the rainy afternoon.

Sorcha had no way of knowing what time it was, due to the heavy cloud cover, but it seemed darker than when they'd arrived, and she figured night was falling. She'd be grateful for the cover of darkness if they encountered Coghill traveling this way from his own visit to Baile a' Chaolais. She pulled her *plaide* over her head and wished Aonghas could do the same. She would need to look for a *plaide* they could afford for him.

The three sailors had gathered several passengers. Besides her and Aonghas, four other men were walking with them down into the dark glen. She was curious about why they were traveling south at this time of year, when crops and animals at home would need tending. But because she wasn't willing to share her own explanation for her travels, she didn't ask, and they walked in silence, listening only to the sounds of the rain and wind punctuated occasionally by a cough or sniff. No sign of the *glaistig* remained, and Sorcha was glad of it.

It didn't take long for her fatigue to catch up with her again. The food and short nap had helped a great deal, and she couldn't deny that her body had grown stronger from the last week of almost constant walking, but she needed a full night's rest. Once they were on the ship, she planned to find a place to curl up and sleep the entire passage.

She lost track of time as they walked. Darkness enveloped them entirely, but the rain let up enough to ease visibility, and two of the sailors carried lanterns that allowed the group to see the rough and muddy track they followed. As long as they didn't fall behind the rest of the group, they wouldn't lose their way. The rough terrain and deep shadows of the glen did, however, bring to mind the many terrifying stories she'd heard of the massacre that had happened here, and she couldn't help but worry that unsettled spirits walked beside her.

After what must have been at least three hours of walking, they finally reached a small sleeping village, and Sorcha thought they'd reached their destination. But no, the sailors kept on walking, ignoring the dogs that barked from the cottage yards and Sorcha's own plea for water.

"There's water on the ship," growled the sailor walking behind her, at the rear of the group. "We're nearly there."

But his definition of *nearly* was quite different from Sorcha's, because they continued to walk another half hour and through a second village.

When that settlement was behind them, she started to notice a hint of saltiness to the air, but it wasn't until the sailor in the lead stopped abruptly and told everyone to sit on some stones to wait that she noticed the ship anchored offshore lit by a handful of lanterns on the deck.

One of the sailors climbed into a rowboat and started making his way to the ship to, he said, alert the captain of the new passengers before they'd be allowed on board. Sorcha sat, as instructed, and used the time while they waited to study what she could see of the ship.

It had two tall masts and another long pole sticking off the front of the sleek, narrow body. Something about its appearance didn't feel right to Sorcha, and it took her another moment before she figured out what it was. The sailors had told Aonghas they were carrying a load of slate. While Sorcha didn't know much about ships, nor had she ever sailed on one before, she doubted the ship in front of her was loaded with heavy stones. Where would they put them all? This one looked like it was used for carrying people, or even for going into battle, what with the line of cannons poking from its side.

And why were the two remaining sailors standing on either side of the passengers sitting on the beach, as though guarding them? Were they protecting them from some unseen danger? Or were they assuring none of them escaped?

To test her theory, Sorcha got to her feet, attracting the attention of one of the sailors. She smiled, even though she doubted he could see her face in the darkness. "I need to relieve myself."

He just grunted and jerked his chin over his shoulder as though telling her to go that way to do her business.

Okay, so maybe he wasn't trying to keep her here. But what about Aonghas? She feigned a need for his assistance. "Archie, come with me, son. I cannot see so well in the dark."

The sailor stepped forward as though to stop Aonghas. But then, seeming to catch himself, he stopped. "Don't go far. We'll board in just a few minutes."

As she and Aonghas walked toward some nearby trees in search of privacy, Sorcha looked back and, in the light bouncing off the water from the ship, saw the sailor's head turned their direction, keeping his eye on them.

Not on *them*. On Aonghas.

As soon as she stepped into the shadow of the trees, she grabbed Aonghas's hand and, leaning her head close to his, whispered, "I need you to listen very carefully, and don't argue."

When he nodded in agreement, his head bumped against hers. She went on. "These aren't mere sailors. They're crimps. Your da told me about them."

"What do you mean? What are crimps?"

Sorcha felt her hand reflexively squeeze tighter on Aonghas's arm and forced it to soften so as not to overly alarm the boy. "It's their job to press men into service in the Royal Navy. If you get on that ship, you'll not be stepping off in Glaschu, I assure you that."

He pulled out of her grasp. "Ma, don't be ridiculous. You're here, aren't you? They don't press women into the king's service."

She couldn't allow him to return to the beach, so she grabbed his arm again and held tight. "They were never going to allow me onto that ship. Didn't you see how willing that man was to let me go just now, but when you stood up, he tried to stop you?"

"I wouldn't leave without you. If they try to make you stay, I'll refuse to go."

Sorcha shook her head. "Aonghas, you don't understand. They'll force you onto the ship, and they'll not care what is done to me as long as I don't stop you from going. We're not safe."

"But we paid them for our passage!"

Just then, they heard a boot scraping over stone nearby, and they froze.

"You there—it's time to board. What's taking you so long?"

To avoid suspicion, Sorcha called back in as calm a voice as she could muster, "I'm nearly finished. Just a moment, please!" And then, to Aonghas, she whispered, "We must go—now. Before it's too late."

The boy did not argue further, although Sorcha would have dragged him away even if he had, and they turned from the beach to make their way deeper into the dark trees.

A cry sounded from the beach, followed immediately by the sounds of a struggle, and Sorcha knew the other men had realized what was happening and were putting up a fight. "Run!"

Too soon, they reached the edge of the forest and found themselves on the road they'd recently walked. With no other options, they ran away from the beach and hoped they hadn't been seen by the guards.

No such luck. "Hey! Come back here!"

Aonghas was faster than her, and she was glad he pulled ahead, putting more distance between him and the press gang.

When they reached the first village, Aonghas darted off the road between two buildings. Sorcha followed, not knowing where they were going but happy to be off the main road.

"Psst! Over here!"

At the hushed call, she saw Aonghas stop and then turn toward the barn where the call came from. Sorcha caught up to him and, looping her hand through his arm, cautioned, "This could be a trap."

"It might."

The barn door pushed open farther and a head poked out. "You can hide in here."

The voice sounded familiar. She took a step closer. "Iain?"

The boy stepped out fully from the building and hurried to them. He grabbed Aonghas's other arm and started tugging him toward the barn. "I saw you walk through earlier and thought you might be in trouble. Hide in here. Quickly."

Inside the dark barn, Sorcha heard animals rustling in their stalls. The three humans froze and listened for any sounds outside.

There were footsteps outside the closed barn door. If the sailors found them, there would be no escape.

Just when she thought whoever was out there had passed by, the barn door creaked open.

CHAPTER TEN

Keaka

Day two, afternoon; along Loch Lomond

I feel like we've walked several miles from Morag and Rachel's house, but when I look at the map in Colin's guidebook, we aren't anywhere close to Rowardennan, our destination for the night.

I really wish we'd accepted Rachel's offer to drive us. We would have been there by now.

And to make matters even worse, I'm feeling what Colin calls a "hot spot" on my left heel. The beginning of a blister. I would stop and cover it with a bandage, but I'm afraid that if I do, I won't be able to get my legs moving again.

The trail this afternoon is different from anything we've experienced yet. The farmlands and wide valleys have been replaced by a huge sparkling lake, rocky beaches, and hardwood forests just starting to show their autumn colors. The trail undulates gently, yet there are enough uphill sections to make me silently curse. Conic Hill used up all my leg strength for the day.

Colin has entertained me with stories from his backpacking trip in the Cascade Mountains last month with a group of high school friends, and I told him my own stories of the trip I took with friends through Germany, France, and Spain when I was his age.

But when Colin starts to reminisce about his father, my fatigue more than doubles and I find it difficult to stay engaged in the conversation. I fake it the best I can, for his sake.

That's what I've been doing for the last ten months: Faking it. Pretending to be a devastated widow. But really, I felt only relief when Adam died, because our secret died with him. With him gone, I wasn't a wife whose husband left her for another woman. I wouldn't have to go through divorce and everything that came with that. I wouldn't have to watch friends choose between me or Adam.

This way, I am a widow.

But hearing Colin talk about his dad fills me with deep shame at my selfishness. What kind of person is happy about the death of her child's father?

There is something very wrong with me.

I look up, and what I see makes me feel like crying. We're at the bottom of a set of stairs built into a steep hillside. The stairs climb high up the hill, then turn and keep climbing until they disappear into the trees. I can't tell how high they go. "How much farther until we get there?"

Colin pulls out the guidebook and flips through. After studying the map, he finally answers, "Two miles, max. Dad wrote in the margin here that this is the last climb for the day."

Two miles. We've come about twelve miles already, and that doesn't even address the elevation gains and losses. I can do two more measly miles, and then I'm going to take my boots off and throw them across the room. I shake my arms to ease my tension. "Let's do this."

Colin laughs. "Need a push?"

"Ha ha, funny man. Just go."

Colin gives me a cheeky grin, then heads up the steps.

Just when I think I'm reaching the top, I feel my blister tear open. Damn. I ignore it and keep going.

But it's not the top. Just a turn of the trail, and there are more stairs ahead. My heel stings where my wool sock rubs at the open sore.

I can't see Colin. His steady pace has led him far ahead.

Dropping my pack, I sit on a wood-and-gravel step and tug off my boot. When I peel my sock off, a bit of skin comes with it and reveals an oozing, raw mess.

I let my heel air out as I dig through my pack, looking for bandages. Birdsong fills the woods, and I realize how quiet it is out here by myself. I can't even hear Colin's footsteps, he is so far ahead of me.

I'm still digging through my pack looking for a Band-Aid when I hear the unmistakable sound of someone coming up the trail. I crane my neck to see and spot two Asian men climbing slowly toward me. I'm startled by the realization that they are the first brown faces I've seen on the trail besides my own.

"Hello," the first man says as he reaches me. His accent is strong, but I can't place it. He eyes my foot. "That looks painful. Do you need help?"

My instinct is to refuse, but that would be ridiculous since I can't seem to find any Band-Aids. Adam used to get so irritated with my refusal to let him help me when I clearly needed assistance. It was even one of the things he told me when we were arguing about his affair. "You never need me," he accused. "It's like I'm nothing more than your roommate, for how often you treat me like I'm in your way."

I saw the truth of his statement as he'd said it, but instead of acknowledging it, I grew defensive and snapped, "You used to say you liked how strong and capable I was. Now you want a needy wife who can't get through the day without her big, strong husband taking care of her?" Adam just shook his head and walked out the door, having no idea how badly I'd needed him to pull me into his arms and tell me we were going to be okay.

I force Adam from my mind and smile at the man. "I can't seem to find my first aid kit."

His companion has caught up to us, and he smiles at me. The first man says something to him that sounds like Chinese, and he slings off his pack and retrieves a small zippered case, which he hands to his friend.

"We have three sizes of plasters." He pulls the Band-Aids out of the kit and holds them out to me.

Thanking him—and smiling my gratitude at the second man, who must not speak English—I take the biggest Band-Aid he has and peel it open. "My son told me to stop if I started noticing hot spots, but I didn't listen and now I'm paying the price."

The man laughs. "Think of it as a souvenir of the trail."

As they disappear up the steps, I slide my sock and boot back on and then follow.

The top of the hill isn't that much farther, I find, and I reach it to discover Colin sprawled on the grass. "Those guys told me you were right behind them," he says as I drop onto the ground next to him.

"Yeah, they were a big help." I make a face and admit, "I have a blister."

Colin sits up. "Mom! I told you to stop the minute you started feeling something." He reaches for his pack as though to get the bandages, but I stop him and tell him that it's taken care of. I'm bemoaning all those stairs when Colin interrupts me. "Mom, where's your ring?"

Reflexively, I wrap my right hand over my left as though to hide my missing wedding ring. Then I force a light laugh. "Oh, my fingers swell when I walk, so I took it off this morning. Don't worry, it's safe."

He dubiously accepts my explanation, and we're soon back to walking, though I can't help but wonder what he's thinking about me not wearing his father's ring. I get my answer a short distance up the trail.

"Mom, are you dating other men?"

"What? What makes you ask me that? Just because I'm not wearing my ring?" I stop talking, knowing that I'm protesting too much. Then, deliberately, I tell him, "No, I'm not dating other men. But I could, you know. I'm single. Your father has been gone almost a year now."

"Yeah, I know." He seems to think about this for a while. "You're right. I'm sorry for freaking out about it."

"That's okay." His "freaking out" renews my decision to never let him know about his father's girlfriend. Adam isn't here to explain himself, and the burden of feeling disappointed in his father would be too much on Colin. He should remember his dad in a positive light.

The rest of our walk is mostly in silence. When we finally see the white bulk of the Rowardennan Hotel come into view, I could dance with joy—if I weren't so exhausted.

The next hour is spent settling into our room and taking turns in the shower before slipping into flip-flops and waddling—at least, I feel like I'm waddling—downstairs to have dinner at the hotel bar.

The bar is crammed with people, and we take our food and drinks to the picnic tables outside. I catch bits of conversations as we wade through the crowd and realize that some people are here not for the West Highland Way, but to climb Ben Lomond. When we sit down, I see the Chinese guys from earlier sitting nearby, and I smile and wave at them.

I'm not in the mood for socializing, and so I sit hunched over my food as Colin moves from one group to another. The sound of his voice and his laughter echoing across the grass makes me smile. At least he's having a good time. That's the whole point, after all.

"Hey, Mom!"

I turn to find Colin walking toward me.

"Kirsten and Terese are here, and there's a German woman who's a lot of fun. Come hang out with everyone."

I feel grumpy and tired and know that I'm not fit for company. "I don't know, Colin. I'm exhausted. I think I need to call it a night."

"But . . ." He looks back over his shoulder to the group, where bursts of laughter fill the evening air. "It was your idea to meet up with them tonight, remember?"

I'd forgotten all about running into the Danes in Balmaha at lunch today and inviting them to meet for drinks.

I give in, figuring I can manage half an hour. I place my dishes in a bus tub near the door, then walk with Colin to join the group. I greet Jorgen and his daughters, noting with some discomfort how Jorgen's eyes light up at seeing me, and then do my best to remember the other three people's names. None of them stick. There is the woman from Germany whom Colin mentioned and two men from Amsterdam. I sip at the hard cider Colin brings me from the bar and mostly listen to the group chatter. After the agreed-upon half hour, I give a small wave to Colin so he knows I'm leaving and then head upstairs. I'm so tired I feel delirious.

And, illogically, part of me feels like I've already lost my boy, a whole week earlier than expected.

CHAPTER ELEVEN

Sorcha

Baile a' Chaolais (Ballachulish)

Sorcha moved backward, deeper into the shadows of the barn, tugging Aonghas along beside her. All sounds were muffled by the pounding in her ears, and she knew her son was likely feeling the trembling that had taken hold of her entire body, but she couldn't make it stop.

The barn door creaked open wide enough to allow a body to slip inside, then banged shut.

Sorcha held her breath, knowing the intruder must be the sailor who'd chased them from the beach. A pinprick of light moved farther into the interior of the barn—a lantern turned low. If she waited just long enough, until the crimp had moved deep inside the barn, they might be able to slide behind him and escape.

But the pinprick light stopped moving right outside the stall where they hid. Sorcha dared not move a single muscle.

"Iain?"

The whisper confused Sorcha at first. How did the sailor know Iain's name? But then she realized Iain had been working with the crimps all along and had trapped her and Aonghas in here on purpose. Anger burned through her. Slowly, she slid her hand into Aonghas's so they wouldn't be separated when it was time to run.

"Son, are you in here?"

Sorcha cocked her head to the side to better hear the whispered words.

"Da?" Iain answered from the darkness on the other side of Aonghas. "Is that you?"

Suddenly, light filled the barn as the man turned up the wick of the lantern he carried. In the orange glow, Sorcha immediately recognized him from the settlement at the top of Loch Lìobhann. He'd been the one holding the reins of Coghill's horses. She shrank back even farther, holding tightly to Aonghas, until her back was pressed against the cold stones of the barn wall.

Iain's father lifted the lantern higher to look them over. "Who've you got with you, son?" His bonnet was pulled low and cast a shadow over half his face.

Iain stepped into the circle of light and proudly introduced them to his father. "They are the two I told you about, who I met by the river. The crimps had them, but they got away just in time."

The explanation seemed to erase the father's distrust, and he visibly relaxed, which helped Sorcha to relax. If Iain's father connected them to the pair Coghill was pursuing, he showed no sign of it. He even seemed to trust them based solely on the fact that Iain knew them.

"I'm glad to hear it." Iain's father spoke directly to Sorcha now, and she found herself warming to him. "That gang came through the village early this morning, before Iain, his brothers, and I arrived to start work at the quarry. The townspeople recognized their kind and urged them on their way, then set up a watch in case they returned." He spit onto the straw floor and shook his head. "If you ask me, it's a sorry state of affairs when the king needs to force men to serve him."

Her fear had finally settled enough for words to come. "We're deeply grateful to your son for helping us. I don't know what I would've done if they'd gotten my Ao—my Archie here aboard their ship." She squeezed Aonghas's hand even tighter.

"You're safe now, but you should stay out of sight until morning to be certain." Iain's father turned toward the door as he went on. "Bed down here for the night where it's warm. We'll keep watch until the bastards set sail."

With that, Iain and his father slipped outside and closed the door softly behind them, leaving Sorcha and Aonghas in total darkness.

"Come," she whispered to Aonghas. "Let's try to sleep."

They settled onto the clean straw with Sorcha's *plaide* wrapped around them and listened to the rustling and grunts of the animals as they, too, settled back down. Within moments, Aonghas breathed slowly and steadily, and she knew sleep had claimed him.

Sorcha, on the other hand, took much longer to find rest. Her mind whirled with the knowledge that she'd almost lost her son today. If he'd been pressed into service and forced to sail away from her, she may have never seen him again. The idea was unthinkable.

Her stomach turned as a startling thought came to her: if he'd sailed away on the ship, he would've successfully eluded Coghill and Baltair. Although forced, he would've been in service to the king, just as his father and brother had been. He might have even thought it thrilling.

He would've escaped the gallows.

He moaned in his sleep, and she pulled him closer to her side to try to ease his nightmare. Immediately, he relaxed and his breath grew steady.

No, she'd done the right thing by taking him away from the crimps. She was doing the right thing in keeping him with her, where he was safe, and loved, and had a chance to grow into whatever future awaited him.

She would do everything it took to ensure that future was one of freedom.

She tucked her *plaide* tighter around him as though he were still a youngster, knowing full well he would complain if he were awake. It soothed her aching mother's heart to tend to her boy, though, so she even planted a kiss on his sweaty forehead.

This boy was her life. She would stick to her plan to get him safely to Dùn Èideann, where they'd be lost in the crowds of the big city. Somehow, she'd keep them away from Coghill and Baltair. She'd keep Aonghas safe from crimps and anyone else who wanted to tear him away from her.

She closed her eyes to try to sleep, but her stomach churned with worry and kept her awake late into the night. There were too many things in this world, too many people in this world, trying to tear the last of her family apart. How was she going to fight them all?

⁓

Sorcha felt like she'd not slept at all, but she must have, because when she opened her eyes, she found sunlight filtering through gaps around the barn door. She didn't want to emerge from her warm bed in the straw, but she knew they needed to keep moving, if for no other reason than to put distance between them and the crimps.

Coghill! She'd nearly forgotten he might be in this very village. The last time she'd seen him, he and Baltair had been heading down Loch Lìobhann toward Baile a' Chaolais, where she found herself now. They could be right outside, for all she knew.

"Aonghas," she hissed, reaching for him. "Wake up—"

He wasn't there. The space in the stall beside her was empty, and after a hurried search, she found he wasn't inside the barn at all. A cry sounded from outside, sending her heart to her feet. "Ao—" She stopped herself, remembering just in time, even as she headed for the door, carrying her *plaide* in her arms. "Archie! Archie, where are you?"

The scene outside stopped her short. Aonghas wasn't hurt, nor at the mercy of any captors. He was running at full speed past the barn with a shinty caman in his hands. As he reached the leather ball, where a group of lads played in the middle of the road, he swung at it with all his might just as Iain did the same from the opposite direction.

Iain's caman struck Aonghas's shin and he fell face-first to the ground. Sorcha cried out in alarm and rushed toward him. The game continued, and the other boys chased the ball down the road with several other legs and feet falling victim to the sport.

When she caught up to him, Aonghas was still on his belly on the dirt, and she feared he was seriously hurt. The moment she touched his shoulder, though, he rolled onto his back. Only then did she see that he was shaking with laughter. "Iain!" he shouted. *"Contrachd ort!"*

Aonghas froze when he saw her and flinched, knowing she wouldn't approve of the insult. But, just as quickly, he jumped to his feet. "Good morning, Ma. The ship is gone!"

Only now did she think to look toward the bay and found it blissfully empty. One threat gone, but another very big one could still be in the village.

By the time she turned back to her son, he was already jogging away from her to join the game again. "Archie!"

He stopped, and she was grateful he'd remembered to respond to the false name. "We must be going. Now."

"Oh, do you have to leave so soon? My employer's wife just sent me to invite you to breakfast." Iain's father was walking toward her from a cottage behind the barn.

Her stomach rumbled at the mention of food, but Sorcha ignored it. The longer they stayed here, the sooner someone—maybe even Coghill himself—might identify them as the murderers he was searching for. "Thank you, but we really must be on our way."

At that moment, Iain ran up to join them, laughing and calling to Archie to get back into the game. When Aonghas told him he needed to be leaving, Iain asked, "Are you traveling south like you said before?"

Sorcha nodded even as she looked at the faces of the villagers coming and going, most of them heading toward the slate quarry she could see against the mountain. No one resembled Coghill.

"Can I come with you? Can I, Pa? Can I go with them?"

The question surprised Sorcha, and her gaze flew to Iain's father, who seemed to be considering the idea.

"No, no," she quickly answered before anyone got bigger ideas. "I don't think that would be a good idea. We're not even sure where we'll settle. It depends on what work we can find . . ." She trailed off, worried the more she spoke, the more she would rouse suspicion.

Iain hugged his caman to his chest and begged his father, as if Sorcha hadn't spoken. "Please, Pa? You know I don't like quarry work. If I go south with them, I can live with Aunt Peigi in Dùn Èideann and work in one of those cotton mills we heard about. I'll send you and Ma all the money I earn, I promise!"

His father cast a glance Sorcha's way as though to determine her thoughts on the subject. Before she could say a word, Iain spun toward Aonghas. "And I can teach you to spear fish; do you know how to spear fish? I'm the best there is. And not only that, I know how to set a grouse trap." Now his attention shifted to Sorcha. "I won't be any trouble, I promise. Please can I travel with you?"

"Can he, Ma? I want to learn to catch fish with a spear." The excuse was weak, but Sorcha knew Aonghas wanted much more than a fishing teacher. He wanted a friend.

But it was too dangerous to allow someone to get close to them right now. They couldn't trust anyone. And, really, they shouldn't expose young Iain to the dangers that Coghill and Baltair present.

No, having Iain come with them was a terrible idea.

She was already shaking her head when another thought occurred to her: Coghill was looking for a woman and her son. He wasn't looking for a woman with two sons, and that would be exactly how they would appear. Iain's company would be a disguise. And if he really could help them find food, all the better.

She stared hard at the boy's father. "You would allow your son to go with strangers?"

The man laughed and shrugged. "Iain hasn't met a stranger in his life." He slung his arm around his son's shoulders and went on. "Iain is right, though. He could find work down south—and better-paying work, at that. We would all go if my wife and I weren't about to be blessed with another child. If you're willing to mind him on his journey, I'm willing to let him go with you, and I'll write to my sister-in-law right away telling her to expect him."

Sorcha looked again at Aonghas to see if she could gauge his thoughts on the matter. The eager grin he gave her was all the answer she needed. Relenting, she smiled at Iain. "Go pack your things."

With a whoop of joy, the boy ran off and returned in record time with a leather bag looped across his chest. He also handed each of them a warm bannock with a sausage patty tucked inside. Sorcha felt tears sting her eyes at the sight and smell of the very welcome food. She took a big bite that scorched the roof of her mouth.

Iain hugged his father goodbye, and then the three of them set their feet on the road, heading back through Gleann Comhann in the direction from which they'd walked yesterday evening.

Just as they reached the edge of the village, sunshine broke free of the heavy clouds to spear through the glen where they would be walking, as though lighting their path. The two boys, with their exuberant energy, led the way into the moody glen, talking and laughing together all the while. Sorcha, trailing behind them, smiled. Maybe their luck had finally changed.

Since leaving Baile a' Chaolais early that morning, they'd passed the King's House, skirting it by a good distance, and made their way onto Mòinteach Raineach—Rannoch Moor. At least, that was the name Iain gave to the wide, moody landscape that seemed to go on for miles with not a soul in sight. The sun's appearance that morning had been fleeting, and now a heavy, dark sky cast a gloom over all, even dimming the orange-yellow birdfoot deervetch and white heath bedstraw growing along the sides of the military road.

So far, the rain had held off, and the huge mountains bordering the edge of the moor and at whose base they walked blocked the worst of the westerly wind. She was grateful for that wind, though, because it kept the midges away and, for once, she let her *plaide* drop to hang around her waist, leaving only her short jacket and shirt to protect her from the chill.

Iain and Aonghas had become fast friends, and their laughter and stories helped the time pass quickly. She'd had her misgivings about allowing Iain to come with them, but so far, he'd been no trouble. A pang of guilt sliced through her every time she considered the danger she was exposing Iain to simply by his being in their company. She would do her best to protect him and see that he reached Dùn Èideann safely.

They'd been walking all day, and Sorcha was considering making camp in the patch of forest they were passing through. But then the sound of rushing water and laughter hit her ears, moments before she emerged from the trees and found a cottage on the bank of a swiftly flowing river. The contrast from the still and silent woods to the flurry of activity in the yard made Sorcha stop in surprise.

Two small boys were playing a game of keep-away with their dog and a stick. Their little sister toddled after them, trying to keep up. A handful of chickens in pursuit of grains clucked in anger as they darted clear of the children and dog.

It was achingly familiar, as though Sorcha was back in Srath Ghlais. She wrapped her arms around her waist as she took in the sights, sounds, and smells that should be her daily life but had been stripped from her.

Suddenly, the little girl tripped and landed on her hands and knees. Then she burst out crying.

Sorcha helped the little girl up. "There, there, little lamb. It's only a scrape."

The girl's mother appeared and took her into her arms. "Poor little Beathag, always trying to keep up with your brothers. Let me look at you."

After the mother kissed the girl's knee and sent her off to play again, she invited Sorcha to rest a spell on the bench in front of her cottage. Seeing that the boys had gone off to watch a man fishing in the river, Sorcha accepted the offer. "I'm grateful for the rest."

"Where are you coming from?"

Sorcha could not risk giving away her true identity, so she answered vaguely. "Baile a' Chaolais." And then, to distract the woman from asking more questions, asked one of her own. "Do you get many travelers passing by here?"

The woman went back to her milking, nodding. "We do. Drovers, seasonal workers, traders. Just this morning two men rode through on horseback. Seems they're after a couple of murderers, a man and a woman, both ruthless and cunning as they come. Go by the name of Chisholm. Take care, should you encounter anyone of that description on your travels."

Sorcha had two immediate reactions upon hearing this. First, her stomach turned over at the realization that Coghill and Baltair hadn't followed the coastline as she'd hoped, and had instead turned inland onto this very road. She would have to stay alert.

Her second reaction was surprise at Coghill's description of her and Aonghas. Ruthless and cunning? It was ridiculous to think that she, a widow, and her young son could be those things—and yet it could work in their favor. No one would look at her and Aonghas and see ruthlessness, nor cunning. "Oh, dear!" She pretended to be shocked. "I shall be certain to take great care. Thank you for your warning."

The woman's gaze went from Sorcha down to the boys on the riverbank, making Sorcha wonder if she suspected her after all. "Where is it you three are traveling?"

Sorcha could see no reason to lie. People traveled to the capital all the time, for numerous reasons. "Dùn Èideann. To find work."

The woman nodded, unsurprised. "I should think your sons would have no trouble finding work. They appear strong and healthy."

Her tension eased, knowing that her disguise of having two sons was working.

"Ma!" Aonghas raced up to her, followed closely by Iain. Both boys looked at her with barely suppressed glee. "The boys are going up the glen to bring down the cattle before sunset. Can we go with them?"

They were so eager that she wanted to give permission, but she knew the longer they stayed among these people, the more something about their true identities might slip out. They needed to get to Dùn Èideann and blend into the crowd there. She got to her feet. "No, I'm sorry, boys. We must keep moving if we're to find a place to camp before dark."

"You can stay here," the woman offered as she pushed to her feet and wiped her hands on her apron. "We have room, and I'm certain my husband could give your boys work, if you've a mind to stay for a while."

Both Aonghas and Iain looked at her with such pleading on their faces she nearly laughed. She wanted to give them what they wanted, and could use a rest from walking herself, but wasn't it too much of a risk to stay? What if Coghill returned? Or what if one of them slipped and revealed their true identities?

As she was thinking all this through, the woman added, "We have a rock wall that needs repairing, and I know my husband would appreciate the help."

Iain puffed out his chest. "I can do that. I helped my father build walls all the time."

The woman smiled at Sorcha in a manner that told her she knew the ways of boys. To Iain, she said, "Your assistance will be welcome, and we can pay you for your time." She seemed to think twice and shot a questioning look at Sorcha. "If that's all right with your mother."

Iain laughed. "Oh, she's not—"

"That would be just fine," Sorcha interrupted, saying the first thing that came to mind, just to keep him from revealing the incriminating truth.

The boys whooped with glee.

Realizing what she'd done, Sorcha knew that if she tried to back out now, she'd only make it worse. Accepting the situation, she admitted, "We could use the money."

Aonghas, his whole face lit up, asked, "So can we go with the boys?"

The second Sorcha nodded, Aonghas and Iain took off running, presumably in the direction of the cattle.

The woman laughed and called to her young children, who had tired of playing with the dog and were now throwing rocks into the river. "Goiridh, Raibert, come away from there. You know your sister cannot swim!" To Sorcha, she said, "Talk with my husband about pay, but for now, I can give you a hot supper and a place to sleep. I am Mrs. Fleming."

Sorcha returned her warm smile. "Pleased to meet you. I am Mrs. Macdonald, and that was Archie and Iain." Since she didn't outwardly claim Iain to be her son, she felt better. Allowing Mrs. Fleming to misunderstand wasn't really a lie, after all.

For three lovely days, Sorcha and the boys stayed and worked with the Fleming family, harvesting the spring barley, repairing rock walls, and, for Sorcha, weaving baskets from willow branches and spinning and dyeing wool while also helping mind the three youngest children.

This life suited them, and Sorcha found herself thinking about making this beautiful glen their new home. Coghill was, by now, well away from here. Surely they were safe.

CHAPTER TWELVE

Keaka

Day three; Rowardennan

This morning, I still feel exhausted but I manage to drag myself out of bed. The moment we walk into the bar in search of breakfast, Colin finds his friends and chatter starts right up.

Disappointment digs into my gut right alongside the joy I feel at seeing him so happy. I expected all week to be special time spent bonding with Colin, and like a child, I don't want to share him with anyone else. The idea is so shamefully selfish that I'm glad no one else can hear my thoughts.

After breakfast, we move as a group onto the trail. As much as I try to leave it behind, the dark cloud hanging over my head comes with me.

Even Jorgen gives me a wide berth this morning. He is walking with Clara, the thirtyish solo German hiker whom I'd met last night. I can't imagine traveling anywhere solo, and certainly not in a foreign country. This woman has guts.

A flash off the lake catches my eye, and I turn to see a boat full of tourists snapping pictures of Ben Lomond. The tour guide's voice comes over a loudspeaker, relaying Ben Lomond's elevation and how it is the southernmost of Scotland's munros.

I look up at the mountain but can't see its height from this angle. I do see gorgeous rolling brown hillsides, immense gray rocks, and dancing leaves on trees catching the morning sun. The single-track gravel road where we walk has yellow and white wildflowers growing on either side. I am missing all this beauty by being stuck in my head.

Up ahead, I hear Colin, Kirsten, and Terese raise their voices in song. *"Twas there that we parted in yon bonny glen, on the steep, steep sides of Ben Lomond!"* They continue belting out the words to "The Bonnie Banks of Loch Lomond," and I feel a smile crack across my face.

I lift my chin and pull in a deep breath of cool morning air, pungent with the scent of fallen leaves. So far this morning the sun is shining, but I can see heavy clouds blowing in from the west, and I know this perfect morning won't last.

Colin and the girls turn off the trail ahead, and when I reach the same spot, I do the same. The kids, Jorgen, and Clara are gathered in front of a signboard that reads WELCOME TO ARDESS LODGE AND BEN LOMOND. While I wait for the group to finish reading the information, I use the opportunity to apply midge spray. Already the pesky bugs are biting and raising itchy bumps on my arms and neck, and I have to keep waving my hand in front of my face to avoid inhaling any.

A white-haired man dressed in brown linen pants and a loose-fitting, long-sleeved shirt emerges from a tiny thatched cottage and welcomes us with a smile. *"Fàilte gu Ardess."*

"Tapadh leibh," I reply, distracted by the midge spray.

His eyes light up. *"Tha Gàidhlig agad! Cò às a tha sibh?"*

"Tha mi à Aimearaga." I put the cap on my midge spray and return it to my pack. As I stand up again, I find the rest of our group gaping at me, especially Colin.

"Mom, what are you saying? Is that Gaelic?"

"No, of course not. I don't know Gaelic." Even as I say the words, the whispers of Gaelic that had come to me at the top of Conic Hill and before, in Glasgow, float through my brain. Had I just spoken Gaelic? I turn to the man standing beside the hut. "I wasn't, was I? Speaking Gaelic?"

"Aye, ye were, lass." His warm eyes dance with laughter. "Can't say as I've ever heard a Yank with the Gaelic. Surprised me, ye did."

I am more than a little freaked out by my sudden understanding of a language I do not know. Embarrassed by the attention, I change the subject. "What is this place?"

"Ah, this here is the Ardess Hidden History Trail, where ye can learn about the farming community that once populated the area."

Colin perks up at the mention of history and launches into a campaign to convince the others to take the one-mile path that loops up the hill, but no one is biting.

"Sorry, but today is supposed to be the most challenging terrain of the entire Way." Clara is carrying a backpack even larger than Jorgen's. "I'm not going to walk any more miles than necessary."

The others concur, so Colin reluctantly shakes the man's hand and promises to return someday. As we turn back toward the West Highland Way, I fall into step with him. "If you really want to see it, you should. I'll do it with you. Let the others go on ahead."

Colin pats my sticky arm, then makes a face and wipes the midge spray off on his pants. "Thanks, but it's not a big deal."

He trots ahead to catch up with the girls, and I'm left on my own again. With nothing more to occupy my mind, I start obsessing over what just occurred. I understood Gaelic. I *spoke* Gaelic. What the hell is happening to me?

Until now, I blamed the weird stuff on jet lag, lack of sleep, stress. But I can no longer deny that something else is going on here. Something strange. Maybe even mystical. People don't just suddenly know a foreign language.

Could I be channeling memories from a past life? I immediately reject that idea.

But something beyond my comprehension is happening, and it seems to be happening only to me. Colin is showing no signs of seeing visions of fire or ghostly women standing over his bed. He isn't spouting a new language. Neither are any of the others. I'm not psychic. I don't have any special powers or abilities. I'm just a mom, a widow, a parent facing an empty nest.

The phrase sticks in my mind and repeats: *Mom, widow . . . Mother, Widow . . . Mother, Widow, Innocent.*

Sorcha Chisholm: Mother, Widow, Innocent.

Does all this have to do with that woman? That murderer?

Maybe I am cursed. Maybe Adam cursed me upon his death for denying him his freedom and this is how that curse is manifesting—in his favorite country, doing an activity with our son that he wanted to do himself.

It all feels crazy and wrong.

I just need to turn my world right again with a good, long nap and a soak in a bubble bath with a glass of wine.

But that nap, bath, and wine are nowhere at hand. Right now I have fourteen miles to walk over what Clara says is the toughest terrain of the entire West Highland Way. I will focus only on that and worry about the rest later.

And tough it indeed becomes. Immediately after I follow the others off the wide gravel road onto a trail that traces the side of the loch, the path narrows and angles down, then up, then over tree roots, around huge boulders, up wooden ladders to wooden footbridges over the many streams falling into the lake; and then it repeats all over again. It takes all my concentration to maintain my footing.

The group drifts apart with Clara heading off first, her huge pack not slowing her down the slightest. Jorgen and his daughters also move at a quicker pace, and I know Colin would like to keep up with them, but instead he hangs back with me. For that, I am grateful. Already I've slipped down a wet rock and landed on my butt. I'm not hurt, but if something bad did happen, I'd need his help.

I try my best to sound upbeat as I pull Colin into a conversation. "Can you imagine walking along here before all these footbridges were built? I don't think it would even be possible."

"Yeah, back in Rob Roy's time, he probably traveled this area by boat, or maybe it's more passable higher up the hillside." He eases down a steep section, then turns to offer me a hand as I descend the tricky roots and rocks.

It doesn't take long for my legs to start burning with the strain of the constant ups and downs, starts and stops, looking for footholds. Thankfully, my feet don't hurt as much as they did yesterday due to the fresh blister bandage I put on this morning. Colin pushed me to buy hiking boots with good ankle support, and now I understand how much they help on terrain such as this.

I'm watching the trail so closely to avoid tripping that I forget to look at the view of the lake. When I stop to pull out my water bottle, I do finally see it and immediately feel a sense of peace come over me. Water laps gently at huge boulders marking the shoreline only feet from where I stand. All around me grows a profusion of ferns, grasses, wildflowers, and mosses. Oak trees grow between the rocks, their leaves just starting to turn red and gold. The numerous trees provide constant shade and make me want to sit right here for the rest of the afternoon. "Gorgeous," I breathe, not expecting a response.

"Yeah, it is." Colin pulls out a bag of butter tablet and offers me some.

I pop one in my mouth and marvel at how it is the best thing I've ever eaten, which probably has more to do with my needing a pick-me-up than the actual candy. "Hey, Colin, I need to apologize to you." I wait for him to look at me before continuing. "I was pretty tired and grumpy last night and again this morning. I hope I didn't ruin any of your fun."

He shrugs and looks back at the lake. "No big deal." He chews a candy before adding, "I'm going to miss you, too, you know."

Tears sting the backs of my eyes, and I'm shocked at his ability to see beyond the surface of the situation. "You're a pretty cool guy, do you know that?"

Colin laughs and hides embarrassment by busying himself, tucking his water bottle and candy away in his pack.

We let the subject drop and continue hiking.

But Colin's mind must also be on my missing him this coming year because he suddenly asks, "What did you and Dad plan to do once I was out of the house? Did you talk about going on a cruise or renting an RV and driving around the country or something?"

Or something. "We didn't really talk about it," I answer vaguely.

"Come on, you must have looked forward to doing something together. Dad was always interested in hiking the Grand Canyon. Maybe he would've talked you into doing that with him."

"Yeah, maybe," I mumble.

"Or you might have talked him into going to Hawaii again. I know you've missed it."

"Yeah, that would've been nice."

"Do you miss him?"

I love that Colin wants to have a conversation with me, but I hate the topic. "Yes."

Colin stops so fast I bump into his back. When he swings around to face me, anger comes off him like a wave. "Why are you like that? Why do you barely talk about him? He was your husband!"

Startled by the intensity of his questions, I can form no reply. I study his pinched lips and narrowed eyes full of heat. I can also see the shadow of pain there, and that is the thing that finally helps me find words. Softly, with no hint of the bitterness and anger I feel over my failed marriage, I tell him, "I'm grieving in my own way. I'm sorry I can't talk about him as much as you want me to, but I can listen. Please know you can talk about him as much as you want. I want to hear your memories of your dad."

The anger vanishes from his face, and he draws in a deep breath that has a hint of shakiness to it, making me ache. Then Colin just nods and mutters, "Thanks. Sorry I yelled."

"It's okay." Now I feel worse than I already did. I just lied to my son and caused him guilt for being angry with me. If he knew what happened to his parents' marriage, he would understand why I don't fondly reminisce about my dead husband. But I'm not about to explain it to him and tarnish Colin's memories of the father he'd idolized.

And so I'll carry the weight of it on my own. It feels one hundred times the size of Clara's pack.

CHAPTER THIRTEEN

Sorcha

Inbhir Dhòbhran (Inveroran)

The fiddle was singing by the time Sorcha, the boys, and the Fleming family arrived at the inn. Although it was well into evening, the sun still glowed brightly over the western mountains. A bonfire had been lit in the field across the road from the inn, and even though the evening felt warm, several people were gathered around it, listening to the fiddler play and enjoying a dram. Aonghas and Iain headed off with the older Fleming boys. On the packed earth of the road itself, young people danced together under the watchful eye of mothers and fathers standing nearby. One of the couples looked to be the newlyweds, the reason for this wedding *cèilidh*, judging by the new blue dress on the bride and the smart *fèileadh-beag* and tailored jacket on the groom. Mrs. Fleming's youngest three joined the children racing about, causing a great commotion. Sorcha loved all the energy. To be part of a community again felt like she was reborn and no longer a ghost wandering forgotten through the countryside.

She followed Mrs. Fleming and the scent of roasting mutton into the inn's kitchen, where they found a knot of women laughing and gossiping as they prepared food around a central fire. Sorcha set the bowl of peas she carried onto the *ciste* where other food had been deposited, and then Mrs. Fleming introduced her to those she'd not yet met. All welcomed her, which added to her growing feeling that the village of Inbhir Dhòbhran could be home.

As the night grew darker and the fiddler was joined by a piper, Sorcha felt warmed by all the music, stories, and songs. She ate the meat, cheese, oatcakes, and potatoes, and wondered if An Siosal was right now eating the potatoes from her kale yard and cheese made from the milk of her own cow, Flòraidh.

But tonight was not a time for resentment, so she pushed the thoughts away and focused on her new friends.

Dòmhnall Òg, whose gray hair and stooped back belied the *young* in his name, was telling those gathered at the fire the story of Fingal's fight against Orla on the heath of Lena. Tàm used to tell the same story at gatherings, and Sorcha missed his telling of what came next in the Ossian tale. The depth of Fingal's sorrow over the death of his son, Ryno, never failed to make her weep.

Lost in the story and memories, Sorcha didn't notice when the stranger arrived and was offered a seat on the *sèis* near her, which had been carried out from the inn to accommodate guests.

It wasn't until she heard the word *murder* that she realized Dòmhnall Òg was no longer speaking. Instead, this stranger, dressed in a smart black suit and shoes that looked incapable of lasting a mile, was telling the assembled group a story of his own.

"Beat him unconscious and left him to die in the flames, they did," he was saying now. Several of the women gasped and covered their mouths with their hands. One woman reached for her husband's hand and clasped it tightly.

Sorcha held herself very still.

"Did you know the victim?" asked one man, leaning his elbows on his knees. "Is that why you're on the road this night? To bring the murderers to justice?"

The stranger shook his head. "I'm only a solicitor, traveling north to meet with a client to draw up estate paperwork. No, I heard the story from the cousin of the estate factor, whom I met in Taigh an Droma. He and his companion are in pursuit and promise they'll track the heinous villains as far as it takes. They are telling the story to everyone who'll listen in hopes that someone will find and apprehend the murdering duo."

Coghill was factor Macrath's cousin? This was news to Sorcha. And he was recently in Taigh an Droma, a town not far from here.

"Where did this horror take place?" Dòmhnall Òg seemed to be trying to memorize all the details so he could repeat the story at a later gathering.

The solicitor motioned toward the darkening moor. "Up north. Srath Ghlais, I was told. It seems the outlaws were last seen moving south, so be on the lookout for a young man and old woman by the name of Chisholm. They are quite dangerous."

Sorcha felt the hairs on her neck and arms stand up, as though all those assembled were staring at her, suspecting her. She forced herself not to move or show any emotion other than idle interest. She must not give herself away.

"Outlaws, you say? Were they put to the horn?"

"Oh yes." The solicitor nodded vigorously. "They failed to appear at court, so they were proclaimed outlaws at the Great Cross in Dùn Èideann, and, as is the custom, the horn was blasted three times."

They had been outlawed. The word shook her to her very core.

"What are we to do if the murderers do come through here?" asked Mr. Fleming, a gentle man who was quick with a smile and a kind word. His face was now pinched with fear.

The solicitor gave Mr. Fleming his full attention. "Do not put yourself or your family in any danger, but if it's within your power to do so, you must detain them—or if they prove to be volatile, it is within your legal power to do whatever must be done to keep them from remaining a threat to society."

"You mean . . . kill them?"

The solicitor's calm demeanor could not hide the fact that he was thrilled to be sharing such a dramatic tale. His chest puffed up as he leaned back and crossed his legs. "Yes, that is what I mean." His lips curved up on the corners in a chilling smile.

This brought another round of gasps and cries from the women gathered. Sorcha wrapped her arms around her middle to hide the fact that her hands were shaking, and she hoped the others would see her distress as being no different from that of the other women.

But different, it was. She and Aonghas were in more danger than she'd even realized. Any one of the people they encountered could take them captive or—her heart stuttered at the thought—take their very lives.

She dared not jump up from her seat and draw attention to herself, but she couldn't keep from looking at every nearby boy to see if he was Aonghas. She needed to know he was safe. She needed to ensure he wasn't letting their secret slip. She'd warned him that first night here in Inbhir Dhòbhran, but he was only a boy, after all.

She couldn't see him, which made her chest clamp tightly around her lungs. The flames of the fire seemed to grow taller and bend toward her, and all she could do was stare at them and will air into her body.

"*Obh obh*, Mrs. Macdonald. Are you quite all right?" Suddenly, Mrs. Fleming had her arm around Sorcha's back and was lifting her from the bench. "Come with me, a cool drink of water will do you good."

As Mrs. Fleming led her away from the fire, Sorcha heard Dòmhnall Òg say, with much regret in his voice, "Perhaps we should save this subject for later when the women aren't around."

Mrs. Fleming helped her into the inn and to a stool by the fire, where an old woman was holding a sleeping infant. As she waited for the water, Sorcha smiled at the old woman, who smiled back, though neither said a word.

Sorcha's head ached with all the thoughts bouncing around inside. Did Mr. Fleming or the solicitor suspect anything of her? Did anyone? Had Aonghas or Iain told someone that Sorcha was not Iain's mother? Were the men out there by the fire right now discussing how Sorcha could be the outlaw? Was she about to be tied up?

Where was Aonghas?

"Here. Drink." Mrs. Fleming shoved a horn cup into her hands and helped her lift it to her mouth. The cool liquid soothed her burning body, but she couldn't calm her racing heart.

Sorcha wanted to jump up, run out of there, and find her son. But to do so would bring unwanted attention. Forcing herself to act normally, she smiled at her friend. "Thank you. I don't know what came over me."

Mrs. Fleming waved her hand in the air. "No bother. I was happy to get away from that talk, myself." Rather than sitting down beside her, as Sorcha expected, Mrs. Fleming moved toward the doorway. "I'm going to gather my little ones and take them home to bed. You rest here for as long as you like. I'll ensure Mr. Fleming walks home with you and your boys."

A heavy weight dropped into Sorcha's stomach, but she hid her fear and smiled. "Thank you. I'll see you in the morning, then. Good night."

The moment Mrs. Fleming left, Sorcha got to her feet and returned the horn cup to the dresser shelf. With a quick smile at the silent old woman, Sorcha dashed to the door, where she paused to look out.

Mrs. Fleming was at the fire, saying something to her husband, who was nodding. The solicitor was still there, as were most of the others. The young people were still dancing and carrying on as the piper played. Again, Sorcha searched each face for that of her son.

There. Finally, she spotted him just as he dropped a clump of moss onto the head of a pretty girl and then took off running into the darkness as the girl squealed in feigned horror.

Forcing herself not to hurry, which would draw attention, she wandered in the direction he had gone. As she walked, she slipped her hands into the slits on the sides of her skirt to take stock of the possessions in her pockets. She never let herself be separated from her coin purse, so that was in the pocket, right where it should be. In her other pocket, she felt the dry, rough clumps of dirt and grass that she carried from her children's graves. Touching them reminded her of their sweet little faces, which calmed her slightly. As long as she had this connection to her family, to her home, she'd always be able to find a small bit of peace.

As she rounded the corner of the inn and moved toward the dark cattle stance behind it, she placed her fingers over the silver brooch at her chest and whispered a small prayer to her husband's memory. "Please keep us safe. Let me find Aonghas and keep him safe."

A motion in the dark made her stop. Laughter drifted across the grass toward her, and she recognized Iain's voice.

"Iain?" she called to him. "Is Archie with you?"

"I'm here." Aonghas's voice did more to calm Sorcha than anything else could. She swallowed, and then called to him, "Come here, I must speak with you."

A laughing Aonghas appeared with Iain beside him. Both boys looked like they'd been wrestling in the grass, and both wore wide smiles. She hated to take Aonghas away from his new friends as much as she hated to leave this community herself. But it was time.

Before she could open her mouth to tell him, however, a new thought hit her: Iain. All she'd been focused on was gathering Aonghas and the two of them escaping into the night before anyone thought to question them. But they'd have to take Iain with them. The Fleming family and all their neighbors believed Iain was also her son. She would attract more suspicion if she left without him.

She steeled herself for an argument but hoped her words would be enough to get them both to leave with her, right now. "Boys, we must be on our way. The Flemings have told me that they've no more work for us and they cannot have us eating their food any longer. We need to go now."

Aonghas scowled but didn't say a word. Younger and more outspoken, Iain raised his eyebrows at her. "What did you do to make them force us out in the night like this?"

Aonghas shoved an elbow into the boy's stomach. "Don't speak to my mother that way."

Iain lunged toward Aonghas, and the two went down to the ground.

"Boys, that's enough!" Sorcha pulled Iain off Aonghas and gave him a slight shake. "I didn't do anything, thank you very much. They told me earlier and said we could leave in the morning after the *cèilidh*, but I don't want to overstay our welcome. We can easily make camp somewhere else for the night and get an early start on the road in the morning. Come along."

"Wait." Iain touched her arm, then immediately dropped his hand. "I need my satchel."

Sorcha tried to come up with an excuse that would make him leave it behind, for she didn't want Mr. or Mrs. Fleming to know they were sneaking away in the night like this, but she couldn't think of any believable reason that Iain would accept. Besides, his satchel was in the byre where they'd slept. He could get it and return without anyone noticing. "Go. Be quick. And not a word to anyone. We don't want to spoil their fun this night."

Iain darted off into the darkness. Aonghas looked at Sorcha, and in the dim light from the bonfire and torches, she saw disappointment in his face. "They don't know we're leaving, do they?"

Sorcha shook her head and stepped closer to her son. "A man was at the fire tonight, telling everyone about the dangerous murderers traveling this area. He said they've been declared outlaws." Aonghas's eyes widened and he looked like he was going to ask her a question, but then Iain reappeared, his satchel hanging from his shoulder.

Before either boy could say another word, Sorcha led them around the back of the inn and onto the road, being sure to stay to the shadows where no one would see them.

After an hour of walking through the grove of oak trees that curved around the southern shore of Loch Toilbhe, and then alongside a river too swift and wide to cross in the dark, Sorcha felt they had put enough distance between themselves and Inbhir Dhòbhran and could finally stop for the night. Uphill, in the shelter of the forest a good distance from the road, they wrapped themselves in their *plaideachan*—Aonghas had borrowed one from the Flemings for the wedding festivities and now had his own—and lay down on the cold ground to sleep.

As Sorcha listened to the boys' breathing deepen, she kept watch late into the night, worried that someone from Inbhir Dhòbhran had followed them, or that someone else might come upon them and, suspecting their guilt, plunge a dagger into their sleeping bodies.

Despite herself, sleep took her into its depths, but images of capture and torture tormented her all through the night.

Sorcha woke with a start to find herself alone in the little clearing. Fear sliced through her, and she yearned to call for the boys but didn't want to attract the attention of anyone else who might be out this morning looking for them.

By the time she had her *plaide* refastened around her shoulders, she could hear the boys' laughter up the hill and knew they weren't injured or captured. But as their voices continued to bounce through the forest as they came toward her, she had to clench her teeth together to stop herself from yelling at them to be quiet. What if someone was nearby? What if *Coghill* was nearby? The boys' shouts would lead him straight to them.

She would need to have a word with Aonghas, and soon. He needed to be told of all that she'd learned last night, and be warned to take care of all he did and all he said to Iain. Maybe she'd made a mistake allowing the boy to accompany them.

Both boys wore wide grins as they neared the campfire, and Sorcha knew they were up to something. Aonghas held his hand behind his back, and when he reached her, he proudly brought out his surprise. "We caught breakfast!"

A fat grouse hung limply by its feet from Aonghas's hand. Sorcha could have wept with delight at the knowledge that they would be able to fill their bellies before the long walk ahead. It would delay their start, and put them at risk of someone finding them should anyone from Inbhir Dhòbhran be looking, but a grouse didn't take long to roast, and they needed the energy. Besides, Iain would grow even more suspicious than he might already be if she kept them from eating. "Well done."

Soon they had a fire lit, and over it, the boys turned the cleaned bird on a makeshift spit. Sorcha's mouth ached in anticipation as the delicious aroma filled the air.

Finally, she laid the roasted bird upon a flat rock to cool just enough to handle. When she could touch it without getting burned, she used Aonghas's *sgian-dubh* to cut the bird into three portions, giving the more generous ones to the growing boys.

As they ate, the sky lightened overhead and Sorcha felt a growing urgency to get moving. She shoved the rest of the meat into her mouth and chewed as she threw dirt over the coals to put out the fire.

Something snapped in the woods behind her, and Sorcha's heart leaped into her throat. She spun around to peer into the wall of green and brown, but she could see nothing moving. Neither of the boys seemed to have heard anything, so she convinced herself she'd imagined it and returned to her task. She wasn't used to forests, having always preferred the open moorland and wide strath around her home. If there was anything out there, it was likely only an animal looking for its own meal.

"What have we here?"

When she heard the unexpected voice, she cried out in alarm. She whipped her head around and found herself looking at a man.

He was dressed all in brown, from his bonnet pulled low over his eyes down to his knee-high boots. In one elbow he cradled a fowling piece that, although not pointed at them, caused fear to slice through Sorcha. When her gaze returned to his face, her heart stopped. His thin lips were pinched tightly together, and his eyebrows and lids were lowered so that only a small gleam could be seen of his eyes. The man's tall, thin body seemed to be held taut, as though at any moment he could lift the gun and fire at them before they saw him move.

She swallowed and told herself to pretend that all was well and not upset him further. Their very lives could depend upon it. "Good morning, sir. My sons and I were only camped here for the night as we travel south." She shot Iain a look to keep him from revealing her lie about their relationship. "I'm sorry we don't have any food left to share with you."

The man didn't relax at all but eyed each of them in turn, as though he could see right into their very souls. No one said a word.

He very deliberately picked up the roasting stick and poked at the picked-clean grouse bones in the ashes. With the stick, he pulled the bones out and squatted down to inspect them.

When he raised his gaze, Sorcha felt a chill crawl up her spine.

"This land and everything on it belong to my employer, the Earl of Breadalbane, and I know for certain that he has not given you leave to take his game." He pushed to his feet as gracefully as a dancer and towered over them. "Poaching is punishable by death."

Panicked, Sorcha looked at Aonghas and found him looking back at her, his wide eyes begging her to find a way out of this. Iain, beside him, had his gaze on the ground, his shoulders hunched. Only his heaving chest gave an indication of emotion.

She looked back at the man, who must be the earl's ghillie, or maybe his factor. They didn't come all this way only to have a grouse be their downfall. "Good sir," she began, trying her best to keep her voice from shaking, "I assure you, we meant no harm to his lordship. It was an honest mistake by the boys here. I'd be happy to pay you the value of the bird and promise that we won't make the same mistake again. Right, boys?"

Both boys mumbled agreement and ducked their heads in shame. *Good for them,* she thought, hoping the man believed their contrition.

The ghillie pinned her with his dark eyes. "Two guineas."

All the moisture drained from her mouth. For that price, they could have, no doubt, purchased a hundred grouse from a public house. It would leave her with only a couple pence left over. They'd truly be destitute after this.

But what choice did she have?

Nodding, she silently pulled her purse from her pocket, counted the coins, handed them to the man, and made certain to keep as much distance between them as possible as she did so.

He, too, did not say a word as he accepted the coins. Then, with a finger to the brim of his cap, he nodded and said, "You'd best remove yourselves from the Breadalbane estate forthwith."

With that, he melted back into the woods from which he'd come, leaving Sorcha wondering if he remained there, just out of sight, watching them. The idea made her skin crawl.

As promised, they left their campsite immediately and continued southward and across the river on a stone bridge, where Sorcha risked evoking the ghillie's wrath again by carving her mark in a stone at the far end. It was the first mark she'd carved since Gleann Comhann and she made certain to point out to Aonghas that this road led through Inbhir Dhòbhran and directly to the King's House. They then continued south past dozens of scattered houses, over hills, and through dips where they often had to ford narrow burns.

Only an hour into the walk, Sorcha noticed increased activity as other roads that appeared from branching glens along the way joined with their road. Herds of cattle were being prodded along by drovers. Travelers in all manner of conveyances passed them, leaving deep troughs in the mud with their wagon or coach wheels. With each new person they saw, Sorcha battled with herself between feeling fear that this would be the person who would discover their true identities and arrest them, and joy that they'd be able to blend into the crowd and evade notice.

She kept her *plaide* over her head so that it shadowed her face. When Iain wasn't looking, she motioned for Aonghas to do the same with the Flemings' *plaide* he still possessed. The steady drizzle of rain had others doing the same, so Sorcha felt confident they would not draw attention for it. As she watched Aonghas pull the faded green-and-blue tartan cloth from his shoulders over his head, a stab of guilt shot through her. The *plaide* had only been a loan and now it was stolen. They were now thieves as well as murderers.

With nothing to be done about that now, Sorcha turned her attention back to the road and noticed it led through a gap in the hills to a village a fellow traveler called by the name Taigh an Droma, House of the Ridge, and though her gaze wandered over all surrounding ridges, she could not identify which held the house in question.

The town itself seemed to be flourishing, if one were to judge by the tidy cottages, public houses, smithy, and cattle stance. It was the people that captured Sorcha's attention, and she had to remind herself not to stare. There were cattle drovers and laborers, but there were also finely dressed men and women who stepped from their coaches with the assistance of servants who were nearly as well kitted as their masters. Most of the voices she heard spoke the *Gàidhlig*, but others spoke Scots English or the King's English, and a few spoke languages she couldn't identify.

It all thrilled and terrified Sorcha in equal measure. If there were this many people in a Highland village, how many more must be in Dùn Èideann?

Despite their grouse breakfast, the boys were hungry again and begged her to inquire at the next public house about a meal. Sorcha shook her head and continued walking.

"It's not because of money, is it?" Iain caught up to her. "Didn't the Flemings pay you our wages before we left?"

Sorcha ignored him.

When Iain touched her sleeve, she finally stopped and looked at his rounded, freckled face. Then she looked to Aonghas, who stood behind Iain and saw by his expression that he understood what had happened, even though she'd not yet had a private moment to speak with him. His eyes widened in what could only be described as fear, and then his head swiveled left and right, as though he only now remembered Coghill was searching for them.

Sorcha had no idea what to say to Iain about their missing wages without raising his suspicions.

"They cheated us, didn't they?" Aonghas stepped in front of Iain, and Sorcha saw on his face a look that warned her to play along. "And then that ghillie back there took it all."

Sorcha nodded and forced her eyebrows to lower and her mouth to pucker in feigned anger. "Yes, that is what happened. Dwelling on it now won't change matters, so let's keep walking. I'm sure there will be nettles or chickweed, or maybe even some wild garlic we can find once we get away from all these people and animals."

As she resumed her walk, she silently blessed her son for his quick thinking.

The boys followed, each lost in their own thoughts until, half an hour later, Iain announced, "We could find work in the mines."

Sorcha turned to see if he was serious. His eager young face was turned to Aonghas, but Sorcha saw the dark shadows around his eyes and under his cheekbones. The poor boy was hungry and tired.

"Come." She motioned toward the grassy bank of the river. "Let's rest for a spell."

As they settled in the cool grass, Sorcha rubbed her sore feet and watched the boys carefully as they talked.

"Mines? What mines?" Aonghas leaned back on his hands with his legs stretched in front of him. His ankles stuck out the bottom of his too-short trousers, and the soles of his boots looked paper thin. He'd need new clothing before winter.

Iain tossed a pebble into the water and pointed to the hills across from them. "There are all sorts of lead mines around here. They say it's disorienting spending all day belowground, but it pays well enough."

Sorcha's gaze traveled over the hills, but she could find no evidence of mines—not that she'd know what to look for other than a hole in the ground. "Is that what you wish to do, Iain? Stop here and work the mines?"

She saw his eyes dart toward Aonghas as though to gauge his feelings on the matter before he could know his own. When Aonghas did not make comment, Iain just shrugged and threw another rock.

Aonghas looked up at the sky, where the rain clouds still lingered. "I think I'd rather work in a mill than a mine. I'm going to hold out for work in Dùn Èideann."

After that, Iain, too, stretched onto his back and seemed to doze. With her *plaide* pulled up to cover half of her face, Sorcha watched people pass on the road and listened to their conversations when she could understand the language. Most were too preoccupied with the logistics of their travels to notice the woman and boys in the grass.

But then a wagon carrying a man and woman drew to a stop. "Could you point us in the direction of Saint Fillan's Priory?" the man called to her as he rested the reins on his knees. "I thought we'd have come upon it by now."

Sorcha shook her head and was about to tell them she wasn't from around here when Iain jumped up and pointed behind the wagon. "It's down that way. Look for the path leading from the main road next to the holy pool."

She wanted to ask Iain how he knew the area when he lived miles to the north, same as her, but she kept silent to avoid raising the travelers' suspicions.

"Thank you, boy." The man touched the edge of his bonnet, then turned his attention to Sorcha. "Forgive me, but are the three of you traveling south? We can give you a ride as far as the holy pool, and that way your son here can make certain we don't miss it again."

Iain and Aonghas jumped up like they were one body and clambered aboard the back of the wagon. Trapped, Sorcha thanked the man but waited until he'd turned the wagon around before climbing up herself and settling between the bags and boxes piled there.

"You must take care when traveling this country," the man told them with a glance over his shoulder. "They say there is an outlawed, murdering mother and son heading down to Dùn Èideann. We heard about it at the inn where we lodged last night. Two men looking for them told us to be watchful and to relay the message to everyone we come upon. Said their clan chief is offering a monetary reward for information leading to their arrest. Until the pair are captured, be wary of anyone you meet who fits that description."

His words sent shivers down Sorcha's arms even as sweat dampened her back. Telling herself to remain calm, she forced a lightness to her voice and replied, "We've heard talk of that awful happening. It is a tragedy, indeed." And then, after a moment of silence, she asked, "Where is this inn you mention?"

The man pointed to a gap in the mountains at the end of the strath. "In Cill Fhinn, about, oh, fifteen miles from here on the road to Loch Tatha."

She glanced over and found Iain studying her with a heavy brow. Her stomach turned sour, but she smiled at the boy, hoping to ease his obvious suspicions.

The wagon bounced painfully, and Sorcha had to hold on to the side to keep from falling out. The woman looked back at Sorcha with a kind smile. "We are Mr. and Mrs. MacInnes. I'm going to my sister's in An t-Òban to help with her older children when her newest arrives."

Sorcha knew her next words would be taking a risk with Iain, but she'd talk with him later and say whatever she needed to in order to make him believe they weren't the wanted murderers. Besides, he'd played along with the Fleming family, so why should this couple be any different? "I am Mrs. Macdonald, and these are my boys, Archie and Iain."

Iain's eyes narrowed, but he remained silent. Aonghas's gaze shot toward Iain and quickly down to his lap.

"It is lovely to meet you, Mrs. Macdonald. Where might you be traveling?"

Although she figured it was probably safe to say Dùn Èideann, she decided to answer vaguely. "To find work. After my husband died at war, it's just been me and the boys here, and we're hoping for opportunities in the city."

Mrs. MacInnes was nodding all through Sorcha's answer. "My sister's boy goes every winter to Glaschu, where he works in the city stables and then returns home to An t-Òban for harvest. Back and forth every year. We are truly blessed to have our farm in Peairt, where the crops don't suffer as much from the weather as they do up north or on the coast."

"This is it, sir," Iain spoke up for the first time since they'd boarded the wagon. "This is the holy pool, and that's the road you want to take to the priory."

The man stopped the wagon to let them off, then the couple cheerfully waved to them and continued on their way.

As silence descended upon the three of them again, none of them moved.

Finally, Sorcha gathered up her nerve and positioned herself directly in front of Iain to force him to look her in the eyes. "I don't know what you are thinking, but I assure you, we're not murderers."

Iain seemed to take this in, and then he angled his head. "Are you the two everyone is looking for?"

At that, Sorcha had to look away while she pondered how to respond. She didn't want to lie to the boy, but if he believed them to be criminals, they wouldn't be able to trust him.

Aonghas took the decision from her. "Yes, we're the ones they are looking for."

Sorcha dropped her head and felt all energy drain out of her.

"We murdered no one," Aonghas went on. "You must believe me. He was burning our house down on top of us, and he was trying to steal our valuables. When I tried to stop him, he fell and split his head open. We didn't mean for him to die, I swear it!"

Sorcha latched on to Iain's arm, forcing him to look at her again. She got very close to his face. "We cannot be captured for a crime we didn't commit. Aonghas tried to pull him from the fire, but the roof was caving in. We are innocent, but they would see us hang. Do you understand?"

Iain jerked his arm out of her grasp and took a wary step back. "I understand."

Sorcha had to be sure, or they must part ways now. "Iain. This is very serious. Can we trust you not to give us away?"

Something must have resolved itself in Iain's mind, because suddenly the muscles in his face eased and he smiled. Clapping Aonghas on the back, he said, "You can trust me, *Aonghas*."

Only when he said the name with such emphasis did Sorcha realize she'd been the one to slip. Now Iain not only knew they were outlaws, but he knew Aonghas's true name.

Aonghas laughed and slung his arm around Iain's shoulders. "It is Archie, my friend. Remember that." Arm in arm, the boys continued walking along the road like old mates. Sorcha stood rooted to the spot, wondering if they were making the biggest mistake of their lives in trusting this boy they hardly knew.

"Ma? Are you coming?"

Aonghas's call got her feet started, and she continued her walk several paces behind the boys. All she could do now was be wary and watchful, she decided. And when the time came, they would leave Iain far behind.

CHAPTER FOURTEEN

Keaka

Day three; Rowchoish

"Mom, it's a bothy! Wait till you see this." Colin turns off the main trail to follow a spongy moss path cutting through a mixed-wood forest. His destination is a small stone building squatting behind trees as though trying to hide.

We've just passed several rock walls and mounds thickly covered with moss. They are the first signs of dwellings we've come across since leaving Ardess, and I've felt all morning that we should be encountering more. I've been looking for the people I, for whatever reason, expected to be living here, but there aren't any.

Rowchoish, as Colin calls it, was clearly once a community. The building ruins are being swallowed by moss, grass, trees, and bushes. The bothy stands out from the rest because it is the only one still fully intact.

As I follow Colin to the bothy, I become increasingly uneasy. Is this someone's home? Are they going to be angry with us for trespassing? Why is Colin walking up to it like he knows the owners?

I open my mouth to call him back when he pushes open the dark wooden door and steps inside. Confused and concerned, I hurry to follow him.

When I enter, I find not someone's home but a large open room divided into three distinct sections. The first third, where we stand, has a dirt floor, where two round stumps have been placed in front of a small stone-and-cement fireplace. Someone has left small stacks of kindling sorted by size.

The second third has wood-plank flooring; a wooden picnic table; and on one side, a makeshift counter of some sort of sheet metal hammered onto wood held up by two-by-fours.

The final third of the room is a high stone step-up from the eating area and is separated from it by metal pipes with a grid of fencing material for walls. The surface of the raised stone platform is flat and smooth, and obviously meant for sleeping. I think about Clara and Jorgen's family who are camping along the Way and wonder if any of them plan to sleep here.

Surprisingly, the entire building is well lit by skylight panels in the corrugated tin roof. Besides me and Colin, it is deserted. "Colin, what is this place?"

He is poking around the counter area, where someone has left a cooking stove and various pots and utensils. "It's Rowchoish Bothy. You can find bothies all over Scotland in remote areas. They're free for anyone to use when out hunting or hiking. Dad and I found one when we were hiking on Skye. We thought we might sleep in one on this hike—but then, you know."

Yes, I know. His dad died, and when I agreed to come instead, I'd talked Colin out of camping and booked us hotels, bed-and-breakfasts, and luggage-carrier service. Guilt gnaws at me as I watch his excitement as he explores every corner of the room and reads every sign. I should have sucked it up and camped with him.

I think again of Clara. How does she find the courage to do this alone? To sleep in places like this, or a tent, all alone in the middle of nowhere? I certainly don't have what it takes.

But still, for Colin, I should have tried.

When he's gotten his fill of the bothy, he insists we poke around the stone ruins nearby. I find myself enchanted by one roofless building that has a tree growing in what was once someone's living room. Another tree has sprouted on the stone windowsill, and its roots, along with moss and ivy, completely envelop the wall on either side of the window opening. I feel like we've come upon a storybook land, or a secret garden. And yet I also feel a sense of melancholy here. Where did the people go, and why did they leave? Had all the work and hope they'd put into building these stone walls by hand been for nothing? Were the families happy living here? Or had it been a struggle for existence, followed by an admittance of failure?

I lay my palm against the stone to the side of the doorway and imagine that the woman who once lived here had placed her hand on the exact same spot as she called her children in for dinner. "I hope you were happy," I whisper to the woman, or maybe to the house itself.

Colin appears from around the side of the ruin, and I quickly drop my hand. "Should we get moving?" He takes a photo of me standing in the doorway, then flashes a cheeky grin. "We're getting close to Inversnaid Hotel, where we can stop for lunch and a cold drink from the bar."

"That sounds perfect." I follow him back to the trail, but not until I look one last time over my shoulder at the community now being consumed by the forest. A niggling unease won't leave me, as though I have unfinished business here. But I don't know what it could possibly be, so I shake it off and follow Colin just as raindrops start splattering on my head and arms. We pull raincoats from our packs and put them on.

Colin's "getting close" turns out to be nearly three miles, but we finally arrive at a roaring waterfall alongside the Inversnaid Hotel. I would have loved to sit by the falls to eat our lunch, but the rain is falling harder and heavier, so instead we duck into the walkers' entrance of the hotel. A sign orders us to remove our boots and packs and leave them in the vestibule before entering the hotel.

We find who I've come to think of as "our gang"—Jorgen, Kirsten, Terese, and Clara—sitting around one of the high tables in the walkers' lounge. After greeting them and seeing how their morning was, I ask them to save us seats as Colin and I go off to find the bar.

I feel strange padding around a nice hotel in only my socks, but all the other walkers are doing the same. At the bar, we both decide to leave our packed lunches in our bags and instead order a hot meal to warm us up and sustain us for the afternoon ahead.

With plates in hand—fish and chips for Colin, soup and fries for me—we rejoin our gang and settle in for a much-needed rest. Unlike last night, I find myself enjoying their company.

With full bellies, rain outside creating a cozy feel inside, and good company, we're all surprised when Jorgen glances at his watch and tells us, "It's nearly three. With over six miles to go, we should get back on the trail."

We scramble to throw out trash, put on boots, refill water bottles, and hoist our packs. Soon we're heading north again along the loch, and I'm happy to find myself walking with Jorgen and Clara, who is telling us about the miserable night she had last night with a tent full of midges. I notice some swollen bites on her neck.

The rain is falling steadily, but I've donned my waterproof pants and raincoat, so it doesn't bother me much. My only real concern is the slippery mud of the trail, which, I quickly learn, is even rougher than this morning's section.

Jorgen, bless him, stays nearby and even offers me one of his trekking poles, which saves me more than once from a nasty fall. I surprise myself by laughing at the absurdity of the situation I find myself in. No one back home would have me pegged as someone who would be out in the wilds of Scotland, walking along a remote section of a lake with a Danish man, risking life and limb. Yet here I am.

And, strangely, I'm having fun.

CHAPTER FIFTEEN

Sorcha

A' Chrìon-Làraich (Crianlarich)

Not long after Iain discovered their true identities—for which Sorcha was watching him closely—they came upon a two-story building sitting at the junction of three roads from three glens. Aonghas eyed the horses tied out front and offered to go inside to find food. Sorcha handed him the last pence from her purse, then sat down under a dripping oak tree rather than face a room full of people.

As she waited, she wrapped her *plaide* tightly around herself to ward off the cold wind and watched with interest as a young boy and his spaniel burst out the door of the inn and caused the horses tied there to dance away in alarm.

"That's a fine dog you have," she said to him.

The boy stared at her through shaggy fringe hanging in his eyes, reminding her of the sweet face of the cow she'd lost when they were evicted. "Good day, missus," he finally muttered, warily.

"Can you tell me what this place is called?"

"It is A' Chrìon-Làraich. My ma runs this pub, and my pa cares for the horses." He tossed the hair out of his face and squinted at her. "Do you need feed for your horse?"

Sorcha smiled and shook her head. "Which direction does one take to get to Dùn Èideann?" A huge mountain sat directly in their southerly path, so it was either east or west from here.

The lad pointed a dirty finger down the road to where the river they'd been following curved to follow the glen to the east. It was the same direction the man in the wagon earlier had pointed as he talked of the men he'd met pursuing murderers.

She looked in the opposite direction. "And where does that road lead?"

The boy, seeming to accept that she was harmless, shuffled over to sit beside her in the grass. "That way is Gleann Falach. It takes you to Loch Laomainn and further on to Glaschu."

"Have you been to Glaschu?" she asked him, impressed by his knowledge.

His angel face darkened in a scowl. "I have not. My pa says it's a dirty, stinking place full of Lowlanders and Englishmen."

She was charmed by the vehemence of his words, but she dared not embarrass him with anything other than serious contemplation. "Yes, I've heard such things."

The scowl cleared and he grinned. "But I have been on a boat on the loch that stretches as far as I could see! It is a grand loch with islands, coves, and beaches, and someday I want to live there."

"That's a fine plan."

"Did you know Vikings carried their longboats over the land from the sea so they could raid the people living on Loch Laomainn?" His excitement had him bouncing on his knees.

He reminded her of Aonghas at that age, and she felt she could sit here all day listening to his stories. He had just launched into a gory account of the marauding Vikings when Aonghas returned and handed her a wooden bowl of potato soup. "Do you want to come inside and get warm by the fire?"

Sorcha considered the offer but decided to stay where she was with her entertaining companion. Aonghas smiled at the boy and headed back inside.

When she was finished eating and the boy had wandered away, she carried her bowl inside and found the room dark and smoky. People sat at all the tables and along the bar, where a sturdy woman poured ale. Sorcha found Aonghas at the fire with an empty pint glass. "Where is Iain?" she asked, moving to stand as close as she dared to the flames, only now realizing how cold she'd been outside.

Aonghas motioned toward the back. "Relieving himself."

Taking the opportunity to speak with him privately, Sorcha lowered her voice. "Even though he knows, be careful what you share with Iain." A barmaid arrived to take her empty bowl and offer a drink, but they declined and she moved away. Sorcha leaned closer to her son. "We're going to change direction. Thus far, we've told people we're heading to Dùn Èideann. Let's keep saying that, but actually go to Glaschu. Coghill is heading east."

Aonghas nodded, though his face clouded with worry.

"Mrs. Macdonald," Iain said, appearing suddenly, "thank you for the soup."

Something seemed off about him, but she couldn't place what it might be. Probably it was only her wariness of him now. "You're welcome." To both boys, she said, "Let's get moving."

When they stepped out of the pub, Iain immediately turned right, eastward, but Sorcha stopped him. "We're going this direction, Iain. Toward Loch Laomainn."

Confusion darkened his face and his eyes shifted to the pub, then down the road to the east. "But this is the way to Dùn Èideann."

She only nodded and started walking without waiting to see if he followed. "This is the way we are going."

He did follow, and soon it was back to only the three of them in the quiet countryside. Not far from A' Chrìon-Làraich, they passed a stone sheep fank where shepherds busily sheared and sorted the animals.

Sorcha quietly steered the boys away from the farm and closer to the burn winding through the glen.

As the distance grew between them and the farm, Sorcha felt her body lighten and stretch. This was where she felt safest. Felt most like herself. Where green and golden mountains reached into the dark sky, shaggy cows grazed in pastures, and leafy trees shaded a swift-flowing burn.

Soon, well out of sight of the farm and any houses, Sorcha stopped at a large stone and carved her mark, making sure that it pointed slightly toward the left and the strath that led to Taigh an Droma and the way home.

As she carved, the boys entertained themselves with carvings of their own on the same rock, which amused her. Since she and Aonghas shared one knife between them, he used the edge of a sharp rock to do his carving.

When they were finished, she saw that Aonghas had carved a simple cross while Iain, in the short time he had to work, carved the image of a stag.

"An artist, are you?" she asked him as they admired his work.

The boy blushed and shrugged one shoulder. "I like pictures."

Aonghas teased the younger boy as they resumed their walk, but Sorcha ignored them. These hills, the trees, the wildflowers, and flowing burns... she loved every little thing she saw, and all of it reminded her of home. Even in the rain and cold, she was happy. She had Aonghas beside her and they were staying out of reach of those who would cause them harm.

She felt good about her decision to turn toward Glaschu. They'd be able to find work there just as easily as they would in Dùn Èideann, and no one would look for them in Glaschu. They would be safe.

The rain made the burns swell and a small one coming off the mountain soon grew into a raging river that tumbled over black and gray rocks on its way down the narrow glen. A coach pulled by four horses passed them on the military road heading toward A' Chrìon-Làraich, and Sorcha kept her face turned away and hidden by the *plaide* she still wore over her head. She hoped Aonghas also hid his face, but she didn't have time to remind him before the coach was upon them.

When it passed without slowing, she lifted her chin and faced the road once more.

The rain and the roar of the river drowned out their voices, so they didn't converse. They simply kept walking. She knew not where they would sleep for the night, but it would have to be someplace off this road, away from curious eyes. She would prefer to sleep somewhere out of the rain, beside a fire. But she would settle for less, as long as no one else was around.

When they came upon a hulking three-story stone building with a signboard that Iain read aloud, declaring it to be the Inbhir Àirnein House Hotel, they gave it a wide berth and continued down the track. Even if she had money, she wouldn't risk drawing more attention. They had to stay away from other people until they arrived in Glaschu.

About a mile south of the inn, Sorcha decided they were safely far enough away from it. A meadow separated the road from the river, and next to it were the remains of a stone building under a grove of alder and birch. Only two walls remained, but that was all they needed to block the worst of the cold wind. They used her *plaide* over all three of their heads to block the rain, and she shared Aonghas's stolen *plaide* for warmth. By huddling together, she hoped to manage a full night's rest.

Even with her stomach growling, Sorcha fell asleep fast and deeply. When she woke some untold hour later, the night was black as pitch and the rain had increased so that it pounded loudly on the trees and grasses. Her feet were freezing, but all she could do was tuck her skirt over them. It was then that she noticed Iain was gone. He'd fallen asleep on the other side of Aonghas, who was lightly snoring beside her. But now Iain was nowhere within sight.

She considered calling out to him but didn't want to wake Aonghas. She thought about going to look for him to be certain he'd come to no harm, but he was a growing boy who wasn't a member of her family, and wouldn't take kindly to her stumbling upon him should he be relieving himself. So she stayed where she was and fought to keep her eyelids open, waiting for his return.

But fatigue got the better of her, and she fell deeply asleep.

The next time she awoke, she startled into confusion. A bright light blinded her, and she blinked until her eyes adjusted. Beside her, Aonghas stiffened.

She brought one hand up to block the worst of the lantern light. "Iain?"

The deep rumble of men's laughter sent a shock wave through her entire body. It wasn't Iain. Or, rather, as the lantern shifted, she did see Iain standing behind three grown men, all dressed in black, carrying clubs. But when she focused on the one holding the lantern, she felt her lungs burst.

Coghill. The sneer on his face was the same as the day of the eviction when he'd sliced a goat's throat for no reason other than to prevent the villagers from having it. She'd seen the darkness in him that day and feared that violence more than anything else.

She knew immediately what had happened: Iain had betrayed them. The factor's man and his helpers had now caught them, and it was over. Their journey was over, their hope was over. Their lives were over.

She could hardly move, so great was her terror, but she managed to scoot her body so that she sat between the men and Aonghas. "Take me. Only me. The boy did nothing wrong. Let him go." She pushed against his leg, silently urging him to run away.

"No, it was me." Aonghas's words hollowed her. "It was an accident, but it is my fault the man died."

Sorcha shook her head, but before she could protest, one of the men roughly dragged her away from her son and then tightly tied her wrists together with a scratchy rope. She stretched her neck around to keep Aonghas in sight and saw him also hauled up and bound. Sorcha stared at Iain with pure hatred. "How could you, Iain? We trusted you!"

The boy briefly met her gaze, then he looked down.

"Boy! Take their weapons." Coghill planted himself in front of them like a chieftain himself, puffed up and proud, his beard twitching.

Iain did as he was told and quickly divested her of the knife she carried in her belt. He then moved to Aonghas and patted his waist as though looking for a knife there, even though he knew Aonghas didn't have one.

Sorcha could not tell if one of them said something to the other, but suddenly Aonghas roared and lunged at Iain, surprising the man holding his rope so that it slipped from his grasp.

Aonghas and Iain fell to the ground wrestling, with Aonghas trying to throw a punch at the younger boy's face but doing little damage with his bound hands.

Iain tried to roll away from Aonghas but didn't get far before Aonghas was on top of him again, beating the younger boy with his bound fists, elbows, and knees. Anything that could make impact with the boy did as Aonghas vented his fury on his former friend.

Iain, for his part, didn't hit back at Aonghas, but only held his hands up in front of his face and took the beating. When Aonghas pitched forward to hit Iain again, Iain rolled away, causing Aonghas to fall hard on his shoulder. He shouted in rage and leaped again for Iain, who, this time, didn't move quickly enough to evade Aonghas's attack.

Sorcha felt tears slide down her cheeks as she watched, knowing there was nothing she could do for her son now to protect him or save him from the pain of this betrayal.

The three men did nothing more than stand and laugh as the boys fought, which made Sorcha wish she had the strength to attack one of them. When Aonghas rolled his larger body on top of Iain and started pummeling him again, Sorcha knew she needed to stop this violence.

"Aonghas, stop! He is not worth the trouble."

Somehow, her words took the spirit out of her son, and his entire body seemed to wilt, although he remained sitting on top of the younger boy. In the short moment when the two boys stared at one another, all fight gone from them, Sorcha felt as though she could see the hardening of both their hearts, and she knew each was forever changed, his boyhood lost.

She had to look away before she shattered.

"Move!" Coghill barked into her ear, making her flinch.

She stumbled as the man holding the other end of her rope pulled her into motion, and she realized her feet had gone numb with the cold. The way the man yanked on her arm sent waves of pain through her shoulders and straight up into her head, but she didn't cry out. She wouldn't give them that satisfaction.

Aonghas was being jerked around just as roughly. At his yelp of pain, she couldn't keep a moan from escaping her lips.

As they walked, she tried to catch her son's gaze, but it was too dark, and besides, he was looking down at the ground, his body drawn in on itself like a wounded animal.

She wanted to scream for help, but who would help them? She wanted to fight these men and run away, but knew she'd be overpowered. The men had greater strength, and there were more of them. Three against two. No, make that four against two. Iain was one of them.

There was nothing she could do but allow herself and her son to be dragged away and hope they survived the night. Surely they would be taken to trial, probably in Inverness, and there they could explain the mistake. The man's death had been an accident. There might still be hope. The court might let them go free.

But even as she thought those words, her heart clenched in fear, for she knew the truth. The court would never believe her and Aonghas over the estate factor and these men. She'd already been shown how much her chief and her country valued their lives. If strangers could come into her home and force her out, if they could savagely beat grown men for the crime of being Highlanders, as she'd witnessed several times over her lifetime, they could tear a mother and son apart and condemn them for a crime they did not commit.

Firelight in the distance caught her notice, and she focused on it as she stumbled closer and closer to its source. She recognized the Inbhir Àirnein House Hotel from when they'd passed it earlier, but it now looked different in the shadows. Bigger. More threatening.

Fiddle music poured onto the track when the door opened and reminded her of all the nights back home in Srath Ghlais when a neighbor, or her own dear Tàm, had brought out the fiddle and everyone gathered to listen, tell stories, and dance. She'd always assumed they would have many more such *cèilidhean* in their future, but now she knew she'd already enjoyed her last.

Coghill shoved aside the man holding her rope and dragged her himself through the front door of the inn. As they entered, a cheer went up from those gathered.

"You got your murderers!"

"Make them sleep with the pigs!"

"Let's hang them right now!"

Coghill stopped in the doorway of the room housing the bar and called out, "Pour us a dram. We'll return in a few minutes to celebrate."

She tried to catch Iain's gaze, but he stoically avoided looking at her as he hung back behind Aonghas and the man holding him.

Coghill pulled Sorcha to an uneven flight of stairs and tugged so she climbed behind him. At the top of the short flight, the stairs split left and right, and Coghill pulled her to the right. The lanterns on the walls made their shadows jump and grow, and Sorcha felt a cowardly need to cringe away, as though the shadows were demon beings reaching for her.

She craned her neck to see if Aonghas was also being brought upstairs and saw him being pushed up the stairs to the left. Their separation had already begun. "Aonghas!"

Coghill slapped her face, bringing the sting of tears to her eyes. "Shut your mouth, murderess."

She blinked hard. Aonghas was gone. Defeated, Sorcha stopped struggling as she was pulled up even more stairs. She caught her toe and jammed her knee painfully into the edge of a step, but the man did not falter as he dragged her down a dark and narrow passage.

She said nothing and did not resist as he pushed her into a tiny room and slammed the door between them. She stood mutely as she listened to the sound of a key turning in the lock, sealing her inside what she knew would either be the first of many prisons to come or the last four walls she saw in this life.

As the sound of Coghill's footsteps died away, she looked around. A single brass bed sat in one corner, taking up over half of the small room. Across from it stood a narrow carved-wood table, upon which a single candle flickered in the cold draught coming from the cracked window. Beside the candle sat an empty plain white basin and pitcher.

Sorcha crossed to the window to see if it might be an avenue for escape but immediately saw it was not to be. Pointed iron bars had been attached to the exterior window frame, but even if they had not been there, the ground was a long drop down. To risk that fall would mean risking her life or, at the very least, her limbs. A broken leg would not carry her very far away. Not that she could even attempt a climb from a window with her hands still bound together.

She turned away in defeat. There was nothing left for her to do but sleep and wait for whatever tomorrow might bring. And pray that Aonghas wasn't hurt. Pray that she would see him again.

As best as she could without the full use of her hands, she pulled back the blanket on the bed and climbed underneath, hoping that Aonghas also had a room with a warm bed on this night.

Thoughts of her son twisted her heart, squeezing all the water from her body up and out through her eyes. Her pillow grew damp from her tears, but she couldn't stop crying.

CHAPTER SIXTEEN

Keaka

Day three, afternoon; along Loch Lomond

When people say this section of the trail is the hardest, they aren't joking. I start up what feels like the millionth climb of the day. Up rock steps, down tree root steps, up man-made stairs, across footbridges, down rock and root obstacle courses. Over and over and over again. It goes on so long that when I come to a stretch of flat path, I think the trail difficulty is finally easing. But no, it only leads to a new challenge.

Our group has been sticking close together this afternoon, and it's been surprisingly enjoyable. I really expected that Colin and I would be alone in the wilderness, and it's taken me some time to get used to that not being the case. But I can't deny that the people we've met are a lot of fun.

Only a mile or so after our lunch stop at Inversnaid, we poke around huge boulders, trying to find the famed Rob Roy's Cave. It involves balancing on a narrow ledge along the water to maneuver around a stone before we can even see the word *Cave* spray-painted on the side. Unimpressed, I abandon the exploration and wait on a bench carved to look like an oak leaf as I skim through Colin's West Highland Way guidebook. It's the first time I see the numerous notes that Adam made in the margins, and I finally understand why Colin has been so protective of it, keeping it in a Ziploc bag and reading through it periodically throughout the day.

I turn a page and see more of Adam's writing. *Colin would love this!* My heart catches, and I have to close my eyes and draw in a slow, deep breath. He sure did love our boy.

There was a time when Adam cared about what I would love, too. Whenever he stopped to put fuel in his car, he'd always go inside and buy me my favorite peanut butter M&M'S. When Colin was a baby and woke up hungry in the middle of the night, Adam insisted that I stay in bed while he brought Colin to me to nurse, even when he had to be at work early the next morning. We'd snuggle on the couch to watch TV but miss the show because we had so much to talk about. He was always interested in anything I told him, even the silliest of stories from my day.

I miss that Adam. The one who loved me. The one who made me laugh and feel like the most important person in the world. Even though I was so angry with him, and hurt, I would've taken him back after he cheated. Despite all our problems, I still loved him.

But then he died. Now I'll never get him back.

I hear the others coming and quickly wipe tears away.

The rain lightens, then stops, and an hour later, when we come to a sandy beach with a view of a tree-covered island that Colin says holds ruins of an old castle, the teenagers beg to stop and swim. The water is much too cold for me, so I sit on the beach with Jorgen, talking about his work as a city planner and their life in Copenhagen. Somehow, our conversation turns to the subject of being single parents and how difficult it is going to be for each of us to see our kids go off to university. It makes me feel closer to him, and I realize we are becoming friends.

Clara chose not to stop, so it's just the two of us on the beach. I lose track of time talking with Jorgen, and when his hand accidentally touches mine as we're both swatting away midges, I'm shocked to feel excitement jump in my belly.

Finally, the kids decide they're ready to get back on the trail. As I walk, I keep an eye on the loch to monitor our progress northward, and it seems we're finally nearing the top. Our hotel tonight is just north of the loch. We must be getting close.

I'm excited for the stop tonight, not only for the obvious reasons but also because we'll be staying at the Drovers Inn at Inverarnan, Scotland's most haunted inn. Or maybe it's Scotland's oldest inn? Aren't those practically the same thing? Either way, I doubt any ghosts will be able to wake me from the sleep I've earned today. I could sleep for a week.

As I crest a small hill, the view ahead opens up and I can't help but swear out loud. We aren't at the top of the lake at all. In fact, a good chunk of blue water still lies ahead. I might be seeing the north bank, but it could only be an illusion and the lake might actually curve around the clump of trees on the shoreline and keep going. It might stretch on forever at this rate, and I'll be stuck in a purgatory of hiking for the rest of my days.

We're nearing a grouping of buildings in various states of disrepair when Clara steps from the most intact one holding a hip flask of whisky. She lifts it into the air. "Welcome to Doune Byre Bothy! Care to join me for a dram?"

I glance at the time and am surprised that it's nearly six o'clock. Still, we all follow her inside.

Half an hour later, Jorgen and the girls decide to call it a night at the bothy, and Colin and I are left alone to walk the remaining nearly three miles to Inverarnan with night rapidly descending.

We tread in falling rain through waist-high bracken ferns, over stiles, across meadows, and through forests. I spy old stone walls and more ruined cottages, and I wonder again about the people who once lived in these forgotten homes and why they left.

My mind is so deep into these imagined people's lives that I'm not watching my footing as I should, and when stepping across a narrow ditch, I suddenly find myself knee-deep in muddy, ice-cold water. My momentum carries me forward, and with my foot lodged firmly in the muck, my knee bangs hard against the sharp flagstone edging the top.

Pain shoots up my thigh, and I cry out.

Colin hurries back to me. Without a word, he loops an arm around my back and lifts me straight up and out of the stream, then helps me hobble over to sit on a large boulder.

My rain pants are ripped at the knee, and I can see blood through the hole. As Colin digs out his first aid kit, I roll up my pant leg and feel sick at the amount of blood that is running down my shin and soaking into my socks.

"Here, put pressure on the wound." Colin hands me a wad of tissue, which I press to my knee.

"I don't know how that happened," I tell him as I waver between embarrassment and shock. "One minute I was walking and the next I was in the stream. My foot must have slipped."

"You're tired. That's when most injuries happen." Colin wipes away the blood and soon has my knee covered in bandages. He looks at me carefully, worry etched on his face. "Can you walk?"

I move to get to my feet when suddenly a wave of dizziness rolls over me, and I drop back to the rock with a thud. Before I can stop it, darkness descends like a cloak over my eyes, and I see flames flickering in an otherwise black night. The man holding the flame stares at me, a mixture of glee and hatred on his face that, in the dancing shadows from the lantern, makes him look like the devil himself. I can smell him, a combination of horse, sweat, and body odor. Other men are standing behind him. I feel rain falling on my head. The sound of nearby water is loud, like that of a flowing river. Abruptly, the man lunges toward me, and I cry out.

"Mom? What's wrong?"

Suddenly, the man and the darkness are gone and I am back in the rainy evening with Colin. He looks scared. "Mom? Can you hear me?"

I try to act like nothing happened, even though I feel shaken. "Of course I can hear you, Colin. I'm right here." I push with my hands against the rock and this time make it to my feet. My knee aches and feels stiff, but I can walk. "I'm okay. Nothing to worry about."

Colin looks like he wants to say something, but he simply gives a quick nod and then focuses on packing away his first aid kit.

I limp through a few steps, but after a bit, I find I can walk almost normally, just slower. Thank goodness I don't need stitches. The adrenaline dump leaves me feeling nauseated, but I'm not going to tell Colin about it. He is hovering near me like he expects me to shatter into pieces at any moment.

After a short distance, his voice breaks the silence. "What happened back there, Mom?" He sounds like he did when he was little and would run into my room in the middle of the night after having a bad dream. "You looked like you'd gone somewhere else. Your eyes were open, only you didn't see me. You saw something that terrified you, and you didn't respond when I talked to you."

Maybe I should tell him the truth about the strange visions I've been having. But wouldn't that scare him even more? All this is certainly scaring me.

But then again, Colin has proven already this week just how grown-up and strong he is. He can probably take it. Plus, with his active imagination, he's probably coming up with scenarios that are even worse than the truth.

"I'm sorry to scare you, sweetie. I think I was just in shock from the fall." I wait to see if he believes that, watching him closely as he helps me maneuver over a stile.

He presses his lips together and sighs, and I know he isn't buying it.

I'm wavering on whether to tell him when, suddenly, Colin stops walking and turns back to read a small sign on the side of the trail. "Mom, look at this. There's a ferry down this way that can take us across the lake. The highway is on that side. I bet we could get a ride to the hotel from there."

I look down the short trail to the lake, then back to the path going north. "Aren't we almost there?"

Colin pulls off his backpack to retrieve his treasured guidebook. He flips through the pages, then squints at a map. "My best guess is that it'll be another hour of walking. Maybe more if we keep at this slow pace."

I look at the mountains across the lake and see the sun is hidden behind them. It will be dark soon. I nod. "Let's take the ferry."

We make our way to the shoreline, where we find a pole with a sign telling us to pull the red ball to the top to signal the ferry to come. Colin does as instructed, then ties off the rope to hold the ball in place. We sit on the wet grass to wait.

I pop a couple of ibuprofen to dull the pain in my knee and stretch my legs out in front of me, feeling strain in my lower back and hips. My injury makes me worry about the hike tomorrow and whether I'll be able to walk in the morning. I don't plan to mention this to Colin until I have to, though.

Since he hasn't asked about my strange behavior again, I decide not to mention the visions to him. There's nothing he can do about them, anyway, and I certainly don't want our week together to end with him thinking his mother is losing her marbles.

We sit for a solid thirty minutes with no sign of activity anywhere on the loch. The light is fading fast. "I don't think the ferry is coming."

"Yeah, I was thinking the same thing." He screws his mouth to the side in a scowl. "We're going to have to walk the rest of the way."

I search the sky. "We're not going to make it before dark."

Colin grabs his pack and unzips the main compartment. "I'm glad I threw in flashlights at the last minute. I didn't think we'd need them, and I almost left them in the suitcase this morning." He hands one to me, then shrugs his pack on.

Before we leave the lochside, Colin lowers the ferry signal. As I follow him back up the slope to the main trail, I can't help but feel a tremor of fear course through me. Colin said it will take about an hour to get from here to our hotel. I've never hiked anywhere in the dark.

The rain seems to be staying away for now, but heavy cloud cover makes the twilight feel even darker. I clutch the flashlight Colin gave me, but I don't click it on just yet. There's still enough light to see by, and I don't want to risk using up the batteries too early.

To my left I see the huddled shadows of more ruins from a former settlement. One house, however, still has a roof, and I see a faint light in one of the windows. Maybe other hikers are sleeping there tonight, or maybe someone lives there. The feeling that I'm trespassing comes over me, and I try to make my steps as quiet as possible until we're well past the dwelling.

Soon Colin switches on his flashlight, and I do the same, realizing that it's now gotten quite dark. Although there are patches of forests to our right, we're mostly walking across open, rolling ground along the route of a small valley.

Although I can't see beyond the circles of light cast by our flashlights, I sense that the loch has fallen away, and I have to believe that we've finally reached the top. I want to get off this trail and into our hotel. Neither of us speaks; we are focused on keeping our eyes on the trail and making sure we don't get lost.

Colin leads us across planks of wood laid down to mark the trail across boggy ground, and I'm grateful that it's mostly flat here, rather than the constant up and down of earlier. If I had fallen earlier in the day, I don't think I would have been able to finish the hike. All the ascents and descents would have put too much pressure on my aching knee.

Every now and again, I lift the beam of my flashlight to see if I can see any markers, or landmarks that might tell us we are getting close, but mostly, I concentrate on the ground in front of me.

The trail takes us through a section of forest that makes the skin prickle on the back of my neck, and twice, I shine my light back behind me into the pit of blackness. If something is back there following me, I can't see it.

The image of the man from my vision comes back to me, and I shudder. If he—or his ghost—is out here lurking in the darkness, I'm doomed. I stick close to Colin and, thankfully, we soon emerge onto moorland again.

When my flashlight catches a pile of stones, I gasp and my heart shoots into my throat. Did someone just duck down behind that wall?

I shine the light on it, but nothing moves, and I decide my imagination is running away with me. It's nothing more than a crumbling stone wall beside a long-abandoned home.

Five steps later, I hear what sounds like a muffled cough coming from the direction of the ruin. "Did you hear that?"

Colin glances back at me. "Hear what?"

"A cough."

The look on his face tells me he thinks I imagined it. "Nope."

I close the distance between us and give him a gentle push. "Let's get out of here. It's spooky."

Up ahead I see the twinkle of a far-off light. We must be getting close now. Please let us be getting close.

Another section of forest is even darker than the last, and I'm desperate to distract myself from all the spooky goblins I keep imagining in my mind. I ask the first question that comes to me. "Colin, if you could eat any food in the world right now, what would you eat?"

He thinks about it a moment. "Cheese enchiladas."

"Ooh, good answer. I'm craving pad see ew from the Thai place at home." A snapping sound in the forest makes me jump, but Colin doesn't flinch. He has much more experience being in the woods at night than I do, so if he's not worried, I'll try not to worry, either. "And after that, I want a liliko'i malasada for dessert."

"Or great-grandma's haupia cake," Colin adds. I'm following as close behind him as I can without stepping on his heels.

When lights appear through the trees ahead, we both pick up our pace.

After what seems like forever, we make our way through a campsite, across a river, alongside a main road, and finally arrive at a historic building that takes no stretch of the imagination to believe there are ghosts lurking inside.

The Drovers Inn is larger than I expected—three stories—and made completely of stone, including what looks like a slate roof. Colin told me earlier that the hotel is over three hundred years old, and I can believe it. If it wasn't for the electric lights alongside the road and on the building, I would think that I'd just traveled back in time.

"Can you believe this inn has been here longer than the US has been a country?" Colin opens the front door for me and I hobble through, shaking my head. This kind of history is difficult to wrap my brain around.

I'm startled by the magnitude of taxidermy animals in the lobby. I know hunting is an industry that has brought much-needed funds into the country, so I try not to think about how the animals might have suffered.

To my left is an open doorway to a bar packed with people eating, drinking, and singing. I can't tell if the music is from a sound system or a live band. The scents coming from the room make my stomach growl, but I first need to drop my pack and use the restroom before I eat.

As soon as we have our room key, Colin heads to the shed out back to retrieve the suitcase our luggage transporter should've dropped off. Alone, I slowly and painfully climb the stairs to our room on the top floor.

I find our room at the end of the hall, and I unlock the door and push it open. As light from the hallway spills inside, I'm startled to see a woman lying on the bed. I hesitate in the open doorway. "Oh! I must have the wrong room."

The woman sits up, and I get another shock. It's the woman from the painting.

It's Sorcha Chisholm.

CHAPTER SEVENTEEN

Sorcha

The Inbhir Àirnein (Inverarnan) House Hotel

She had no idea how long she'd slept, but the sound of a key in the door jerked Sorcha awake. She sat up quickly and had to fight through a wave of dizziness.

When she could see straight, she realized it was still dark. The candle was burning low, but it gave off enough light for her to see the door opening and a strange woman stepping into the room.

Although Sorcha could clearly see the door behind the woman standing open, she also saw it firmly closed, as though there were two doors. She could make no sense of it, and so turned her attention back to the woman.

She could make no sense of her, either. Long, dark hair left uncovered, dark eyes, dark skin. Even more strange was her immodest clothing. She wore a man's trousers, ripped at one knee, and a shirt without buttons or ties that revealed the skin of her arms right up to her shoulders. How she'd managed to pass the men downstairs without being accosted was a mystery.

And then Sorcha noticed the woman's strange satchel hanging on her back and strapped around her chest and hips with buckles the likes of which she had never before seen. No, she *had* seen it once before. That evening near An Gearasdan when this woman—it had to be the same woman—emerged from the trees with a man in short pants, and yet Aonghas had not seen them.

Alarmed by the strange woman's arrival and odd clothing, Sorcha felt her heart beat even faster when she saw that the satchel on the woman's back almost glowed, so vibrant was the green of the shiny material. Nothing in nature could produce a fabric or color such as this.

This woman was not from here. She was not from this world.

Alarmed by the realization, Sorcha scrambled back on the bed until she felt her shoulder blades press against the brass headboard.

The woman must be a Good Woman, one of the Fair Folk. She must have stepped from her underground kingdom to visit Sorcha here in her jail. But why?

The woman stared back at her with equal surprise, as though she hadn't expected to find Sorcha in this room. Her lips moved as if she were speaking, but no sound came out.

"Who are you?" Sorcha asked the only question she could think of, but the woman's mouth continued moving. She seemed to be asking questions of her own, which Sorcha couldn't understand. But because her facial expressions and body movements didn't seem threatening, Sorcha slowly relaxed.

"Can you help me?" Sorcha threw aside the blanket covering her and swung her feet to the floor to stand. "I need to find my son and leave this place."

The Good Woman's eyes widened when she saw the ropes binding Sorcha's wrists. Helplessly, Sorcha lifted her arms. "Have you a knife?"

The woman stepped forward, and Sorcha instinctively stepped back. But when she lifted her empty hands as though to show she meant no harm, Sorcha allowed her to approach.

But then the strangest thing happened. When the Good Woman reached to touch the rope, her hand passed right through it and through Sorcha's hands. She felt nothing of the touch, but her heart started pounding loudly in her ears.

The Good Woman's inability to touch Sorcha must have surprised her, too, for she took a step backward and looked at Sorcha in shock.

As she stared into the Good Woman's eyes, Sorcha felt a strangeness come over her. It was as though she'd always known this woman and the woman had always known her. Without words, they understood each other and, even more surprisingly, cared for the other.

The Good Woman slowly blinked her big brown eyes, and then she looked away from Sorcha, her gaze roaming as though in search of something.

When she found it, her eyes widened and a dazzling smile spread across her face. Even her gleaming white teeth were evidence that she was from the kingdom beneath the mounds.

As Sorcha watched with interest, the Good Woman walked to the end of the bed where the side butted up against the dingy wall, and pointed. Confused, Sorcha cautiously drew closer.

She looked to where the Good Woman pointed and saw that a piece of the brass bed had broken off the post, leaving a jagged edge. When she looked back for an explanation, the woman pointed to the ropes binding Sorcha's wrists together, then back at the broken metal.

Finally understanding, Sorcha felt a spurt of hope surge through her.

The Good Woman stepped back, and Sorcha got to work sawing the rope against the jagged metal. At first it didn't budge, but when she put more pressure against it by pulling her hands apart as far as the rope allowed and pushing down as hard as she could, the rope finally frayed, and then snapped apart.

She dropped the rope and smiled her gratitude to the Good Woman, who returned the smile and lifted a fist into the air in some sort of strange Fair Folk celebration.

Now all Sorcha needed was to free herself from this room and find Aonghas.

When she looked back to the door, she again saw it both closed and open at the same time, which made no sense.

Crossing quickly to it, she soon learned that the open door was just as real to her as the woman of the Fair Folk. She could see it, but there was no physical substance to it. That left the closed door.

She curled her hand around the handle and turned.

Nothing. The door was still locked.

The Good Woman looked just as confused as she by the two doors. As Sorcha watched, she walked past Sorcha and disappeared through the closed door, only to reappear a second later, coming back into the room. The Good Woman's brows furrowed, and she placed her hands on her hips in frustration. She said something to Sorcha, but no sound came from her mouth and Sorcha was unable to make out the words.

Before either of them could think of something else to try, a noise at the door made both women jump back. Someone was inserting a key into the lock!

Sorcha shuffled backward to put distance between herself and whichever of her captors was entering.

The rope! Her captor would see that her rope had been cut, and he would bind her again. Quickly, before the door could open, Sorcha grabbed the cut rope from the floor and wrapped it over her wrists so it would appear intact. Then she pressed her hands to her midsection to hold the loose rope in place.

The door swung open. "Ma?"

"Aonghas!" Forgetting all about the rope, Sorcha hurried to the now-open doorway and pulled her son into her arms. "How are you here?"

Aonghas hugged her. *"Ist!"* he said in a voice so low she had to strain to hear him. "Come, we need to go now while Coghill and his companions are in their cups."

"How did you find me?"

"Yours was the only locked door on this floor."

"How did you escape your room?"

"I'll tell you the story later. Come, we must go."

Only now remembering the woman of the Fair Folk, Sorcha tugged Aonghas's hand to make him wait. "First I must thank—"

The Good Woman was gone. Sorcha peered into each darkened corner but saw no sign of the woman who'd helped her. Confused by all that had happened, she shook her head. "Never mind. Let's go."

With her *plaide* lost during their capture, she had no choice but to grab the thin, dirty blanket from the bed and wrap it around her and over her head. Her brooch was still fastened to her skirt, where she'd placed it for safety as they settled down to sleep last evening; the men must not have noticed it, or surely they would have taken it from her.

As she followed Aonghas out of the room, she fastened the blanket at her chest with her brooch and hoped she appeared like any other woman staying at the inn.

Together they crept down the stairs, staying to the sides of each step to avoid creaky spots in the middle of the treads.

The last section was the worst. Loud music and voices echoed into the inn's reception room, and Sorcha had only to glance down the last remaining short flight of stairs to know they ended right at the door of the barroom, where Coghill had been promised a dram.

Aonghas led the way and she followed. As she pressed her back against the wall and descended into the reception room, she could feel the pounding of the drum on the other side of the wall. With the drum and fiddle and voices raised in song, she doubted anyone would hear them, but all it would take was one lull in the din and an errant sound from her or Aonghas and they would be caught.

Aonghas quickly slid from the bottom step and disappeared down the shadowed corridor opposite the barroom.

With a deep breath like she was about to plunge underwater, Sorcha took the final step and followed Aonghas, feeling like something evil was breathing onto the back of her neck. Only now did she see a desk where the innkeeper worked, but thank heaven, it was empty.

At the end of the dark corridor, she found Aonghas waiting by a door. As soon as they stepped into the rain and fresh air, Sorcha pulled Aonghas around the side of the building. A few cows had been left in a small field as their drover took refreshment inside, but they only shifted and snorted as Sorcha and Aonghas ran past.

They were free.

CHAPTER EIGHTEEN

Keaka

Day three, evening; the Drovers Inn, Inverarnan

The woman on the bed, Sorcha Chisholm, shuffles awkwardly backward under a brown tartan blanket until her back is pressed to the headboard behind her. She is clearly afraid of me.

I reach back and flick on the overhead light but, disconcertingly, even though it illuminates the room, it does not penetrate the darkness around Sorcha, who is lit only by a burning candle on a side table.

Sorcha is filthy. Her hair, which had been uncovered when she was standing over Colin's bed and covered by a white hat of sorts in the museum painting, is now escaping from under the same white hat, now dingy and tied under her chin in a limp bow. She's wearing a brown waist-length jacket and a dark-blue skirt with vertical red stripes. Pinned to the skirt at her waist is a flat, round brooch the size of my palm. It is dulled by use, or maybe it only seems so in the low light.

I quickly scan the room and see a barred window, an empty bowl and pitcher on the table next to the candle. Straw is spilling out from one corner of the mattress.

I look back at Sorcha. "I'm sorry to frighten you, but I don't understand what's happening."

Sorcha's brows lower in confusion, but she doesn't seem as scared as she was when I first opened the door. Her mouth moves as though she's speaking, but no sound comes out.

"I know who you are," I tell her, as I wonder whether I should move closer or run away. "You're Sorcha Chisholm, right? Your home was burned and a man died?"

She doesn't answer, but she no longer seems afraid as she kicks off the blanket, swings her feet to the floor, and moves toward me.

That's when I see the rope tying her hands together. It looks painful. So when Sorcha lifts her hands toward me as though asking for help, I don't hesitate. She may be an outlawed murderer, but I know she's getting the raw end of the deal. I step toward her.

Sorcha steps back, her big eyes watching me. Fear has returned.

I raise both my palms toward her. "I won't hurt you. I'm just trying to help." I try another step forward, and this time Sorcha doesn't retreat.

I reach for the knot over her wrists, but my hand slips right through the rope and even through Sorcha's hands as though they are made of water. Horrified, we both jump backward.

I stare at her as my mind races. What, exactly, is this woman? Is she a ghost? A time traveler? Am I the time traveler? How are we able to see each other so clearly when she isn't actually, physically here at all?

Several emotions flash over Sorcha's face as I stare at her, and I realize she's just as confused as I am. And she's scared—not of me, but of the situation she finds herself in. She needs help. And murderer or not, I want to help her.

If I can't free her from the rope, from this room, then she's going to have to free herself.

I scan the room again. The candle. She could burn the rope with the flame until it breaks apart. But, no, she would burn her own skin along with it.

The window. She could climb out the window. I look at it and again see the bars firmly attached to the stone outside the wavy glass. No, that's no good.

Think, Keaka. There must be a way to help. I scan the room again. The side table doesn't hold anything that could help, and it's made of thick, gleaming wood that looks strong enough to withstand everything but a saw. No help there.

I look at the bed and see that it's made from some sort of metal that was probably once shiny but is now blackened with tarnish.

And then I see it.

On the bed leg that is against the wall, a section is jagged and sharp, as though a piece was broken off. It looks sharp enough to cut the rope. I smile at Sorcha in triumph and move closer to the bed so I can point it out to her.

She comes closer, but is careful not to come so close to me that we accidentally touch. I don't blame her. It was freaky to see my hand pass right through hers.

When Sorcha looks at the bed leg and then back at me, confused, I point to her ropes and then back to the jagged piece. I put my hands together as hers are and make a sawing motion with them to illustrate what she should do.

But she's already hunkering down and positioning her hands over the makeshift saw. I step back to allow her room and watch as she works.

It's taking longer than I expected to cut through the fibers, but she's not giving up. She exerts more downward force on the ropes as she moves them back and forth over the sharp metal, and then, suddenly, her hands snap apart.

When Sorcha turns to show me, her face is alight with joy and hope, and for the first time, I realize she's not as old as I'd first thought. In fact, she's probably in her early forties, same as me.

I pump my fist in celebration, which seems to confuse Sorcha, but she only smiles wider.

Seemingly energized by her ability to use her hands again, she moves past me to the open door. But then, instead of walking through it, she stops and reaches for the space where a doorknob would be if it was closed.

I'm confused. "Just go, Sorcha. It's open."

She doesn't respond, and I remember that she can't hear me. I slip past her, careful not to touch, and walk out into the hallway, hoping she will follow. When she doesn't, I walk back into the room and turn to study the doorway. Maybe she sees something I don't. I get ready to demonstrate walking through the threshold again.

Just then, Colin appears in the open doorway, pulling our suitcase behind him, and I jump in surprise. "Colin! You scared me!"

He raises one eyebrow. "Really? You didn't hear me banging this monster against every step on the way up?"

"No, I was talking to—" I turn to introduce the two, but Sorcha is gone. In fact, everything in the room has changed. I spin around to take it all in.

The room itself has more than doubled in size. A wall must have been knocked down at some point to convert two rooms into one. The wood flooring has changed to carpet woven in a blue-and-red-tartan pattern. Where Sorcha's single bed had been shoved into a corner, there now stands a twin-size oak bed, a matching nightstand holding a lamp and a digital alarm clock, and a second bed beside that. A television is mounted in the corner over a long, narrow table with an electric kettle, sugar packets, and teacups.

I look to the window and find it a clear black square. No bars in sight. Blue drapes hang down either side.

"This will do." Colin must not have heard me or he figures I was talking to myself, because he doesn't ask who I was talking to. He places the suitcase on a luggage rack next to the door. "I saw the bathroom just down the hall. I hope you don't mind this isn't an en suite. When I made the reservations, I really wanted to stay in the original historic building. This was all they had left."

I shake my head to clear out the fog that crept in during my time with Sorcha and drop my backpack on one of the beds. "No, it's no problem at all. Besides, it's only one night. I'll survive." I force a grin for my son. "But I am starving. Want to check out the pub downstairs?"

Colin drops his backpack on the floor, and we head for the stairs after a quick pit stop in the bathroom. As we walk down the uneven steps to the ground floor, I can't help but look at the historic paintings and photos on the walls, at the tartan carpeting and flickering old chandeliers, and wonder what Sorcha saw when she passed through here. I feel like she's still around since I just saw her, but I know her time here happened over two hundred years ago.

It makes no sense to me that I saw her and she saw me. There's no logical reason for our connection.

The stairs end in the small lobby. I avert my eyes from the taxidermy bear standing on its hind legs in one corner, silently growling toward the entrance. After what I'd just experienced, it wouldn't surprise me one bit if the bear turned its head and growled at me.

I follow Colin into the pub and find it busy, but we manage to secure a tiny circular table under the window, where we're given menus and instructed to order at the bar.

Once I've ordered and returned to our table with whisky for Colin and hard cider for me, I tentatively broach the subject. "So, uh, what did you think about that woman we learned about from Morag yesterday?"

Colin sips his whisky, then makes a face and reaches for his water glass. "You mean the murderer? Sorcha something?"

"Yeah. Do you think she really was a murderer, though? I mean, the painting at the Kelvingrove calls her innocent."

He sips from his glass and gives an absent-minded nod as though it tastes better now. "Yeah, but Morag said she's the woman who killed the man whose body her husband found under their barn. So she's not as innocent as the painter believed, is she?"

Oh God. I'd forgotten about the dead man near Milarrochy. Strathglass, Sorcha's homeland, is much farther north from here, which means that she was likely traveling southward. And I know she came through Inverarnan, because I just saw her upstairs, which means that in her timeline she has not yet reached Milarrochy and killed the man. By helping her escape just now, am I to blame for that man's death? If I hadn't helped her, would she have been put in prison and the man would have survived?

I imagine my own photo on the flyer beside the drawings of Sorcha and Aonghas, and feel a cold sweat break out over my entire body.

Musicians arrive and start opening their instrument cases to set up on the tiny stage near the door. "I really don't think she did it." I'm telling myself this as much as I am Colin. "Or, if she did, I think both murders were purely self-defense. Aonghas was innocent, too."

"Wait a minute." Colin holds his hand up as he drains his glass. "I need another drink before we go any further. Want another?"

Just then, the server arrives with our food, so we lean back to allow her room to set our plates down. When she leaves, Colin excuses himself to order another round at the bar. As I wait, I pick absently at my side salad.

Colin gets right to it when he sets my cider on the table in front of me. "Why do you care so much about this story?"

All I can do is answer vaguely. "I don't know. I just find it interesting."

He nods and digs into his steak-and-ale pie, and I think the subject is dropped. But then, after he swallows, he tilts his head to the side. "If I was evicted from the only home I'd ever known, and I had nowhere else to go, I think I would feel pretty angry about it. I'm not saying I would murder someone over it, but history is full of murders motivated by much less."

I think about that as I eat my own dinner. Of course Sorcha was motivated to murder the man evicting her from her home. And if she did end up killing the second man in Milarrochy, well, the little girl who witnessed it had called him a bad man, so he must have been hurting Sorcha in some way at the time.

I will not lose you again, bitch. I cringe at the memory of the words I'd heard in the woods at Milarrochy. It must have been the murdered man who'd said those words to Sorcha and, somehow, to me. He was intent on causing her harm. I'm certain of it.

I've looked into Sorcha's eyes. I've seen the fear there. And the worry. I feel deep in my gut that if she did kill either of the men, she had good reason. I don't believe she was an evil person herself.

My guilt eases a bit at that, and I turn my attention to the musicians, who have started playing a lively jig. The noise level in the room cuts off all chance of further conversation, so I don't even try. Colin joins in the clapping and seems to have forgotten all about Sorcha.

But I haven't. I can't. She's as real to me as any person in this room, and I'm dying to know what happened to her. And why is she haunting me?

Could it be because we are both moms traveling alone with our sons?

I can't possibly be the only mom who's walked the West Highland Way with her son. Does that mean she's haunted other moms who've come through here?

I have to admit, if I heard of some other woman experiencing the visions that I have, I wouldn't believe her. It's all too weird. My head hurts from all the thoughts banging around in it.

We stay long enough to hear three songs, then Colin begs the bartender for a bag of ice for my knee and we head back upstairs to our room. Each step sends a stab of pain through my leg, and I want nothing more than to be off my feet for the rest of the night.

But I still can't get Sorcha out of my head. As we're climbing the last flight of stairs to our room, I say to Colin's back, "Sorcha didn't feel only anger after her eviction. I'm sure she also felt rejected and scared of her future."

Colin is pulling the room key from his pocket, but he stops and turns back to me, his face pinched. "Okay." He tilts his head to the side. "Mom, are you scared of your own future?"

His maturity and insight catch me off guard. I try to make a joke of it. "Of course I am. My baby will be living on the other side of the planet, not needing me anymore."

I take the key from him and unlock our door, half expecting to see Sorcha in the room but finding only the modern room. Colin follows me in, and I start gathering the items I need to go down the hall for a shower. He sets the ice bag on a towel on the table but doesn't move farther. "Mom . . ." His voice sounds timid. "I don't mean to make you feel rejected. I'm always going to need you." He looks down, then up at me again. "Is it because I'm going to school in another country, or is it because I've been walking with Kirsten and Terese so much?"

The guilt on his face steals my breath. "Oh, sweetie, it's not you. I promise. I'm excited for you to go to school here, and I'm happy you're making friends. Really." I pull him to me and squeeze him tight, knowing a hug won't solve anything like it did when he was a toddler but needing to try all the same.

Colin doesn't let the subject drop. Even as we're hugging, he says, "But something is making you feel rejected. I know you weren't just talking about Sorcha Chisholm."

I could kick myself for letting that slip. The rejection and fear I feel have nothing to do with Colin and everything to do with the way my marriage ended. I can't tell that to Colin, though, any more than I can tell him about my visions and why I'm feeling so connected to Sorcha. "You amaze me, my boy. Do you know that? The fact that you're even asking me this shows me how grown-up you've become. It means a lot to me that you care."

I let him go and turn to the suitcase to dig out fresh clothes. Colin shuffles to the bed and plops down. "So you're not feeling rejected and sad about something?"

I can see he's not going to let this go. I search my brain for an explanation that he'll accept, and finally decide on, "I think it's just an ancestral-memory kind of thing. Sorcha belonged to something so much bigger than herself. A community, an identity. When she was evicted, that was all stripped from her. To be pushed out was akin to being told you don't matter, you never mattered, you will never matter."

Which was exactly how I felt when Adam told me he wanted a divorce. As though I was being evicted from community, kinship, belonging, identity, home, security, legacy, feelings of worth. I shove the thoughts away and return to my flimsy explanation. "I think that's how my dad's parents felt when they were forced into internment camps during World War II. It's how our Hawaiian ancestors must have felt when European settlers took over their land, stripped away their culture, and killed so many of their loved ones through the diseases they introduced to the islands. It's probably how any refugee from anywhere in the world feels when they lose their home, their country."

"Oh, wow, I hadn't made that connection before." Colin toes off his shoes and stretches out full length. "You're right: the Highland Clearances weren't unique, in that one class of people was the victim of another, and the social, emotional, and economic repercussions are still playing out today. And what's really crazy is that the Scots who were displaced by sheep went over to North America and Australia and displaced the Indigenous people living there. It's a sad cycle."

I love seeing his mind spin off on the subject. It reassures me yet again that he is going to thrive at university, studying history and having discussions like this with his peers. We discuss it a bit further, and soon, with his attention off my emotions, Colin finally allows me to leave the room to take a shower. When I return, he leaves to do the same, and I settle on my twin bed to place a fresh bandage on my knee and then cover it with the bag of melting ice.

As exhausted as I am tonight, I'm eager for Colin to fall asleep so Sorcha can return, either in her ghostly form or in a vision. I need to know what happened to her.

CHAPTER NINETEEN

Sorcha

Somewhere near the top of Loch Laomainn (Loch Lomond)

Sorcha didn't stop running, nor did she release her hold on Aonghas's hand as she dragged him through the pounding rain away from the inn, away from those men, away from young Iain, who had betrayed them.

When they reached the river, she didn't pause to think about the danger of the swift current. Though the water was in spate, she and Aonghas were both strong swimmers. The men in pursuit wouldn't expect a woman and boy to survive a crossing here, so they wouldn't think to look for them on the other side. They would look to the south, or to the north, or possibly even to the west up the great mountain that cradled the inn at its base.

She plunged in, pulling Aonghas with her. "Swim for the other side as fast as you can. Don't worry about me; I'll be right behind you."

She watched him wade in farther until the dark night swallowed him up. The sound of splashing reassured her that he was swimming. She had to trust that he would make it across.

Taking only a moment to tie the *plaide* around her waist so her arms were free, she followed her son and felt the water pull on her skirt. It twisted around her legs and threatened to drag her under with its weight.

She started to pull up her skirt to free her legs for kicking, but the bottom of the river disappeared and she plunged underwater, into an iciness that fogged her mind and paralyzed her limbs. It would be so easy to stay here, to give up fighting and drift away to where Tàm and the children waited for her.

But then she remembered Aonghas, who should be on the opposite shore for her. He needed her. He would be all alone without her.

With her last remaining ounce of strength, she clawed at the water until her head broke through the surface and she was able to draw in breath. Delicious, life-saving breath.

She flipped onto her back in hopes that she could half float as her arms pulled at the water and her legs—still encased in heavy, wet wool—kicked as much as possible.

The dark night became a confusion of black water and black sky and raindrops and waves splashing over her face, making her cough and gag. She struggled on, hoping she was moving in the direction that would take her across the river to Aonghas.

When her head hit a rock, she yelped in pain. To her surprise, she found she could stand, and she struggled, one straining step at a time, to shallow water. When she pushed her hair out of her eyes, she discovered that her mutch was gone, snatched away by the river.

When she reached the riverbank, she grabbed whatever her hands landed on—which turned out to be ferns, grasses, and saplings—and pulled her weary and freezing body up the slope. At the top, she dropped onto her belly and spent several moments working to draw air into her body, even as shivers squeezed it back out of her.

Aonghas. She had to find Aonghas.

She pushed up to her hands and knees, then struggled onto her feet. She had no idea where she was, although she was almost certain she had successfully crossed to the other side of the river from the inn. The dark, wet night prevented her from seeing more than a couple feet in front of her.

The sound of coughing came from upriver. As only a mother who'd tended to her child through all his illnesses could, she knew it was Aonghas. Suddenly, she couldn't get to him fast enough.

She followed the sound. Her forehead banged painfully on a tree branch that she didn't see, her wet skirt tripped her countless times, and her shivering limbs slowed her considerably, but she made progress through the tall grass, and when the coughing sound grew louder, she risked calling out, "Aonghas?"

"Here." More coughing, which told her his crossing had been even worse than her own.

She followed the sound and found him on his hands and knees on the riverbank, dripping wet and freezing cold. The Fleming *plaide* that had been draped around his body at the inn now lay in a soggy pile beside him.

Dropping onto the ground, Sorcha wrapped her arms around his shivering body and rubbed her hands vigorously up and down his back and arms. She felt the cold down to the middle of her bones and she shivered uncontrollably, yet all she cared about was warming her son.

She pounded on his back to loosen the worst of the water, and when his coughing finally subsided, she helped him up. With one arm looped around his back, she snatched up the heavy, wet *plaide* with her other hand. "We must go away from here before they come looking for us. Move."

They stumbled together across a field and into a woodland, where the rain lessened under the tree canopy. All the while, Sorcha felt the blade of danger poking at them from behind, urging her faster, away from the inn, away from the men there.

Another coughing fit overtook Aonghas, and he had to stop and rest his hands on his knees. "I can't go on," he told her once he caught his breath.

"We need to put more distance between ourselves and those men before we stop."

He placed a hand on her shoulder like his father used to do and said in a grave tone, "We won't last the night if we don't find shelter."

She knew he was right. Her muscles were growing stiffer by the minute, her mind foggier. But where could they go?

"Come," Aonghas said, taking hold of her hand. "I smell animals. We must be near a farm."

She pulled on his hand. "We cannot speak to anyone. They'll turn us over to Coghill, just as Iain did."

Aonghas simply squeezed her hand. "Trust me. I'll keep you safe."

Comforted despite herself, and surprised by his maturity, she followed.

But the night was devoid of a moon and the rain clouds obscured any starlight. Completely blind in the dark, they struggled to find their way, often tripping on tangled vines, twice banging their heads against tree limbs, and even once falling over a low stone wall.

Sorcha was ready to huddle together on the ground and see if they survived until morning.

But then she spotted something. A light, bouncing through the forest. "Someone is coming. I see a light."

"Where? I don't see it."

"Ist!" She pulled Aonghas down behind the wall as the light shone over them, and then, as they were plunged into darkness again, she risked peeking over the wall.

The strange light continued toward them through the forest. At one point, it shone upon a building and Sorcha took note of its location, hoping that whoever was holding the light would keep moving.

The light was strangely bright. Brighter than any lantern or bog pine torch she'd ever seen. And it seemed to point in one direction only rather than illuminate all around it.

As the light came closer, Sorcha forced herself to remain completely still.

Aonghas coughed. She squeezed his arm to remind him to be quiet.

Suddenly, a woman's voice spoke into the darkness, and Sorcha jumped in fright. Yet it soon became clear that the voice was not directed at them, but at the woman's companion. Sorcha couldn't make out the words, but the voices sounded friendly.

Sorcha slumped against the wall. It wasn't people pursuing them, but merely travelers stranded out on this miserable night, same as them. She closed her eyes and breathed until her heart settled back into its natural rhythm.

For several moments after the voices and the strange light disappeared, Sorcha held Aonghas beside her, behind the wall. Finally, when it seemed the travelers were gone, she released him. As Aonghas got to his feet and helped her up, another coughing spasm hit him and he couldn't suppress it. She pushed his soggy *plaide* to his face to muffle the sound and, again, pounded his back to loosen the phlegm.

When he calmed, Sorcha grabbed his hand in the dark and whispered, "This way. I know where we can find shelter."

She led him to the building the strange light had revealed.

"Wait here." Aonghas pushed her gently against the corner of the stones and disappeared along the length of the wall. When he reappeared on her other side several moments later, he whispered, "We're in luck. It's a detached byre. There must be a house nearby, so stay quiet."

He led her to the door and gently eased it open. The animal smells were familiar to her and their accompanying warmth welcome. As they stepped inside, cows shifted in their stalls and a goat bleated. Aonghas quickly pulled the door shut behind them and the animals quieted, although they still stirred in their stalls, uneasy from the smell of strangers in their midst.

But the warmth. Oh, the blessed warmth. Fresh, dry straw covered the floor, and the heat from the animals' bodies filled the small space with a warmth she had not thought she'd ever again feel.

"We'll have to leave before sunup," she told Aonghas. "We cannot be discovered here."

"We will. Now, lie down here and go to sleep."

She first draped their wet blankets over the stall walls to allow them to dry, and then she did as her son told her and lay down on the straw near a cow's warm, sleeping body. Aonghas stretched out beside her, and she felt around in the straw until she found his hand again. "You did good, son."

"So did you, Ma."

"I don't understand how you escaped, though. How did you do it?"

"Iain."

The answer was so surprising Sorcha sat up. The cow stirred but didn't get to her feet.

"You know when I attacked him, before we were taken to the inn?" His voice held a note of wonder. "Iain slipped my knife back into my belt and pulled my *plaide* nearly off me so that it wasn't seen by those men. I think he wanted us to escape."

"Then why did he turn us in?"

Aonghas took a long time to answer, but when he finally did, his words made Sorcha feel ill. "I didn't want to tell you of it, but at that inn yesterday, where we purchased soup, I saw a paper tacked to the wall with our likenesses drawn on it. I couldn't read what it said, of course, but I did see an amount of money written there. I think Iain also saw it before I tore it down and, being able to read, he knew what it said." He coughed again, smothering the sound in the crook of his arm. Once he had recovered, he finished his story. "I think a reward was offered for our capture. We know Iain's family needs money. I would venture that's why he turned us in, but his regard for us made him return my knife."

Sorcha didn't know what to think of Iain's actions, but she was deeply bothered by the news that An Siosal had ordered Coghill to pursue them so relentlessly.

But, of course, the man who'd died had been Lady Chisholm's cousin. Sorcha and Aonghas had personally offended their betters by harming one of them. They would not be allowed to get away with it.

Her mind reeling, she lay back down beside her son.

The warmth of the byre was starting to seep through her clothes, and she felt her fatigue settling heavily over her, pushing her down into sleep.

She gave into it, grateful for the escape from her jumbled thoughts.

⁓∽

Morning arrived clear and dry. For countless long hours, and with exhausted bodies and pounding heads, they moved south along the eastern shore of Loch Laomainn. Sorcha's empty belly twisted and sent a burning pain up into her throat. The occasional leaf or flower did little to ease her hunger. It was too early in the year for berries or nuts, but still she yearned for both. All she could do was drink from the burns and hope the water would fool her stomach.

The mountains seemed to grow from deep in the loch itself, leaving little shore or ledge where they could walk. She'd lost count of all the boulders and tree roots she'd clambered over.

Some burns and waterfalls were narrow enough that they could step across and stay dry on the rocks. Many others fell from high overhead down a sheer rock face and their only option was to enter the loch and swim until they were past the worst of it. The only thing keeping them from freezing to death was the June sunshine.

Sorcha felt like the day would never end. She was constantly wet, and the tender area where her thighs touched felt chafed and raw. Her feet had gone from pained to numb, and she wondered if they were damaged beyond healing.

"We need rest, Aonghas. And food."

"We do." Aonghas clambered up yet more boulders and craned his neck to see what was ahead of them. "A boat is coming."

"Come down!" she hissed, panicked. As soon as he got within reach, Sorcha pulled him the rest of the way off the rock and as far from the edge of the loch as they could get, tucked behind tumbled-down boulders. "Say not a word, nor move a finger until the boat has passed."

Her muscles screamed for relief from her crouched position, but she dared not move. She could hear the splash of oars and knew the boatman was close. Next to her Aonghas breathed fast and heavily, bringing Sorcha's attention to the fact that she was doing the same. She forced herself to breathe slower, deeper, as she listened to the sound of oars splashing and then the rub of wood against rock.

And then Aonghas coughed.

"Feasgar math!" She flinched at the man's call, but she didn't make a sound. "Do you need passage? A farthing to cross to An Tairbeart, or I can take you for free to Inbhir Snàthaid, as I'm going there anyway."

She looked at Aonghas and found hope in his eyes. Carefully, she shook her head at him to keep him silent.

"Are you there?"

Sorcha squeezed Aonghas's hand and kept silent.

"I mean you no harm. It's my job as ferryman to assist travelers, and I'm happy to do so." After a long pause, he added, "Suit yourself, but know there's a landslip a short distance down the loch that will be difficult to pass."

"Wait!" Aonghas shot to his feet and shook off Sorcha's grasping hands. "You can take us to Inbhir Snàthaid for free? Where is that?"

Resigned, Sorcha got stiffly to her own feet and stepped out from behind the boulder. The ferryman sat in his three-seat rowboat with a beefy hand clutched to a tree root to hold him against the shore.

The ferryman touched a finger to the brim of his bonnet, pushing it up to get a better look at them. He did not seem to recognize them as wanted criminals. "Inbhir Snàthaid is, oh, two miles south of here. It is where Loch Aircleit drains down the mountain into Loch Laomainn."

Aonghas turned to Sorcha. "What do you say, Ma? He can save us a difficult journey."

Sorcha studied the man's weathered face behind his scruffy beard. She had no doubt he could hold his own in a fight, but his eyes met hers square on, which she liked. She hoped she would not regret it, but she decided to trust him. "We have no money, nothing to pay you for our passage."

He shrugged. "If your boy will help me row, my own arms can rest."

Aonghas stepped carefully into the boat, and Sorcha followed, settling herself on a bench at the opposite end from the man. Aonghas sat on the middle seat and took up the oars. The ferryman instructed him and then settled back with his face tipped up to the sky. Soon they were well away from shore and heading quickly south.

The ferryman started singing: *"Iomairibh eutrom hò rò..."*

Aonghas matched his pull on the oars to the song's rhythm. Twice, he was interrupted by a coughing fit, but he quickly recovered and the boat sped across the water.

"... Huraibh o na hoireanan..."

For the length of the journey, Sorcha let herself forget that they'd lost everything and were wanted criminals. She let herself feel the air against her skin and blow through her hair, and only then thought about what a mess it must be since she'd lost her mutch. Later, in private, she'd need to brush out her hair with her fingers and re-plait it. Still, to be in public with her head uncovered shamed her. She pulled the dirty *plaide* over her head and adjusted her brooch on her chest to hold it there.

Her gaze traveled down the length of the loch and over the tops of the mountains, and she wondered what life would be like here. She and Aonghas could live on one of the tree-covered islands in the loch and never see another soul if they didn't choose to. It sounded like a grand plan, but one available only to someone with a boat and money to pay rent to whoever owned the islands, as well as money to build a cottage and buy a cow and seeds for crops... She forced her gaze away from the islands and resigned herself to life in the city.

With Aonghas facing her as he pulled on the oars, she studied him—his feet planted wide and firm on the bottom of the boat, the bulging muscles of his arms, his sweet face now spread open in a joyful grin. His mouth and eyes were white-rimmed, which Sorcha knew was caused by his hunger, though he didn't let it dampen his enthusiasm for the task. He loved this, she realized. He loved being out on the loch, relying on his own strength to propel them.

When the ferryman told him to turn toward shore, Aonghas's smile dropped and settled into a determined press of his lips. A grown man in a young man's body. The knowledge both saddened her and filled her with pride. He was going to make some girl a fine husband one day. Sorcha could practically see the man he would be with a wife and children of his own. Strong, honorable, loving. Just like her sweet Tàm had been.

But Aonghas wouldn't have the opportunity to be any of that if he was arrested. She had to stay focused on that right now and keep him safe. She'd let down her guard with the ferryman, and that had been a mistake. He knew their faces. He knew in which direction they were traveling.

"You said Loch Aircleit is up that mountain?" she asked him as they pulled alongside a dock near a waterfall. When the ferryman nodded, she then asked, "And can one travel to Dùn Èideann from there?"

Again, the ferryman nodded distractedly as he tied ropes to the dock. Sorcha looked at Aonghas but made certain the ferryman heard her next words. "We shall take that route to the city, then."

Aonghas nodded in agreement as he helped her from the boat and then followed.

"Do you need a place to sleep this night?" the ferryman asked as he finished tying up. "We don't have much, but what we have you can share." He motioned toward the small cottage tucked into the trees. Sorcha saw firelight glowing through the open doorway, where a young boy appeared, carrying a pail that looked to be heavy. He waved to the ferryman but turned and went around the back of the cottage.

Aonghas's eyes pleaded with her to accept the man's offer, but she couldn't take that risk. "Thank you, but we must be on our way. We'll not forget the kindness you've shown us."

"Don't worry about the garrison you will pass up the hill. There are only a handful of old soldiers who live there now, and they won't bother you."

The news of the nearby garrison alarmed her. She had no desire to go anywhere near English soldiers, old or not. She didn't let her fear of the soldiers show, however, and soon she and Aonghas were heading up the rough footpath in the direction the man had indicated. Aonghas, bless him, waited until they were well enough away that the man wouldn't hear before asking, "Are we really going to Loch Aircleit?"

She shook her head. "I only wanted him to believe that, should anyone come asking. No, we'll cross the burn as soon as we find a safe place to do so, and we'll continue south along the shore of Loch Laomainn."

"To Glaschu?"

She nodded. "To Glaschu."

They found a place to safely cross the rapidly flowing stream out of sight of the ferryman and his family, and were soon surprised to find a well-trod path through the trees.

It didn't take long to discover the reason the path was there, for they came upon several scattered settlements. Cottages were tucked amid oakwood and fields planted wherever a plot could be dug in the narrow land between loch and steep mountain. In several places, she spied coppiced oaks, evidence of a leather-tanning industry in the area.

As the day was drawing to a close, most of the inhabitants of the cottages were inside, no doubt eating their supper, which allowed Sorcha and Aonghas to pass undetected, except by the dogs who barked at them but didn't accost them in any way.

Sorcha was wondering at the wisdom of going in this direction where they would be potentially witnessed by so many, but what could they do now? It was growing dark, and their best course of action would be to continue, sleep somewhere away from the path, then rise early to keep walking.

The smell of bread wafted through the trees, causing Sorcha's knees to buckle. They needed to eat tonight. They couldn't go another day without food.

Ahead of her, Aonghas stumbled and nearly fell but caught himself on a tree.

Sorcha put a hand on his arm. "Are you unwell, son?"

He avoided her eyes. "I am fine."

He clearly was not. He was weakening. He needed rest and he needed food, and she needed to find both for him.

She looked more closely at the next settlement. Several scattered cottages were clustered just off the path. Unlike at her home in Srath Ghlais, the byres for these homes were detached from the houses.

"Come," she whispered to Aonghas and tugged on his arm. As silently as possible, she guided him to the shadows behind a byre set apart from other buildings. With a glance around to be certain no one could see them here, she motioned for Aonghas to sit in the shadows. "Wait for me here, and be silent. I'll return shortly."

The fact that her son did as he was told without argument and without question told her just how weak he had become. It worried her.

A collie rounded the corner, startling her, but he only sniffed at her skirt and wagged his tail in greeting. She took a moment to rub his head and let him satisfy his curiosity about her so that he didn't warn his master of their presence. When the dog moved on to Aonghas, she hurried away from the pair.

Staying in the shadows, she ducked into the byre and waited for her eyesight to adjust to the dim interior. When she could see, she took stock of the inhabitants—two cows and a lazy cat curled up in the corner. No baskets or sacks of meal on shelves; no potatoes; no pots, pans, or anything of use to her.

She slipped out into the night air again and moved to the closest cottage, her senses on alert. Voices drifted through the open door, and she carefully ducked around the corner and made her way to the next cottage.

When she heard no noise, she carefully pushed the door open a crack and looked inside.

Silence greeted her, save for the crackling of the fire that was lit in the fireplace at one end of the single room. Thick shadows clung to the perimeter, and she knew there might be someone sitting there in the darkness or asleep in the box bed. "Is anyone home?" No answer.

Her cramping stomach pushed her farther into the room. She was no thief, but what was a person to do when her survival and that of her son was at risk? She knew the law would dictate that she should go without, but the men who'd created that law, and who upheld that law, had never had to watch their child go hungry.

She would only take what she and Aonghas needed. Nothing more.

When no one raised an alarm at her entrance, she crossed quickly to the open box bed and looked inside, just to be certain. Empty.

Moving as fast as her weak body allowed, she grabbed what she needed from the shelves and cupboards and wrapped it all in a cloth she found draped over the back of a chair. With the corners tied together, she tucked the bundle into a cooking pot, slid a dirk into her belt, and made for the doorway with the pot in her arms.

She made certain the way was clear before she left the cottage and hurried back to the byre.

Just then, a whistle pierced the gloaming, and she dove into the shadows of the stone building. The dog, who must have stayed with Aonghas this entire time, raced past her, his tongue flapping.

She pressed a hand to her racing heart. It had only been the dog's master whistling for him. She had not been seen.

It had scared her, though, and she wanted nothing more than to collect Aonghas and be gone from this place. But she had one more chore first.

Quickly, she ducked back into the byre and crossed the small, musty space to the largest of the two cows and found, with much relief, that she'd not yet been milked. With soft words of comfort for the beast, she squatted beside her and placed the pot she'd stolen onto the ground.

The cow protested and tried to shuffle away from her, but the small space kept her pinned. "There, there," she murmured softly as she gently stroked the cow's flank to calm her. "I know you don't know me, but I won't take it all. I promise."

When the cow calmed, Sorcha set to work, softly singing a milking song as she did so. When the pot had a good amount in it, she patted the cow's hip. "You are a fine lady. I thank you."

Carrying the pot very carefully so she didn't spill the treasured contents, she slipped back outside and around the corner to where Aonghas waited. He was lying on his side, curled into a ball, fast asleep.

"Aonghas!" she whispered to him. When he did not stir, she set the pot and bundle down on the ground and placed her palm on the side of his face, worried he'd fallen ill. Blessedly, his skin was cool to the touch. "Aonghas, wake up. We must away. Just a bit further until we can rest, I promise."

Groggily, he blinked and looked up at her, then around at the trees and the byre wall. Seeming to remember where they were, he silently nodded, then pushed himself wearily to his feet.

Seeing that he had nothing in him to fuel even a short walk, she pushed the pan of milk into his hands and motioned for him to drink as they walked. He hesitantly took a sip, and then proceeded to gulp the warm liquid as fast as he could.

When the pan was empty, he shot her a guilty look, which she waved away. Then, as furtively as they could, they skirted the edge of the small village and continued south along the loch, breathing easier with each step. It was dark under the trees, but the lingering summer light helped them find their way.

After another hour, they had long left behind the last dwelling, and Sorcha felt safe enough to stop. "Aonghas, rest here while I look for firewood. I'll have you warm and fed before long."

He had been standing bent over with his hands propped on his knees, but at her words, he pushed upright. "No, I'll help."

Together they gathered all the dried wood they could find and even some dry moss from the sides of trees. When she returned to their chosen campsite, she found Aonghas breaking apart small sticks into kindling with his eyes glazed over. Her poor boy needed more food, and a full night of sleep. "Thank you, Aonghas. You rest while I prepare supper."

She squatted on the ground next to the stacked wood and opened the bundle of goods she'd taken from the cottage. She'd been excited to find a tin with the tools for starting a fire and now took from it a striker, flint, and char cloth. Iain had been carrying their flint and, she presumed, still had it with him, wherever he was now.

Thinking of him and his betrayal made the familiar burn of anger flare inside her chest. She pressed her lips tightly together and refocused her attention on the task at hand.

Working quickly, she placed the cloth on top of the flint and set to work hitting the striker onto the edge. Before long a spark smoldered on the cloth, and she gently blew a flame to life.

When the ember was big enough, she set it in the middle of the dried moss bundle and continued blowing on it until it was ready to transfer to Aonghas's kindling.

Soon the warmth of the fire reached her body, and she closed her eyes for a moment to soak it in. This day had been difficult. The last weeks had been difficult. Until last night, she'd believed there were still good people whom they could trust, but Iain had ruined that illusion.

A flickering memory of the boatman came into her mind, but she pushed it away. If they'd stayed in his company any longer, he would've turned them in. She was certain of it.

Iain had helped Aonghas at the end by returning his knife, but that wasn't enough to erase his betrayal. In the short time they'd known him, Iain had become part of their family. She'd started to think of him as a second son, and she knew Aonghas loved him like a brother.

Now it was only the two of them again. From now on, it would only ever be the two of them. They would trust no one but each other.

Together they would survive, as long as they stayed ahead of the factor's man and any other authorities, and took care not to reveal their true identities to anyone. No more mistakes.

Aonghas coughed, pulling her from her thoughts. He had coughed on and off throughout the day, a lingering effect from his swim across the cold river last night, and it worried her.

Eager to get warm food into his belly, she set the pan onto the fire and got to work mixing the oats she'd taken from the cottage with water from a nearby burn. This mixture she formed into small cakes, which she dropped onto the hot pan. Once they were cooked, she set them on a flat stone to cool. As another batch cooked, she spread cheese over each of the first two cakes and handed both to Aonghas.

As he ate, the color slowly came back into his face, and she wanted to weep with relief. Of the second two cakes, she kept one for herself and gave Aonghas the other. Afterward, Aonghas melted onto his side and went to sleep. Sorcha scrubbed the pan clean and wrapped up the remaining oatmeal to save for tomorrow.

Finally, her chores done, she returned to her spot beside the fire. Her heart felt heavy tonight, and so, as she often did, she touched her fingers to the brooch Tàm had given to her on their wedding day, thankful she still had it.

The pin felt cold to her touch, but it warmed quickly and she pretended for a moment that she was touching Tàm's hand, feeling his strength bolster her.

But, still needing more comfort, she slipped her hand into her pocket to touch the grass and dirt clods that she'd taken from her children's graves.

They were gone.

"No." She dug her fingers deeper into each pocket but felt only a few gritty particles. The rest had disappeared. Suddenly, whatever had been holding her together these last few days fell apart, and a keening moan tore from her throat.

Sobbing, she hugged her knees to her chest and dropped her forehead onto her arms. She'd lost them. Probably in the river last night, or all the times they'd had to swim around obstacles today. With all that they'd experienced, she'd not once thought to feel for the dirt and grass. If she'd remembered they were in her pockets, she would have untied her pockets and held them over her head each time she entered the water. How could she have forgotten?

But there was nothing she could do now. Her last remaining contact with her lost children was gone. As gone as they were. She couldn't return to the kirkyard where they rested. She might never be able to return there.

Why was this happening to her? Was this God's punishment for her sins? What had she done to deserve his wrath?

Long into the night, she watched the flames dance and felt her heart harden. She welcomed the numbing anger and hatred she felt, for it didn't eat away at her as completely as did sorrow and the pain of betrayal.

No, she much preferred to focus her mind not on what she'd lost, but on all those who had taken away every bit of joy from her life. She listed them all in her mind: An Siosal, Lady Chisholm, Factor Macrath, Coghill, Baltair, the unnamed shepherds bringing sheep to the Highlands, the sheep themselves, young Iain, the cold, the rain, the river, the loch, the lack of food, the laws preventing common people from hunting or fishing . . .

She fell asleep with the list running through her mind, anger warming her from the inside as much as the fire did on the outside.

CHAPTER TWENTY

Keaka

Day four; the Drovers Inn, Inverarnan

I'm disappointed not to have had any visions or Sorcha sightings all night long. I don't even get a glimpse of floating orbs or other ghostly signs from a Drovers Inn spirit. I do, however, get a good night's rest, which feels wonderful. I wake up eager to start the day.

My leg, however, has other ideas. It aches from my fall yesterday. Just under my knee, where I slammed against the edge of the rock, a scab is forming on the top of a swollen bruise. Walking is uncomfortable.

After hobbling downstairs for breakfast in a quirky side room with the unfortunate name the Poachers Den, I beg our server for another bag of ice. Back in our room, I prop both legs on pillows and ice my knee while Colin tries to repair my torn rain pants with duct tape.

Out of the blue, he asks, "Have you ever heard of second sight?"

Amused, I shake my head. "Nope. What is it?"

Colin cuts the tape with his teeth and presses it into place on the pant leg. "It's something that keeps popping up in Scottish stories. Basically, it's the ability to see this world and another. Usually, people with the sight see future events, or they see something in a vision that they otherwise would not know. I think it's usually understood as the ability to see the living and the dead, which explains the two sights."

I'm intrigued but don't want Colin to see how deeply. I fiddle with a loose thread on my sleeve. "So, it's like being psychic?"

Colin shrugs. "I think the definition probably changes with who you ask. But maybe?" He presses a second piece of tape to the pant leg. "I hope I get to meet someone who has the sight. That would be so cool!"

I agree with him but silently wonder if he already has met someone. Me.

"We told you Scotland was a magical place." He gives me a playful wink. "You feeling it yet?" I laugh, remembering all the times he and his father tried to ignite my interest in this country. A memory surfaces of my husband in the kilt he wore on our wedding day. I'd loved cornering him all that day in private rooms so I could reach up under that kilt. He'd loved it, too.

I have to clear the knot in my throat and force my attention back to the conversation at hand. "I fully admit, Colin, I can finally see what you guys were talking about. It is a very special place, and I'm happy to be here with you." I reach out a hand to him, and when he takes it, I give his hand a strong squeeze. "Thanks for letting me tag along on your adventure."

He releases me and looks embarrassed but says, "Thanks for coming with me. It's been fun."

Shame stabs through me because I know I haven't been all fun on this trip. But not anymore. Even with a sore knee and fatigued legs, I feel lighter today. Happier. Excited to be on this journey. I am with my boy on an adventure. Plus, I'm somehow communicating through time with a woman traveling through Scotland with her own son. What could be more exciting?

I move the ice off my knee and swing my feet to the side of the bed. My leg is now extra stiff from the cold. Gingerly, I put my weight on my feet and get up to slowly walk around the room, waiting for my legs to warm up.

My right knee is still painful. As I watch Colin stuff things in his pack, I ask, "Any chance you have an ACE bandage in that first aid kit?"

"As a matter of fact, I do." After digging out the compression bandage, he hands it to me and watches as I lean over to wrap my knee. "If you need more pain meds, I have plenty." He waits a beat, and then: "Do you think you can walk?"

I hear the emotions in his voice and understand what he's not saying. He's worried that we'll have to end the hike early, which would disappoint him deeply. "I'll be just fine," I tell him honestly. "I might move a little slower than normal, but I bet once we get going and I'm warmed up, I'll barely notice the pain."

Although he tries to hide it, the relief on his face is evident. "Let's get going, then; it's already past ten."

Surprised, I glance at the bedside clock and see he's right. We rush to lace up our still-damp boots and hoist our packs. As I follow Colin out, I can't help but look back one more time to see if Sorcha has returned. The room is empty.

We leave our suitcase in the shed behind the building, refill water bottles from the faucet in front, then head up the road, across the river, and back to the trail behind Beinglas Farm.

The morning is glorious, with only a few wispy clouds in the sky. With Loch Lomond behind us, it's like we've entered an entirely different Scotland now. We're walking through a narrow valley bordered on each side by high gold, green, and purple mountains. Threading through the middle of the valley is a red-brown river flowing over black and gray boulders and shaded by oak trees. I try to capture all of it with my phone camera.

I decide to bring up a topic I've been thinking about over the last few days. "You know, I'm starting to understand why so many Americans research their genealogy here." I look to see if he's listening, and I'm happy to see a gleam of curiosity in his eyes. "It's because the US is so young and made up of immigrants. Other than Native Americans, we all came from somewhere else, and we lack that soul-deep connection to a place or a community like people have in these older countries with a long, known history. We're hungry to belong, and we think we'll find that by learning where our people came from."

"Makes sense." Colin scratches his head, then readjusts his baseball cap. "It's man's constant striving for meaning. We want to feel like our time on Earth matters, and we accomplish that by connecting with something bigger than us that will remain after we're gone."

"Exactly!" I love getting into these grown-up conversations with my son and learning how he thinks. "And Scotland, with its history and tradition of clans, where a person knew to the very depths of their soul that they belonged, is something that appeals to us Americans. I would argue that's especially true today, when we're feeling society is fractured more than ev—" I absently touch a boulder and jerk in shock as a vision floods my mind.

I am cold, and tired, and so very anxious. I am mourning my lost home and all the people I left behind there, both living and buried. My breath comes shallowly, as though I've been running, but I know that I have not. This is how my breath has felt for the last several days, and I wonder if I'll ever be able to draw a deep breath again. I look down and see a knife in my hand. I am carving a flower petal onto the stone, and I feel like I have to finish this because only the symbol will guide my son home again.

I look up and see my son, Aonghas, carving his own markings onto the rock. He tosses back his head and laughs, and that's when I notice a second boy beside him, also carving. Iain Ramsay. The boy who is traveling with us who is a true friend to my Aonghas. I smile at their innocent antics and return to my carving. The flower petal is nearly finished. We must be on our way. We must find shelter away from the road. And food. What will I feed these boys?

"Mom? Mom, are you okay?"

A hand on my arm pulls me away from the rock, and the vision abruptly ends. I blink.

The two boys are gone, but Colin is standing before me, his face bleached of color. "You did it again. Just like yesterday. You totally spaced out on me."

I nod, distracted by the echoes of the boys' laughter still reverberating inside my skull. But I have to ease Colin's worry. I take off my pack and grab my water bottle. "I was just feeling a little dizzy, that's all. I must be dehydrated." I take a long gulp of water and pray that he believes me. I feel fine, physically, but my heart is racing and I feel scared, like I need to hide from danger. I drink again.

Oh, Sorcha, you were right to feel afraid here. You were about to be captured.

I squat down to replace my water bottle in my pack, and to give the boulder a closer look.

There it is. Just as in the vision. The flower petal, pointing up the glen but slightly turned. I look past the rock and see that this valley is about to meet another that turns north. I would bet anything that Sorcha wants us to turn that direction.

I stand to put my pack back on and step to the side of the rock. There they are. The boys' carvings. One is made of two straight lines carved in a cross. The other is much more complicated. Despite the sandpaper of time and weather, I can clearly make out the image of a deer with antlers. From the vision, I know it was Iain who carved the animal.

Who the heck was Iain? Only Sorcha and Aonghas were listed on the Wanted poster. Was Iain another son? No, that doesn't seem right. In the vision, Sorcha was thinking of him as a friend. A boy who is traveling with them.

What happened to Iain?

"What are you looking at?"

I jerk my attention away from the carvings and remember that Colin has no idea what they mean to me. I point. "Look. There are some cool carvings on this stone. Will you be studying things like this at school?"

After he excitedly inspects the carvings, we resume walking and Colin starts telling me all he knows of Pictish rock carvings and a place called Kilmartin Glen, where the Kingdom of Dal Riata left a carving of a footprint on an ascension stone. I'm grateful that I've successfully diverted him.

At a tight tunnel that crosses under the railroad tracks, I duck my head and walk through, wondering how tall people with huge backpacks manage this. A short distance farther, I enter a circular metal tunnel that takes me under the road and out the other side. I stop to wait for Colin, and then together we continue up the path that climbs up a hillside. He's fallen silent, and we walk a good distance without speaking. The quiet is comfortable.

Another mile farther, I notice Colin nibbling on his lower lip. "What are you thinking about?"

My question takes him by surprise, but he quickly recovers. "I was just thinking about life during the time of the clans."

As we climb up the open hillside, my knee and feet ache, but I welcome the pain because it helps bring me back into my own body again, in the present moment. "Oh, yeah?"

"Before the clan system was destroyed after Culloden, people felt they would give their lives for their clan and that others in the clan would give their own lives in return for them, if necessary." Colin stares out through the valley as he says this, and I wish I had the deep knowledge he has of Scotland's history. "Because we lack that deep connection to our neighbors today, are our souls suffering? Is that why so many people are suffering from mental illness and why we have societal atrocities like mass shootings?"

Stunned by the places his mind went to as he connected what, to me, had previously held no connection at all, I can only gape at my son. "How did you get so smart?"

Colin blushes and smiles bashfully. "Good parenting, I guess."

I laugh with him at that, but inside I'm glowing.

We pass through a kissing gate and turn right into the remains of a recently felled forest to take a diversion off the West Highland Way and down to the town of Crianlarich for lunch.

At a café, we order sandwiches, and Colin asks the woman behind the counter for a bag of ice. I spend the entire time we're eating with my foot propped on the chair opposite and an ice pack balanced on my knee, which helps my pain immensely.

As we eat, Colin and I pass his West Highland Way guidebook back and forth so I can see the route we'll be taking this afternoon. I'm mostly interested in the maps, but Colin reads a few paragraphs aloud about the area's lead-mining history and how a gold-and-silver mine opened nearby in 2018. As he finishes his sandwich, I study the map again to calculate how long it should take us to reach Tyndrum, where we have a hotel room and hot showers waiting for us. Adam scribbled on the side of this page a note about a restaurant he wanted to try in Tyndrum, and I memorize the name so I can suggest it later to Colin. I love that Adam put so much thought and effort into researching this trip with his son. When did he stop putting any effort into our marriage?

When did I?

I flip back through the pages and see other notes that Adam made, and realize with a start that when Colin suggested a swim in Loch Lomond yesterday, he had probably been planning it all along because Adam had circled the beach with a pencil and wrote *Swim?* in the margin.

It seems my dead husband is accompanying us on the trail after all.

After lunch we retrace our steps back up the hillside to the trail, where we follow a snaking track through a dense forest that feels spooky. These woods are nothing like the forests back home, which are rich with plant life in the understory. Here, it feels like nothing grows between the trees but moss. Dark shadows play with my imagination and leave me jumpy.

Colin starts talking about his dad, reminiscing about their hikes in Oregon and campouts in the Cascade Mountains. After Colin confronted me about it the other day, I feel like I need to add a memory of my own, but I struggle to dredge one up and instead lamely comment that his dad sure loved going camping with him. I'm still angry with Adam and still deeply hurt by his betrayal, even though he's long gone.

Colin tells me about a time they took a wrong turn on a forest road leading to a trailhead and ended up on the wrong mountain entirely, with no option other than to keep driving on a precarious track until they found a place to turn around, well after dark. I do my best to smile in all the right parts. I remember that weekend, too. Adam promised to help me paint our bedroom, but instead he took off with Colin and then called me late that night, laughing about their wrong turn and that they'd rented a hotel room and would go up the mountain again to do the hike the next day. The room was painted by the time he got home, and he never thanked me for doing it alone.

It's amazing how all the tiny cuts and stabs in a relationship can add up to become a traumatic wound.

By the time we descend through the forest and come to a beautiful stone viaduct, I am wound up tight. Normally, walking helps my emotions loosen from where they are stuck in my body, but now they feel like they are festering and growing. My painful knee, my worries over leaving Colin in Scotland alone, my inexplicable connection to Sorcha, and my failed marriage are all combining to feel like I'm about to burst out of my skin. Not only that, I'm disappointed in myself. I thought I'd put this negativity behind me.

Soon after passing under the viaduct, we cross a busy road and enter a horse pasture on the other side. Even though the ground is muddy, I quicken my pace in hopes that getting my blood pumping will unstick my emotions so they'll finally ease.

But Colin keeps talking about Adam.

"Remember that time Dad took us to that improv show and he somehow ended up on stage?" Colin tips his head back and laughs. "I didn't even know he knew who Taylor Swift was, let alone knew the words to her song. He was terrible!" I force a smile. It was later that same night that I first found a text from his girlfriend.

We are passing a farmhouse with several outbuildings when a sign next to the track informs us we have reached Saint Fillan's Priory, which makes Colin excited. "Dad told me a story about this place. He said that Robert the Bruce himself had taken refuge here after losing a battle with Clan MacDougall. Isn't that cool?"

I murmur agreement.

Colin is shaking his head in wonder. "Man, Dad knew so much."

"Yeah, he did." I bet he impressed his girlfriend with all his historical knowledge, too.

"Why was he an engineer? He should've been a historian or professor or something."

"His family convinced him that a career in history wouldn't pay the bills." Was Adam's entire adult life a big disappointment to him, starting with his choice of wife?

"That's so sad." Colin was silent after that, which I am grateful for.

The gravel road we follow passes through rolling grass fields and deposits us at another farm, this one with public restrooms, which couldn't have come at a better time for me.

When I reemerge, I find Colin talking with two men several years older than him. The taller of the two has the sides of his head shaved, with the hair on top sticking straight up four inches and dyed purple. An earring glints from one lobe, and his arms are completely covered in tattoos of dragons and Celtic symbols. The man next to him is unmarked and unpierced, and I wonder what they have in common that makes them friends. The three are laughing about something.

When I step up beside Colin, he introduces me to them. "This is my mom, Keaka. Mom, this is Peter and Grant. They live near Edinburgh."

I shake their hands and notice Peter, the spiky-haired and marked one, has rough calluses. "It's great to meet you. I think I saw you in Balmaha the other day."

"Aye, this yin is hard to miss." Grant jabs his elbow into Peter's side. "I'm always sayin' he looks a right cockerel with that ridiculous hair." He stares at Peter adoringly as he says this, and I wonder if the two are more than friends.

I'm glad to have the men—who we learn are a married couple—to walk with for the rest of the afternoon, all the way into Tyndrum. They keep Colin laughing with their stories and creative insults, which gives me a chance to think about all that's happened today and, more importantly, gives me a break from talking about Adam.

Adam might not have been a great husband at the end, but he was always a great father, and that is what I want Colin to remember. To that end, I'll stay vigilant about everything I say about him. As far as Colin is concerned, Adam was the love of my life right up to the end.

Which wouldn't be a lie, really. I did love him, even though he shattered my heart.

CHAPTER TWENTY-ONE

Sorcha

Alongside Loch Laomainn (Loch Lomond)

Although the oatcakes and a good night of sleep did wonders for his energy, Aonghas seemed different today. He was quieter than usual and seemed to be deep in thought about something. Sorcha wondered if his nightmares had returned, but when she asked, he waved off her concern with excuses.

The going was rough again, even though they found a footpath up the hill away from the loch that allowed them easier passage than what they experienced yesterday. It was the numerous burns flowing down the mountain that they had to cross, and countless boulders and roots that they were forced to navigate around or over, which made the going so difficult. To make it even worse, the midges were swarming. With no rain and little breeze, the tiny beasties were everywhere, making it nearly impossible to draw breath without sucking some into the nose or mouth. They tangled in Sorcha's eyelashes and bit every inch of exposed flesh they could find. She'd long ago coated her hands, feet, ankles, and face with mud from a burn, and she wore her stolen *plaide* tied around her head despite the warmth of the day.

With Aonghas not talking much, she was left with only her thoughts for company, and they kept returning to the woman of the Fair Folk who'd helped her at the Inbhir Àirnein House Hotel.

Who was she? And why had she appeared to Sorcha as she had?

She certainly was not Scottish—but then again, the Fair Folk weren't, were they? They were of an ancient race that had lived on this land long before the Scots or Gaels arrived. When they were forced to move underground, they took their magic with them and only came out at night when the mounds opened.

Whatever the Good Woman's reason for being in that room, she'd helped Sorcha.

She could use her help again, she thought as she climbed over a tumble of boulders after Aonghas. She would ask the Fair Folk for a boat they could row down the loch all the way to Glaschu, and she'd ask for that boat to be filled with all the food they could eat. And, while she was thinking of impossible things to ask for, she'd also ask that the boat be shielded from the eyes of all who would wish them harm. She'd ask for safe passage to the city and well-paying jobs waiting for them when they arrived. She'd ask for An Siosal and factor Macrath and the government to drop their search and declare that Sorcha and Aonghas were innocent of all charges.

If she was going that far, Sorcha thought, she might as well go all the way. She would ask for the return of her home in Srath Ghlais so that she and Aonghas could live out their lives in peace in the only place where they belonged.

But as she moved farther along the path and failed to find the Good Woman waiting for her around each bend, she knew it was wishful thinking. The Fair Folk would not save her today. Maybe the woman was only located at the Inbhir Àirnein House Hotel. Maybe she was not a woman of the Fair Folk at all, but something else entirely.

By nightfall, she was exhausted and starving again. The worst of the terrain was behind them, and the way seemed easier now, through softly undulating woodland interspersed with farms and fields. She was grateful for the change and hoped that meant they would be able to travel farther and faster tomorrow.

For now, though, it was time to rest and eat. She had some oats left from those she'd stolen last night, and all day she'd tucked edible leaves into her pockets to add to their meal.

They decided upon a small clearing in the trees in which to camp, well away from the cottages and the busy inn they'd passed an hour earlier. They'd keep their fire small tonight and extinguish it as soon as dinner was cooked.

"We should expect the rest of the way into Glaschu to be more settled," Aonghas said after blowing gently to get the fire going on the tinder bundle in his hands. As he set about stacking the kindling over the flame, he went on. "I don't think we can avoid people from now on. We'd best be vigilant."

Sorcha, who was stirring oats and water in the cooking pot, agreed. "And I think we need new names, considering Iain likely told Coghill the names we've been using."

She set the stick she was using as a spurtle aside and glanced around the small clearing, searching for inspiration. When she saw the tiny buds forming on a wild rosebush, she made her decision. "Ross. I will be Mrs. Ross. And you will be—"

"Anndra," Aonghas interrupted with a quick glance at her and then away.

Sorcha knew he was thinking of his best mate from Srath Ghlais and felt a heavy weight settle over her. Aonghas may never see Anndra MacRae again. The poor boy had lost too much for one so young.

Forcing a cheeriness she did not feel into her voice, she resumed stirring the oats and said, "Yes, Anndra Ross. That suits you."

All through the night, Sorcha was startled awake with each creak of a branch, rustle of a mouse, or sigh from Aonghas. Near dawn, she fell into a deep sleep and dreamed that Tàm was kissing another woman, which made no sense at all, for he'd been faithful to her from the day they married to his last breath.

She awoke cold and stiff and with her mind still full of dream images. It took several moments to remember where she was and all that had happened. And then she realized that Aonghas no longer lay next to her on the spongy forest floor.

He had been so quiet yesterday, so somber. As she fastened her *plaide* around her shoulders, she tried to imagine where he might have gone off to this early without saying a word to her. Did it have to do with Iain?

She headed through the trees back to the path they'd been following along the loch. If only she'd learned how to track from Tàm. Was that broken branch a sign that Aonghas had passed by here recently? Or had she herself broken it yesterday on her way to the clearing?

She shook her head at her uselessness but kept moving. Maybe he was at the loch, bathing in the water.

She found herself at the top of a bluff that towered several feet over the loch. Desperately, she scanned the water below, then the shoreline to the north. No sign of him. To the south, a rocky beach curved toward a wooded promontory that blocked further view. The only movements on this calm, sunny morning were gently lapping waves and a pair of ducks swimming near shore. No Aonghas.

But then a scraping sound caught her attention. Something was moving down on the beach, where the bluff on which she stood blocked her view.

Moving as silently as possible in case it was a stranger, Sorcha followed the sound, her bare feet moving without noise over moss and stone.

When she saw Aonghas alone on the beach, relief swelled through her. "Aonghas!"

He turned to look over his shoulder, then back to whatever he was crouched over. When she caught up to him, she saw he was skinning a red squirrel with his dirk. "Did you catch that?"

"I did," was his only response, his attention focused on his task.

She thought about the trouble they had gotten into with the ghillie on Breadalbane land. "Was that wise?"

His hands stilled and he finally lifted his gaze to meet hers. What she saw there made her heart stop. He no longer looked like her fourteen-year-old son, but someone much older, much more hardened by life. Someone who had given up. "Aonghas?"

He didn't respond until he'd finished cleaning the meat, which he then handed to her by what had been the squirrel's back legs. "You can roast this now, or you can wait until supper."

The way he spoke sounded like he wasn't going to be with her later. She put a hand on his arm and moved her face in front of his so that he was forced to look at her. "Aonghas? What is on your mind? Did something happen to you?"

His gaze shifted so that he stared across the loch. A gentle breeze ruffled the curls on his forehead, and she ached to push them back, but the tense way he held his body told her he wouldn't welcome her mothering touch.

"I'm going back. I saw a ferryman at that inn we passed yesterday. I'll have him row me across to whatever town is on the coaching road."

Sorcha felt like her lungs were on fire. "And then what will you do?"

The look on his face told her his mind was set. "I'm going to turn myself in. I'll tell them it was I who killed that man, and then only I will have to serve the punishment. You'll continue to Glaschu, where you can live free."

Sorcha would sooner be dead. "No, I'll not let you do this. You'll remain with me and we'll live free together. We'll find a way. Trust me."

Aonghas's face crumpled before he looked down at the ground. After releasing a deep sigh, he looked at her again. "Don't you see, Ma?

We cannot live like this. We cannot keep running, hiding, starving. If it's not the factor who wants to harm us, it's someone we thought was a friend. We will never have a friend again. We cannot trust anyone."

Sorcha looked down at her feet, ashamed. She had only wanted to keep Aonghas safe. She'd never wanted to force a life of loneliness and suspicion upon him. She opened her mouth to say something, anything, but he kept talking. "The truth of the matter is . . ." He paused. When he spoke again, his voice was shaking. "The truth is that I am guilty. I did kill that man, and only I should pay for that."

She refused to hear it. "No, you did not, Aonghas. It was an accident. That is all. He fell. He tripped and he fell and he accidentally hit his head. It wasn't your fault."

Aonghas drew back his shoulders and lifted his chin. Quietly, yet in a voice that brooked no argument, he told her, "It was on purpose. I saw the stool behind him and I pushed him over it to stop him from taking our things and because I was angry. When I saw all that blood, I didn't regret it, either. I was happy he was dead. I did that. And I deserve to be punished for it."

Sorcha knew she should be horrified that her son was capable of these sinful feelings and actions, but if she were honest with herself, she might have done the same thing, had she been the one at home that morning.

She would think more about all this later, though. Right now her dear boy was hurting. He'd struggled under the weight of his guilt all these days, and she'd not known. She dropped the squirrel and pulled Aonghas into her arms. With her face buried in his hair, she struggled to sort her thoughts into something coherent that would convince him to stay with her.

"You are not to blame for that man's death." She repeated her words to be sure her son heard them. "Do you understand? You may have pushed him, but you could never convince me that you wanted to kill him. It was an accident. An accident that you shouldn't have to pay for with your life." She kept talking, saying anything that came to her mind that might convince him not to turn himself in.

When his shoulders started shaking and she knew he was crying, she hugged him tighter. "Stay with me, Aonghas. I need you. I need you more than An Siosal needs to punish someone. You're all I have left in this life, and my heart would not beat were it not for you. Don't leave me. Please."

He suddenly jerked himself out of her arms and walked away to stand at the water's edge, his back to her, his arms crossed. "I cannot keep doing this, Ma. This hiding, running, sneaking, stealing, not being able to trust another soul, being betrayed by those we think are friends. If I turn myself in, then at least the truth will be out in the open and we'll have nothing left to hide."

Sorcha thought about this. He had a point. Even in Glaschu, they would always be looking over their shoulders, waiting for someone to recognize them and turn them into the authorities. They wouldn't be able to trust another soul with their true identities, their true selves.

What kind of life would that be? Not just for her, but for her sweet boy, who still had his whole life ahead of him?

Theirs would be a half life. A shadow life. A lonely life.

A boat floated into view on the far shore of the loch, and she thought about pulling back into the trees to stay out of sight, then decided the boat was too far away for its inhabitants to see them.

Where was the woman of the Fair Folk when she needed her?

The Good Woman could take Sorcha and Aonghas back to the mound with her. She could take them far from this place, where their life had burned to ashes along with their home.

But the Good Woman was not here, and Sorcha had to stop hoping for something so improbable. She'd likely imagined the woman at Inbhir Àirnein House, anyway. No one had been there to help her, and no one would arrive at this lochside to help her now.

"I'll find a place for us that is safe, Aonghas," she promised her son, even though she had no idea how or where she could accomplish this. "We'll go to Glaschu and we'll find work, and we'll save every coin until we have enough to start a life somewhere else. Alba Nuadh, or America."

She could tell by his expression that while he still doubted such a thing could happen, he was intrigued, and that was enough to keep her talking. "I'll find a way. I promise you this."

Now a spark of hope was aflame in Aonghas's eyes, and the relief that flowed through her was so great she started to cry. With tears rolling down her cheeks, she smiled at her son. "What say you, Aonghas? Will you stay with me?"

He hesitated, but then he nodded. "I'll stay."

CHAPTER TWENTY-TWO

Keaka

Day five; Tyndrum

Today will be our longest day on the trail, and it starts terribly.

When I come out of the bathroom, I find Colin digging through my backpack. The contents of his own backpack are spread across his bed.

"What's up, buddy?"

He doesn't look at me. "Where's Dad's guidebook? I haven't seen it since you were reading it at lunch yesterday." He pulls out the gloves and hat that were stuffed at the bottom of my pack and tosses them on the floor. He looks devastated. "You didn't leave it in Crianlarich, did you?"

I get a sick feeling deep in my gut, and I join the search.

The book is gone.

I find the receipt from our lunch yesterday and am grateful to see it has the name and phone number of the café. A quick chat with the owner turns up nothing. She hasn't seen the book, and it's not in the tub where her staff places items that are left behind.

I feel terrible. Colin is barely speaking to me.

We ask the front desk if they know of a lost and found of any sort for the trail, and they suggest posting to the West Highland Way Facebook group, which I do. I have no other ideas, and I promise him I'll buy him another guidebook just like it, but we both know it won't be the same. A new book won't have his dad's handwritten notes throughout.

It's like losing his dad all over again. I can't fix it for him this time, either.

We pop into the Green Welly Stop to buy food for lunch later, and then we leave Tyndrum and head north on the historic military road through a glen and alongside both the A82 main road and the tracks for the train line up to Fort William.

Today is going to be pure torture if Colin doesn't speak to me the entire way. It might be pure torture anyway. Twenty miles. I've never walked twenty miles in one day in my life. What scares me the most is that the majority of the day will be spent out on remote Rannoch Moor, far from roads, train stations, or civilization of any sort. If the miles prove to be too long for me, or if one of us is injured, there will be no calling a taxi or hopping onto a bus. Our only recourse will be to call Mountain Rescue—if we have cell service.

I vow not to need them. I'll crawl if I have to, but I am going to make it on my own steam for all twenty miles.

I eye the skies warily. The rain is holding off, but dark, swirling clouds and mists cloak the mountains in the distance. Despite the dark weather ahead, for now the morning is pleasant and my long-sleeved T-shirt is keeping me plenty warm. I really didn't expect to enjoy this morning's walk, considering the proximity of the road and train tracks, but the glen is gorgeous. We are walking toward a towering conical mountain, which I know must have an impressive name and history, but I don't dare ask Colin and remind him about his lost guidebook.

For some reason that I can't quite put my finger on, I'm surprised at the lack of people, just as I was on the eastern shore of Loch Lomond a couple days ago. Sure, there are other walkers on the trail and a steady stream of traffic on the road down at the bottom of the valley, but there are few houses. It feels as though some giant has come through and plucked the houses from the ground and carted them off, leaving no trace behind that anyone ever lived here. But I know they had. This glen used to have dozens more people living in it; I am sure of that. I could even draw a map of the area with the missing houses labeled on it.

Which does not, of course, make any sense at all. This is my first time setting foot in the area.

This strange *knowing* has to be because of Sorcha. I have no other explanation for the deep sadness I feel as I take in the view and see only the absence.

Does Strathglass look this empty?

I don't know if the thought is my own or Sorcha's, but I do know I couldn't point out Strathglass on a map if someone asked me to, despite Morag showing us just a few days ago.

As we cross the Bridge of Orchy, I start to feel raindrops. "Should we put our waterproof pants on now?" I ask Colin.

He's already wearing his raincoat, as am I, and he pulls up the hood. "Let's just see if it gets worse." He clicks the waist strap of his pack into place and shoots me a scowl. "By the way, don't say 'pants' here. To Brits, the word *pants* means *underwear*. Call them *trousers*." With that, he marches away from me.

My mature son has disappeared right along with his guidebook. There's nothing I can do about it but ignore his tone and follow him across the stone bridge and up the mountain behind the hotel.

My knee is feeling much better, but by the time I catch up to Colin at the top of the hill, where he's waiting next to a huge stone cairn, I am ready to pop some more ibuprofen. The view grabs my attention. "What's the name of that lake?" I ask Colin, forgetting that he isn't speaking to me.

"Loch Tulla." He jabs a finger toward the vast expanse to the north. "Rannoch Moor."

The landscape is stunning, even on this wet, gray day. I swallow two ibuprofen and drink deeply from my water bottle as I take it all in. The wind is blowing strongly up here, and I feel the occasional sting of raindrops against my face.

"Think we can make it to that building down there before stopping to put on rain *trousers*?" I emphasize the word *trousers*, hoping to make him smile. He doesn't. He just nods and starts down the hill.

The Inveroran Hotel has an outdoor storage room for walkers to store their gear before going inside, so we drop our packs on the shelf and duck inside just as the rain starts pounding.

It is a tiny space, but welcoming. Colin's bad mood cracks, and his excitement loosens his tongue. He tells me that the famous English poet William Wordsworth and his sister, Dorothy, visited here in 1803. "Dorothy wrote in her journal that the food they ate was terrible, but she loved the scene in the kitchen, where eight drovers ate porridge around a peat fire in the middle of the floor with children playing around them. I wish I knew how much this place has changed since then."

I open my mouth to tell him it was only a small cottage, and smoke from the fire made it difficult to breathe, so everyone sat low to the floor, but I catch myself just in time. It's shocking how clearly I can see the former building that stood here as though I'm looking at a memory of a place I saw with my own eyes.

Once I have my full waterproofs on, the rain doesn't bother me at all. I even find myself enjoying the walk now that the ibuprofen has kicked in.

We cross over a stone bridge at the small river behind the hotel, and I suddenly find that I'm standing in sunshine in a small, well-tended village surrounded by fields of grain, where men are spreading manure and women in long skirts, aprons, and white caps on their heads are singing together as they waulk a large cloth on a table in front of one of the cottages. Warmth fills my chest, and I want to join them.

I blink and everything changes just as quickly as it first appeared. The sudden change makes me stumble, and I stop to catch my balance. Colin shoots me a look, but I ignore him.

The village is gone, the grain fields are gone, the people are gone. All I see now is what looks to be wild grasslands stretching from the imposing mountains at my left all the way down to the lake at my right. The paved single-track road where we walk stretches on toward a wooded area in the distance.

Sorcha again. It must be. For whatever reason, I am seeing the area through Sorcha's eyes, and it feels bittersweet.

All those people, vanished without a trace. Their homes erased. Their land left untended and swallowed by the encroaching moor.

But I am seeing it. I'm seeing how it was, how it is, how it could be again. I see that the land that seems ignored today was once cared for, worked, lived on.

"Mom? Did you hear me? I said I want to stop and eat lunch."

Colin's voice makes the image disappear, and I find my son standing directly in front of me. I manage a nod, my mind still on the memory.

I follow him to a second river, this one bigger than the last and lined by trees. Colin ducks off the trail and I follow him to a somewhat-sheltered spot under the trees, where we sit on two boulders and dig out our lunches.

We eat in silence, which suits me fine. I'm struggling with Sorcha's memories and emotions. Sorrow flows through me like the river flows through this valley, constant and pushing, filling voids along its boundaries, trying to spread out and overtake.

Like Sorcha, had the people of this valley been evicted from their homes one terrifying, fire-consuming night? Had they been beaten or killed? Where had they gone? Did anyone remember they had lived here, loved here, died here?

Looking around the valley now, I can't help but feel the slimy, black oiliness of anger. Good people had been removed from this land, and for what? So hikers could walk through here two hundred years later?

Surely if it had been necessary to cause such brutality to people, it had been for a good reason. But by the way the land seemed left untouched, it had not been for any lasting nor positive reason.

"Why were people cleared from the Highlands again?"

Colin blinks. Then he clears his throat and answers, "To clear the way for landowners to bring in more profitable sheep farms and, later, to create hunting estates for the wealthy elite to come on holiday."

My gaze follows the river down to where it joins Loch Tulla, though, in my imagination, I see rich fat men wearing full tartan, stomping through the grasses as servants follow behind carrying long rifles. "Was it all as lucrative as they hoped it would be?"

"For a time. Until it wasn't. Now some claim that the agricultural and commercial practices of that time devastated the land. A rewilding movement in Scotland is trying to heal that damage."

I nod. One only had to look around at the empty hills and valleys of the Highlands to see that the economic schemes of history had not lasted in any positive way. "So really, none of the heartbreak and ruined lives were worth it in the end, were they?"

Colin wraps up the garbage from his lunch and stuffs it into his pack. "That's still being debated. There are some who look at the Clearances as being a necessary agricultural and economic reform. Others, like Dad, see it as a tragedy to humanity and to biodiversity. I can't tell you where between that continuum the truth lies."

I follow Colin's lead and wrap up the remains of my lunch to stuff into my pack. The heaviness in my soul persists as we rejoin the trail, cross the river, and pass through the gate placed to prevent vehicles from continuing onto the old road leading across Rannoch Moor to Glencoe.

The surface underfoot immediately becomes more difficult. The stones laid in the 1700s are about the size of my palm, and are sharp. They are set close enough together to provide a hard surface for water to run off but far enough apart to make it uneven and difficult to traverse without risking a twisted ankle. Tall grasses and stiff heather grow on either side of the road, making it impossible to step onto flatter soil better suited for walking.

A mile in, my feet are screaming in pain, but there is nothing I can do about it but keep on and hope the road changes soon. How did people tolerate riding in a carriage over this road for all those years? They must have been tossed about and rattled until driven to madness.

And yet I can't deny the impressive engineering of the road, for it has lasted all these years, through all kinds of weather.

"Did I tell you about these military roads yet?" Colin asks me, and I know he's making an effort to change his surly mood. I give him a look of encouragement, and he continues. "They were built by the British military to allow for easier travel through the Highlands by the soldiers sent here to subdue the clans after the Jacobite uprisings failed."

I ask questions and keep him talking about the history, even though I really don't want to hear about yet another time when people were terrorized and persecuted. Although I want to believe the opposite, I'm starting to fully realize that humans are truly ugly to one another, in every time and place.

That knowledge saddens me and, right at this moment, makes me very happy to be out on Rannoch Moor, far away from other humans.

The afternoon proves to be a long one, but the moody moor and low cloud cover fit me perfectly, so I don't mind the miles. The farther I walk, in fact, the more I start to feel like I don't want to be anywhere else.

I'm even loving the walking itself. It allows me to simply exist. All else fades away, and I am at my most fundamental self, which I like. I don't have anywhere else to be and nothing else to do but walk. I can think more clearly or not think at all. I feel stress and worry slip away as I watch the landscape pass slowly by.

This place is stunning. Unlike in the hot, treeless expanse of Eastern Oregon, this treeless expanse feels full of life. Small lochs, dozens of rivers and creeks, and all kinds of grasses, bushes, and flowers intersperse the red and gray lichen-covered rocks and make every direction I look seem like a postcard.

I even start to enjoy the feeling of my body moving. The cobblestones eventually fade to gravel, and the trail is mostly flat with slight inclines, so my muscles aren't being strained at all. My knee isn't bothering me, and even my blister is hardly noticeable under the cushion of the blister bandage. I hear gravel crunching under my boots, which takes me back to my grandparents' farm on the Big Island of Hawaii and the sound of lava crunching under flip-flops.

It is all connected. This big, beautiful planet is all connected, and all the people on it are connected. I feel a spark deep in my belly that makes me want to throw my arms wide and shout into the wind because I finally understand why Colin wanted to do this hike.

The gravel, the aching limbs, the wind, the rain, the smell of wild thyme on the air . . . it all connects us. I am connected to the people who walked here before me and to the people who will walk here after me. The moor knows this. The mountains know this. Only people have forgotten that we are one with everything around us.

Did Adam know this? Is that why he wanted to take me hiking in the early days of our marriage and why he wanted to bring me to Scotland? I wish I paid more attention to his interests. If I did, maybe our marriage would have been stronger. It may not have saved it, but at least I'd have more happy memories with him.

Maybe I didn't make enough of an effort for him. Maybe his cheating wasn't the only thing that wrecked our marriage.

The realization is so shocking my feet stop moving.

For years, I didn't make any effort to connect with him and his interests. I thought we were fine with him going his way, me going mine, and meeting up at the end of the day over dinner. I even congratulated myself for being so independent and not clingy.

Maybe all Adam wanted was to connect with me like we used to do on the couch and talk about something other than our son or the mortgage bill. He tried and I turned away, too busy with chores around the house or rushing off to a Boosters meeting.

And so he found someone else to share his passions with. In the case of Scotland and history, he found Colin. In the case of everything else, he found . . . her.

"Mom?" Colin had walked twenty feet ahead of me before he noticed I stopped.

I force all thoughts of my marriage and husband out of my mind to examine later and paste on a wide smile for my son. "Just admiring the view. The pictures you showed me don't do it justice."

Colin's face lights up at my words, and I can tell it means a lot to him that I'm enjoying this, finally. I catch up to him and we fall into step side by side.

His moody-teenager side from earlier has disappeared, thankfully, and we spend time talking about Colin's friends back home and what they are doing now, which of them he plans to keep in close contact with as they scatter around the world. I feel free and alive alone out here with nature, and the thunder rumbling in the distance only adds to that sense of being right where I'm supposed to be, at just the right moment.

As we pass a spur trail leading up to a cairn, Colin tells me that the cairn is a memorial to someone famous who died out here, but he can't remember who and we don't have the guidebook to refer to. I make a mental reminder to log into the Facebook group later and see if anyone responded to my post.

Colin doesn't dwell on it, though, and is soon talking about the Glencoe Massacre. I have my gaze on the path in front of us and am working hard to focus only on Colin's story and not the pain that all these long miles are igniting in my feet and hips.

"Mom, look."

I look at Colin, then in the direction he is pointing, and when I see it, my breath sticks in my throat. The view in front of us is the very definition of *awesome*. I have to stop walking to give the moment the honor it deserves. I stare with wonder at the massive pyramid-shaped mountain rising from the moor floor and marking the beginning of what looks to be a dramatic valley stretching into the distance. The late-afternoon sun, absent all day until now, is setting behind the mountain, which makes it look even more commanding, more majestic.

"That's Buachaille Etive Mòr. 'The great herdsman of Etive,'" Colin tells me. "Glen Etive is the valley stretching to the left of the mountain. Glencoe is on the right side."

I know about Glencoe since it is arguably the most famous landscape in the Highlands and has been featured in countless television shows and movies. Plus, Adam and Colin showed me photos from their trip here a few years ago. But none of that is the same as being here in person, standing on the moor, looking up at the mountain and down to the valley.

For the first time, I feel a surprising new emotion stir to life in me. Envy. I am envious of my son because he is going to live here for the next few years and he'll get to explore all the nooks and crannies of this country to his heart's content.

And I'm feeling deep sadness. I could have been enjoying all this for the past several years, if only I listened to my husband more and come here with him when he invited me to. How long ago did Adam give up on me? How long ago did he shut down and start to look elsewhere for connection? Why didn't I notice until it was too late?

And yet he made the last few years miserable, and I've got to stop allowing him to continue to make me miserable now, after he is gone.

Colin points to a cluster of buildings surrounded by clumps of trees in the distance and tells me that is Kingshouse Hotel, our stop for the night. It's in the middle of nowhere, with a two-lane road passing beside it on which there's a good amount of traffic.

By the time we reach the hotel, every joint in my lower body is screaming. Twenty miles was a lot.

As I'm checking us in at the front desk, Colin is beside me, but all his attention is on his cell phone, texting someone. When we get to our room, I learn what he's up to.

"Kirsten says they're all down in the bar and we should join them." He tosses his phone on the bed, pack on the floor, and sits down to pull off his boots. "Mind if I jump in the shower first?"

"No, go ahead." So it's going to be another night like that. Socializing. Drinking. Laughing. Telling stories. Maybe it's time I show our new friends that I'm not the grump I've been behaving like until now. After today's long walk, I've earned myself a drink—that much is certain.

After his shower, Colin dresses and heads downstairs. I take my time, relishing the steaming-hot shower and a long rest on my bed with my feet propped on a pillow. An hour after Colin, I finally venture downstairs and find him in the bar with the Danish family, Clara from Germany, and even the Scottish couple, Peter and Grant. They'd pulled tables together and are already well in their cups, judging from the collection of empty glasses in the center.

I take the only open seat at the end of the table between Jorgen and Grant and laugh as Grant immediately pours me a dram of whisky from the bottle in front of him. "Did you have a good walk today?" I ask him after taking a cautious sip of the fiery liquid.

Grant laughs from deep in his belly. "Aye, but we nearly didna." He points to his husband in the chair beside him, deep in conversation with Colin and Kirsten. "This eejit had us stop at the Bridge of Orchy for a midday pint and again at Inveroran for coffee. 'Tis a wonder we're here at all."

Peter, having heard the jab, puts a tattooed hand on Grant's face and pushes him back as though to get him out of the way so he can speak to me. Leaning toward me, he states, "I'll hae ye know, lass, that I would still be oot there, daunderin to Kinlochleven at this verra minute, if not for this old hen here who demanded we stop in 'just for a wee bite to keep me from fainting away like ma granny at a boxing match.'" The last bit is said in a falsetto that is so opposite Peter's usual deep tone that everyone at the table bursts out laughing.

Grant is also laughing as he pushes his husband's hand out of his face. "Aye, and it's a right good thing we did stop or we'd hae missed this craic company."

To that, Jorgen lifts his glass and calls out, "To craic company!"

We all drink to that, while inside I am marveling at Peter and Grant's relationship. How they obviously love teasing each other mercilessly while making it clear to everyone around them that they are devoted to one another. Even their insults feel like terms of endearment. Maybe I should have teasingly insulted Adam a bit more and let him do the same to me. Maybe then we would have had more fun together. Shaking my head, I turn my attention to the menu in front of me. The others are already in various stages of their own dinners, so when the server arrives, I order a portobello burger, fries, and side salad. Like Grant, I'm feeling ravenous after the hike today.

The whisky warms me and goes straight to my head. By my second glass, I hear myself giggling but don't care. Everyone at the table is in high spirits, and I want to have fun right along with them. No thinking about Sorcha or our mysterious connection. No thinking about Adam and his betrayal. No thinking about leaving Colin in this country all alone next week. I will stay present in the moment and simply have fun with our new friends.

Two hours later, night has blackened the view outside the bar's wall-to-wall windows, and we are still drinking and having a great time. I've told stories of my own; listened to theirs; traded jokes; sang along to songs playing on the sound system, plus a few others that someone or other in the group decided we should sing.

I learned that Peter and Grant married in a small ceremony at a castle on the Isle of Skye last autumn and took their honeymoon in Spain. Peter is a blacksmith artist and Grant a university professor. Clara works as a software engineer at a large company in Hamburg and is close to burning out, which is what prompted her solo hike in Scotland.

Kirsten will be starting university in a couple weeks in Copenhagen, and Terese is the star of her school's handball team. Although I'm not entirely sure what handball even is, the others seem impressed.

Being that Jorgen and I are the oldest two at the table, I find myself drawn to him. As the whisky warms my limbs, it feels natural to lay my hand on his arm as we talk, and after Jorgen tells a story about a cycling accident that left him with a broken clavicle, I even subconsciously lean into him as he shows me his scar.

When he feels me against him, heat rises in his eyes. I want to drown in that heat. No man has looked at me with such interest, such hunger, in more years than I can remember.

A longing rises up in me so intense I can't even breathe.

The others at the table fade away, and before I even know the thought is in my head, I lean forward and kiss him. His warm palm cups my cheek and his mouth opens to mine, sending a shock of delight through my entire body.

It is only when Grant coughs loudly that I realize the group has fallen silent. Jorgen must realize it as well, because he pulls back and panic flashes across his face.

I turn my head and find our children and friends staring at us with varying degrees of shock, horror, and amusement. My heart slams painfully in my chest, and my vision darkens around the edges as I look down at the table.

Peter sets his glass on the table with a clunk. "I thought there might be something between you two!"

Startled, I look up at him, and he gives me a saucy wink that makes me want to laugh and cry at the same time.

I look at Colin at the other end of the table, and my throat closes up when I see the look of stunned betrayal on his face. As his eyes meet mine, his expression flashes to shame and then quickly to anger. I can see his chest rapidly rising and falling with his breath. I don't know what to say to him. I don't know how to explain what I've just done. Even if I did know what to say, he doesn't give me the chance. He jerks to standing, making his chair fall over backward and crash onto the floor behind him. His eyes narrow. "Dad's only been gone ten months. You can't forget him fast enough, can you?"

The injustice of the remark hits me deep. I wasn't the one who forgot my spouse. I wasn't the one who cheated. And besides, my husband has been gone nearly a year. No one would expect a man to wait this long before moving on. I haven't felt desirable in too many years to count. I shouldn't have to wait any longer. The need to defend myself roars up and spills out. "He's been gone from me a lot longer than ten months, Colin."

Surprise flares in his eyes but is quickly replaced with disbelief. He opens his mouth to say something else, but then he clamps it shut and he walks away.

Oh, God. I've gone too far. Self-loathing makes my hands and knees shake as I push back from the table to go after him. Grant stops me with a hand on my arm. "Give him a moment."

"I'll make sure he's okay." Kirsten disappears out of the bar after Colin.

I glance at Jorgen and our eyes meet for just a second before we both look away. After a beat, I hear him telling Terese that it's time they call it a night.

I am so embarrassed that I could melt into the floor right here. After Jorgen and Terese leave, I keep my gaze averted from the others remaining at the table as I pull cash out of my purse and leave it on the table. Then I clumsily get to my feet. "Good night, everyone."

With my head down, I head straight for the elevator and the sanctuary of my room.

CHAPTER TWENTY-THREE

Sorcha

Loch Laomainn a deas (South Loch Lomond)

They traveled slowly, not because of rough terrain, nor bodily injury, but because of the heavy weight Sorcha carried in her soul that pulled on her heels. She needed to rest often, and each time she sat, her gaze turned to the north, to the mountains and the sky over her precious Highlands.

She'd promised Aonghas that she'd get them to safety outside of Scotland. It was a promise she would keep, but it would cost her dearly. If they left Scotland, they would never be able to return. Who would she be without her homeland? She had no language other than the *Gàidhlig*, and she did not wish to learn. She especially did not wish to learn the King's English—that hateful language that had been used her entire life to spit insults at her people.

But she'd promised her son, and that was that.

The first step in fulfilling her promise was getting them safely to the city, where they could become one of thousands—thousands, that number of people was impossible to imagine—and thus, be hidden. And then, safe as they could be in the city, they would work. They would save until they had enough, and then they would sail for another land.

"Ma, I have something for you."

Sorcha was sitting on a rock by the lochside, soaking her aching feet in the cool water of Loch Laomainn. She turned and found Aonghas standing on the beach beside her with a bashful grin on his sweet face.

"What is it, *a ghràidh*? That look means you're up to something."

Aonghas kicked at the pebbles on the shore. "I know you're heartsick from losing the grass clumps from my siblings' graves." He shyly brought his hand out from behind his back but kept his fist closed over whatever was in his palm. "This doesn't replace any of it, but I hope you can look at it as a new treasure. One that won't wash away."

He looked absolutely pained saying the words but they, and the words of love he didn't say but she knew he meant, brought tears to her eyes. When his fist opened to reveal a stone in the shape of a heart, she felt her own heart swell.

Gingerly, as the precious moment dictated, she accepted the gift and closed both hands around the stone. "It's perfect. I will treasure it for all my days."

Embarrassed, Aonghas gave her a quick nod, then turned away to pick up a handful of pebbles that he then proceeded to toss far out over the loch one by one.

Sorcha examined the rock in her hand and felt all her aches from their travels diminish. Even the pain and humiliation caused by being branded an outlaw eased some. The stone had stripes of different colors, from red to gray to black, and sparkled throughout with shining flecks. She rubbed her fingers over it, feeling the rough texture and the love from her son that it held in its cool hardness. He was right: this was a treasure.

Her new treasure restored her energy and resolve.

"We should be away." She pushed to her feet and slipped the rock into her pocket before stepping gingerly across the sharp stones back to the smooth path. "I'm seeing more boat traffic the further south we go, and that last one turned behind that point up ahead where there is smoke over the trees. We must avoid the people there."

"But if there are people, there is food."

The leaves they'd been nibbling all day weren't enough, and they'd eaten the last of their stolen oats early that morning along with the squirrel Aonghas caught. She shook her head. "We cannot risk being recognized."

Aonghas stopped under a tall oak tree and turned back to face her. In his hunger-bruised eyes, she saw a strength that reminded her of his father. "I'll go alone. Wait for me here, and I'll go into the village to find food. Single men travel all the time by themselves. No one will look at me twice."

He was right, of course. Men and boys—girls, too, for that matter—traveled from the Highlands every year to farmlands in the south to earn a wage while women like her stayed home to tend the crops and animals and children. It was she who would draw unwanted attention, or she and Aonghas together. But Aonghas on his own was another matter.

She nodded before she changed her mind. "Go, and try to find food honestly." Aonghas had not meant to steal the Flemings' *plaide* so, possibly, that thieving was not a sin. He would not commit the crime intentionally if she could help it. "Do any work they ask of you in exchange, but be quick about it. If you are not back by the time the sun touches that mountain across the loch, I'll come looking for you."

She watched him turn to inspect the mountain and the sun's position in the sky, and then he nodded. Before he could turn away, she grabbed his arm and whispered, "Remember that you are Anndra Ross."

With a very serious expression, he nodded, and then he turned and trotted down the path, soon disappearing behind the trees.

Sorcha looked around and decided to head back to the lochside, where there would be distance between her and anyone who might be traveling on the footpath. Near to the southern end of the beach she spied a burn draining into the loch. The elder and sweet briar growing there would hide her well.

As she settled herself onto a cushion of moss and leaned back against a tangle of tree roots to wait, she tried to keep her mind from traveling with her son and worrying about all the dangers that might befall him.

But, of course, she worried anyway, and the worries exhausted her. She must have fallen asleep, because the next thing she knew, she jerked awake and immediately heard footsteps coming toward her on the gravel beach. In her drowsy state, she forgot to be cautious and she jumped to her feet with her son's name on her lips.

Her sudden appearance startled the man as much as the fact that he was not Aonghas startled her.

Her sleep-addled mind took a moment to catch up to what her pounding heart already knew.

Coghill. His greasy black-and-gray hair, his trimmed beard and mustache, his black clothing. He looked exactly as he had that night at Inbhir Àirnein House and every night since in her nightmares.

Stunned, she could only stare at him and watch as recognition bloomed in his eyes and then quickly shifted to the gleam of triumph.

She turned and ran. As fast as she could, she ran from him with tree branches and bramble thorns tearing at her skin, sharp rocks spearing her bare feet. She slowed for none of it. She was a hare at the mercy of hounds and, like a hare, she would only stop if her heart gave out.

She followed the burn away from the loch and then to the left, toward denser forest, where she hoped to escape.

Just when she thought she was making progress, claws tugged on her arm and she fell, hard, landing with all her weight on her other arm and shoulder. Pain stabbed through her, but she refused to think about it, refused to even feel it.

Her only thoughts were, *Go! Run!*

But Coghill had his gloved and impossibly strong hand clamped around her arm. The momentum of her fall had made him stumble, but he was able to maintain his feet, and now he yanked her up, wrenching her shoulder in the process. She jerked her arm trying to get free, but her struggle only made him laugh.

"I will not lose you again, bitch." Spittle flew from his mouth as he spoke, and she cringed away from that as much as his devilish promise. "You and your murdering son will hang. You can count on that."

Like the captured animal she was, Sorcha allowed her most basic instincts to take control. With all her strength, she drove her fist upward into Coghill's face, catching him in the nose. A satisfying crunch sounded and had him bringing his free hand up to feel the injured appendage. Before he could do anything more than bellow in rage, she grabbed her knife from her belt and drove the blade into the arm still holding her tight.

She missed driving it deep into his flesh but managed to slice enough that his grip loosened and gave her an opening to jerk free and run.

His curses followed her, and she knew he was close. She ran as fast as she could, knowing at any moment he would grab her, and this time he wouldn't let her escape. She had to get away. Aonghas needed her. She darted around trees, never slowing, never looking back. She didn't need to look back because she knew Coghill was there. She felt his presence like hot iron against the back of her neck.

The trees were thinning, and up ahead she spied smoke. A house. Everything in her told her to run there for protection, as she'd been trained from birth that no Highlander would turn away a person in need. But this was different. This was no longer the Highlands. And she was an outlaw.

She changed course to avoid the farm, and that was her mistake.

Coghill tackled her to the ground, the weight of his full body landing hard on top of hers, knocking the wind out of her. The knife she had not realized she was still holding flew from her hand, leaving her defenseless.

For a stunned moment, she struggled to draw air back into her lungs, but she didn't have the luxury of a moment. As Coghill moved to regain his feet, she rolled away from him and pushed to her hands and knees, trying her hardest to stand, but her skirt tangled around her legs, hindering her.

Coghill launched his body forward, grabbing her leg and dragging her onto her stomach. With her other foot, she kicked back at his head and face. His hands loosened from her ankle, and she scurried away enough to stand, grabbing a palm-size rock along with her.

He lunged to his feet and came toward her. She swung the rock as hard as she could and caught him on the side of his head. The momentum of her swing knocked him sideways and he stumbled, crying out in pain and rage.

Before she could do anything else, Coghill smashed his fist into her jaw, the force of it sending her backward to fall into thick bracken.

Pain from the blow shot from her jaw, throughout her head, and down her spine. She had to blink to clear the stars and tears from her eyes.

Coghill, clearly thinking she was down for good, was dabbing a cloth against the blood on the side of his face, not even looking her way.

Now was her chance. She had to go. Now.

She turned her aching head to the side, looking for an escape route. But then, what she saw caused everything else to stand still and horror creep over her.

A little girl, no older than five or six, sat crouched in the tall bracken no more than three feet from Sorcha. Her pretty floral dress attested to the fact that she was loved and cared for. Long, blond hair hung loosely along the sides of her face. Her eyes were big blue saucers that stared at Sorcha in fear as her tiny, heart-shaped lips hung open as though in the middle of a cry.

Sorcha's eyes met the little girl's, and then, to Sorcha's surprise, the little girl lifted her hand from where it had been hidden in the thick foliage, revealing an iron jockey, used to hold a kettle over a fire. Sorcha flinched, thinking the girl was going to strike her with it, but she only held it out to Sorcha as though offering it to her.

Sorcha shot a quick glance toward Coghill and saw him spitting blood on the ground as he muttered about the *damned woman*.

Moving slowly so she didn't attract his notice, Sorcha reached her arm out toward the little girl and clasped the jockey. Then, with her other hand, she brought her finger up to her lips to signal the girl to stay silent.

With fear in her eyes, the little girl nodded, but then her eyes slid sideways and widened even further.

Turning, Sorcha saw Coghill advancing toward her, his face bloody and tight with rage.

Before she could think twice, she brought the jockey up just as Coghill lunged for her. With a sickening sound, the jockey pierced deep into his belly.

Coghill's eyes flared in shock as his hands came around the iron rod. Sorcha twisted the rod, thinking only of stopping Coghill from getting to her.

With his gaze still wide and full of pain, Coghill grasped the rod and stumbled back, pulling it from Sorcha's hands.

Blood pooled around the black gloves that clutched at his belly and poured down his legs.

Horrified and fascinated by what she saw, what she'd done, Sorcha could not look away as he struggled to pull the jockey from his body but failed.

He dropped to his knees and lifted his face toward Sorcha as she cautiously neared him. He struggled for breath but managed to speak; his words were faint but clear. "Burn in hell."

He fell to his side and lay there unmoving, his eyes staring sightlessly at the trees.

A sound tore her attention away from the gruesome sight in front of her, and Sorcha turned to see a little blond head running away from her toward the farmhouse.

The little girl. In the horror of the attack, she'd forgotten about her. The poor little thing had seen it all. The realization caused Sorcha's heart to painfully clench.

But there was nothing to be done for her now. Sorcha had to think of herself, and her son. She had to get away from here before the girl's father or other adults arrived, for surely that was where she had run to.

Sorcha started back in the direction of the beach but stopped when she spied her *sgian-dubh* lying on the dirt. Snatching it up, she slipped it back into her belt and took off running.

She did not stop until she neared the beach, and then she hid in the trees. Where was Baltair, Coghill's companion? Surely another man or two had been traveling with him. So why weren't they here?

Aonghas! The companions were probably in town, where Aonghas had gone. They would recognize him. Might have already captured him.

She would have to go into the village to look for him.

Sorcha started in that direction but stopped short when she realized what she must look like. The screaming pain in her head and arm was enough to addle her wits, but the injuries Coghill had inflicted on her face must surely be visible. She lifted a hand to her cheek and flinched at the stinging there.

Backtracking to the burn, she carefully knelt and cupped her hands in the water. Only now did she realize she was shaking, as she had trouble keeping water in her hands long enough to bring it to her face.

She had killed a man.

The realization made her stomach spasm, and she retched over and over into the grass, although there was nothing to bring up but bile.

Exhausted, she laid her forehead against the cool ground and sobbed. How was she going to live with the knowledge that she'd taken a man's life?

No, she could not think about that now. Aonghas. She needed to think of her boy, who needed her. She forced herself to get back onto her knees by the side of the burn. With hands still shaking, she drank the cool water until it eased the burning in her throat. Then, taking care with her injuries, she washed her face and neck and arms. When that was done, she sat back on her heels and smoothed her hands over her hair, wishing again for her lost mutch to cover the mess and for the respectful appearance it would've provided.

Only now did she realize that she'd lost her *plaide* as she ran from Coghill. She'd need it for warmth as well as to hide her new bruises and cuts from Aonghas. She pushed painfully to standing and set off on tender feet.

It was easy to retrace her path from the beach. In their race, she and Coghill had torn limbs from saplings and crushed ferns and grasses with each step.

She found the *plaide* at the beach, where it must've fallen when she'd awoken from her nap. She shook it out and wrapped it carefully around her shoulders and over her head, drawing it close to the sides of her face and securing it with her beloved brooch.

The village was farther than she realized, and she walked for several minutes without reaching any dwellings. She stayed in the trees away from the path to remain out of sight. Not only were Coghill's companions likely looking for her, but now also were the adults belonging to the little girl.

Thinking of that, why hadn't she heard an alarm raised? If the body had been discovered, surely there would be shouts, men on horseback and on foot combing through these woods looking for her.

The thought spurred her feet onward at a quicker pace until she was running as fast as the undergrowth allowed.

A voice in song drifted to her ears, and her body jerked with fear.

It was coming from a short distance away, in the direction of the loch where the path must be.

"*Amadan gòrach gòrach, amadan gòrach saighdear . . .*"

The voice sounded just like Aonghas. It was Aonghas!

"*Amadan gòrach gòrach, chunna mi 'g òl a-raoir thu . . .*"

Sorcha moved through the trees toward the voice, toward her son. When she saw him walking on the road, as carelessly as though he were back in Srath Ghlais walking home from church, she wanted to weep. Tears did, in fact, spring into her eyes, and she had to blink them away before she could see enough to move the remaining distance through the forest.

She stopped behind a tree. "Aonghas!"

His feet stopped and he looked, questioningly, her direction. "Ma?"

She beckoned him toward her. "*Ist!* Come, this way."

He shrugged and turned off the path to join her under cover of the trees. "Why are you here? I was to meet you at the beach."

She tugged the *plaide* so it hid her bruised cheek. "I saw some men and didn't want them to see me. We need to be away from here. Did you see anyone in the village?"

He nodded but then saw her look of alarm and amended, "I mean, I saw a minister who gave me a baked potato. Look, it's still warm!" He unfolded the corner of his *plaide* to reveal the potato cooked in its skin.

Her mouth watered as she looked at it. "Well done, son."

"I thought we could camp here for the night, fill our bellies, and get an early start in the morning. The minister told me how to get to Glaschu. He said the best way would be to hire a boat to take us down the loch and then down the Uisge Leamhain to the Abhainn Chluaidh, which, if we follow it upstream, flows through Glaschu."

She'd wanted to camp here for the night, too, until everything changed. "We can't pay a boatman."

He nodded. "I know. That's why I asked if there are other routes by foot. He said we can walk south from here along the loch until we come to a river he called Endrick Water. We follow it until we reach a wide strath positioned north to south, which we follow south to the city."

Sorcha nodded as she listened to him, and pulled gently on his sleeve to draw him farther away from the path and into the forest. "But wouldn't Coghill and his men expect us to take that route? Maybe we should find another way."

"But Coghill doesn't know we're on this side of the loch, does he? The last he knew, we were on the main road on the west side, where the Inbhir Àirnein House Hotel is located. Logically, we would follow it south, and so he'll be looking for us there."

How had Coghill found her on this side? It was a question she might never know the answer to—and besides, it didn't matter now. He had found her, but he wouldn't ever again.

His companions, however, were still out there somewhere. "All the same. I would feel better if we stay off the main path."

They'd moved through the section of trees as they talked and now found themselves staring at a wide moor that rose up the side of a lump of mountain with what looked like two rocky knobs at the top. Moving across the open moor rather than staying to the trees alongside the loch would be risky, but what choice did they have? They each wore *plaideachan* woven with colors of the moor, which would help hide them even as they walked. "I say we walk this way, around that mountain, before moving south. That would put some distance between us and anyone looking for us, don't you think?"

"Well, yes, but why? We haven't seen Coghill in days. No one is looking for us here."

If only he knew. She vowed he never would know what she'd done this terrible day. "All the same. We're here; let's continue."

He gave in and followed as she picked a path across the rough ground. As they walked, they passed the potato back and forth between them, taking bites until it was gone.

Every bit of Sorcha's body ached. She wanted nothing more than to curl up and sleep for hours, but knew she would find no rest until she'd put distance between them and the men looking for them.

At least Coghill would no longer be looking. Relief warred with guilt in a greasy tumble in her belly.

Now she really was a murderer and should be hanged for it.

Why hadn't she heard shouts of alarm echo through the forest after Coghill's body was discovered?

Was it not discovered? Had the little girl not told anyone?

She quickly dismissed the thought. Of course she'd told someone. Her mother. Her father. Someone now knew and was surely raising the alarm among the neighbors.

But maybe not.

The thought brought her feet to a standstill. Was Coghill's body still slumped inside that clearing where she'd left him?

If she could get back to it and bury it, then no one would find it and come after her. And when Coghill failed to appear, would his companions give up their chase and go home?

The possibility was too great for her to ignore.

"Aonghas." He'd kept walking when she stopped, but at her call he turned with a question on his face. She pointed to the trees beside a close burn. "Let's make camp there for the night. I'm too tired to go further."

He nodded and angled his course. She followed, devising a plan in her mind.

⁂

When Sorcha jerked awake, she saw that night was upon them, dark and heavy. Aonghas slept beside her, his breath steady and deep.

It was time.

Moving as silently as possible, and biting her lip hard to keep from crying out when a lightning bolt of pain shot down her injured arm, Sorcha got to her feet and carefully crept away from camp.

She'd made certain to notice the route she would need to take as they had arrived here, and now followed that route back to the forest. Stumbling through the dark over rough ground made the going slow and frustrating. No moon lit up the sky, but enough stars shone to allow her to see her way.

After an impossible amount of time, where she started to worry that she'd never finish her task and return to Aonghas before sunup, she finally found the clearing she was looking for.

The dark form of Coghill's body remained slumped on its side where she'd left it, the iron jockey jutting from his midsection.

Sorcha's own stomach spasmed, and her body suddenly felt cold with sweat.

She'd done this. She'd taken this life. No matter how cruel and heartless this man had been, he had not deserved to lose his life this way, by her hands.

Her stomach convulsed. She retched into the bushes until her body felt hollowed out. Afterward, she rubbed her hands over her face, taking care not to press onto her damaged cheekbone and jaw, and then she dropped her hands to her sides. Time to do what she had come here for.

She returned to the body but refused to glance at the man's face. Seeing only the rod, she braced her feet, grasped the cold iron in both hands, and pulled it out with a sickening sucking sound that made her shudder with revulsion.

For a long time, she could do nothing more than stand over the body with her face lifted to the night sky and her eyes closed. She wished with everything in her that she didn't have to do this.

But she did have to. For Aonghas. And yes, for herself as well.

She swallowed and clenched her teeth together. A stab of pain in her jaw reminded her that he had hit her there, which helped. She set to work digging.

With no other tools—a flaughter spade would have been useful—she used the jockey to cut through the soil. When the ground was loosened enough, she got onto her knees and scooped the dirt out with her bare hands, ignoring the pain in her shoulder and arm. Over and over, jockey, then hands, she dug and dug.

When she judged the hole big enough, she finally looked up and realized the sky was growing lighter. Soon the sun would crest the eastern horizon, and the people living in the nearby cottage would begin their morning chores. She needed to finish and be away from here.

Quickening her pace, she didn't allow any thoughts to come into her mind about this being a human being with a family who loved him. She just grabbed the legs and pulled the body into the hole, bending the limbs so it fit. Then, again using her hands, she shoved the loose soil over the body until it was completely buried.

With a cringe, and an admonition not to think about it, she walked over the grave to pack the dirt.

She then tossed the jockey far into the forest and was about to return to Aonghas when she looked again and realized the loosened soil would draw suspicion.

The cock from the farmhouse crowed. The family would be stirring.

She quickly ripped out a handful of bracken and used it like a broom to sweep away her footprints and smooth the soil. Then she scooped up handfuls of loose debris from the forest floor—dead leaves, needles, cones—and scattered them around the clearing, over the grave.

It wasn't perfect, and anyone looking would spot something amiss in the ground here, but it was all she could do.

A voice sounded from the direction of the farmhouse: a woman's voice, calling to her child a reminder to not dump the chicken feed all in one pile.

Sorcha wanted badly to run away, but she forced herself to step carefully, make no sounds. She moved steadily and purposefully until she reached the edge of the moor. Then she ran.

She approached their campsite from farther up the burn and took several minutes to wash the dirt off her hands and arms. Then, moving downstream, she found Aonghas already awake, washing his hands and face in the stream.

Deep breath. Smile. "*Madainn mhath,* Aonghas."

"Oh, there you are. Good morning to you." He cupped his hands in the water for one last drink, then stood up. "Where were you?"

Her heart was pounding, but she pretended nonchalance. "Just stretching my legs a bit before our walk. Are you ready to go?"

He started to nod, but then his eyes narrowed and he reached out to push her *plaide* from her head. "What happened to your face? Is that blood on your jacket?"

Alarmed, Sorcha looked down and saw with horror that Coghill's blood had splattered across her front. The brown wool disguised much of it, but this closely, both she and Aonghas saw the spots for what they were.

And the bruise. She'd forgotten all about the bruises Coghill had left on her. She'd been so worried about burying his body and returning to Aonghas that she'd forgotten the other evidence of her encounter yesterday.

Thinking fast, she laughed and stepped away from Aonghas as she drew her *plaide* back up. "This is nothing. I was clumsy yesterday in the forest when you were in the village. Fell right on my face, I did, and got a bloody nose. Silly, wasn't it?"

He didn't seem convinced, but he finally allowed a smile. Then, as he drew his own *plaide* over his shoulders, a gleam lit up his eyes. "I was looking at that mountain this morning and thinking." He wiggled his eyebrows. "Let's climb it. I know you're tired and so am I, but we're nearing the city. This could be the last hill we can climb and our last view of the Highlands."

She blinked. She'd had no idea Aonghas was also feeling the weight of being forced to leave the Highlands. He'd had enough to worry about with Coghill after them and she'd kept her longing to herself, but now she saw that he felt it just the same. They were both losing the only homeland they'd ever known.

Climbing the hill would be a detour that prolonged their time in the area when they should be moving far away from here, and away from Coghill's companions.

But Coghill himself was no longer pursuing them. The truth of that sent such a wave of relief through Sorcha that she almost didn't feel the aches from yesterday's battle, her restless night, and this morning's shameful activity. Coghill was gone, and so far, it seemed that no one knew. The little girl must not have told her family, because the body had remained untouched through the night and no one had been scouring the woods looking for the killer.

She was safe today. The only possible threat was if Coghill's companions were still looking for her, but it had been clear all along that Coghill was leading the effort. Without his leadership, would his men continue?

Likely not. They would return home to wherever it was they lived and go back to their lives.

Despite the crushing fatigue she was having to hide from Aonghas, she felt lighter. She felt safer today than she'd felt in weeks.

Turning to look at the hill that Aonghas called a mountain, she saw the top lit up by the rising sun and knew it was a sign. Aonghas was right: they should climb up there and turn their gazes to the north one last time. "Yes, let's climb it. It's a beautiful morning."

They followed the burn, then crossed over a grazing moor to the bottom of the steeply sloping hill.

As they climbed, Sorcha became keenly aware of how exposed they were. Anyone might glance up at the mountain and see the two of them. If the wrong people saw them, their freedom would end.

The thought made her climb more quickly, even using her hands at the steepest parts to pull herself up. Aonghas, bless him, sprang up the hillside like he'd been born to it, which she supposed he had. The boy had been climbing mountains with his father and brother from before he could walk.

At the top, he plopped down on his rear end and exclaimed, "It's even grander than I'd hoped!"

When she finally dragged herself up, sweating and panting, her head, shoulder, and bruised face aching with every heartbeat, she sat beside him and took in the view. Immediately, it reached inside her chest and squeezed. Up here, she could still hear her home, singing in the wind. If she listened hard enough, she could make out the sounds of the pipes and her neighbors' laughter, the women's voices raised in a waulking song and the steady beat of their hands on the cloth along with it. Even though they were not yet in bloom, she smelled the heather and wild thyme and could have been sitting at this very moment on their own mountain at home.

The loch below stretched far into the distance, and she marveled at the fact that they'd walked along its shore from the very top. Although this loch was much bigger, seeing it took her back to Loch Afraig, where she'd spent many a day with her husband and children. The loch even took her further back to when she was but a girl herself, running with her sister along the shore of Loch Cuaich and riding with their father as he rowed across to visit relatives, stopping to catch pike to bring as a gift.

Would there be mountains and lochs where she and Aonghas ended up? She could not imagine a life without them. From where does the morning sun rise if not from behind a mountain? How does one mark the coming night if not by marking the glow and shadows as the sun dips behind other mountains? Where do the cows graze in summer? Where do women gather the wild herbs that not only seasoned their food but also brought down fevers, healed wounds, eased aches, and provided dye for wool? Mountains and lochs were vital to life, and she had no idea how to live without them.

Aonghas, lost in his own thoughts, let out a deep sigh. She wrapped her arm around his shoulders and squeezed. "Do not worry, *a ghràidh*. We will be just fine." She didn't believe the words herself, but she wouldn't let him know that. "Mark this moment and this view so you can remember it on those days when we are far from here. The memory will warm your heart when nothing else can."

They sat leaning against one another for several long moments, watching the rising sun light up the loch and the hills all around it.

Sorcha could've stayed here forever, up above the rest of the world with her beloved Highlands in her sight, but then Aonghas stiffened. "Someone is coming."

She followed his gaze and saw two figures down the mountain, slowly and steadily climbing up. They didn't look to be Coghill's men, for their clothing was lighter and looser, but she wasn't about to take any risk. "We must go."

Aonghas bounded to his feet and took off along the ridge of the hill in the opposite direction from the men. It took Sorcha longer to get her aching muscles and joints to cooperate, and then, once she was on her feet, her heart clenched painfully and she had to take another moment to cast her gaze far to the north, to the purple mountains in the distance, to home. The words came straight from her soul and slipped from her lips. "Will I ever return to my beloved Highlands, where Gaelic can be heard on the lips of its people?" She swallowed hard as she took one last look and then whispered, "With beautiful views now at my back, it breaks my heart."

"Ma!"

Aonghas's call broke the spell, and she finally turned to follow him, swallowing the tears that burned her throat.

They hurried down the backside of the hill, which went much more quickly than the climb. The only inhabitants here were two sheep, who did nothing more than idly lift their heads as she and Aonghas raced past.

Once at the bottom, they took a moment to slake their thirst in the burn, and for Sorcha to mark a stone, before splashing across to the moorland on the other side. She wanted to follow the burn, as it flowed to the south, but the trees and brambles grew thickly there and prevented passage. All the same, they stayed along the edge of the trees, moving across the moor, which allowed them fast movement but kept them close enough that they could duck into cover if someone appeared.

For several miles, they followed the burn until the moorland turned into pastures enclosed by stone walls and wooden fences. They did not want to draw the ire of any farmers, so from there on, they stuck to the coach road that meandered through the wide farming glen.

"The minister said to follow the north and south going strath. Do you think he means this one?" Aonghas pointed to the right, where a wide and fertile valley between two mountains seemed to be narrowing toward the southern end.

They were at a crossroad marked with a signpost. Sorcha stared at it a long moment, hoping the words there would unlock their meaning to her, but she'd never learned to read—and besides, it was probably English, anyway. They were in the Lowlands now, after all. "We may need to risk asking someone for direction, but for now, let's continue along the course of this strath." She found that carving her symbol into the wood of the signpost was much easier and quicker than marking stone.

The mountains were noticeably smaller now, the flatlands wider. Just as she had on the side of the mountain this morning, she felt exposed. Her skin prickled as though a thousand eyes were upon her, and she worried that someone—a stranger, Coghill's men, thieves—would accost them at any moment. She jumped at every sudden sound. A raven croaking from a tree, just as she passed underneath it, made her flinch sideways. A voice across the field that sounded like a woman calling to her neighbor made Sorcha hunker down behind a gorse bush. At this rate, they would not get far.

"There are too many people about." She looped her arm through Aonghas's to keep him close as they walked. "I fear the next person we come upon will be Coghill, or someone who turns us over to him." *Heaven forgive me for lying to my son,* she silently pleaded.

"I feel the same."

They chose their path carefully after that, staying off the road as much as possible and out of sight of houses and farms. They cut across fields, followed a curving river, walked on the other side of hedgerows from the road.

Sorcha had been watching Aonghas's steps grow slower all afternoon and knew he needed food. He'd even started rubbing at his belly as though it pained him, although he made no complaints.

"If we could find a kirk, we could see if the minister is in." She forced her voice to reveal none of the fear the idea caused in her. "He would share his supper with us, I'm certain of it."

Aonghas looked at her askance. "And how would you answer his questions?"

"He doesn't need to know our real names or that we're being sought. We could tell him only that we're traveling to find work."

"And when he asks where we are from?"

Sorcha thought about that. "Not Srath Ghlais. That would put him on alert if he's heard of our accused crime."

Aonghas scowled. "So you'll be lying to a man of God now, will you? I know you better than that, Ma."

Sorcha dropped her head in shame. He was right, of course. She couldn't lie to a minister. Nor would she be able to look one in the eye knowing that she'd committed the worst sin possible.

The scent of roasting meat danced on the breeze, making them both stop short as though by mutual consent, although neither said a word. With eyes closed, Sorcha drew in the mouthwatering aroma. The last time she'd smelled anything so enticing was at Hogmanay last, when she and her neighbors had pooled their resources to make a fine shared supper. She'd contributed butter and potatoes. Aileach Fraser had contributed beef from her cow, who'd broken its leg wandering in a bog and had to be put down. Someone else had contributed turnips, another cheese, another whisky. They'd feasted like they had not in years prior, nor in the months since.

The memory of it made her mouth ache and fill with saliva. She opened her eyes and looked at Aonghas. His face had paled, and the shadows under his eyes had darkened. It was as though the smell of the food had wasted him away right in front of her eyes.

She knew what she must do.

She was already a thief and a murderer—what did she have to lose by stealing again? Her son needed to eat, and the Lord knew they may never be able to buy food so fine on their own.

With her plan in mind, Sorcha didn't stop to question it. "Come, Aonghas. Sit here and rest. I'll return shortly." She guided him closer to the burn they were following where bright-green moss created a soft bed.

"Where are you going?" He sat on the moss with his back against a tree. A flash of relief across his face told her she was doing the right thing.

"Never you mind that. Just rest." She helped him tuck his *plaide* over his body, then she left the cover of the trees and followed the delicious aroma across a field.

Soon she spied its source. A cottage sat tucked amid a grove of oak and birch trees. On the ground in front of the house was a fire with a large iron pot hanging over it, sealed tight with a lid. A woman tended the fire, but no one else was about. Sorcha squatted behind a tree for several long moments, watching to make certain.

The man of the house must be out in the fields or tending his animals. No other person made an appearance.

She decided she would introduce herself as a poor woman traveling to the city to find work. That much would not be a lie. She would then weave a tale of a sickly child who needed food—a small stretch of the truth. Surely the woman would find it in her heart to share her supper.

Just as she was preparing to step out from behind the tree, an infant's cry sounded from within the cottage, and the woman hurried inside.

Sorcha didn't waste a moment. She dashed to the fire and lifted the lid of the pot to find four meat pies baking inside. The golden crusts made her mouth water. Using her skirt to protect her fingers from the heat, she quickly snatched up two of the pies, then she returned the lid to the pot and ran back to the trees.

She dropped down behind a leafy bush and waited, her heart pounding in her ears and racing so fast she felt like it would burst out of her chest.

No cry of alarm sounded behind her. The woman hadn't seen her. The man hadn't returned.

With the pies wrapped in the cloth of her skirt, she hurried back to Aonghas. She found him asleep against the tree, his mouth hanging open. He jerked awake when she touched his shoulder. "Ma. You're back."

"Yes, and I have supper." She unfolded the fabric to reveal her treasure.

His eyes widened with delight, and in one motion, he grabbed the pie and bit off a huge bite. Immediately, he opened his mouth again and panted. "Hot!" After a moment, he chewed carefully and then closed his eyes and moaned. "I could eat this every day for the rest of my life and never get enough."

Sorcha broke off a corner of the second pie and popped it into her mouth, immediately agreeing with Aonghas's assessment. The meat inside wasn't beef. Perhaps it was lamb? Whatever it was, it was cooked to perfection and mixed with carrots and peas, all swimming in a rich gravy and enclosed in a flaky, buttery crust.

As they ate, Sorcha watched Aonghas and felt satisfied by his joy. She'd provided for him this night, and she was happy about that. They ate every tiny crumb and then licked their fingers clean.

After washing it down with fresh water from the burn, they resumed their walk. She didn't want the woman or her husband to come looking for the thief who'd taken their supper.

They finally stopped as the sun dipped below the horizon and the temperature of the air cooled. With their backs against a stone wall and their *plaideachan* wrapped around them, they settled down side by side.

Despite all that had happened, despite taking a man's life, Sorcha felt the glow of contentment. She'd provided for her child this day. It was a good day.

CHAPTER TWENTY-FOUR

Keaka

Day six; Kingshouse

I awake from strange dreams of fiddle music and laughing sailors to a pounding headache and a cotton mouth. The room is dark, and I have no idea what time it is.

Sitting up hurts my entire body, and I don't know if it's from the long days of walking or the alcohol I consumed last night. Both, probably. But water will help. So will food.

Nausea rolls through me. Okay, maybe not food.

Moving as quietly as I can so I don't wake Colin—he came in late last night, and, like the coward I am, I pretended to be asleep—I shuffle to the bathroom and wince as the light pierces the back of my skull. Squinting to block most of it out, I drink deeply straight from the faucet.

Still feeling shaky, I wash my face and study myself in the mirror. I'm annoyed to find the bags under my eyes have darkened but the rest of my face has gone a shade of green. Two—no, make that three—ibuprofen. I down these with more water and wish I had some anti-nausea medicine.

Just before I flick off the bathroom light, a shaft falls onto Colin's bed and makes me pause. I flick the switch back on again. My eyes weren't fooling me. His bed is empty.

Concerned, I click on the bedside lamp and grab my cell phone. I'm shocked to see it is just past ten in the morning. I drop my phone back onto the nightstand and skirt around Colin's bed to the window, where I fling open the heavy drapes.

I flinch at the sunlight, but then my eyes adjust, and what I see makes the pain worth it. Where yesterday had been dark, moody, and damp, today the moor and mountains are bright and textured with layers of color, from red to green to purple to yellow. I push my face close to the window to see down into Glencoe and am instantly enchanted by the steeply sloping green mountains meeting in the valley with a single road snaking into its depths.

I'm surprised to feel a stirring inside me. Despite feeling nauseated, I want to get out there and follow the trail to see where it takes me. I want to step into the morning sunshine and breathe in the mountain air, hear the crunch of gravel underfoot, smell the heather, discover whatever I'll find over the next rise.

I've changed. I've become a hiker. Who would've thought? Certainly not Adam.

Adam. Colin's words last night echo through my mind. *Dad's only been gone ten months. You can't forget him fast enough, can you?*

I kissed Jorgen. In public. In front of our kids and the rest of the bar.

Heat flames my face, and I drop my forehead against the cool glass window. What was I thinking? How am I going to face any of them today? Worse, what will I say to Colin to fix this?

The ringing of my cell phone snaps my eyes open, and I rush back to the bed to grab it. "Colin?"

"Oh, good, you're up. Checkout is at eleven, so we need to pack and head out. I'll be up in a minute to get my stuff."

"Why didn't you wake me when you got up?"

"You seemed like you needed to sleep." He pauses, and I wonder if he is going to say something about last night. But all he says next is, "See you in a minute."

"Okay. I'll get ready." We hang up, and I force myself to get dressed and pack up my bags when all I really want to do is crawl back into bed and hide.

Colin walks in smelling of coffee and fried meats, which sends another wave of nausea through me, though I succeed in swallowing it back. I force a bright smile for my only offspring. "Good morning! Sorry we're getting such a late start today."

"No big deal. We only have nine miles to go today. Three or four hours, tops, I figure." He steps into the bathroom to brush his teeth, and I turn back to stuffing the last of my things into my pack.

When he emerges from the bathroom, I'm sitting on the bed, waiting for him. "Colin, about last night . . ."

His face darkens, and he turns his back to me to shove his toiletry kit into the suitcase.

"I'm really sorry about what happened. It's no excuse, but I drank too much and I wasn't thinking."

He zips the suitcase closed without a word, then slings on his backpack and looks at me without emotion. "Let's get going."

Clearly he doesn't want to talk about last night. I swallow the desperation I'm feeling to make things right between us, and I reach for my own pack.

I'm relieved when the elevator doors open onto the lobby and none of our friends are in sight. At the Way Inn, a small café off the other end of the lobby from the main restaurant, I purchase a large coffee and a scone for my breakfast, and we both get sandwiches for lunch on the trail later.

The moment we step outside, I feel another stirring of the excitement I felt standing at the window earlier. Fresh, moist air soothes my wonky stomach and energizes me. I am happy to follow the track that winds behind the hotel, and I'm eager to see the views the day will bring. Other hotel guests are milling about and taking photos of deer that are nibbling grass at the edge of the parking lot. Surprisingly, I don't feel like I'm one of the tourists. I walked here, and my feet are going to carry me away from here, too. How many people at the hotel can say that?

As we cross the bridge over the river behind the hotel, Colin points to a grassy area to the right. "That's where Clara, and Peter and Grant pitched their tents last night. Clara said the midges were swarming like mad, and she had to sleep with a bug net over her head all night."

"She must have a hole in her tent since that keeps happening." A night like Clara's sounds miserable. It also takes my feeling of satisfaction down several notches. I may have walked here, but I'd slept in a luxurious bed and had a warm shower. Clara walked here carrying ten times the weight I had, and she slept on the cold hard ground while being pestered by tiny biting bugs all night. Clara clearly had more fortitude than I did. "What about Jorgen and the girls? I thought they were camping, too."

Colin stiffens at hearing Jorgen's name out of my mouth, and I want to kick myself for bringing him up. But rather than pursuing *that* conversation, Colin only answers my question. "They stayed in the bunkhouse over there. It's cheaper than the hotel and provides actual mattresses, toilets, and showers, which is better than camping."

I nod to show I heard him, but my mind is deep into the shame of last night. How could I have lost control so thoroughly? How could I have forgotten for even a fraction of a second that my son, my singular priority, was sitting at the same table? I'd promised myself that I would leave Scotland with our relationship on solid ground, but my actions last night destroyed that, and I have no idea if I'll be able to fix it.

We walk in silence for a while, hearing only the sound of our boots on the gravel and the trickling of water in the many small streams we step across. I can see cars moving along the A82, but we are far enough up the mountainside that the traffic noise does not reach us.

Colin's pace is much faster than mine this morning, and he's a good distance ahead, leaving me alone with my thoughts, which continue in a never-ending loop of shame and embarrassment.

To distract myself I start humming, and then quietly singing aloud, "The Skye Boat Song" from the television show *Outlander*. For a good distance I even imagine myself as an eighteenth-century heroine traveling through the glen when the road and traffic did not exist, which must have made the valley quite remote. It's surprisingly easy to picture.

"This is the famous Devil's Staircase."

Colin's words snap my attention back to the trail, which rises up the side of the steep mountain with numerous switchbacks. I swallow. "I suppose it's named that because it's so challenging?"

"Actually, no. Grant told me this morning that it was christened as such, either by the soldiers who made the trail back in the 1750s or the laborers building the Blackwater Reservoir Dam in the early 1900s who took this route to the Kingshouse for a drink. A number of them died trying to walk back to camp in poor weather." He loops his thumbs under his pack straps. "Ready?"

"As I'll ever be." I follow him and, again, soon find myself trailing far behind.

Although each step is upward, it isn't so bad as long as I don't let the idea of the climb freak me out. I focus on putting one foot in front of the other, and before I know it, I have climbed a good distance.

Stopping at one switchback to catch my breath, I turn to look at the view and am rewarded for my climbing efforts. From this vantage point I can see farther, to more mountains down the glen and far to the south. My body is still dehydrated from last night, so I take a moment to pull out my water bottle and drink deeply. Our hike is shorter today, I reason, so I don't need to ration my water as much as I have on previous days. Only half the bottle is left when I replace the cap.

Several people pass me, and I am greatly relieved that none of them look familiar from the bar last night.

I return my water bottle to its pocket and slip my pack back on, then I continue upward. Up, up, up, until finally, I reach the top, where Colin is waiting for me next to a large cairn.

"Take a good look," he tells me. "This is the last we'll see of Glencoe."

The news disappoints me even as I'm suffused with relief that Colin is talking to me again. "Will we come through here on the way back to Glasgow?"

He shakes his head. "No. The train from Fort William goes further east. We'd have to be in a car to come back here."

I spend several long moments taking in the view, trying my best to imprint it into my memory. The awesome Buachaille Etive Mòr is directly across the valley from us, and numerous mountains are bunched up behind it. Sunlight spears through clumps of clouds, which creates a spotlight effect on an outcropping of immense boulders here, the furry green slope of a mountain in shades of purple and red there. At this moment, I don't want to be anywhere else on planet Earth than right where I am. The scenery stirs my soul, and I silently promise myself that I will come back someday to explore Glencoe's nooks and crannies more thoroughly.

I look at Colin beside me and see he is also drinking in the view. I study his profile and wonder how we're going to clear the air about last night. I hope he'll eventually allow us to discuss it rather than pretend it didn't happen.

Turning my back to the view, I face the trail that winds over rolling hills leading to Kinlochleven. "Shall we go?"

He nods, avoiding my eyes.

As has become our habit, Colin leads the way on the narrow trail. For at least an hour, all we do is walk; our only words are when Colin points out where to step as I cross a stream or when I ask him the name of the lake I see in the distance (Blackwater Reservoir). I can feel his disappointment in me like a living thing between us, but I'm afraid if I pressure him to talk about it, he'll only retreat more.

When we are somewhere on the grassy mountain moorland between the two valleys, we stop to eat our sandwiches at a grouping of rocks beside the trail with a view of Blackwater Reservoir and the Mamores mountain range to the north. As we eat, Colin tells me the names of the different mountains along the skyline.

Buoyed by the fact that Colin is talking to me, I work up the nerve to broach the subject again. "I'm so sorry for last night," I blurt out. "I drank too much, and I'm really embarrassed by my behavior with . . . with Jorgen."

Heat flushes through my entire body and my stomach knots, causing the sandwich to sit like a lead ball inside. I wrap up the second half and put it away, my senses on high alert for Colin's reaction.

He takes his time responding, which torments me. He eats his sandwich and keeps his gaze on the distant mountains. Finally, still without looking at me, he quietly asks, "What did you mean when you said that Dad's been gone from you longer than ten months?"

I hunch forward, feeling like I've been punched. I have no memory of saying anything about my marriage, and hearing that I did is worse than everything I do remember. Never in a million years would I choose to say anything of the sort to Colin. The fact that I did makes me want to rip out my own tongue.

The silence stretches between us, and I know he is waiting for an answer. The walls he built between us overnight are only growing taller. But what do I tell him? The truth about Adam's affair? That wouldn't be fair to Adam or Colin. So, a lie? What lie could possibly explain away something as huge as saying that my marriage died long before my husband did? And wouldn't lying risk wrecking our relationship even more?

I swallow and then force a lightness to my voice that I don't feel. "I'm surprised to hear that I said that." I keep my gaze on the pebbles at my feet. "I wish I could say that it's not true, but I don't want to lie to you. Your dad and I . . . well, we were having some problems in our marriage."

I glance quickly at Colin to see how he's taking that news, but he's looking down at the ground and I can't see his face. I go on. "Just know that we both love you very much and neither of us wanted our problems to affect you at all."

Colin doesn't say anything for a long moment, and then he balls up the sandwich wrapper between his fists. "Did you have an affair? Did you kiss another man like you did Jorgen last night?"

"What? No!" I slam my lips shut before the fact that it was Adam who cheated slips out. "I loved your dad and wanted only him for the rest of my life. We just . . . had some issues to work through. Marriage is hard work." It's true that I wanted Adam, even after I'd learned about his affair. I begged him not to leave me in hopes that we could work on our relationship and he'd fall in love with me again. I used the excuse that we shouldn't disrupt Colin's last few years at home with a divorce. Adam agreed to wait until Colin graduated high school, and that's why he spent the last three years sneaking around, both of us lying to Colin that it was Adam's work keeping him away for longer periods of time.

All for nothing, as it turned out. He didn't love me anymore.

Colin seems to be thinking this through, so I don't push him, and instead sit quietly beside him, listening to the wind blow through the grasses.

Colin's voice is timid when he next speaks. "So, you and Jorgen. Are you, like, dating now?"

I feel my face burn as I shake my head. "No, we're not. We were both drinking too much, and we got caught up in the moment. It shouldn't have happened, and certainly not in front of all of you. I'm so sorry that it did happen and that I embarrassed you."

His eyes rake my face as he thinks about this, then he looks away. Shuffling his feet in the dirt, he admits, "I understand that you must be pretty lonely without Dad. I shouldn't have made such a big deal about it. I guess I just forgot that you are anything but my mom." His mouth twists into a wry smile, and all traces of anger disappear.

I smile back and wrap my arm around his shoulders. "I'll always be your mom first and everything else second. And for the record, you can make a big deal about anything that upsets you."

He does a little shrugging motion like the words embarrass him but also make him feel great at the same time. My worry evaporates and my nerves calm. Maybe we're going to be okay after all.

"I'll apologize to the group when we see them later—if we see them." I pause. "Are they all stopping in Kinlochleven tonight like we are?"

My arm drops as Colin turns to stuff trash into his pack. "Yeah. I'm not sure about Grant and Peter, but the others plan to stay at the MacDonald Hotel campsite. Our B and B isn't far from there."

"Okay, good." I force a lightness into my voice even though the thought of seeing the others—seeing Jorgen—makes my stomach flip. "I'm glad we'll see them. Ready to get moving?"

Colin nods and hoists his pack. He seems preoccupied, and I wonder if he's nervous about meeting up with Kirsten later. Or if it's me and Jorgen that he's nervous about.

Not even a hundred yards down the path, Colin abruptly stops and spins around to face me. My heart starts ramming my chest. "Colin?"

"Mom . . ." He stops and shakes his head, then shoves a hand through his hair. With a loud sigh, he says, "I've gotta ask you something."

"Okay."

He looks away, uncomfortable. "I saw how often Dad was gone, supposedly for work, and how you always seemed a little sad or angry, but then he would come home, and you'd go back to being normal and I let it go. Until it happened again and again." He pauses, his gaze searching deep inside my soul. "Were you getting divorced?"

I want to deny it. I want so badly to keep up the lie. But standing here now, studying my boy's face, I wonder if I should come clean. There are shadows in his eyes. His lips are firmly set as though he is steeling himself for a blow. His skin is so pale I see the smattering of freckles across his nose that usually only appear when he has a sunburn. I see the little boy inside him, who is afraid and needs reassurance. But I also see a layer of something deeper. An adult strength that he will be able to take whatever I might tell him.

If I'm not honest with him now, he'll know. More lies will drive a wedge between us.

I cannot leave him in another country with this unresolved. Emotional distance will only grow wider with physical distance.

I slide my gaze over the faraway mountain peaks as I decide what to do. From the corner of my eye, I see Colin's head and shoulders drop in disappointment, and I realize he thinks I'm refusing to answer his question. I look down at my feet and hope I don't blunder this. Then I admit, "Yeah, Colin. We talked about divorcing. I thought I was protecting you by keeping that from you."

He silently nods and seems to be thinking this through. "Thanks for telling me." He heads down the trail, leaving me with my mouth open. Doesn't he want to talk about this more?

But no. Clearly he wants to be left alone with his thoughts, and I need to give him space to process all that I just told him.

Damn you, Adam, for causing all this pain.

With heavy feet, I follow my boy to Kinlochleven.

◆

The town of Kinlochleven feels serene. It lies in a bowl at the end of a fjord with a single road leading out of town alongside the sea loch.

There is little traffic, with only locals and a few tourists in town to visit the ice-climbing center inside the old aluminium smelter.

The River Leven flows right through town, and as Colin and I walk across the bridge on our way to dinner, I spot two kayakers taking on the mild rapids. We stop to watch them. The river itself looks dark and foreboding, with white surf outlining jagged black rocks. Each bank is thick with bushes and trees in all shades of green. The whole valley is green and lush with trees, mosses, and ferns. It feels like an enchanted grotto where I wouldn't be surprised to encounter a dragon or a unicorn.

I fill my lungs with the moist air in an effort to soothe my frazzled nerves. The closer we get to the hotel where we are meeting the others for dinner, the more I feel myself slipping into a shame spiral. What am I going to say to the them? To Jorgen? Is he as embarrassed by our public kiss as I am? He kissed me back, after all. But maybe he was just being polite and hadn't wanted to hurt my feelings by pushing me away.

I really don't want to see any of them.

But Colin does want to. So I'll go and face the music.

We follow signs to the Bothy Bar in the back of the hotel and see our group on the deck outside, gathered around two whisky barrels that serve as tables. Colin tells me his order, then he slips out the sliding door and sits next to Kirsten. Their heads immediately tilt toward one another.

I place our order at the bar and then carry our drinks—only soda for me—outside.

"There she is!" Peter hollers the moment I step through the sliding glass door. "Now the group is complete."

I see Colin's body stiffen. His eyes meet mine briefly, and then they slide toward the other end of the table. I follow his gaze and feel myself blush when I see Jorgen getting to his feet to greet me. I awkwardly step up to him and accept his kisses on my cheeks before taking the only empty stool right beside him.

"*Och*, Keaka, tell me." Grant props his forearms on his crossed knees and leans toward me. The intense expression on his whiskered face reignites my nerves, and my mind races with all the possible questions he might ask me. "Were ya feelin' peely-wally this morning as much as I suspect? Because my heid was sair aff, I can tell ya that." He winks, and I know it's to tell me there is no judgment coming from him. Then he lifts his whisky glass into the air. *"Slàinte!"* He tosses back his drink as though to say headache or not, he plans to drink just as much tonight.

Spontaneously, everyone at the table lifts their glasses and calls out a toast.

"Cheers!"

"Skål!"

"Prost!"

I laugh and add my own. "Kāmau!"

Terese smiles shyly. "I have not heard that one. What language is that?"

"Hawaiian." I smile at her and silently beg her not to hate me for kissing her father. "I'm American, but my ancestry is half Hawaiian and half Japanese. My grandmother still lives on the Big Island of Hawaii."

"Tell me of Hawaii. I have seen it in movies and would like to visit someday." Terese had revealed herself in earlier conversations to have a hunger to see the world, so this does not surprise me in the slightest. I finally relax as I tell her about the islands and answer all the questions the teenager asks, enjoying talking about a place that is so close to my heart.

"Who's having the vegan burger?"

I look up to find a server holding my dinner and looking impatient, as though he's asked more than once. I shoot him a smile of apology. "Right here."

Since empty plates are stacked in front of the Danes and the others are halfway through their meals, I don't hesitate to dig in, only now realizing how starved I am. As I eat, conversation turns to today's walk, and I find myself looking out at the water. The view is stunning. Loch

Leven stretches to the west, where the setting sun casts a red glow over the steep-sided mountains on either side. In the distance I see a pointy-topped green mountain that looks too perfect to be real, yet it is. The whole view reminds me of pictures I've seen of China, or Middle-earth, and I have to take out my cell phone to take a photo right now, before the light changes.

I get up from my seat to go closer to the railing so that nothing but the loch and mountains will be in the shot.

After a moment, Jorgen joins me and rests his hands on the wooden railing. "It is very beautiful here."

I'm suddenly nervous again. "Yes, very beautiful."

"They say that is called 'the Pap of Glencoe.'" He must see my confusion, because he steps closer to me and points at the knob-topped mountain I had just been admiring. "That one there."

I smell his cologne, and my blood pounds in my ears. I have to swallow before I'm able to speak. "Look, Jorgen, I need to apologize about last night. I shouldn't have kissed you. It was inappropriate and I'm terribly embarrassed." I look away from him back to the water.

He pats the hand still clutching my cell phone. "Take heart, my friend. You have made my Scotland adventure quite enjoyable, and I do not regret anything."

I search his face, looking for clues to the meaning behind his words. Was his choice of the word *friend* intentional, meaning he wants only that from me? Or does him saying he has no regrets mean that he enjoyed kissing me and wants to do it again?

"Jorgen, I . . ." I stop, having no idea how to finish that sentence. I have no idea what *I* want from *him*.

He must see my discomfort and confusion, because he smiles kindly. A memory of the feel of that mouth on mine makes my heart stutter. "You and Colin have become treasured friends to me and my girls, and I hope that we all can stay in touch once we return to our home countries."

Ah, so we are in the friend zone. Okay. I realize that I'm relieved. Relaxing, I place my hand on his arm and give a brief squeeze before dropping it to my side. "I'd like that. And I think Colin and Kirsten will be making plans to see one another again very soon." I nod toward the kids, who are whispering to each other. From where we stand, I can see that the two have their knees pressed together like they can't stand to be near one another and not touch.

"Ah, young love. Nothing else burns quite so bright, does it?"

A deep yearning sparks to life inside me. Do old people like me feel the giddy excitement of a new relationship? I hope I get the chance to find out one day.

I watch Colin a moment longer and suddenly feel melancholy. My baby is all grown up. I'm sad that I won't see him every day, but I'm so excited for all the experiences he has ahead of him. He's going to break hearts and have his broken in return, he's going to take leaps and suffer falls, he's going to discover parts of himself he didn't know existed . . . and I'll get to watch it all from the sidelines.

Adam won't get to see any of it. Our beautiful boy has so much in front of him, and Adam is missing it all. Tears spring to my eyes, and I have to blink several times to keep them from falling. Jorgen notices but does not comment, for which I'm grateful.

When we return to our seats, we find the Scots and Clara discussing other long-distance walking trails in Europe. Terese is clinging to their every word.

"The Tour du Mont Blanc is nice," Clara is saying. "I think you would enjoy the challenge but also the stunning mountains."

"How long is that yin?" Peter seems more interested than Grant, but he is the more fit of the two, which likely explains his interest.

"One hundred seventy kilometers, which is . . ." She pauses as she calculates it in her head. "One hundred five miles. It takes you through the Alps of France, Italy, and Switzerland."

Grant seems put off. "What aboot walks in Germany? What are some choices there?"

Clara sips her beer. "I've done the King Ludwig Way in Bavaria, which is one hundred fifteen kilometers—er, roughly seventy-two miles. You would like it for all the historic towns along the way with pubs for a beer and *brezel*."

Grant seems to like the sound of this walk, but before he can comment, Clara goes on. "Or there's the Moselsteig, which follows the Moselle River through Germany's oldest wine-growing region. It is three hundred sixty-five kilometers, but you could easily choose to do only a section of it if you like and stop often, of course, at the wineries."

I don't join their conversation, but I do listen with interest. I had no idea there were so many established long-distance walking trails. All I've ever heard of were those in the States like the Pacific Crest Trail or the Appalachian Trail, which are for hardcore backpackers. But, listening to the group talk, it sounds like there are numerous other trails like the West Highland Way where walkers can sleep in a bed each night and have a shower and hot meal every day. I've never been interested in backpacking, especially not at my age, but doing it this way, the glamping version of hiking, is something I can see myself doing more. I tuck the names of the hikes they list into my mind for future reference.

A smile spreads across my face that I don't bother to hide. Who is this woman I am becoming? I like her.

Colin catches my eye, and he gives me a sad smile. His gaze slides to the left, toward Jorgen, then back to me before dropping to the beer on the table in front of him. Kirsten shoots me a pitying smile, and I know that Colin has told her everything.

Soon the golden hour fades into twilight, and I feel my energy fade with it. Colin isn't ready to go yet, so I limp back to the B and B alone. Tomorrow will be our last day on the trail, and before I know it, I'll be on an airplane flying home without Colin.

Is it my imagination, or is our relationship still strained, even after our talk today? Did I, by admitting that we lied for years to him, make Colin feel like he can't trust me anymore?

Even though we can talk every day by phone if we want to, I can't help but feel like the clock is ticking. I have only one day left to ensure Colin and I are solid before we become separated by half a planet.

I wish the West Highland Way would never end.

CHAPTER TWENTY-FIVE

Sorcha

Somewhere between Loch Laomainn and Glaschu

Despite the meat pies they ate last night, Aonghas awoke hungry and Sorcha, too, found her mind constantly thinking back to the warm gravy wrapped in flaky pastry. The bitter vetch tubers that Sorcha gnawed on to quiet her hunger pains did not come close to the satisfaction of the peas, carrots, and meat they'd eaten.

Walking was slow today, as they again stayed off the roads. Hours later, as the sun neared its highest point in the sky, they came upon a whisky still hidden among the bushes beside a burn. Most passersby would not recognize it as such, but Sorcha knew the signs—the thread of smoke curling up from what seemed to be the side of a bracken-covered hill, the narrow path worn in the ground beside the stream. The subtly sour scent of the mash. As the taxes imposed by the English on the Scots were so unfair, and unsanctioned stills were illegal, Sorcha knew the owners of this still were hoping to keep it hidden. Which also meant someone was sure to be nearby guarding the still and could appear at any moment wielding a blade.

She motioned for Aonghas to stay quiet, and they moved past the site as quickly as possible.

As they continued south along the fertile strath, they spotted several farms, cottages, and even a small village. Unlike yesterday, when the wide-open strath made her feel exposed, today Sorcha felt like she and Aonghas were only two of the many people traveling along the path, heading south. It confirmed what she had been suspecting all along: that in an area more heavily settled, they would be able to blend in, become lost in the crowd.

The day felt unseasonably warm, or perhaps it was typical this far south. Sorcha had never in her life set foot outside of the Highlands, and she didn't know what was normal down here. Aonghas had long ago shed his wool vest, which he rolled into his *plaide* and carried under one arm. Sweat darkened the underarms of his linen shirt. She had her own *plaide* tied around her waist and wished she could remove her short jacket or even roll up the sleeves to feel any errant breeze against her skin.

"That lochan would sure feel refreshing." Aonghas had been making comments such as this for the last quarter mile, from the moment he'd first spied the small loch.

She looked around, taking in the scattered cottages and farmhouses, well enough away that the inhabitants would not be able to identify them. "Go on, then."

Aonghas's face lit up with such joy she could do naught but laugh. He shoved his *plaide* into her arms and took off down the sloping hill, ripping off his shirt as he ran. At the shoreline he tugged off his shoes, then dropped the rest of his clothing on top of them before running naked into the cool water and diving under.

Sorcha followed more slowly and sat down under the trees. As she waited for Aonghas, she drew out her knife to carve her symbol in the nearest stone, more by habit now than to lead their way back home.

While carving, she listened to Aonghas's splashes and let the memories come to her of all the times she swam in lochs and lochans as a girl. One time, she and her Tàm had swum together, naked as the days they were born. Even now, all these years later, she could remember the feel of the cold water sliding over her bare skin, deliciously caressing her like a lover. But then Tàm's hands, warm and calloused, had slid along her body, and she'd no longer felt the cold.

What she would give to have his hands here now, to hold her and to protect her. Tàm would have known what to do. He would have seen them safe and well out of this dangerous mess they were in.

Would he tell her she was doing the right thing in taking Aonghas to Glaschu rather than turning themselves over to the authorities? He'd been an honest man, never once lying or having a negative word for anyone. If he were here, would he commend her for protecting their son or scold her for running from their crime?

He was not here, and she only had herself and Aonghas to rely on now.

Where was Aonghas? The surface of the loch was smooth. No ripples or bubbles showed where he might be.

Worried, she put her knife away and pushed to her feet, stepping closer to the water. Her heart pounded painfully as she scanned the entire lochan.

Suddenly, he burst out with a howl of delight, then he threw his body back into the water like a fish resisting a line. He soon popped back up again with another whoop.

"Aonghas! *Ist!*" All his calling and cavorting would bring the locals from their cottages and fields. They were trying to pass through here undetected, but Aonghas's antics were going to see them caught.

Chastened, he pressed his lips together and slid backward until only his nose and eyes were above the surface. Comically, he moved his eyes back and forth like a kelpie waiting to devour unsuspecting prey.

She laughed out loud, for she could not help herself. Oh, how she loved this boy! "Come now, Aonghas. We must away."

She shook out his *plaide* and handed it to him to dry off, her arms aching with the memory of all the times she'd wrapped a cloth around her babies after a bath, their tiny bodies squirming to get away. She'd always hugged them tight and planted a kiss on top of their sweet-smelling heads before releasing them to run naked through the cottage. Aonghas was long past the days of needing his mother to help him bathe, and the knowledge saddened her. Had she enjoyed that last bath time? Or had her mind been on all the other chores awaiting her, the cow to milk, the butter to churn, the grain to grind, the wool to spin, the plants to collect to dye the wool? The chores would always be there, she knew well enough, but her babies had all gone—to heaven, to adulthood.

Would Aonghas live long enough to provide her with a grandchild someday? Would she ever hold a baby again? No one had warned her the yearning was a physical pain in her body.

"Coming, Ma?"

She blinked and found Aonghas well up the slope, fully dressed and ready to resume their walk.

She sighed. "I'm coming."

They walked across fields and through woods, following a meandering river she wished she knew the name of. She wished she knew where they were, how much farther they needed to go to reach Glaschu.

From here, she could see no mountains at all, only hills, which left her feeling unnerved in a way she'd never felt. How did people who lived in these parts find their way when the land stretched far and flat? How did they feel alive without the burning of their lungs and legs as they climbed higher and higher? How did they feel close to God without ever standing on top of a mountain and seeing all his creation before them, all the lives tucked into the folds that were the glens and straths where water flowed?

She could not understand this landscape, which meant she would not understand the people living here.

But she was going to have to try. This was to be her new life.

"Aonghas, we shall stop for the night here." She knew he wondered why she wanted to stop when the sun had not yet set, so she pointed across the river to the farmhouses tucked against a slope on the other side of a grassy field. "I'm noticing more and more settlements, closer together. I think we're nearing a town, and I don't want to be caught without a safe place to sleep."

He dropped his *plaide* roll onto the ground near a moss-covered stone. They dared not light a fire and risk someone coming to investigate. For supper they ate wild garlic, dandelions, and red clover. As night fell over this strange land, Sorcha fell asleep feeling nervous about what tomorrow might bring.

CHAPTER TWENTY-SIX

Keaka

Day seven; Kinlochleven

The morning of our last day hiking arrives drizzly and cool, which renews my energy as though I'm no different from the grasses, ferns, and mosses that thrive in the damp. Colin is still quiet, and I'm trying to allow him the space he needs.

We pack up our stuff and thank our host for the filling breakfast and sack lunches she made for us, then we head for the trail.

The steep ascent through a birchwood warms my body quickly, but I wait until we reach a break in the trees before I stop to remove my fleece jacket. Colin notices and pauses on the side of the trail. After I've tied my jacket around my waist, I join him at the edge, where he is admiring the view, and as my gaze takes in the misty loch stretching narrow and long toward the sea and the vibrantly green mountains all around, I feel the deep fullness of gratitude. "Thank you for bringing me here, Colin." He doesn't look my way. "This place is truly special, and I'm honored to have shared it with you."

"We still have sixteen miles to walk today. You might not feel so happy about it in a few hours." He takes some photos of the view.

I keep my eyes on him, my gaze tracing the contours of his face. The stubble on his chin from having not shaved this morning; the arch of his eyebrows, which always reminds me of Adam; the leanness of his cheeks that were once so round and smooth . . . I imprint all of him into my mind so that I won't forget the smallest detail when we are separated by an ocean and a continent. Even if he forgives me for lying to him for years, things between us will change simply from living so far away from each other. I try to tell myself that it'll be okay. Our relationship will change and be different, and that is normal. That is healthy.

I watch the hair above his ear flutter in the breeze and think back to his first haircut, when he'd sat in a chair shaped like an airplane and was so distracted by the buttons and knobs that he hadn't noticed what was happening until he was turned to face the mirror at the end. "Just like Dada!" he'd exclaimed, touching his hair in wonder.

Now look at him. My little boy, all grown up into a bright, caring man. Like his dada. Tears sting my eyes.

"Whose idea was it?"

I blink to clear my eyes, but even then I'm not sure what he's asking. "What?"

Colin finally looks straight at me, and I'm staring at a carefully placed, emotionless mask. "Was it you or Dad who thought lying to me would be a good idea?"

My heart drops into my stomach. I swallow. I open my mouth, but then close it again. I'm struggling to find the right words.

His eyes narrow. "Don't even think about lying again."

My breath catches. That's exactly what I was about to do. I am so desperate to salvage our relationship that I almost lied again to protect myself.

I look toward the loch once more, but I don't see it. What do I tell him? For so long my purpose had been to protect him from the truth, and now I'm still trying to protect him. But am I? Is it only myself I'm protecting now?

I can't lie to him anymore. I'm about to leave him in a foreign country, and if there is anything between us, even one tiny white lie, it will grow and fester and tarnish our precarious relationship. I lift my chin and meet his gaze, determined to be an open book. "Mine. It was my idea to keep the truth from you."

His jaw clenches and he gives a quick nod as if to confirm what he suspected all along. He opens his mouth as though to say something but then clamps it shut again and shakes his head. Then, with a roll of his eyes, he spins around to walk away from me—

—and steps right off the lip of the trail and slips down the steep, grassy slope.

"Colin!" I reach out to catch him, to no avail.

He falls hard onto his rump, but his slide is arrested by clumps of stiff grass. He tosses back his head and lets loose a belly laugh.

"Colin Angus Denney, you scared me!" I reach out my hand to help him up, but a wave of dizziness overcomes me, and I hear an echo of my own voice bouncing over the hillside—not his full name, just the middle. *Angus, Angus, Angus!*

I squeeze my eyes tightly closed until the vertigo fades. When I open them, Colin is clambering back to his feet and wiping dirt off his backside. "Are you okay?"

His face has lost its protective mask, and he laughs again at his fall. "Only my ego is bruised."

"I'm glad that's all that was." I smile at him, and he allows himself a small smile in return, which does much to soothe my aching soul.

Without another word, he leads the way up the rest of the climb, and I follow, just as silent. At the top the path joins a single-lane gravel road, and we find ourselves looking down a wide, treeless valley that stretches far into the distance. Informational and caution signs beside the road identify the area as belonging to the *Allt Nathrach Hydro Scheme*.

"Scheme?" I wonder aloud. "They admit to sneaky practices right in their business names?"

Colin barks out a laugh. "No, Mom, it's not like that. In Britain, a *scheme* is a program or project. The word doesn't have the devious connotations it does in the States."

I laugh, too, happy that my ignorance has lightened the mood between us. "I was totally picturing men twirling their mustaches and chuckling together, 'We'll show them! Ha ha ha!'"

Colin joins in by rubbing his hands together as, altering his voice to sound like a cartoon villain, he says, "They think we're providing them water, but really we're going to take it. All of it!" He throws back his head and gives an evil laugh that sends us both into fits of giggles. It's not a lot, but I'm encouraged that we'll get back to the closeness we had before.

For the next several hours we walk through the sweeping valley past ruins and burns and recently felled forests. Mostly we walk in silence, and I can't tell if that's because Colin is still sad, or even angry with me, or if he's simply lost in his thoughts. Either way, I respect his silence and trust that he'll talk to me when he's ready.

The rain stops, but the wind kicks up and blows icy cold right through the fleece jacket I put back on, and I eventually have to also add my rain jacket, which acts as a windbreaker.

I'm loving the landscape out here, and remember with irony that I used to think Scotland's bare hills were ugly. We pass a couple of stone ruins along the path and stop each time to poke through the structures, wondering aloud about the people who once lived here and why they'd left. For some reason, I keep expecting to find cattle around every bend, but am always disappointed to see no animals at all. Other than the other walkers scattered along the trail, no other signs of human life can be seen. I feel like I'm in the famed wilds of Scotland. I love it. All of it. I love knowing I am seeing areas that all the tourists in their cars and camper vans are missing. I love that my own two—aching—feet have brought me here and will carry me to civilization tonight. That fact makes me feel strong and capable in a way I've never really felt before.

A cairn appears in the middle of nowhere with a sign saying that it was built to replace a stone set on this spot in February 1645 by the MacDonalds to mark where they broke off their pursuit of the Campbells after the Battle of Inverlochy. Colin loves this, of course, but so do I. After reading the story on the sign, I can imagine kilted warriors running through this very valley, bloodied and wounded from battle, eager to reach safety.

When we see a lake in the distance, I ask Colin if he knows the name of it. He scowls and averts his eyes from me. "No. The guidebook would tell us, if we had it. I think it's the one Dad told me had a crannog that King Macbeth lived on for a time."

"Crannog?"

"Yeah, an artificial island built by prehistoric people. Remember when Dad and I read *Macbeth* when I was only, like, twelve?"

"I do. It gave you nightmares."

Colin laughs, though it's tinged with sorrow. "Yeah. And I still struggle to keep straight what really happened to the Scottish king as opposed to what Shakespeare made up."

"Maybe you'll study him at the university."

"Yeah, maybe." He falls silent after this and seems deep in thought about something.

Something he said a minute ago sticks in my mind, and I have to bring it up. "Um, Colin? I'm really sorry about losing your guidebook."

He shrugs and keeps walking. "It's fine. I don't really want anything of Dad's with me right now, anyway."

I grab his arm to force him to stop and look at me. "Why? Because he didn't tell you about the divorce? It was my idea to keep it from you, Colin, not his."

Colin nods but keeps his face averted. "Yeah, but I think you still loved him." He looks straight at me. "You did, didn't you? It wasn't you who wanted the divorce was it? Did he have someone else on the side?"

I drop my chin to my chest and squeeze my eyes closed. This is exactly what I've been working so hard not to tell him. As angry as I am at Adam, as hurt as I was by him, I never wanted his and Colin's relationship to be marred. I never wanted to put that on our boy.

I must be taking too long to reply, because Colin suddenly grunts. "That's what I thought."

He turns to continue walking, but I grab his arm again. "Colin, stop. You don't know what happened between the two of us, and it doesn't matter now anyway. Your dad loved you so much. I love you so much. Don't let anything that might or might not have happened change how you feel about him. Think about all the good times you had together. Remember all the times he was there for you when you needed him, and even when you didn't."

He opens his mouth to say something, but then he clamps it shut and gives me a nod before turning back to the trail. I let him go.

I don't push him to talk, and we spend the next half mile or so in silence. My stomach, though, soon demands attention. "Can we stop for lunch?"

"Yeah, I'm hungry, too. Let's find a place on that hill up here to sit."

We find a grassy ledge on a small hill just to the side of the trail with a view back toward the lochan and, in the other direction, to the awesome Ben Nevis, whose top is obscured by clouds. Below us, to the north, I can see fields and a handful of farmhouses.

"That's really the UK's highest mountain?" I take a bite of my vegetarian ploughman's sandwich and think about the mountains at home near Portland. "How does it compare to Mount Hood?"

"Mount Hood is over eleven thousand feet. Ben Nevis is only something like four and a half thousand." He crunches into an apple, and juice runs down his chin.

I hand him a napkin. "We don't have to climb it, do we?" I doubt my legs will last if I do have to go over it, no matter how much I'm enjoying the hiking now.

Colin laughs. "A lot of people do include it in their West Highland Way journey, but no, the official trail does not summit Ben Nevis."

"I'm relieved to hear it." Then, after seeing him staring at the hulking gray mountain, I say, "You want to climb it, don't you?"

He just shrugs. "Yeah, someday. Don't worry, I won't drag you up it."

A part of me feels sad hearing that, and I have to sit for a moment to figure out why. I really don't want to climb a four-thousand-foot mountain today, or even tomorrow. But next week or next summer, after my body has rested from this trek? Sure. Why not? I've already proven to myself this week that I can do hard things and, more importantly, that I love having adventures with Colin.

Is that it? Am I sad that he will have that adventure without me?

A certain knowing settles into my gut. Yes, that's it exactly. I want this to be our thing now. The thing Colin and I share. But we found it too late. He'll be going off having most of his adventures without me, and that saddens me.

Maybe we could plan another hike together for next summer. Maybe even Ben Nevis. I clear my throat. "Did you and Dad plan to climb Ben Nevis if he had done this walk with you?"

Why? Why did you ask that? I want to drag the words back into my mouth and swallow them away.

Colin shoots me a glance but quickly turns back toward the mountain. "Yeah, we talked about it but never said for sure that we would."

I stare at the mountain, too. "Now that we're only a few miles away from the finish, did it go okay for you? I mean, did you have fun this week?" I suddenly feel very vulnerable, so I hide my face by looking down at the remains of my lunch in my lap.

"What? Yes, of course, Mom. Well, except for the last day or so, but that has nothing to do with the trail."

We sit in silence as we finish eating and watch the other hikers as they pass. I want to hang on to this moment for as long as I can because once we finish this hike, we'll be too close to our final goodbye.

"I get it, Mom," he says, startling me from my thoughts. I look at him and see him resting his chin on his crossed arms. "I understand why you lied to me, and I'm not mad about it anymore."

"Thanks, buddy. That means a lot to me."

He nods and gives me a sad smile, then he straightens his legs and reaches for his backpack. "What do you say? Should we finish this thing?"

I look at the trail as it winds toward Ben Nevis, then I nod. "Let's do this."

We stiffly and clumsily get to our feet, our muscles and joints having tightened from sitting so long. When we have our packs on and are about to start walking, I put a hand on his arm. "I sure do love you, Colin."

His smile is indulgent as he opens his arms, inviting me in for a hug. Tears sting my eyes as I hug him as hard as our awkward packs allow, so grateful that he is allowing me this. "I love you so much."

"Me too."

I smile through my tears. He rarely says the word *love*, but that's okay. I know he feels it.

We get back on the trail and walk mostly in silence for the next few miles. When we reach a sign with information about an Iron Age hill fort up a side trail, Colin convinces me to go see it, even though my feet and legs feel swollen and achy. When we reach the top of the hill and find nothing but a wide, grassy bowl, I am at first disappointed. But then we walk to the lip of the bowl and peer down into Glen Nevis, the valley separating the mountain we're standing on from Ben Nevis only a short distance away.

The mountain drops sharply below me, and the view captivates me.

In every direction, I see vivid greens made richer by the gray sky and gray rocks jutting from the tops of the mountains. Wind whips my hair across my face and pushes at my backpack, making me feel like it's going to blow me over the edge and down thousands of feet to the valley below. Moving carefully along the rim, Colin and I take selfies together with the moody, misty, green mountains behind us and again in the opposite direction, northward toward Fort William and the end of our hike.

I'm turning toward the trail to head down when Colin stops me. "Wait, Mom, there's something I want to do here."

I give him my full attention and see that he's nervous. His throat is convulsing like he's swallowing a lot, and his hands are fidgeting on the straps of his pack. His eyes meet mine, then dash away, then return again. "I, um, I did something you might not like."

Everything inside me freezes. Now what? "Okay. What did you do?"

CHAPTER TWENTY-SEVEN

Sorcha

Glaschu (Glasgow)

The shocking sights came quickly the next day, starting with the village they walked through that had an enormous building made of red stones. When Aonghas inquired of a townsperson if this was Glaschu, the man had laughed and told him that it was the village of Muileann-Gaidh. Sorcha had never known a village to hold such towering buildings. She counted windows going three high and at least a dozen long, and imagined being inside would feel like being inside a mountain.

She'd been glad to put that village behind them even though the man had told them that the river flowing through the village would lead them to Glaschu by nightfall. It was the city they needed to go to in order to disappear, but she dreaded it.

They followed the river until late in the afternoon, and they kept following it even after they could see more mountainous buildings, black with smoke and soot, across the fields. When the river dumped into a larger, wider one and they could go no farther, they considered sleeping among the trees but decided they would be safest in the city, where they would be just two among thousands, no matter how frightened the prospect made Sorcha feel.

The first thing she noticed as they drew near was the immensity of the buildings. It was as though the behemoth in Muileann-Gaidh had been reproduced here, over and over and over again, with variation in the color of stone, the shape and number of windows, and ornamentation. She could not tell where one building ended and the next started, as they flowed one to the next, stretching down the street as far as she could see.

And the smell! She had known the city would not smell like the fresh crops and fertile soil of home, but she'd not expected all the human waste, animal waste, tobacco smoke, and acrid stenches billowing from various buildings that made her wonder what could possibly be being produced inside.

But this was going to be their new home, so Sorcha marched forward, unsure of where she was going but knowing the answers lay ahead.

"What do you suppose that tastes like?" Aonghas's voice came from behind her. When she looked back, she found him peering through a storefront glass at more meat than she'd ever seen in one place.

"It hasn't been that long since you ate meat," she reminded him. "Remember the pies?"

"No, I mean that meat." He pointed to meat shaped into squares and displayed one leaning against another.

Just then, a man pushed Aonghas roughly aside so he could enter the shop, but not before he glared at them both and snapped an insult at them. They could not understand the words, but they understood their meaning. They were not wanted here. This man hated them without knowing them.

Sorcha pulled Aonghas's sleeve to get him moving again. This time, as they walked deeper into the city, she was not noticing the buildings or the smells, but the way people looked down their noses at them. When she asked a kindly looking woman for a place to sleep, the woman spit at Sorcha and shouted something that could only have been a command to speak English.

By the time the sun disappeared behind the towering buildings, Sorcha gave up looking for help, for the scene with the woman repeated three more times, leaving Sorcha shaking.

They slept in the only green space they could find, doing their best to hide in the shrubbery.

The growl of Aonghas's stomach woke Sorcha early the next morning, and she knew then what she had to do. Her son needed food—they had not eaten at all yesterday—and she still had in her possession one item that might be worth some coins.

She lay for a minute longer in the early-morning fog that blanketed the grass and made her feel safe, unseen. Carefully unclasping her betrothal brooch from her skirt where she always fastened it when it was not holding her *plaide* closed, she rubbed her fingers over the silver and let her tears fall.

The brooch was her last physical connection with her husband. It had been her only remaining possession that Tàm had once touched. It represented his love for her and his lifelong commitment to her. It had belonged to Tàm's mother, and her mother before her, and was supposed to one day be given to Aonghas's bride. But Aonghas needed to eat today more than he needed a betrothal token for a mystery woman he did not yet know.

She ran her thumb over the circle of interwoven knots and then over the design in the middle with tiny roses, a symbol of the Jacobite cause. Then she blocked it from her sight by clamping her fingers around it, so tight the edges cut into her palm.

After Aonghas awoke and she told him her plan, they walked to the busy street nearby where most vendors and shops seemed to be located. Most people she approached ignored her outright; some scowled or responded in anger. But then she found a Gaelic-speaking man and his wife who she could finally communicate with. They helped her sell the brooch and buy a small satchel of food. They were not, however, able to help her find a safe place to live or work.

For the rest of the day, and the following two days after that, Sorcha and Aonghas wandered the streets of the city, looking for work and a place to live. They learned the names of streets and neighborhoods, and more importantly, they learned how to avoid the gangs of young men who lived on the streets and caused havoc wherever they went. They also learned to avoid members of the newly created Glaschu police force. At night they returned to their patch of bushes in the Green, where they slept.

On the third day their food was gone, and they were no better off than they'd been when they'd arrived.

"Maybe we should keep walking." Aonghas lay huddled on the ground under his *plaide*, trying, as they did every night, to think of where they might find work.

"Walk to where?" Sorcha wished her voice didn't sound so bitter, but she could not help it. "Dùn Èideann? How will there be any different than here? Lunnainn? Do you know how far away that is?"

Just then, she became aware of a woman standing over them, and Sorcha looked up at her, alarmed.

"No, no, do not be frightened; I only want to help." The woman spoke Gaelic and did not seem threatening. But her appearance did frighten Sorcha, for the woman was reed-thin under a gown that was cut low in the front in a way that told her this woman worked a scandalous trade in the company of men. "I've seen you here the last few nights. Do you need food? *Plaideachan?*"

Sorcha could not bring herself to speak to the fallen woman. When she noticed Aonghas staring up at her with blatant curiosity, Sorcha stretched her toes and gave him a poke so he would look away. The woman only nodded and then retreated.

The next night she was back, only this time she did not say a word. She simply handed Sorcha a loaf of bread and walked away.

The bread filled Sorcha with shame.

Two nights later, when she saw the woman walking past, Sorcha called to her, "Wait! Have you a moment?"

The woman stopped and regarded her with caution.

"Thank you for the bread. That was very kind of you."

The woman nodded and looked like she was about to walk away, but then her shoulders dropped and she said, "I'm Ealasaid. Who are you?"

They ended up talking for several minutes, until Ealasaid realized the time and had to hurry away. The next night she returned, but earlier, and Sorcha found she had a new friend in the younger woman. Two days later, Ealasaid invited Sorcha and Aonghas to live in her tenement flat with her and her two young daughters.

CHAPTER TWENTY-EIGHT

Keaka

Day seven; Dun Deardail Iron Age Fort

My heartbeat is louder in my ears than the whistling wind. What has Colin done?

He turns toward Glen Nevis. "Don't be mad, but I—well, I brought some of Dad's ashes with me." He rushes through the rest as though afraid I'm going to be angry. "I thought he'd want to be scattered on the trail, but I didn't find the right spot until now."

My first reaction is worry. There are probably laws against bringing cremation remains into a foreign country. "You carried him with you the whole way?"

Colin nods, his face red.

I give up the worry because what's done is done. I squeeze his biceps. "I think Dad would love that you hiked with him. I'm not mad. Really."

He relaxes, and a sad smile clears the remaining tension there. Without another word, he sets down his backpack and then carefully, so the wind doesn't rip it out of his hands, he digs out a plastic bag containing the gray coarse sand of my husband's remains.

Seeing them, an unexpected sob escapes my throat and hot tears sting my eyes. Despite how it ended, I loved Adam fiercely, and yes, even enduringly. I love him even now. And I miss the friend that he was to me through most of our years together.

"Colin, wait." I grab his wrist to keep him from opening the bag, and he looks at me in surprise. "Can I have a minute with him?"

Colin carefully transfers the bag to my hand, both of us conscious of the wind trying to snatch it from us. I cup my hands around the remains, and even though I know the bulk of him is still in the urn on my fireplace mantel at home, I feel Adam here with us today.

I clutch the bag to my chest and whisper, "I forgive you, Adam, and I apologize, too, for my part in breaking us. The best of you is standing beside me here on this mountain, and I promise to take care of him and guide him as you would've wanted." My throat convulses, and I can't go on until I take several breaths. I can't see anything through my tears. "Thank you for our life together, and thank you for our sweet boy. Now, go, be free in your beloved Scotland."

I turn to hand the bag to Colin, but I think of one more thing. With my hands cupped to my mouth, I whisper to Adam, "Oh, and you were right: Scotland is amazing."

Wherever he is, I know Adam is laughing at me right now, which makes me smile. He always loved when I admitted to being wrong about something.

Carefully, I place the bag into Colin's hands, and then, together, we walk to the edge. With one hand gripping the plastic so it doesn't go flying, Colin carefully unzips the bag, and then he lifts it into the air to release his father's ashes into the wind.

We watch them fly toward the glen and the mountain, and I feel at peace. Maybe the next time Colin comes home, I'll send the rest of Adam's ashes with him to scatter elsewhere in Scotland.

Colin turns the bag inside out to make sure all the ashes are gone, and then he carefully tucks it into his pocket. When he doesn't make any motion to turn away, I squeeze his biceps again. "I'll give you a minute with your dad."

I wait for him on the other side of the hill fort, near the stone trail.

Surprisingly, all my anger toward Adam is gone, like it was never there to begin with. Whether that is due to finally saying aloud what happened between us or to something else, like the magic of this hike, I cannot say. But our failed marriage is no longer eating away at me.

I feel different now. Lighter. Free.

When Colin finds me ten minutes later, he is smiling, and I can see he's also found peace with his father. For that, this long and difficult week was worth it.

As we return to the main trail, I feel incredulous that our walk is almost finished. For the last seven days my life was walk, eat, sleep, repeat, and I've come to love the simplicity of that. I'm walking on top of a mountain right now, but once I make it to the bottom, and a few miles farther into town, I will be done.

My body will welcome the rest tomorrow, but my mind and soul will feel something is missing.

I finally understand why people walk trails that are several hundred miles long all in one go. I would happily take a rest day or two, then get right back on the trail.

I'm contemplating all this when I see the boulder, and the carving on the side, low to the ground. Sorcha's flower-petal carving.

Colin doesn't notice me stop, and I let him go on. I trace the carving with my finger and am disappointed when no vision appears. I haven't seen Sorcha in a couple days, and I have no idea what that means.

I'm still thinking about her and her trail markers pointing to home when I catch up to Colin on the descending gravel forest road. "Random question for you," I begin. "Were any of the people who were evicted in the Clearances ever allowed to return home?"

"No, never. The Clearances changed the Highlands forever. Thousands emigrated and, of those that remained in Scotland, the potato famine of the 1840s killed hundreds more."

This news worries me, and I'm suddenly desperate to learn what happened to Sorcha. I'll look her up when I get to a computer.

As we're heading down the mountain, Colin reaches into his pocket and pulls out his cell phone to read a text. He smiles wide. "It's Kirsten. They're at the Glen Nevis Visitor Centre and say they can wait there for us if we want to walk to the finish together. What should I tell her?"

I can see by his expression that he wants nothing more, so I agree. "Sounds like fun. Tell her we'll be there soon."

Near the bottom of the mountain, way markers lead us off the forestry road and through a short section of mixed woodland, alongside a sheep pasture, and onto a paved sidewalk beside a two-lane road. Soon we see a sign pointing to the visitor center, so we follow it to a building with a gift shop and restrooms. The number of people milling around the grounds surprises me until I realize this is the starting point for the Ben Nevis climb.

Kirstin suddenly appears on the path as though she's been watching for us. Behind her, I see Jorgen stretched on the grass, his head resting on his pack. Terese sits cross-legged beside him, eating a candy bar.

"Can you believe we're almost finished?" Kirsten asks, her ponytail swinging. "It was a long week, and yet not long enough."

"I completely agree." Colin's fingers intertwine with Kirsten's as they walk. I trail behind.

After getting to his feet and greeting us, Jorgen says, "We weren't sure if you were in front of us or behind us today. I'm happy Kirsten decided to text Colin and find out. We didn't want to leave without saying goodbye to you both."

"Aren't you staying in Fort William tonight?" I drop my pack on the grass next to theirs and roll my shoulders to ease the kinks.

"No. We'll be on the 19:50 train to Edinburgh."

"Unless you three have other plans, want to have one last dinner together before you go?"

Jorgen tips his head toward Colin and Kirsten, who are still holding hands. "We'd all enjoy that." His warm smile assures me that he includes himself in that statement.

I use the restroom and emerge to find that Colin has zipped off the bottom of his convertible trousers. Only now do I realize how warm the afternoon feels with the mountains blocking the cold wind. I strip off my jackets and stuff them into my pack.

Once the five of us return to the trail, we learn it will be all pavement to the end point, and we grumble over the extra strain it puts on our battered feet.

The glen feels tranquil, despite the cars and camper vans passing by. Leafy trees and green grass give the area a rural feel, even though we're close to the second-largest town in the Highlands.

Colin makes us all stop at a huge round boulder perched just off the path and tells us that it, reportedly, spins around three times on an unknown but specific night of the year. "If you see it spinning," he says dramatically, "ask any three questions and you'll receive the answers."

Even though the stone is not spinning and the legend has nothing to do with wishes, all three teens walk around the stone and make a silent wish. With a little urging, Jorgen and I join in, and soon we're all laughing at our silliness. Even though I feel ridiculous making it, I desperately want my wish to come true. *I want Colin to be safe and happy in Scotland.* With his father's ashes floating in the air here, how could our wishes not come true?

I'm still laughing when I spot the flower-petal carving, and my heart stops. Sorcha was here. *Sorcha, you'll watch over Colin while he's in your country, won't you?* I place a palm flat to the cold stone, and then I silently turn away.

I'm surprised when Colin falls into step beside me. At my questioning look, he just shrugs. "I came here to walk the Way with you and I want to finish it with you, too."

My heart melts right out of my chest, so I sling an arm around my son's waist and give him a side hug. "Thanks, buddy." We bump awkwardly into each other, which makes us both laugh out loud.

We hear the hum of increased traffic and know we are nearing a busier road. I think back to all the hikers at the visitor center and nudge Colin's arm. "Are you sure you don't want to go back and climb Ben Nevis?"

"Naw, it's okay, Mom. I can come up some weekend and climb it."

As Colin answers, I feel the hairs on the back of my neck stand up as though we're being watched. I look back over my shoulder and find the road and sidewalk behind us completely deserted. In fact, no other soul is around except for the Danes, who are ahead and paying us no attention.

I must be imagining it. Returning to the conversation, I say, "Strange as it may sound, I might be a little envious that you'll get to climb it. I bet the view is breathtaking up there."

"I'll be sure to take pictures for you."

"Or maybe I'll fly back over next summer and we can climb it together." Colin's smile looks skeptical but he doesn't turn me down, so I tuck the idea away as a possibility.

The last mile is through the town, and my senses are overwhelmed by road traffic, people, and buildings. The Danes keep a quick pace, which Colin easily matches. I push my exhausted legs to keep up and feel the pain in my feet increase exponentially. They burn and feel swollen inside my boots, and my ankles now hurt as much as my knees and hips.

When we come to a small park with statues scattered about, I forget about my discomfort. The town of Fort William is different from the smaller towns we walked through along the Way. There's a certain energy to it. Like if I squint in just the right way and tilt my head just so, I might see the ghosts of old Highlanders walking past.

We're soon funneled onto a street paved with setts, with businesses lining both sides. As we walk, we take note of the various stores we want to come back to explore tomorrow before we catch the train. Colin is most excited about a whisky shop, and my interest is piqued by a bookstore.

Before I'm ready for it, I'm suddenly standing on top of a metal line set right into the stone pavers with the words WEST HIGHLAND WAY engraved into the stones on one side and the Gaelic equivalent—SLIGHE NA GÀIDHEALTACHD AN IAR—on the other. Stunned that I've done it, I can't seem to take another step. I really did it. Despite serious misgivings, I walked all ninety-six miles on my own two feet. Not only that, but I *enjoyed* it. That was probably the most shocking thing of all.

My eyes fill with tears, and I look for Colin through the blur.

I find him hugging Kirsten and high-fiving Jorgen and Terese. When he looks at me and sees how overcome with emotion I am, he laughs and pulls me into a hug. "I'm proud of you, Mom. We did it!"

I laugh through my tears. "Yes, we did! Woo-hoo!" The whoop makes everyone laugh, and then Jorgen and his daughters make a beeline for a statue off to the left, where they sit and copy the statue's pose—right ankle propped on left knee. Kirsten calls for Colin to take their picture.

I stand next to Colin as he takes their photo and explains for my benefit, "This is *Man with Sore Feet*. It's tradition to have your picture taken with him when you finish the Way." He hands the phone back to Kirsten, then immediately gives his own to her before smiling at me. "Now it's our turn."

Thrilled that I'll have a photo with him to remember this by, I sit in the prescribed pose and feel my muscles protest at the stretch. I plaster on a wide smile anyway and wait for Kirsten to take several photos of us. When she hands the phone back to Colin, I say, "Let's get one with all of us."

They readily agree, and Kirsten asks a passing stranger if he will be our photographer. When he kindly consents, Kirsten sits next to Colin, Jorgen sits down next to me, and Terese stands behind the statue. This time when I smile, I'm wishing our whole gang could be here with us, and I'm sad that I hadn't thought to get photos of any of them along the way.

But then a new and disturbing thought enters my mind. Does being finished with the hike mean I won't see Sorcha again? Will I have to return to the Drovers Inn to feel her spirit, or is she gone for good?

Of course she is gone, you idiot. The woman was alive in 1801. She's dead now. Whatever you saw might have been a weird anomaly of time and space but was probably just your own imagination.

Even though I know it's improbable, I still search the shadows behind every building and tree as we make our way to our B and B to drop our bags before meeting up again with the Danes for dinner.

I'm not ready to be finished with Sorcha. I still have questions for her, and worries about her and her son.

As for the West Highland Way, I may be done, but I suspect it's going to stay with me forever.

CHAPTER TWENTY-NINE

Sorcha

Eleven weeks later; 12 September 1801; Glaschu (Glasgow)

Even as the morning lightened, a waning moon lingered in the sliver of sky Sorcha could see between the tall, stone buildings of Gallowgate. Smoke and soot blanketed everything, and she could not make out if it was only smoke making the moon look hazy or if fog had rolled in during the night.

She turned to lug the bucket of water she'd filled at the pump up to the fourth-floor one-room flat she and her son shared with three other people. Sorcha and Aonghas slept on pallets on the floor, but neither minded. They were in from the cold, and safe.

Over the nearly three months since she and Aonghas had moved in with Ealasaid and her daughters, Ealasaid had slowly revealed her story to Sorcha, and it made Sorcha care for the woman more than she'd thought possible.

Ealasaid had grown up in Inverness, where she'd fallen in love with a man who told her he was bringing her to Glasgow to meet his family and to make her his wife. For three years he'd provided for her and visited her often, but he never introduced her to his family or friends, and he never married her, though he sired two children on her. And then, one unexpected day, another man knocked on her front door and ordered her off the premises. The man she'd thought would be her husband was married to someone else and was no longer paying rent on her flat.

Shame prevented Ealasaid from returning to her family in Inverness. She now worked most days as a washerwoman, and when that wasn't enough to feed her daughters and herself, she worked nights going to strange men's beds.

The way Ealasaid had told her that, with her chin raised high and only the slightest wavering of her voice, made Sorcha respect her and trust her, despite her sins.

When Ealasaid could not be home with her two young daughters, ages one and three, they were cared for by an older woman in the flat below theirs. Sorcha also helped as often as she could.

It was Ealasaid who'd found Sorcha a job at the washing house on the High Green.

Sorcha's days were long and backbreaking. Her hands were raw from the constant hot or frigid water, lye, and scrubbing. Even though the walk here had made her entire body ache, she would much rather still be walking than doing this work, which made her shoulders, elbows, and hands swell, her head feel as though it was too heavy for her neck to hold, and every muscle on the back of her body feel as though they were clenched in the fist of an angry demon.

But at least she was earning money, paltry amount though it was.

Sorcha entered the flat and found the two girls sitting sleepily on the bed they shared with their mother. Ealasaid tied the laces on the oldest one's shoes, and then, wishing Sorcha a good morning, she gathered her girls and disappeared down the stairs. Sorcha would be following soon to start her own shift. Aonghas stood at the window, eating a bowl of porridge. He didn't greet her, nor look her way.

Aonghas couldn't find work. He'd applied to several linen, cotton, and muslin warehouses, the pottery warehouse, even several grocers. He was turned away from all with claims of needing no help or derision for his being a Highlander. One calico printer had given him a job sweeping floors but had fired him the same day for, they'd claimed, not working quickly enough. Sorcha suspected it was actually because the manager had grown frustrated that Aonghas could not understand his English commands.

He'd given up on finding paying work and now spent his days wandering the city, which worried Sorcha greatly, for it put him at risk of catching the notice of the city police.

Sorcha also worried about the company Aonghas was keeping. She knew he'd met boys his age, but he wouldn't tell her what they spent their time doing, which told her all she needed to know. Late each night, he returned to their room and often silently set a gift into her hands before going outside to sit alone on the steps. These gifts were sometimes a hunk of bread, an apple, a sack of bere meal, a potato. One time it was a pair of shoes in her size.

He was most assuredly stealing these things, and she hated the danger that put him in. But they needed the food. She needed the shoes. Her pay was not enough for their survival. She'd hoped she'd be able to save money for their passage to America and a new life, but she couldn't see how that was possible.

She set the bucket down on the chest of drawers that held Ealasaid's belongings and also served as their work surface and eating table. Aonghas handed her a bowl of porridge, and she wrapped both hands around it, savoring the warmth. "Thank you, *a ghràidh*." He didn't reply.

The worst part of their new lives was that Aonghas never smiled anymore. Her ears ached to hear his laughter. He used to tell her stories of his day as they ate supper each night, but here their meals were in silence, Aonghas's only response to her questions a grunt or a sigh.

This life would not do. She had to think of something else, somewhere else to go.

Dùn Èideann? But how would that city be any different?

South to England? What would be the point? They would be pursued as outlaws no matter where they went. At least here in Glaschu they were invisible to the upper class.

She dreamed of a cottage by the sea in the Western Isles, where they'd spend their days fishing and catching gannets. But that life was out of reach, too. She'd met others in the city who'd been evicted from homes in the islands. It seemed that landowners across Scotland had been infected by a lust for the money to be gotten from sheep. Even after all that the people had given to their clans for centuries, chiefs considered them expendable.

It was this that had changed Sorcha the most, she now realized. The knowledge that she was absolutely without worth. She, a living, breathing human being who once was a valued member of her community, was now seen as no more than a sack of meat taking up space that could be used for more fruitful endeavors.

The knowledge made her afraid of people. She walked through the streets of Glaschu with her head down, her *plaide* held tightly to the sides of her face and under her chin. Her blood pounded loudly in her ears, and more than once she'd caught herself moaning without realizing why. When she reached the washing house in the mornings, she always needed to stop first into the privy to calm her frazzled nerves. Her days were spent flinching away from people, hiding her face, staying silent.

Aonghas spooned the last of the porridge into his mouth and set his empty bowl next to the water pail, knowing she would wash it along with her own bowl. Wordlessly, he slipped out the door and into the dark of the stairwell, closing the door quietly behind him.

She listened to the sound of his footsteps fade and didn't bother to wipe her tears away.

CHAPTER THIRTY

Keaka

Two days later; Glasgow

Now that the hike is over, I have less than a handful of days left with my son.

It feels too soon. I'm not ready.

But it's going to happen whether I'm ready or not. And so, for Colin's sake, I vow to hold it together until I get home.

We left Fort William yesterday and took the train down to the city, which took about four hours. It amazed me that the distance that took us seven days to walk could be traveled so quickly by train. Colin and I both spent the entire journey either dozing or watching the gorgeous scenery pass by. On the section from Bridge of Orchy to Inverarnan, I loved spotting hikers on the West Highland Way and felt a kinship with them. I know intimately what awaits them on the trail.

But then again, each hiker has her own experience, and that is part of the fun.

My body feels stiff and congested, like it needs to be out on the hills walking instead of sitting in a cramped hotel room or on public transportation. Not for the first time, I marvel at how much this week has changed me.

In Glasgow, we checked into our hotel and picked up the extra suitcases we'd paid to store during our hike that contain things Colin will need at university, then we'd shopped for everything else—cooking utensils, dishes, bath towels.

Today we're settling him into student housing, and I'm doing my best to stay busy to hold back a flood of emotions.

"I made your bed and put towels in your bathroom." I join Colin in the kitchen area of his new flat and lean against the counter to watch him wash his new pots and pans. The flat is small, but perfect as a first apartment. Colin has his own bedroom and bathroom, which are attached to this shared living room and kitchen area. One of the other two guys sharing the flat is settling into his own bedroom, and the second hasn't yet arrived. Jin is from South Korea and speaks flawless English. He and Colin seemed to hit it off right from the start, which helps ease my anxiety tremendously. At least Colin will have one friend when I leave. "Want to run out and find a grocery store? We'll stock your fridge with anything you want, my treat. Maybe we can explore campus a bit, too, and grab lunch somewhere?"

A flash of panic widens Colin's eyes, but before I can figure out what is causing it, Jin struts into the kitchen. "Hey, man, you about ready to go? They're going to meet us at Ashton Lane."

That's when I realize Colin has made other plans. He is already starting a new adventure with new friends.

Several emotions flit across Colin's face as he looks at me. "Uh, I'm not sure."

He's clearly torn between going out with his new friend and staying with me. I must save him from himself.

I paste on a bright smile and reach for my green backpack, which I'd used to carry some of Colin's things here from the hotel. "Perfect timing. Colin's all settled and I need a nap. We'll meet up later, Colin—or tomorrow, whatever. Go have fun, and don't worry about me."

I know I've made the right decision when his shoulders visibly relax. I swallow the lump in my throat and pull him in for a hug, then I head for the door. "Bye! Love you!"

I manage to get out to the street before the first tear falls.

Colin will be coming outside any minute, too, and I don't want him to see me crying. I turn my feet east, toward the city center, and walk.

Here it is, the moment I've been dreading. The moment I find myself all alone. I knew it was coming, and yet I don't think I ever truly believed it would happen. I'd believed that Adam would change his mind and come back to me, but he died before that could happen. But Colin had been there all that time. He's always been there with me. My little buddy. My heart. Being away from him is something that I've refused to think about for too long.

And now the moment has arrived, and it hits me as suddenly and painfully as though I've stepped in front of a moving bus. I was fine one minute, writhing in pain the next.

My thoughts make me cringe. *Get over yourself, Keaka!* Kids move away from home all the time. This is nothing unique. Husbands leave their wives. Husbands die.

But he wasn't really my husband, was he? Not there at the end, at least. He was honest with me, asked for a divorce. And I refused him and begged him to stay with me, using Colin as an excuse, and he gave in.

That was a mistake. I should have let him go.

My feet stop right in the middle of the sidewalk. *I should have let him go.*

It's a thought that has never entered my mind before, and it requires all my attention. I should have let Adam go when he first asked. It was true. I should have freed him to live authentically with the woman he loved. If I'd been brave enough to let him go, that might have opened up space in my own life for love to enter. Instead of spending the last four years fighting with my husband, I might have been able to create a friendship with him as we co-parented our son. I might have found peace and a new direction for my own life. Instead, I stewed in my misery and delayed the inevitable.

"Feckin' bampot."

The grumbling man bumps into my shoulder, making me realize I am blocking pedestrian traffic. Shaking my head, I get my feet moving again, but now my tears have dried. I understand now. Ours wasn't a happy marriage those last few years. I wasn't happy nor fulfilled in that relationship any more than Adam was. What if I'd been the one to find love elsewhere? Would I have stayed if Adam asked me to?

That sounded miserable. Like a prison.

All the pain, shame, and misery that I've been carrying around for all these years lessens, and I'm surprised to find that I feel sad for Adam. I no longer blame him for ruining our marriage, ruining our family. He simply fell in love and wanted to be happy. He was so close to living the life he wanted, but then his heart gave out.

I want to feel love again. The idea rocks me. I have connected the concept of love with Adam for so many years that it seems strange, frightening—maybe even a little exciting—to think of a new man in my life.

A memory of Jorgen's kiss floats through my brain, and I feel my lips tingle. Interesting.

Or maybe it's not even a man that I need in my life right now. Maybe love will come into my life in the form of a new career, a new pastime, a group of friends. I've always wanted to learn to paint. That could be fun. Or play the violin. Am I too old to learn an instrument?

Am I too old to be loved by another person again?

Did I waste the best years of my life holding on to a failed relationship?

My stomach feels queasy, and a headache pounds in my skull.

In my misery, I pay no attention to where I'm walking and only numbly give notice to crosswalk signals and traffic. If not for the painted words LOOK BOTH WAYS on the streets, I would have forgotten to look for cars coming in the opposite direction from what I'm used to. One close call with a blue sports car has my heart racing and adrenaline spiking throughout my body. It's that wake-up call that finally makes me look around and take notice of my surroundings. I'm surprised to find myself in front of my hotel, with no recollection of how I got here.

I could go to my room, take that nap I mentioned. But I don't want to. I want to keep walking. Even with the nerves in my feet and hips still zapping and twinging from my long hike, I feel good. Maybe walking will be my new thing. I keep going, content to wander the city with no destination in mind.

"Did you know they filmed scenes in *Outlander* here?" asks a voice standing next to me at a crosswalk.

Surprised, I look up to see who is speaking to me and only then realize the fifty-something American woman in an I HEART EDINBURGH sweatshirt is talking to her companion, who is probably her husband.

"Yes, you've told me," he answers patiently. Then, as the crosswalk signal changes and I follow them across the street, I see him smile down at her. "The hospital in Paris where Claire works, right?"

The fact that he knows this makes his wife beam up at him, and then she clasps his hand in hers and practically drags him to the entry of the Glasgow Cathedral. I follow them but don't go inside the stunning medieval church. Instead, I take a walkway along the side of the cathedral and across a bridge to where I can see gravestones and monuments tightly packed on a rounded hill. A sign welcomes me to the Glasgow Necropolis, created in the 1830s for the merchant patriarchs of the city, many of whom had made their fortunes from the slave trade in tobacco, sugar, cotton, or ships.

I wander the pathways winding around the hill and read the names on monuments, interested in the history they illuminate but mostly looking for Sorcha's name. Or her son Aonghas. Had they made it to Glasgow and made a life for themselves? Had they become one of the city's class of merchants, or had they been part of the working class upon whose backs these barons profited?

I remember my vow to research Sorcha and figure out what happened to her and her son. I can't leave Scotland without knowing. It would be like leaving three people behind when I board the plane on Monday morning, rather than only Colin.

Regardless, they don't seem to be in this cemetery.

I leave the Necropolis the way I came and let my feet wander wherever my fancy takes me, wondering all the while if Sorcha had walked these same streets and set her gaze on the same landmarks and buildings. The architecture of the old stone buildings fascinates me because it's so different from what I'm used to on the West Coast of America. Physical evidence of history at home is in its infancy compared to this. The Indigenous people of the area that is now Portland, Oregon, lived in harmony with the land, which meant they did not leave stone and metal structures that still stood hundreds of years later. People of European descent had "discovered" the area with the Lewis and Clark Expedition in 1806, and settlers had started arriving in the 1830s by wagon train across the Oregon Trail. When I learned that history in school, it felt so ancient. But now, standing in this city with Roman structures and even earlier hill forts and standing stones, I feel the true weight of history, and it leaves me in awe.

I didn't expect to enjoy my afternoon alone, but I do. Very much. I snap photos of interesting old buildings still blackened from coal fires from over a hundred years ago. I miss Colin's company and random historical notes, but I do have a surprisingly good time. I don't have to consult with anyone else about where to turn, when to rest, what restaurant to pop into for a snack. It feels strangely liberating.

I wander down a small street off Gallowgate and am questioning the safety of the area when suddenly I feel lightheaded. Stars sparkle on the edges of my vision. I close my eyes and rub my temples, cursing myself for not bringing my water bottle with me.

When I open my eyes, I'm shocked to find the rundown businesses and littered pavement gone. In their place is a packed-dirt street lined by huge buildings made of a blond stone. Five young boys dressed in wool pants, black leather shoes, and boxy brown coats race past me, chasing a mangy dog and shouting for it to come back. Two women sit on the steps of the closest building, one peeling potatoes into a pail, the other holding a crying infant in one arm while clutching a little girl's arm to keep her from escaping while the woman admonishes her for some misdoing. I smell the acrid scent of smoke, and when a breeze stirs, I flinch at the smell of human waste.

I tilt my head back to look at the upper windows of the building, and though they are dark, I know the place as surely as if I live there myself. I can picture the interior in my mind: the cramped room with a bed shoved into one corner, an ancient iron stove along one wall, tin plates stacked on a shelf, worn and tattered clothing hanging on hooks by the door.

Suddenly, my phone vibrates in my pocket, and the image disappears. I am looking up at the sky, empty but for the patchwork of gray clouds blowing eastward. I drop my gaze to the street and find the children gone, the women gone. A plastic bag caught in the breeze is the only motion on this otherwise deserted street.

Sorcha. It has to be. Sorcha had made it to Glasgow and this was where she'd lived, in that tiny room in a building that has since been demolished. I'm certain of it. She's still talking to me!

Irritated by the interruption, I look at my phone and find a Facebook message with good news. I type a quick response, then return my attention to what used to be Sorcha's street.

I have to look for her. I have to know if Sorcha and her son found safety here or if whoever tied her up at the Drovers Inn found them again. Arrested them. Worse.

I need to know why Sorcha matters so much and why she'd reached out to me across more than two hundred years.

Because Sorcha did matter. And maybe that meant I matter, too.

CHAPTER THIRTY-ONE

Sorcha

End of September; Glaschu (Glasgow)

Sorcha folded the last of the shirts from the line and stacked it atop the others. When she bent to lift the heavy basket into her arms, however, something popped in her lower back, and she had to leave the basket on the ground as she rubbed the sore area.

Pains such as this were nearly a daily occurrence. Trying again, she squatted rather than bent her back and this time managed to lift the basket into her arms.

After carrying it to the washhouse and depositing it on the bench alongside others waiting for their owners to retrieve, she was handed her coins as payment and she was finally free to return home. Her work had taken longer today because of the rain. Washing was done at the river, where fabrics could be scrubbed against stones or washboards. On a dry day, the linens would then be spread on the grass to bleach in the sun. On a rainy day, the wet linens were carried into the washing house and hung on lines to dry in the heat of the fire and hot irons. Sorcha hated the oppressive heat and suffocating enclosure.

Washing faceless strangers' clothing and bed linens was a miserable chore. On days like today, when exhaustion weighed her down following another night dreaming of Coghill's ghost whispering that he was coming for her, it was all she could do to put in a full day's work. Each item of laundry felt three times as heavy as it should.

But now, for the remainder of the evening, she was free. As she left the Green in the gloaming, she felt the pain in her back with each step. She rubbed at it, hoping that a full night's rest would set her to rights. Her feet ached—they'd never been the same after the injuries she'd sustained on her walk here—but she was almost able to walk normally.

Distracted by her fatigue and pain, Sorcha was only partially aware of her surroundings. Normally, she took St. Mungo's Lane, or even Charlotte Street, to their room on Gallowgate Street, but tonight she detoured to Saltmarket to spend the pittance she'd been paid on a bag of meal. Oh, what she'd give for a bowl of fresh peas! Not only were fresh vegetables expensive, but most of the greens sold on Saltmarket were already wilted or rotting.

Carriages and carts, both loaded and empty, jostled along the street, filling the air with noise. A woman tossed a tub of dirty bathwater out her window, narrowly missing Sorcha walking below.

Her feelings hadn't changed since the first day she'd arrived in the city. The busy streets overwhelmed her, with mountain ranges of buildings four and five stories high on each side. Walking between their upright faces made her feel trapped, like she could not breathe.

She had her head down to avoid looking at the hulking buildings and was still rubbing at her aching back when she felt her elbow bumped by a passerby.

Startled, she looked up to find a finely dressed gentleman glaring down at her, his face reddening.

"Pardon me," she told him in Gaelic, knowing the words were expected even if the man could not understand them.

The Gaelic seemed to enrage him even more. He clamped his gloved hand around her upper arm and hollered something she couldn't understand. At his shouts, the people around them turned to stare.

She was used to the looks of contempt; it was being grabbed by a strange man that unnerved her. She tried to yank her arm free, but that only made him hold tighter.

"Let me go!" She struggled, her panic rising. "You have no right to accost me like this."

Suddenly, a policeman was there, pushing his way past the gathered onlookers. From her first day in the city, she'd known to avoid anyone wearing this crisp, all-black uniform and hat, but now here she was standing face-to-face with one. Her bowels turned to water as she dropped her chin to her chest, desperate to hide.

Was this it? Was this the moment she'd be captured and sent away? What would Aonghas do when she failed to return home tonight? Would he think she'd abandoned him? Would he also be captured? Her boss at the washing house knew where she lived. The policemen could track Aonghas down with that knowledge. How could she warn him?

She looked at the gathered faces, hoping to spot one familiar, but all the people were strangers.

Although she couldn't understand their words, the policeman seemed to be asking the well-dressed gentleman what was happening. When the hand holding her loosened, she thought he was releasing her, but his other hand clamped tightly to her arm. His free hand slipped into his pocket and drew out a coin purse.

That's when Sorcha realized the man was accusing her of trying to steal from him.

Her first reaction was one of deep offense, for she was a God-fearing woman who would never pick a pocket!

But then she remembered the supplies and food she'd stolen from the village on Loch Laomainn and the pies she'd taken from the farm south of there. She was a thief. Maybe not today, but it was still a crime she was guilty of committing.

Her guilt must have shown on her face, because the policeman narrowed his eyes at her like he believed the man.

But then he squinted even more, and, stepping closer to Sorcha, he used his wooden baton to force her chin up. A light of recognition widened his eyes, and he said something she couldn't understand but took to mean, "I know you!"

Fear hit her hard and gave her the energy and strength she needed to break free of the other man's hold on her. Without thinking of where to go, she ran, pushing past the people gathered, and anyone else along Saltmarket who got in her way.

She ran north but knew she needed to get off this busy thoroughfare. She turned to duck into a close, but realized just in time that it was a dead end.

On and on she ran, turning down one street, then another, running until her lungs screamed and her feet ached even more than her back.

Turning another corner, she risked a glance back and saw with great relief that no one was chasing her.

She ducked into another close and moved into the shadows before she allowed herself to stop running. That was when the nausea consumed her.

Holding her belly, she hunched over and retched until everything inside her lay in a disgusting puddle on the cobblestones. Without the energy to do more, she stepped back enough to be out of the mess and dropped to the ground, her shaking legs unable to hold her up a moment longer.

Hugging her knees tightly to her chest, she let the tears come. When would she be safe? Where would she be safe? Would she spend the rest of her life running? Always hungry, always afraid?

Aonghas deserved so much more in his life. How could she possibly give it to him when this was what her life had become?

She rocked back and forth and cried until her body stopped shaking. By now it was dark, and she knew Aonghas would be worried about her. If he was home himself.

She needed to get back.

After using her skirt to wipe off her face, Sorcha then took a deep breath and looked around.

She had no idea where she was. The buildings here were still tall but spaced farther apart. A dog barked behind a brick wall, and she figured there was a garden on the other side.

Carefully, she edged to the end of the close and peeked around the corner.

The street was wide. Not as wide as Trongate or Saltmarket, but wide enough for the passage of at least four carriages, she figured, and not traveled enough for the dirt to be packed like busier streets. Muddy puddles glinted in the weak light cast from the gas lamps along the nearest side, while on the other was a dark meadow with grass coming right up to the roadway.

She must have run to the very edge of Glaschu.

A carriage passed being pulled by a pair of matching black mares. It stopped a few doors down from where Sorcha hid, and she watched from the shadows as two people—a man and a woman—alighted with the assistance of a uniformed servant and then disappeared up the stairs and into the building. Judging by their expensive clothing, Sorcha knew they were one of the many families who had grown rich from the money flooding into Glasgow. These huge mansions were full of people who believed that people like Sorcha existed only to serve them.

Even knowing she was likely invisible to the people who lived here, Sorcha still drew her *plaide* over her head to hide her face before she set off walking in the direction the horses and carriage took.

She'd not gone far when another carriage pulled to a stop a short distance in front of her, and she had just enough time to press into the shadows between buildings.

"An Siosal!"

Sorcha's entire body convulsed upon hearing the man's voice calling to the Chisholm, the chief of her clan and the man whose orders led to her eviction from her home and all the horrors that came with it. He was here?

She had to see for herself.

With her *plaide* drawn close, she poked her head out just enough to see with one eye down the street to the carriage.

An Siosal himself was standing beside the carriage and assisting the Lady Chisholm down to join him. The man who'd called to An Siosal ran up to them, calling his name again, but when he reached them, he switched to English, and Sorcha could not understand his words.

Whatever they were, it made An Siosal very excited, and the three of them disappeared into the building, talking rapidly.

Sorcha pulled back into the shadows but stopped when she heard the footman ask the carriage driver in Gaelic what the man had said.

"The murderess they've been pursuing has been spotted here in Glaschu. It's only a matter of time until she's captured and justice is served." At that, he called for the horses to go, and the carriage moved away, drowning out any more of the conversation.

Sorcha stood unmoving, shocked by the sight of the Chisholms as much as by the knowledge that, apparently, there was now a city-wide search happening for her.

She should leave. Go, now. Cross the street and head across that darkened meadow and keep going until she was far, far away from here.

But Aonghas.

She could not, would not ever, leave her son.

Suddenly, the need to be with him, to hold him in her arms, felt like a physical hunger. She pushed from the wall and walked, staying to the shadows as much as possible.

This city always felt threatening to her, but this night it felt doubly so. Each stranger might be the one to grab her and turn her in. Each shadow might hold a policeman or one of the Chisholm's men.

Sorcha felt like her body wasn't taking in enough air, and she had to duck into another dark close and lean against a wall to catch her breath. Her fear of being captured was so great that her entire body shook and her legs felt incapable of movement. If she could hide away in this dark close forever, she would.

Footsteps.

Sorcha whirled around at the sound but found no one in the close.

Turning toward the main street, she was shocked to see a familiar green satchel passing by. The Good Woman! It had to be her. That color, that satchel, could belong to no one but the Woman of the Mounds who had helped her at the Inbhir Àirnein House Hotel.

Sorcha hurried after her, wishing she had a name to call but also knowing the Good Woman likely would not hear her.

With her eyes firmly on the strange green satchel, Sorcha followed her across a grand intersection, past a small fenced meadow absent of animals, and beside a darkened church with a single candle burning in an upper window.

Only when she reached the bank of the Abhainn Chluaidh did Sorcha realize where she was. She could find her way from here back to their flat, but curiosity made her turn the opposite direction and continue to follow the Good Woman.

As they passed the stone bridge spanning the river, Sorcha saw and heard a great commotion that caught her by surprise. Before she could take it all in, the Good Woman disappeared behind a passing carriage. Sorcha waited, but she did not reappear. Giving up her chase, she instead turned to see what this place was.

At least a dozen ships were tied to the wharf, each with two or three tall masts, a few with sailors climbing all over, mending, tying, loading, unloading. She was surprised to see them working after dark, but then again, there seemed to be plenty of light cast by numerous lanterns on the ships, as well as gas streetlamps and the addition of small bonfires spaced evenly on the stone wharf. Sorcha found a spot out of the way where she could watch, fascinated by the process and by the immense ships themselves, so full of promise, whispering of adventure to the very air that whistled through their riggings.

She wished more than anything that she and Aonghas were on a ship right now, riding out to sea toward lands far away from here, the distance growing between them and An Siosal and anyone else looking for them. But it would be months—years, even—before she saved enough to pay their passage.

And then she had an idea.

CHAPTER THIRTY-TWO

Sorcha

End of September; Glaschu (Glasgow)

Sorcha cried all the way back to their building. There, even though she ached to be with Aonghas, she waited in the shadows for a long time, watching the street, watching their building, just to be sure no policemen—or anyone else—were there waiting for her.

Satisfied that all was as it should be, she finally dashed into the close and up the stairs. As soon as she reached their room, she hurried inside and then turned the key in the lock. Aonghas had been sitting on his pallet with his back against the wall, but now he jumped to his feet. "What's wrong?"

The window. She crossed the room and stepped around Aonghas to pull the limp curtains closed, taking care not to stand in the opening herself.

"Ma? Something happened. I can see it all over you. Are you hurt? Where've you been?" He stood as still as stone. Only his wide eyes moved as he watched her sink onto a chair.

"Where are Ealasaid and the girls?"

He shrugged. "They weren't here when I got back."

Back. He never called this place home. She could not help but agree.

"Ma. Tell me."

Sorcha finally met her son's anxious gaze and saw the maturity there, the acceptance of all that their lives had become, the lack of any remaining hope. She swallowed and reached to push back a lock of hair hanging in his face. "I need to cut your hair. It's getting long."

Irritated, he pushed her hand from his head but held on to it as he sank down to his haunches in front of her. "Tell me."

Strengthened by his touch, she finally admitted, "I was almost captured today." She told him of the man who'd thought she was pickpocketing, and the police officer who recognized her, and her escape through the city.

"You got away." He said it like a prayer.

She swallowed again. "That's not all of it, Aonghas. An Siosal is here. In Glaschu. He has men searching for me—for us."

At that, Aonghas shot to his feet and shoved both hands through his hair as he took two steps to the window. There, he stood to the side and peeked out as though expecting someone to be out there, looking back at him. "We've got to go, Ma. Leave the city. Tonight. Now."

"Where? Where will we go where they'll not come looking for us?"

Aonghas clamped his lips together so hard they turned white, and paced the small room. She opened her mouth to tell him the arrangements she'd made, but he cut her off.

"You are innocent." He dropped onto the edge of Ealasaid's bed and leaned his arms on his knees. "It was my fault the man died in our cottage. If I hadn't pushed him down, he'd still be alive and none of this would be happening." He raised a determined-looking face to her. "I'll turn myself in."

If he only knew, Sorcha thought, her mind filling with the image of Coghill's corpse. She shook it away. "We've been over this. It was an accident, Aonghas, and don't ever think otherwise. I won't allow you to turn yourself in for any reason, and especially not for my sake."

"But if I turn myself in, you could go anywhere—even back home to the Highlands—and find work. Or to England. I hear cotton mills need women to work the looms. You could be happy again."

"Oh, dear boy, come here." She opened her arms to him and felt a small part of her world fit into place as he dropped to his knees on the floor in front of her and wrapped his arms around her waist. She laid her cheek on the top of his head and breathed him in. "My heart is near to bursting knowing that you'd sacrifice yourself for me, but I would never want that. Don't think of it ever again. Promise me."

He did not respond, so she put her hands on his shoulders and gently pushed him away from her until they were face-to-face. "Promise me."

His eyes filled with tears, and in that moment, he looked so much like the little boy he had been just a few short years before. Finally, he nodded. "I promise."

"Good." She pulled him back into her arms and held him tight. It was time to tell him. "Speaking of promises, I promised you I would get you out of Scotland. I promised you a life that is safe and happy."

He pulled away and looked at her, his eyebrows heavy over suspicious eyes.

"I have a way for you to leave here, and I need you to agree to go, because only then, only when I know you are safe, will all of this have been worthwhile."

He started shaking his head, but she wouldn't let him speak until she got it all out. "I've arranged for you to indenture yourself to a ship's captain. You'll be part of his crew until you reach Philadelphia, where he'll sell your contract. I don't know what work you'll do then, but it will only be for seven years, and then you'll be free to make your own life. In only seven years you'll be a free man, and you'll be far away from An Siosal and anyone else looking for you here. You leave before dawn."

He'd pulled away from her as she spoke and now paced the room, still shaking his head. "No, I won't leave you."

So she told him, cruelly, of the fate that awaited if they were captured. How they would be locked in the Tolbooth to await sentencing, if they were lucky. As convicted outlaws, they might just as easily be killed on the spot. She told him how they were already presumed guilty for failing to appear at court. How people of their class were always found to be at fault, for any crime, unless someone of higher standing spoke for them. The only person who might have spoken for them in the past was An Siosal himself, but he was the one to convict them now. The only possible outcome for them would be a guilty conviction for murder. Murderers were hung by the neck in front of a jeering crowd.

"If you sign that indenture contract, *a ghràidh*, and sail away with the morning tide, we'll never see each other again, but you'll be alive and you'll have the opportunity to make a life of your choosing once your term is up."

"What will my life be without family—without you, Ma? I need you and you need me. I promised that I'd never leave you."

Sorcha saw that he would not willingly leave her behind. So she added another sin to her long list: she lied. "Your life will be grand, and I will be just fine, too. Don't worry about me. I've found work as a lady's maid with a family moving to London. I'll be living in a fancy house well away from An Siosal or anyone else looking for me. So you see? We'll both be safe."

"I'll work for this family, too." His eyes pleaded with her and nearly broke her.

"I asked. They don't have room for you." She swallowed and had to take in a slow, deep breath to calm her shaking belly.

"You said you'd never leave me!" His face crumbled before he buried it in her skirt. Her heart shattered as she held him.

Sorcha had given up on sleep long ago and now sat at the window, watching the street below through a gap in the curtains. Shadows moved. The night watchman had sauntered past on Gallowgate hours ago, and a gang of street lads raced through the close like they were being chased, but no one came after them.

Soon—too soon—Aonghas would leave for the ship, and she would never see him again. But he would be safe from the gallows. She had to keep reminding herself of this.

The sound of whimpering made Sorcha turn from the window and toward the bed where Ealasaid's daughters slept. The three had returned home only long enough for Ealasaid to put the girls to bed, then she'd disappeared out the door again to her evening's work. Aonghas had fallen asleep despite swearing he would stay up all night.

When the whimpering did not calm after a full minute, Sorcha turned up the wick of the lamp and carried it to the bed, where she found three-year-old Hannah shaking her head and kicking their blankets off. Sorcha bent over the tiny girl to better see her face and was unsurprised to find her still asleep. Both girls suffered from nightmares and often had to be consoled in the night when their mother was absent.

"Shhh . . ." She smoothed the sweaty hair off the girl's forehead until she calmed, then she pulled the blanket back over the girls. When she was certain both slept deeply, she turned away and knelt on the hard plank floor beside Aonghas.

He slept, but his breaths hitched, as though the air caught on something and he had to jerk it free. She felt her own breath catching and knew that with Aonghas across the ocean, she would never again breathe easy.

Something caught her eye and she leaned closer, raising the lantern higher over her son. When she saw the streaks of tears running from the sides of his eyes, she felt her own eyes water.

Setting the lamp on the floor beside her, she reached a hand toward Aonghas to soothe him as she had done for Hannah, but she drew back before she made contact. She did not want to wake him and remind him of the reason he'd cried himself to sleep.

In a few short hours Aonghas would sail away from her, and she'd never see her son again. She would not see him grow into a man. She would not get to know the woman he'd one day marry, nor the children they produced. She'd always thought she'd spend her later years rocking her grandchildren and teaching them the old ways. But after tomorrow, all that would be lost to her.

Aonghas was going to be entirely alone on that ship and in America. She'd have no way of reaching him. Even if she made enough wages to one day buy her own passage, how would she ever find him?

Tears streamed down her own face, and she let them fall. Oh, how her arms ached to gather Aonghas up like she'd done when he was small. She would hold him to her heart and breathe him in, and they would both know that he was safe.

Aonghas's breath hitched again, and his head jerked to the side as though turning away from something in a dream. She reached for him, her mother's instincts screaming at her to hold him, but she stopped before touching him, remembering just in time that he needed his rest.

She clasped her hands together to keep from disturbing him, but when he stirred again, she could not help herself. She smoothed his hair off his forehead, putting all her love into that touch.

Aonghas relaxed, and, still asleep, he let out a sigh, just as he'd done as a baby. Her heart broke anew with the pain of it all.

A noise that sounded like a woman gasping filled the room, and she jerked her head up, only to find the shadows empty. The girls still slept, Aonghas slept. Nothing stirred.

It must have been her imagination.

But it was enough to remind her that dangers were out there, waiting for her and Aonghas. She must see him safely to the ship and safely away from here, where An Siosal and his men were searching for them.

Safety, for Aonghas, would arrive with the morning tide.

CHAPTER THIRTY-THREE

Sorcha

Morning; Glaschu (Glasgow)

Too many people had been taken from her. Her parents, her sister, her three who'd died young, her strong eldest son as he marched off to be a soldier and never came home again, the love of her life as he served Scotland and was cut down on the battlefield. Each time she lost one of them, she'd had another child needing care, a home to manage, animals to feed, crops to tend, neighbors to visit. People and duties to give her focus.

As she stood in the dark and the rain on the busy riverside wharf, she felt bereft of all that had ever made her whole. As soon as Aonghas stepped aboard the ship, there would be nothing left to live for, no one who cared if she woke up in the morning.

"Ma, you cannot tell me I won't see you again. I will not believe it." Tears pooled in Aonghas's eyes, but he knuckled them away with a glance at the sailors walking past them, carrying heavy canvas bags on their shoulders.

Sorcha clenched her back teeth together until she had control of her own tears. "Then I'll not waste my breath." She had to focus on the feel of the stones beneath her feet to keep them planted. She wanted to run away. She wanted to grab Aonghas in her arms and carry him far from here, anywhere, as long as she had him with her always.

All it would take would be to grab his hand and tug him away from the ship. They could cross the great hump of the Broomielaw Bridge and continue south to England, away from here. Away from the ship's captain and away from the arrogant men who wanted them punished for a crime they did not commit.

She eyed the bridge spanning the river. Its arches and circle holes to allow floodwaters through looked like black eyes watching her, and she knew she'd always feel watched. An Siosal, his factor, and all his men would never give up until they saw her and Aonghas punished. They'd pursue them as far as it took. She and Aonghas would always have to be on guard, watching, waiting, not trusting anyone, always moving.

Aonghas didn't have to accept that fate. Aonghas could board this ship and sail away from here without anyone knowing.

As though conjured by her thoughts, the captain suddenly arrived by her side. "I must say, I did not expect to see you or your boy this morning." His gravelly voice did nothing to reassure her misgivings.

She lifted her chin. "You said you'd accept his contract. Are you denying it?"

The captain cleared his throat. His bushy beard twitched. "No, missus, I am not. So . . ." He turned to Aonghas. "This is your boy?"

She placed a hand on Aonghas's back. "Yes, this is A—" She stopped herself just in time, then gave his false name so there'd never be a record of Aonghas Chisholm sailing away from Scotland. "Anndra Ross. He's a strong worker. You'll not regret taking him on."

The captain's gaze took Aonghas's measure, and then he stuck out his hand. "James Malcomb. Call me *Captain*." After shaking hands, he planted his on his hips, his feet wide as though he were standing on the moving deck of his ship. "I agreed with your mother to take you on as an indentured servant in exchange for your passage to America. When we reach Philadelphia, I'll sell your contract and you'll be obliged to work for your new master for a full seven years. Do you understand?" He broke off as he spotted something to his dissatisfaction and shouted an order to the sailors walking up the gangplank of his ship.

In the light shining from the gas lamps, Sorcha saw Aonghas's throat convulse, and when he darted a wide-eyed look her way, she saw fear and a rising panic. For what may be the last time, she took the opportunity to soothe her son by stepping closer to him and placing one hand on his arm with a squeeze, the other on his back. In a voice she hoped eased his fear but did not embarrass him in front of the captain, she said, "Seven years is not so long. When it ends, you'll be free to explore the mountains, build a home, learn a trade. You can be your own man in America, A—Anndra. You can do none of that here."

Aonghas's gaze drifted over her shoulder toward the waking city behind her, and she wondered if he was looking for An Siosal's men, or simply needing one last look at the city that had been his home these last two and a half months.

Then, seemingly finding his strength, he turned back to her and pulled her to him for one last hug. She closed her eyes and clung to him, working with everything in her to keep from sobbing.

When he released her, his face was carefully blank. Following his lead, she hid her own emotion. He nodded once, then turned toward his new employer. "Yes, I—I understand. I'm ready, Captain."

"Good to hear it. Missus." Captain Malcomb nodded once more to her as though in dismissal, and then he slapped Aonghas on the back and pointed toward the ship. "Find Crawford. He'll see you sorted." With that, he turned his attention on the driver of a wagon that had just arrived stacked with crates.

Sorcha was still holding on to Aonghas's arm, and the captain's words had made her fingers clamp tighter to him. She wasn't ready to let go. She could have ten more years and still never be ready.

But the captain was shouting orders to load the last of the cargo quickly or they'd miss the tide.

Sorcha pulled Aonghas against her and squeezed as tight as she could. She breathed in his scent of wet wool and soil and did her best to take note of the exact warmth of his body against hers, the breadth of his shoulders, the way her chin fell level with his armpit so she had to arch her neck backward to hug him properly. She could not allow herself to think she would never again hold her boy. She had to remain focused on the freedom he would have, the safety.

"I must go, Ma."

"I know." With another tight squeeze, she released him and stepped back. His expression appeared confident, but she could see the child inside who was terrified. Knowing this would be the last time she mothered him, she gave him the only thing she had left to give. With a wide and carefree smile, she said, "Off with you, Sailor Anndra, and make your family proud."

It worked and his fear faded. He started to turn toward the ship but paused to look back at her. "I love you, Ma. I'll come back for you as soon as I can."

She shook her head. "Just live your life, *m'eudail*. That is all I've ever wanted."

He gave her a sad little smile, then his shoulders lifted on a deep breath. As they dropped, he resumed his walk, and this time made it all the way onto the ship before he turned to wave.

She waved back, still swallowing her tears.

After that, everything moved quickly. Workers on the wharf motioned her out of the way so they could untie the lines. She did as they directed, but stayed as close as possible to keep her eyes on the ship, searching every man who moved on deck to see if he was Aonghas.

Remembering, she slipped her hand into her pocket and found the heart-shaped rock Aonghas had given her all those days ago on the shore of Loch Laomainn. She curled her fingers around it and squeezed until her fingers ached.

The ship moved away from the wharf and immediately started downstream, caught by the current and the outgoing tide. Only now did she notice that the sky was lightening with the coming dawn.

The ship was too far away now for her to identify Aonghas. Wanting to watch the ship for as long as possible, she hurried to the bridge and up the rise to the highest point at the middle, where she could see downriver without anything blocking her view.

The ship moved steadily downstream, away from her.

"Stop!" she yelled, unable to keep the words inside her. "I cannot let you go!"

Dizziness swamped her and she stumbled. Just then, a body slammed against her, and she heard a woman say, "Excuse me," in Gaelic.

Sorcha didn't bother to look at the woman, nor reply to her apology. She regained her footing and pressed her belly to the bridge railing. Aonghas's ship was now a dark smudge on the silver surface of the river. She leaned forward, feeling as though Aonghas was pulling her to him with ropes she could not see. Never in her life had she wanted anything more than she wanted to be on that ship with her son.

A sob escaped her, and she clapped her hands over her mouth, one fist still clutching the heart rock. The ship disappeared into the hazy distance, and then even the river itself completely disappeared as her eyes flooded with tears.

He was gone.

Her body convulsed. Without warning, she collapsed as though the bones holding her up had disappeared with the ship.

She fell onto the dirty stones and cried, curled into herself and not caring who saw her. Nothing. Nothing was left to make her care. Her soul could flee her body right this very minute. She would welcome it.

She would never again see her boy in this lifetime.

She still did not move from the bridge, as if remaining here meant she kept a part of her son with her.

Knowing she needed to mark this place, even though it wouldn't lead her home, she returned her rock to her pocket and pulled her knife from her belt. She set to work carving her symbol into the smooth stones of the bridge.

A bowen knot for her Tàm.

A flower petal for each of her four older children, gone from this world.

A center disk for Aonghas, the center of her life. Now gone from her.

When she was finished, she placed her palm on the symbol and mourned for all of them.

CHAPTER THIRTY-FOUR

Keaka

Glasgow

I wake for the first time in my life knowing my son has been launched into the world, into adulthood, and it makes me feel both full and hollow at the same time. He texted last night to say he'll be busy today with orientation. I may not see him at all.

With nothing to get up for, I roll over in my hotel-room bed and pull the covers under my chin. As I drift between waking and sleep, dreams filter through my mind of a two-masted ship with heavy ropes tying it to the stone wall of a riverbank. Other ships are tied alongside, but this one holds my focus, as though it is the most important ship in the world.

Gulls squawk as they land on the quay to snag a bit of dropped bread for their breakfast. Carts, wagons, and even one glossy black coach pass by, adding to the noise and commotion of the busy dockside. Voices call out, but I pay no mind to anything they say. As though seeing through a tunnel, I watch my son in the predawn light walk up a wooden gangplank and board the ship and I know, without a sliver of doubt, that I will never see him again. I want to die.

I jerk awake, my heart racing and adrenaline spiking so high I feel sick to my stomach. Suddenly hot, I kick off my covers and look around the darkened hotel room to ground myself in the present.

The dream felt so real. I swear I was just standing on the dock about to watch Colin sail away forever.

But I'm not. I'm in a Glasgow hotel room. I am about to say goodbye to Colin and fly back to the States without him, but it isn't like I'm not going to see him again. I'll be able to see his face every day if I want over Zoom or a FaceTime call. I'll be able to get back on an airplane and fly back here to see him.

But parting from him was brutal. It will be brutal.

With so much adrenaline pumping through my system, I know that sleep is impossible now, so I get out of bed and push back the heavy curtains over the window to let light flood the room. It is a sunny day in Glasgow, at least for now, and I suddenly want to be among the people on the sidewalks below.

The dream may have revealed how upset I am about leaving Colin here, but really, I feel quite happy for him. I wouldn't want him doing anything else. I've witnessed his joy and love for Scotland. He thrives here. He's going to be just fine.

A strange feeling germinates inside my chest, and I wait for it to grow in order to identify what it is. It's an emotion I've never felt before, one that feels like a quickening next to my heart. Like my soul has been shocked to life with electric paddles. A new version of myself is being jump-started.

Colin is settled. I can relax my vigil now.

I can try new things, go new places, make new friends. I can stay out late and sleep in late. I can get into a project and forget about the time, staying up all night if I want, or forgetting to eat during the day. No one needs anything from me. No one expects me to be anywhere. I can jump in my car and drive until I encounter something interesting and stop. No agenda. No expectations.

The possibilities excite me.

I've adored every single moment of being Colin's mom, and I wouldn't trade a second of it for anything. But I've done my job and raised my son to be an incredible young man who is now making his own way in life. Any decisions I make for myself now will mostly affect only me in a way that hasn't been true since the day I married Adam. I can view this new stage of life as a lonely one, or I can see it as an opportunity.

I choose opportunity.

The image of Colin walking up the gangplank onto the ship comes to mind again, and I sigh. It felt like he was sailing away to a new world without me. Which, I guess, he metaphorically is doing. He's starting a new life here in Scotland that won't include me. He'll be having his own adventures from now on, as he should.

But part of me still wishes I was with him on that ship.

Wait a minute. Something isn't right.

I close my eyes to better recall the dream and realize with a shock that it hadn't been Colin walking aboard the ship. It was Aonghas.

Aonghas!

Does this mean Sorcha is talking to me again?

Suddenly, I know exactly how I want to fill my day. I'm going to find Sorcha.

I race for the shower, excited by the prospect of a whole day following the trail of my mystery friend.

An hour later I'm walking along the north side of the River Clyde, searching for anything that looks familiar from the dream. I keep moving westward on the river path and enjoy the sunshine and people watching. But nothing looks familiar, and doubt starts creeping in. Maybe the dock was in another city. Maybe it was farther downriver, toward the sea. That would make sense. The river here isn't that wide. Had ships ever been able to maneuver here? Is it even deep enough?

I receive an answer as soon as I get to the Squinty Bridge and see an old steamship tied up on the south side of the river next to the Glasgow Science Centre. If the river is deep enough for a steamer, then surely it's deep enough for older ships. It seems logical that many of the bridges spanning the river had been built well after Sorcha's time. Without bridges blocking the way, ships could likely have traveled farther upstream than they do today.

Plus, I trust my gut, and it's saying that I'm right. I identified the location correctly from the start when I went to the riverside near the Central train station. I have no proof, but I feel certain that Aonghas boarded a ship on the river in that general vicinity.

I turn and retrace my steps back to that spot, right where a wide bridge crosses the river to deliver trains into Central station. Just upriver, beside the train bridge, I see another bridge that blocks my view of Glasgow Green beyond.

The longer I stand here under the train bridge and stare at the numerous arches of the next bridge, the more an image starts to form in my mind of that very same bridge in Sorcha's time, and it looks nothing like it does today. I pull up Google Maps on my phone to get my bearings. There, I find that the bridge in question is the A77, or the Jamaica Street Bridge.

I open my phone's browser and type in the name. Wikipedia confirms that a bridge had indeed been there in Sorcha's time. The original bridge had been built in 1772 and had been called Broomielaw Bridge. Another quick search for "Broomielaw Glasgow" tells me that the city's first quay had been right here where I'm standing, and it brought shipping right into the heart of Glasgow.

It's all the confirmation I need, and I know I've found the very location that I saw in my dream this morning. Aonghas boarded a ship right here. I'm certain of it.

And then another memory resurfaces. The bridge. I know the Broomielaw/Jamaica Street Bridge. Colin and I walked across it last week, before we left for the hike.

I stash my phone in my pocket and hurry to the end of the bridge so I can walk to the midpoint where I'd seen the first of Sorcha's carvings.

Right at the very spot, I stop and hunker down to see the flower and knot.

But there's nothing there. No carving of any sort at all. Even the stone itself has changed. Where there used to be a solid stone wall is now a row of numerous carved-stone stanchions with solid, rectangular blocks every thirty feet or so to anchor the railing. I walk the entire length of the bridge inspecting every surface, but there are no carvings, only random graffiti and stickers advertising local bands or depicting anime characters.

I feel like I'm losing my mind. I know I saw a carving here. I remember touching it. I didn't imagine it. The carving was there. I traced it with my finger just before I accidentally bumped into a woman and, somehow, spoke Gaelic to her.

The woman. I do remember her. She'd been wearing a dark skirt and had a tartan blanket wrapped around her shoulders.

Could that have been . . . ? No, surely not.

But maybe it was. Maybe that had been Sorcha. Maybe I'd stood with Sorcha on the bridge that day and saw her carving and spoke her language, and we've been connected ever since.

Why? And how?

I look downstream again and imagine away the train bridge blocking my view, as well as all the bridges beyond it.

Sorcha had stood right here and watched her son sail away from her forever. She must have been devastated.

Wait, I know exactly how she felt because I felt it myself this very morning during the dream. I wanted to die.

Did Sorcha die here? Did she jump from this bridge and end her life in the river?

The thought makes my throat clamp shut, and I feel the hot sting of tears. I lean over the railing to stare at the water.

Is that why I see her, know her thoughts, understand her language, feel her emotions? Because we both stood on this bridge thinking about how much we're going to miss our sons?

And her ghost is still here.

I look around, searching for a tiny woman in a tartan blanket, but see only modern jeans, rainproof jackets, and wireless earphones.

"Are you here, Sorcha? I've come to find you."

Nothing—no one—responds.

I wish more than anything that I could open a door and find Sorcha as I did at the Drovers Inn. I don't know what I would say to her, or if I could talk to her at all, but I'm aching to ease her pain.

I stay on the bridge for several more minutes, but Sorcha doesn't appear and neither do any more visions.

I'm so sad for this woman I feel like I've known my whole life. If she did die here after her son sailed away, it seems she's now existing for eternity in that same distraught state.

If only Sorcha could have embraced the circumstances of her life. If only she could have had some help in starting a new life in her beloved Highlands. She'd clung so fiercely to her old life that a new one in Glasgow or elsewhere had likely felt impossible.

That's what I've been doing.

Everything around me disappears as the realization sinks in. I've been fiercely clinging to my old life—as a wife, as a mother, as a family of three—that I refused to see the possibilities that change could bring. Until this morning, I didn't see any possibility of being happy as a single woman with a grown son out on his own. I only saw what I no longer had.

Just as Sorcha could only see all that had been taken from her.

It's time to let it all go. I need to move forward now and find new joy, new relationships, new purpose.

A train rumbles past, and I look around with new eyes. I want some sort of ceremony to mark this occasion, and I think about tossing my wedding ring into the river as a way of releasing and accepting all that

I experienced with Adam and now with letting go of Colin. But I don't have the ring with me. It's tucked inside my suitcase back at the hotel.

Besides, I'd already released Adam at the top of the Iron Age hill fort near Fort William.

But I still want to mark this moment somehow, because it feels significant. With no other ideas, I pull a pound coin from my pocket and clutch it tightly between my palms. I hold my hands in front of my mouth and whisper, "Thank you, Sorcha, for sharing your experience with me and teaching me to let go. Thank you, Adam, for all the years we loved each other and for teaching me that it's okay to pursue joy. Thank you, Colin, for making me a mom and for teaching me to go after my dreams. I love you all."

And then I drop the silver-and-gold coin in the river and watch it turn in the water and catch the sunlight until it sinks too low to be seen anymore.

I feel lighter. I feel free.

I walk, following the Clyde Walkway without any destination in mind. It is simply enough to be here, walking where I know Sorcha once walked, where Colin will soon walk as he becomes acquainted with his new city.

My cell phone rings, and I pull it from my pocket. It's Colin. "Hey, sweetie."

He has laughter in his voice. "Orientation ended and some guys are going to teach us to play rugby in the park, but I wanted to check in with you first. Did you want to do something together today?"

I love that he's making friends, and I love that he's thinking about me. "Rugby sounds like fun. Go with your friends. But any chance you're free for dinner tonight?"

"Sure." A muffled sound comes across the line, and I know he's pulled the phone away from his face. "Hey, Ethan, what time does this end?"

I can't hear Ethan's answer, but Colin comes back to the call. "I'll be free after four o'clock. Want to meet me here or at the hotel?"

"I'll come to you. I haven't seen much of the West End yet, and you can show me around."

After hanging up, I hear my stomach growl and realize I haven't eaten. With several hours until I meet Colin, I decide to take myself out for lunch at a vegan restaurant I passed yesterday.

By the time I waddle out of there, full to my very limit, I am tempted to go back to the hotel and take a nap. Instead, I walk, and I marvel at the fact that the West Highland Way has turned me into a walker. Now that I know how interesting the world can be when viewed at a slower pace, I crave more of it.

Never in my life have I had more fun exploring a city. I pop into museums, art galleries, and shops at my whim, with no one to please but myself. I want more of this in my life.

As the afternoon passes, I head west toward Colin's flat and the university, and it's only when I see the red stone of the Kelvingrove Museum that I remember the painting. Sorcha's painting.

I have to see her again. One last time.

CHAPTER THIRTY-FIVE

Sorcha

Glaschu (Glasgow)

The rumbling of a loaded wagon brought Sorcha's attention back to the bridge, and she realized she was still huddled on the ground against the stone railing. She'd been staring downriver, as though Aonghas's ship would come sailing back to her and deposit him on the quay.

"*Mar sin leat, a ghràidh,*" she whispered to him, one last time. And then, feeling like only half a person, she pulled herself to standing and looked around. Upriver was Glasgow Green and her work at the washing house. To her right, on the south side of Abhainn Chluaidh, were fields of bere and oats stretching far into the distance.

She could go that direction, toward England, away from the Highlands, away from An Siosal.

The idea made her feel hollow.

No more. She would end this today.

Pivoting, she walked off the bridge, back into the city.

She knew exactly where to go, for it had been only a few hours since she was there last, although it felt like a full year for all that had happened.

In the daylight the street looked even fancier than it had in the night. She was out of place here amid the ladies in their fancy dresses and lace gloves, the men in their matching suits and stiff hats. Even the servants, who should be her class, looked different. Better. They wore starched uniforms and carried themselves in a manner that echoed their masters.

Watching them all come and go made Sorcha feel exhausted. She was so tired of it all. One class of people looking down on another. External trappings of clothing or home being the gauge by which a person was judged more than was their character. The injustice of tables on this street being laden with food that went to waste while only a handful of streets over, small children cried themselves to sleep with empty bellies.

And there, inside that fancy building, was a chief and his wife who'd decided that sheep were more important than people. A chief whose father and grandfathers in days past honored *dùthchas*—the understanding that people were rooted by an ancient lineage to a particular place and to all the creatures, nature, and culture living there. But this chief was so disconnected that he'd scratched his pen upon paper, and suddenly the land no longer belonged to his people, but to the sheep.

And his people were left to wander, homeless and alone.

Or, in Sorcha's case, to die by the noose for an accident that never should have happened.

But Aonghas. Her Aonghas would live, and live well. He was safe now.

She was so tired of hiding.

Sorcha tucked her hair under the secondhand mutch Ealasaid had lent her, and then she drew her shoulders back and climbed the steps to knock on the door.

To her shock, a man wearing a *fèileadh-mòr* answered the door. When he saw her standing there, his nose scrunched. "Deliveries are to go to the back gate."

When he started to close the door, she pushed at it with one hand. "I am not making a delivery. I must speak with An Siosal."

He raised an eyebrow. "An Siosal is not taking visitors." He again tried to close the door.

"Tell him Sorcha Chisholm is here."

The doorman obviously recognized her name, because he flinched away as though she was there to murder him where he stood. But then, after collecting himself, he stepped back and opened the door wider. "Come inside."

She entered the hushed and overly grand home, wondering if she was making a mistake.

"Stay there." He shot her a wary look as he closed the door behind her and then hurried off to a back room to deliver the message.

Almost immediately, he returned. "You are to wait here. An Siosal will see you shortly."

Sorcha waited for what felt like an hour under the watchful eye of the doorman, and noticed that in all that time she was not offered a drink of water, let alone a chair to sit on. She rocked back and forth from one foot to the other to ease the strain, knowing this discomfort was nothing compared to what was coming. The opulence of the entry hall distracted her from her fear, so she focused on the details.

A polished-wood stairway led up to a landing, where a window taller than a man spilled light inside the otherwise dark interior. That same dark wood was repeated on the bottom half of the walls and the arches of closed doorways leading to other rooms. Marble statues of embracing couples decorated alcoves set into the wall to her right along a passage leading to the back of the house. Rich red and gold carpets decorated the floors and made her feel as though she should have wiped her feet before stepping inside.

The more she looked, the more Sorcha felt out of place. But even more than that, the greater she felt betrayed by her chief. If he could afford all this luxury, he certainly had not needed to evict all his people to raise sheep.

Finally, a door to her left opened, and out stepped William and Elizabeth Chisholm, dressed in clothing fancier than she'd ever seen them wear in Srath Ghlais. An Siosal's dark-blue waistcoat and matching jacket gleamed as though it was woven from a glossy thread. Silver buttons lined the opening and cuffs and dazzled her eyes.

Lady Chisholm's gown matched the blue of her husband's clothing with an added pink in the delicate flowers embroidered on her skirt. Glittering blue jewels graced her neck and were probably worth more than all the cottages in Srath Ghlais combined, including their contents.

Behind the Chisholms, Sorcha could not help but notice the huge painting hanging over the sitting room fireplace. It depicted a younger Lady Chisholm standing on a rocky promontory overlooking Gleanna Garradh, the very glen where Sorcha had spent her childhood. The very same glen from which the present Lady Chisholm's parents had evicted Sorcha's parents and everyone else she knew to make way for sheep. It had happened nine years after Sorcha left the glen to marry Tàm. Only sheep roamed there now, and Sorcha had never seen her parents again. They died in far-off Alba Nuadh. She should have seen her own eviction coming.

A cloud of perfume preceded the couple into the hall, and Sorcha stepped backward, suddenly embarrassed by her own scent.

"It is you," sniffed Elizabeth Chisholm as she stopped in front of Sorcha. "You occupied the cottage across the river from Comar Lodge, the one nearest the old oak, am I right?"

Sorcha nodded and hid her irritation at the woman's obvious disdain. "Yes, my husband's fourth grandfather built it with his own hands after serving the sixteenth Chisholm in battle." She could not help but remind them that her land was paid for by the blood of her people and was not theirs to hand over to sheep.

Neither seemed to catch her meaning, or care. An Siosal drew himself up. "Are you the Sorcha Chisholm that my men have been searching for, who was put to the horn sixteen weeks past for failing to stand in court to the charges of murder?"

If he was trying to put her in her place, he succeeded. She looked down at the fancy carpet. "Yes. I am she." She lifted her chin again so they could see she was being honest. "It was an accident. I'm telling you true. We were going about our business when the man—"

"James Cumming," interrupted Lady Chisholm. "He was my cousin, Mr. James Cumming, and you will say his name with the respect he deserved."

Sorcha swallowed, then tried again. "Mr. Cumming came into our home, and I didn't know what he was about." She was lying and planned to keep lying to protect Aonghas. No one need know that he'd been involved. "He was taking my belongings for his own, and I tried to take my silver milk pitcher back from him, but he refused to release it to me. In our struggle he stepped backwards and, not seeing the stool there, he fell. His head hit the stones around the fire. He was gone before we could do anything. I'm telling you the truth."

Lady Chisholm arched her eyebrow. "And yet you heartlessly left his body to burn."

"We had no time! The cottage was burning down on top of us." Lady Chisholm looked unconvinced, so Sorcha turned to Mr. Chisholm. "My son and I nearly did not make it out in time ourselves before the roof fell in."

An Siosal seemed to be considering this. When his wife started to say something, he laid a gentle hand on her arm to stay her words before turning back to Sorcha. "And where is your son now? Why isn't he here with you?"

Panic sliced through Sorcha. She should have thought this through a bit more. If she told them Aonghas was on a ship bound for America, they might track him down and arrest him there. She had to tell them something that would make them give up their search for him. She looked down and realized she was wringing her hands. She forced herself to hold them still. "He is gone," she whispered, not knowing what else to say.

"Oh, dear woman, my condolences." An Siosal started to reach for her as though to offer her a comforting pat upon her arm, but then he thought better of it and stepped back. "It is a tragedy to lose a child."

Sorcha kept her eyes downcast so they wouldn't reveal the truth. "Thank you."

"Have you sent for Sergeant Johnston?" Lady Chisholm asked her husband, as though Sorcha could not hear her. "I want her out of my sight."

"Yes, he is on his way." He paused and then addressed his wife. "Perhaps we should ask for a second trial for this woman. She's been through so much."

Sorcha's heart lifted at his words, and she dared a peek up at the Chisholms' faces.

Lady Chisholm stood with her hands on her hips, glaring at her husband. "She had her chance for a trial. A good man, my dear cousin, is dead and this, this . . . woman is responsible."

After having felt a spark of hope, Lady Chisholm's words felt like claws around Sorcha's throat. She opened her mouth to beg for her life, but then her gaze landed on the portrait of a spoiled young Lady Chisholm, and anger overwhelmed her better sense. She leveled her gaze on the woman. "Your father pushed my family off their lands, and I never saw them again." She spat the words into Lady Chisholm's face and did not care when the younger woman paled. "Now you've pushed us off the lands of my husband's family as well, and I've lost everything and everyone. How will *you* pay for that injustice?"

Lady Chisholm drew herself up and, with narrowed eyes, declared, "A man is dead because of you."

Sorcha felt her heart stop. Lady Chisolm was right. She'd taken a life. Not the one the Chisholms believed—she would never accept blame for that accident—but she had taken a man's life. And, for that, she must pay.

Sorcha felt overwhelmingly tired and was just about to ask for a place to sit when she found her arms caught in the clutches of the kilted doorman she'd forgotten was even there.

She did not struggle against his hold, and when the policemen arrived, she said nothing as they dragged her to the carriage waiting outside.

Only when she found herself on the bench seat squished between two uniformed officers did she find words. "Where are you taking me?"

The one on her left surprised her by answering in Gaelic. "The Tolbooth, for now. From there, the gallows. It's what you deserve."

Deserve? Sorcha knew that was true. She may not have taken Cumming's life, but she had taken Coghill's. No one seemed to know that yet, and Sorcha intended to keep it that way, but she knew and her Heavenly Father above knew, and that was enough. She would take whatever punishment was given to her, and she would know that, yes, it was exactly what she deserved.

Now that she was captured, she hoped the end would come soon. A sudden death would be preferable to a lingering existence in this world all alone.

CHAPTER THIRTY-SIX

Keaka

Glasgow

Inside the Kelvingrove Museum, I marvel again that so many museums in Scotland have free entry. I head directly for the gallery where I first saw the painting.

There she is, despair pouring from her motionless face as chaos rages behind her. I walk across the room toward her, paying no mind to anything else. She has my full attention, and I feel like she's about to step out of the painting and talk to me.

Sorcha does not move. I stop directly in front of her.

I feel her sorrow and desperation. If this poor woman's life ended like I believe it did, in the river, then she never again felt joy. She struggled, mourned, and fought, but she never again found a life that made her happy like the one she'd had here, in the village that is burning down behind her.

I don't know how long I stand there staring at the woman who feels like my friend, but then I remember the title card on the wall that I'd forgotten to read the last time I was here. I take a half step to the right and lean toward it. SORCHA CHISHOLM: MOTHER, WIDOW, INNOCENT. 1838. ARTIST: IAIN RAMSAY (1789–1876). OIL ON CANVAS.

Immediately, I see a mental image of a laughing boy bending over a stone as he carefully carves a stag. The image quickly changes, and I see his young face, eyes wide with fear and a little regret as he stands behind a man holding a flickering lantern. Iain.

Iain Ramsay was the young boy who traveled with Sorcha and Aonghas for a time. He had to be the same person.

I pull my phone out of my pocket and type his name into a search engine. From the information that comes up, I learn the painter was born in the year 1789 somewhere in the Scottish Highlands. By age seventeen he was living in Edinburgh and working as an artist's apprentice. His fame erupted in the 1840s when Queen Victoria commissioned him to paint scenes of her beloved Highlands. His painting of Sorcha, however, is considered by critics to be his greatest work. The artist never revealed the story behind the painting or his connection to the subject.

I put my phone away and stare again at Sorcha's image, seeing it now through the eyes of a young boy. Iain clearly respected Sorcha. The title shows he believed her innocent of the charges against her.

I wish I knew more about their story and why the boy had traveled with Sorcha and Aonghas.

If Iain Ramsay had not painted this portrait, would I have ever connected with Sorcha, or even known her name? I have no way of knowing. I like to think that I would have, through her carvings or the land where we both walked, but I'll never know for sure.

And that's okay, I remind myself. I don't need to know. I only need to be grateful for what was and take what I've learned forward into this next chapter of my life.

I snap a photo of the title card and then one more of the painting for good measure, and then I head for the exit. It's time to meet my boy.

It's a short walk to Colin's flat, and I knock on his door right at four o'clock. When he opens it, he already looks older to me, as though he's grown up in the day and a half since I saw him last. I linger in his hug as long as I dare before letting him go. "Where are your roommates?"

He grabs his jacket off the back of a chair and slips it on. "They went to a movie with some girls we met today."

The way he says it makes me pause and consider suggesting he meet up with them since he clearly wants to. But then I remember that I'm flying home the day after tomorrow; he can spend one evening with his mother. "Where should we go?"

Colin tilts his head to the side as he considers, and I find myself soaking up every detail of his face, not wanting to forget the tiniest freckle. He shaved today, and there is a hint of newfound confidence in the way he moves. Already he's finding his groove here, and I'm happy for it. "It's early still. Let's walk for a bit and see what we come across."

"Before we go, I have something for you." I pull the book from my bag and show it to him.

"My guidebook!" Colin grabs the book and hugs it to his chest. "How did you find it?"

"A guy found it on the trail just outside of Crianlarich, and he sent me a Facebook message after he saw my post on the West Highland Way Facebook group page. He brought it down on the train yesterday and left it for me at the hotel front desk."

Colin is thumbing through the pages, as though to reassure himself that his dad's notes are still there. After my explanation, he closes it and hugs it again. "Thanks, Mom."

"You're welcome." I love the smile I've put on his face, and I love that he's able to treasure this tangible connection with his dad again.

He leaves the book safely in his room, and then he grabs his keys and we head out.

We walk through Kelvingrove Park, stopping to watch lawn bowlers and, later, part of a play being performed on an outdoor stage. As we wander, I tell him the highlights of the museums and art galleries I've seen today, and pull out my cell phone to show him photos.

We're walking through campus as he's telling me all the activities planned for the upcoming Freshers' Week. But then he suddenly tugs on my arm to get me to stop walking and smiles expectantly. "Recognize this place?"

I look to see what he's talking about and instantly recognize the medieval-looking stone arches and columns. "I do, but from where?"

He names some television shows and movies. "It's called the Cloisters."

We poke around for a bit and then explore the rest of campus. I take a lot of pictures of Colin in front of various buildings so I can look at them later and not feel like he's so far away.

After a leisurely dinner, we walk down Byres Road in the general direction of Colin's flat. Night has fallen, and the city lights reflect off wet pavement. I hold on to Colin's arm partly for warmth but mostly because I need to have this contact with him while I still can.

The neighborhood feels alive with students, and I can't help but feel wistful when I think of Colin walking these streets, making memories that I'll have no part of, meeting people I'll never meet myself. "It feels strange knowing you don't need me anymore."

Colin looks down with an expression that reminds me of Adam when he was exasperated with me. "Mom, I'll always need you. I may not need you to take care of me day-to-day any longer, but I'll always need to know you're just a phone call away, ready to answer any questions I have. And you know I'll have questions. Expect to hear from me the first time I try to do my own laundry."

I laugh at that. "And I'm only a plane flight away, too," I remind him as we resume walking. "You say the word and I'll be here. You'll always be my baby, even when you have babies of your own." It's something I've said to him since he was just a boy, and he smiles down at me in acknowledgment.

Colin and I are going to be okay. All this time, I've been thinking that my identity as a mother is coming to an end, but that isn't true. I'll be Colin's mom forever. My purpose is not ending; it's simply changing, altering, shifting, evolving. And that's a good thing. That's living.

"You know, Mom, there's something I haven't told you."

Alarm bells go off in my mind. "What?"

He looks away like he's embarrassed. "I'm a little bit scared."

It takes me a long moment to process this. Colin, scared? He's shown no other emotions but excitement and confidence over this move.

My mind races to figure out how to respond. Finally, I simply ask, "What scares you?"

He shrugs and keeps walking. I am laser-focused on him. "Colin?"

He finally stops. "It's just, you know, a big change. And I'll be here all alone."

A group of drunk girls pass by us on the sidewalk, arguing loudly about where to go next. One girl, I notice, is walking with them, but not saying anything. She seems to be the only sober one. I turn back to Colin and find him watching the girl with a gleam of interest in his eyes.

My heart warms. He's got a good head on his shoulders. He's going to be okay. He'll make friends, maybe fall in love. And really, it's good that he's scared of this huge change in his life, because it means he's smart. It means he'll be careful and make good choices. Strangely, the knowledge that Colin is scared makes me less so. I don't have to hold all the fear and worry alone anymore.

I tug on his arm to get him walking again. "It's normal to be scared. I'd be worried if you weren't." A few steps later, I add, "You'll be lonely at times. You'll make mistakes. That's all part of growing up. But you'll also meet interesting people and have all kinds of fun. You'll find people to be your crew, and you can all be there for each other in times of need and you won't feel so alone. For what it's worth, I think you're exactly where you're meant to be."

He seems to think this over as we wait for a crosswalk signal. Again, I watch him as he looks around, taking in all the people, cars, lights, scents, sounds. As the light changes and we step forward, he relaxes and smiles. "You're right. This is where I need to be."

Half an hour later, I climb out from the taxi that brought me back to my hotel. As I do, the sound of bagpipes catches my attention and something in my chest clenches.

On instinct, I walk right past the hotel entrance and keep going, following the sound. A short distance later I arrive onto Buchanan Street, a wide pedestrian-only street that is busy during the day with buskers, shoppers, and locals.

Tonight, though, the crowds are gone. Standing smack-dab in the middle of the walkway, lit only by the soft glow of a streetlight and the lights shining through shop windows, stands a lone piper dressed in full Scottish garb of kilt, sporran, wool socks pulled to just below the knee, and ghillie brogues covered with white spats on his feet. On his upper body he wears a black jacket with a length of tartan pinned to his shoulder that hangs down his back. Perched on his head is a furry hat with a strap under his chin. He could have stepped out from a movie.

What is strange, though, is that there are no other people around. He's playing a sorrowful song with his eyes closed. Even though there is an open black case at his feet, a plea for tips, everything about him says he is playing only for himself.

Not wanting to intrude on his private moment but unable to turn away, I quietly drop a five-pound note in his case and then back away to lean my hip against a flower planter and listen.

In all the years when Adam played bagpipe CDs, I'd always cringed. Always felt it was like nails scraping a chalkboard, and I could not understand why my husband and son loved the music so much.

But now, at this very moment, I understand. Each note the piper plays reaches deep into my body and, there, weaves around my soul, whispering to it of all I'd seen: the heather-covered hills, craggy mountains, trinkling burns, and placid lochs; and the rich history—the sorrow of the Clearances, the hope and fear of mud-covered warriors defending their land, the interconnectedness of the community as illustrated by a group of women singing as they waulk woolen cloth. The music speaks of the heartbreak of lands and loved ones lost, and the endurance of the love that binds them together still. My throat burns with unshed tears, and I want this moment to last forever.

Scotland is a place of mystery, magic, stories told and untold. It is a place of honor, duty, tradition. I finally understand.

Somewhere along the way, whether it was through Sorcha, walking the West Highland Way, or simply experiencing the country and her people for myself, I've fallen hard for Scotland.

If I can fall this deeply for Scotland, what else can I love?

I blink. *What else can I love?*

That's just it. There's so much in this big, beautiful world, and I've been living my life on autopilot. Scotland has woken me up. Instead of fretting over all that I've lost or my empty nest, I can go out and explore.

The piper draws out a long note until it fades to silence, and as it does, I feel my obsession with Sorcha fade along with it, as though the woman herself is saying goodbye.

The piper meets my gaze and gives a short nod before putting the mouthpiece back between his lips. Logic tells me his nod is his show of gratitude for my tip, but I feel it's something more than that. An acknowledgment, maybe, that it's okay to let Sorcha go. That it's okay that I live my own life now, separate from Adam, Colin, and even Sorcha.

As the achingly sweet notes of the next song begin, I sigh in contentment. I have one more day here, and no one to please but myself in how I spend it.

CHAPTER THIRTY-SEVEN

Keaka

Last day in Scotland

I wake up early and head straight for Queen Street Station and a train to Edinburgh. I invited Colin to join me today, but he declined, rather guiltily, citing activities on campus but promising to join me for one last dinner tonight. While I would've loved one more day with him, I find that I'm actually excited to have the whole adventure to myself.

Scotland's trains, as I've already discovered, are comfortable and clean, and I enjoy the fifty-minute trip watching the scenery pass by. Just before the train pulls into Waverley Station, it passes in the shadow of the immense crag that holds Edinburgh Castle on top, and I decide the castle will be my first stop.

Edinburgh feels much older than Glasgow—at least the part that I walk through from the train station to the castle does. For two hours, I poke around the grounds with the self-guided tour playing through earphones I rented at the gate.

Hunger drives me to leave the castle, and I stroll down the Royal Mile looking for sustenance. I end up at a pub that looks like it hasn't changed in two hundred years, which I love. I text Colin a photo and the words **Next time I visit you, we're spending at least an entire weekend in Edinburgh. It's amazing!**

When he doesn't respond, I put my phone away and try not to be disappointed.

After lunch, I head over to the National Museum of Scotland, where I walk through all seven floors telling the story of Scotland, from its ancient origins to present day. I'm especially captivated by the lowest level, where Pictish carvings on stones and other ancient artifacts are displayed. It makes me think about Sorcha's carvings and about Dun Deardail, the Pictish fort where Colin and I released Adam's ashes. I spend two full hours in the Scotland exhibit alone, and have to skip the rest of the museum because my brain feels like it can't take in one more factoid or it will burst.

I emerge from the museum to find the last of the clouds have disappeared, and I want to stay outside, breathing in the fresh air.

Returning to the Royal Mile, I wander down the length of it, looking through shop windows but not going inside. At the bottom, at the Palace of Holyrood, I feel a twinge of longing. If I had more energy and time, I would tour this building as well. But not today. I add it to my list of things to see next time.

I continue past Holyrood and see the massive crags of the extinct volcano known as Arthur's Seat, and suddenly I know the perfect ending to my day, to my entire visit to Scotland. A quick glance at my cell phone confirms I still have a couple hours until my return train back to Glasgow and dinner with Colin.

The path up the hill is easy to find, and soon I'm climbing steadily upward, my heart pounding and sweat dampening my neck and back. Again, I marvel at how much the last two weeks have changed me. I never would have chosen hiking as an activity to do when visiting a new city. But now I know the secret. Getting away from steel and concrete and moving my body in nature helps me to better know a place, for it is the stones, dirt, grasses, and trees that connect me to the land and all who passed here before me. I breathe in scents and microscopic particles, and I become one with all living things, throughout time. By slowing down and replacing the commotion of buses, cars, and crowds with birds, lakes, mountains, and wide-open skies, I connect with my own thoughts and emotions and senses, and, for once, am truly present.

And so I hike up Arthur's Seat. There is still quite a crowd on this sunny Sunday climbing the mountain with me, but I feel a connection to these people more than I did with the tourists below. These people are like me now; they know that trading a little sweat and muscle strain for the experience of seeing what so few others see is very much worth it.

As the trail gets steeper, I long for the hiking boots sitting in the closet at my hotel in Glasgow. When I started the West Highland Way, I hated the clunky things. Now I miss them. I even feel a tenderness toward them, as if they're a comfort item like a stuffed animal or blanket. They've carried me through trying times.

I'm almost to the top now, and the view is opening up. Just a bit farther to go.

A crowd is crawling over the concrete trig point at the peak. I stand for a moment beside it and take in the 360-degree view of Edinburgh, its suburbs, and the wide blue expanse of the Firth of Forth as it stretches eastward to the North Sea. Across the Forth, I can see the shoreline of Fife and, farther, blue mountains humped on the horizon and I feel the now-familiar stirring deep inside me that says, *Go! Explore! See what's out there!*

Other hikers are clamoring to touch the trig point, so I move away and find a spot to sit on the red rocks and take in more of the view.

I think about Sorcha and wonder if she really did die in the river. Maybe there was more to her story. And what happened to Aonghas? Maybe someday I'll try to find answers. But for now I'm grateful for the experience, and I feel satisfied with that. Sorcha helped me through this time of transition in my life, and I don't need to understand how or why. Her life may have been as fleeting as smoke on the wind, but her impact on me has been huge.

Suddenly, I hear the aching melancholy of a fiddle bow being pulled across its strings, and I look around for the source. There, a short distance away, sitting on a group of boulders at the top of the hill, is a young man dressed in jeans and a T-shirt, a mahogany-colored fiddle under his chin. Almost everyone gathered has paused to listen.

Softly, the fiddler sends the first strains of a song into the air, and I feel it hit the back of my throat. *"Auld Lang Syne."*

Every year on New Year's Eve when I hear the tune, it makes me cry. It's a song about remembering friends who are gone, and it feels fitting to hear it right now as I'm saying goodbye to Sorcha and, even more, to Colin.

I turn away from the fiddler to face the view again and let the moment sink deep into my soul. This is how I'll always remember my first trip to Edinburgh, to Scotland. Sitting high on a hill overlooking a city full of stories, solo and free, and listening to a fiddle play. Perfect.

"This song is aboot emigration, ye ken?"

Startled by the voice, I turn to find a gray-haired man sitting a short distance away, facing the same view as me. He wears a tartan hat with a feather sticking from it, and his hands rest on a walking stick that he likely carved himself that has been worn smooth by years of use. He smiles at me, and the way his eyes look deep into mine makes me feel like he knows me, knows all that I've experienced in his country. "What did you say?"

"I said this song is aboot emigration. 'Tis one friend singing to another, remembering good times together picking flowers and swimming in a burn, but now they are separated by an ocean."

"I didn't know that." I'm struck by his words. He could be speaking about me and Colin hiking together through the Highlands and then being separated by an ocean, starting tomorrow. Or he could be talking about Sorcha and all the people she'd lost during the Clearances. Did

Sorcha spend the last of her days feeling the words of this song, yearning for times long past?

The man turns to face the view again, and I see his face cloud with memories. "We've all lost someone. 'Tis why we sing it every year at Hogmanay, even those of us who dinna ken its meaning."

I feel his sadness and want to give him a hug, as I would do if he were my father or grandfather. But instead, I smile softly at him, acknowledging our mutual pain and loss. "Thank you for telling me that."

He gives me a nod and then leans on the cane to push to his feet. "That's me off. Ma tea is waiting." Charmingly, he touches his fingers to the brim of his cap and turns to make his way down the mountain.

I turn my gaze to the northwest, in the direction of the Highlands where I'd walked, and listen to the last few strains of the music.

As the fiddler pauses before playing his next song, I hear only the wind blowing past my ears, and it stirs a restlessness in me. It's time to hike down the mountain, board a train, have dinner with my boy, and then fly home. It's time to step into my own future while also remembering, with love and gratitude, all the people from my past.

Echoing the old man, I whisper to myself, "That's me off. My life is waiting."

EPILOGUE

Sorcha

January 1832; Sydney, New South Wales

The air felt heavy and damp as Sorcha made her way back to her shop after delivering Mrs. Carter's order of flour and tea to her house two streets away. She could have had Janet, her shopgirl, make the delivery, but Sorcha enjoyed getting out early in the mornings before the heat became too intense or the afternoon rain showers broke.

Morning was her favorite time of the day because it was the only time she got to listen to the birdsong, smell the flowers in her neighbors' gardens, and feel her body carrying her farther than simply up the stairs or from her kitchen to the front shop, where she assisted customers.

Mornings were the only time she allowed herself to think of her old life.

Thirty years. She'd lived in this unforgiving land for thirty long and miserable years—the first half as a convict and then, finally, after she'd served her sentence for culpable homicide, as a free person. But now, still, she often glanced up, expecting there to be mountains and waterfalls surrounding her. She still expected to see glens full of bracken and lochs surrounded by oak woods and hillsides carpeted in purple heather. Always, she was disappointed to find land stretching flat as a tabletop as far as her eyes could see, broken only by the choppy blue water of the harbor.

Most days she stopped her memories from going any deeper, because those memories hurt too much. She could not allow herself to think of her Tàm, or her dear lost children, or her home, where their life together had been so happy. Those memories had the power to drop her to her knees.

But she did, occassionally, allow herself to think about Aonghas. She was never without the heart-shaped stone he'd given her because, to her, it was more precious than gold or jewels. He would be a grown man now, if he was still alive. She had no way of knowing. In her mind, he was still the fourteen-year-old boy who'd bravely boarded that ship and sailed away from her forever. She hoped he'd found a good life somewhere, with good people looking after him.

"Mrs. Styles, one moment, please!"

Sorcha recognized Mr. Fowler and stopped to allow him to catch up. She hated her name, but the community knew her as the widow Styles, and nothing short of another marriage would allow her to change that. She would never again marry. Her last husband had nearly killed her on several occasions during one of his drunken rages, and she would never allow herself to depend on a man again. Besides, she was seventy-three years old. No man would want her at this age, nor she him.

She had her mercantile and the two extra rooms above it that she rented out to travelers or new settlers. She owned her property, thanks to her drunken bastard dead husband, and she could take care of herself now.

Even better, no one could come along and force her off the property. She had the deed locked safely away, proving that she owned it, free and clear. Never again would she be without a home.

Mr. Fowler reached her side, out of breath, and had to take a moment to wipe his brow with the handkerchief he kept in his front pocket. "Good morning to you, Mrs. Styles. It's going to be a hot one this day, don't you think?"

Sorcha made small talk with the younger man and, as soon as she could politely do so, steered the conversation to its point, as she was eager to get back to her shop. "What can I do for you, Mr. Fowler?"

"Ah yes." He looked over his shoulder as though expecting his wife to suddenly appear from the hedge. When he faced her again, he lowered his voice. "I was wondering if, perhaps, you might add a bolt of silk to the order my wife placed yesterday. I'd like to surprise her for her birthday next month."

Sorcha smiled thinking of how Mrs. Fowler had fondled the silks yesterday in the shop but had ordered only the practical linen. "Of course, Mr. Fowler. Would you like to come to the shop to choose a color?"

He paled and looked decidedly uncomfortable. "Oh no, I wouldn't know where to start. I'll leave it to you ladies. You know what Mrs. Fowler would like much more than I."

"Of course." Sorcha patted the man on his arm. "We'll choose something lovely for her."

She'd almost made it to her shop when she heard her name called again.

"Sorcha!"

She turned, startled that someone would call out her given name when everyone she knew called her by her married name.

But no one was there. No one approached her.

Deciding it must have been her imagination, she shook her head and resumed walking.

"Sorcha Chisholm Ross, come here!"

She froze. Her heart pounded loudly in her ears as she turned in all directions to look for the person—the woman—calling to her. It was a name she had not heard in a very long time. Not since Srath Ghlais, in fact.

"Sorcha, stop. Come here before you dirty your dress."

A little girl of only two or three raced around the corner of the ship chandlery coming straight toward Sorcha, followed closely by her exasperated mother. The woman wore a rose-colored gown, which looked lovely with her pale complexion and blond hair, though her cheeks were reddened and her hat askew.

Without thinking, Sorcha stepped right into the path of the little girl before she could evade her mother again. "Good morning." Sorcha smiled, charmed by the flash of rebellion in the girl's green eyes. "Where are you off to in such a hurry?"

The girl clearly hadn't expected a stranger to talk to her, because she stopped running to stare up at Sorcha in confusion. Her chubby fingers twisted in the cotton of her knee-length dress.

"Sorcha, do not run away from us like that." The woman caught up to her daughter and grabbed her hand before the girl could escape again. Then she smiled at the adult Sorcha, out of breath. "I cannot thank you enough. I don't know how I would've caught her if she'd kept running."

Only when the woman placed a hand on her bulging belly did Sorcha realize she was expecting. No wonder she'd had trouble catching her daughter.

"Did you say her name is Sorcha?" She couldn't help but ask. It wasn't a popular name, after all.

Dimples flashed in the woman's reddened cheeks. "Yes, it was my husband's mother's name. It means brightness, or light, and our wee girl has certainly brought light to our lives. Oh, here he comes now."

Sorcha looked beyond the woman to see a tall man dressed in a black suit striding toward them, carrying a hatbox under one arm and a leather satchel in each hand. Instantly, she knew him, and a sob caught in her throat.

The man's lips were pressed together, and his worried gaze was on his daughter. "Dinna run away, *a ghràidh*. 'Tis not safe."

Sorcha clutched her trembling hands together at her chest. She had to swallow the emotion clogging her throat before she could squeak out his name. "Aonghas?"

The man's head snapped up, his eyes wide. Eyes that Sorcha hadn't seen in many years. She saw the moment when he recognized her. "Ma?"

She nodded, then reached for him as tears blinded her. He dropped his bags right on the street and launched himself into her arms.

Her boy. Her sweet Aonghas. He was here! Sobs tore from her throat as she buried her head into his chest and squeezed him tight. "Oh, my heart, my boy. I never thought I'd see you again."

His body shook in her arms, and she knew he was crying, too. Her big, strong son was back in her arms, and she never wanted to let him go again. He smelled of the sea, and soap, and tar from a ship. For a long time she couldn't speak. For a long time she couldn't release him. It had been too long, too many years, since she'd held him. All she wanted to do was hold him and breathe him in.

When they finally pulled apart, Aonghas looked at her in wonder. "I thought you were dead. I looked everywhere for you. Every port, every city I ever visited."

Sorcha held tightly to both his hands, noting the calluses there and how much bigger they were than when she'd touched him last. She took in all the other changes she could see in him. He wore a closely trimmed beard now, and his cheekbones stood out sharper than when he was young. His auburn hair was lighter from the sun, and longer, but still tended to fall into his eyes. She could not stop herself from pushing a lock back to tuck behind his ear. "I have a lot to tell you, son. But first, can you introduce me to your family?" Her tongue slid over the Gaelic like an old lover. She hadn't spoken it in too many years to count.

Aonghas's eyes warmed as he turned to his wife, and Sorcha's heart swelled. Her boy had found love. It was what she'd wanted most for him. This alone made all her hardships worthwhile.

"Ma, I'd like you to meet Rebecca, my wife."

Sorcha finally tore her gaze from her son and found his wife smiling at her with tears running down her cheeks. Sorcha kept hold of one of Aonghas's hands and dragged him forward so she could properly meet his wife without letting go of him. Switching back to English, she said, "Rebecca, I'm so pleased to meet you." She leaned forward and kissed the younger woman's cheek, smelling jasmine as she did so, and then she grabbed her free hand. "So pleased."

Aonghas ducked his head to look into her face. "Ma, you learned English!"

She laughed and nodded. "And so, it seems, did you."

"Aye, I'm American now. Captain of a whaling ship."

That got Sorcha's attention, and she returned her full attention to her son. "You got your adventures. You said you wanted to see more of the world."

His smile warmed and she knew he was feeling the joy of being known by someone. He was still so much her little boy, pushing out his chest with pride. "I've been around the whole world, Ma. First with Captain Malcomb, who ended up not selling my contract and kept me on his ship as a crewmember, and then with other merchants and whalers. Now I've got my own crew."

"I'm so proud of you." Sorcha could not imagine a life at sea, as her journey here had been brutal. But maybe it wasn't so bad if Aonghas loved it so much, and even took his family with him.

"What of you, Ma? Why are you here?"

Only then did Sorcha realize they still stood on the street. Neighbors and strangers alike were passing by, eyeing them with curiosity. She wiped the tears from her face and laughed. "Oh, I have so much to tell you, my boy. But let's get out of the sun. My shop and home are just there." She pointed across the road.

Aonghas looked to where she pointed, and his eyes widened. "The mercantile and inn? That is yours?"

She nodded and went to grab the hatbox from where it had fallen in the dirt. "Yes, and I'd love for you to stay with me if you can. Unless you need to be going?" Her gaze darted toward the harbor, where she knew his ship must be at anchor. She found herself shaking again as she waited for his answer.

Aonghas took the hatbox from her and placed one warm palm against the side of her face. "I can't believe I found you. I'm not going anywhere, Ma."

With her heart near to bursting, Sorcha led her family home.

AUTHOR'S NOTES

The Highland Clearances are viewed as a particularly brutal era when entire populations were removed in one fell swoop to be replaced by sheep. The story depicted in this book is not representative of all the Clearances, but of what might've been one woman's experience. I did my best to write Sorcha's story as accurate to the events and era as possible, but know that her story is fiction. The Chisholm chief did clear his people from Strathglass in 1801, but with little information to go on, I gave to Sorcha an experience that was an amalgamation of several people's experiences around the Highlands. Any misrepresentations of the Clearances and any errors in the depiction of Scotland in 1801 are my own.

During a time when many parts of Europe were experiencing agricultural reforms, the changes hit particularly hard in the Scottish Highlands, where deep cultural shifts were also occurring, mostly by force. After the Battle of Culloden in 1746, when the Jacobite uprising was squashed for the last time, the British government made it illegal for Scots to wear Highland clothing such as kilts, or have in their possession any weapons. Many clan chiefs who supported Bonnie Prince Charlie were stripped of their holdings, although many of those were returned in the 1780s. Still, the clan chiefs and landowners who did retain their lands were required to spend the bulk of their time in London, where the government could keep an eye on them. In fact, the English government had imposed similar requirements since the Statutes of Iona in 1609, which, in part, demanded that Scottish landowners educate their heirs in England. This all had the effect of clan chiefs completely losing touch with their people, homeland, and customs. As older landowners died and their sons inherited, many chiefs didn't know a single soul by name in their Highland homelands, nor did they know the Gaelic language. So when these chiefs started hearing that sheep could be the answer to their financial woes, they saw no moral issue with forcing people off the land and replacing them with the animals.

The community, on the other hand, saw it very differently. For centuries folks worked communally to raise crops and animals. When a neighboring clan or outside force threatened, clan members fought beside the clan chief. The chief looked out for the good of all his people, and in return they were of service to him whenever called. To the people, the land belonged to all of them. They all had family members who gave their lives in service to the chief, who now thought he could evict them like strangers.

Some Clearances weren't recorded in history. Some happened peacefully. Some involved terrible brutality. All were horrific to the people evicted.

Once forced out of their homes, some people were encouraged to settle in coastal communities and take up fishing or kelp harvesting, with no training or equipment. Before 1830, the government actively discouraged emigration by making it outrageously expensive. They did this because they needed men to join the military to fight the Napoleonic Wars, among others. This meant that the people evicted in these earlier years couldn't afford to start new lives elsewhere, and instead had to carve out new lives in Scotland on inferior land or in crowded cities.

Some great resources for reading more about the Clearances include:

- *The Highland Clearances* by Eric Richards (academic, well researched)
- *The Highland Clearances* by John Prebble (seen by some scholars as a biased and sometimes false accounting, but is best at explaining the emotional impact on the people)

───

This story was influenced by numerous sources, but one very enjoyable read was the diary written by Dorothy Wordsworth, sister to the famous poet William Wordsworth, who traveled in Scotland with her brother two years after my story takes place: *Recollections of a Tour Made in Scotland A.D. 1803.* Many of Dorothy's observations have made their way into my story, such as the description of Kingshouse Hotel and the ferryman's house at Inversnaid. One detail that Dorothy observed was that most of the Highland women she encountered were barefoot, a detail I confirmed in other sources as well. As a result, I knew that Sorcha would be going about her chores in late May without shoes. She would have planned to slip into her only pair of shoes before going to the Whitsunday church service that morning, but, alas, she ended up losing them in the fire and so had nothing to protect her feet during her long walk.

───

The term *plaide*, or "plaid," probably instills in some readers the idea of a particular pattern especially associated with '90s grunge. Highlanders, however, used the term to refer to a blanket, often woven with a tartan pattern, and worn as an outer garment by both men and women. The Gaelic word is *plaide*, pronounced "plahtcheh." The plural form is *plaideachan*, pronounced "plahtchuhan."

───

If you are interested in Scottish Gaelic or would like to hear the pronunciation of any Gaelic words you encountered in this story, I encourage you to visit the dictionary at www.learngaelic.scot.

⁓

Speaking of the Scottish Gaelic language, as a learner myself, I thought I could do the translation of a passage I wrote for the scenes that take place on the top of Conic Hill. I originally had Sorcha saying something along the lines of "My bones are of the stone, my blood of the rain . . . I am of the Highlands," and so on. When I sent the phrase to a professional Gaelic translator, however, he informed me that the sentiment is not translatable to Gaelic. I'm so glad I asked a professional! He suggested that I instead use an existing song or poem, or hire someone to write a bespoke poem. Many thanks to Michael Bauer of Akerbeltz Translation for stopping me from making a huge mistake and for introducing me to Gillebrìde MacMillan (singer, writer, poet, actor, language consultant for *Outlander*). It was Gillebrìde who wrote the beautiful poem, a part of which appears in the Conic Hill scenes. *Mòran taing do Mhìcheal agus do Ghillebrìde!* Below is the full text of his poem:

Air Cnocan na Còinnich
fo làimh Gillebrìde Mac ÍlleMhaoil

An till mise chaoidh gu Gàidhhealtachd mo rùin
Far an cluinnte a'Ghàidhlig air bilean a daoin'
Le seallaidhean bòidheach a-nis ri mi dhrùim
Gum bris e mo chridhe 's gun tig tost air ar fuinn.

'S ann agam tha sealladh 's mi aig àirde an-dràst
Air Cnocan na Còinnich 's mo chridhe-sa cràidht'

Thionndaidh mi thugaibh—gach beann agus srath-
Is 's e mo dhùrachd 's mo bheannachd gum bi sibh ann slàn.

On Conic Hill
by Gillebrìde MacMillan

Will I ever return to my beloved Highlands
Where Gaelic can be heard on the lips of its people
With beautiful views now at my back
It breaks my heart and makes our melodies fall silent.

What a view I have now, being at great height now
On Conic Hill with a broken heart
I have turned to you—each ben and glen,
And my dearest wish and desire is that you will be healthy there.

Scottish Gaelic Place Names

A' Chrìon-Làraich: Crianlarich
Abhainn Chluaidh: River Clyde
Abhainn Ghlais: River Glass
Alba Nuadh: Nova Scotia
An Gearasdan: Fort William
An Gleann Mòr: The Great Glen
An Tairbeart: Tarbert
An t-Òban: Oban
Baile a' Chaolais: Ballachulish

Beinn Nibheis: Ben Nevis
Cill Fhinn: Killin
Craoibh: Crieff
Dùn Èideann: Edinburgh
Glaschu: Glasgow
Gleann Canaich: Glen Cannich
Gleann Comhann: Glen Coe
Gleann Falach: Glen Falloch
Gleann Nibheis: Glen Nevis
Gleanna Garradh: Glengarry
Inbhir Àirnein: Inverarnan
Inbhir Dhòbhran: Inveroran
Inbhir Snàthaid: Inversnaid
Loch Afraig: Loch Affric
Loch Aircleit: Loch Arklet
Loch Cuaich: Loch Quoich
Loch Garadh: Loch Garry
Loch Laomainn: Loch Lomond
Loch Lìobhann: Loch Leven
Loch Tatha: Loch Tay
Loch Toilbhe: Loch Tulla
Lunnainn: London
Mòinteach Raineach: Rannoch Moor
Muileann-Gaidh: Milngavie
Peairt: Perth
Srath Ghlais: Strathglass
Taigh an Droma: Tyndrum
Uisge Leamhain: River Leven

GLOSSARY

Scottish Gaelic

*To hear pronunciation of Gaelic words, go to http://learngaelic.scot/dictionary.

A chàraidean: "My friends."

A ghràidh: a term of endearment meaning "my dear" or "my love"

Amadan gòrach gòrach, amadan gòrach saighdear . . . chunna mi 'g òl a-raoir thu . . . : A fun gaelic tune. These lines translate to: "Silly, silly fool. Silly fool of a soldier. I saw you drinking last night . . ."

An Siosal: the Chisholm (the name given to the chief of Clan Chisholm)

Cèilidh: literally translates to "a visit," but has come to refer more to a party featuring music, storytelling, visiting with friends, and often drinking

Cèilidhean: the plural form of cèilidh

Ciamar a tha sibh?: "How are you?"

Ciste: a large chest or trunk

Cò às a tha sibh?: "Where are you from?"

Contrachd ort!: "Curses on you!"

Crodh-laoigh nam Bodach: A traditional Gaelic milking song. The title translates to: The old man is milking (or calving) cows.

Deas: south

Dùthchas: A word that translates as "place of birth, heredity, birth-tie" but carries much deeper meaning about the connection and unity between land and people, natural heritage, and cultural belonging. It also refers to the medieval custom that fairly divides up land between families of the clan and gives rights to inherit land that one's ancestors lived on. No written deed of occupation existed, but if you've had three generations on one piece of land, then that's your right to live there (the specific number of generations may change depending on century and specific clan).

Fàilte gu: "Welcome to . . ."

Feasgar math: "Good afternoon/evening."

Fèileadh-mòr: A great kilt; a large piece of fabric wrapped around the body and secured at the waist with a belt. Most-common dress for men from the sixteenth to eighteenth centuries. The knee-length kilt most often seen today is called "fèileadh-beag," or "small kilt."

Gabhaibh mo leisgeul: "Excuse me."

Gàidhlig: Gaelic

Glaistig: a supernatural, malevolent being of the Scottish Highlands, sometimes called Maighdeann Uaine (the Green Maiden)

Iomairibh eutrom hò rò . . . Huraibh o na hoireanan . . . : A traditional rowing song. These lines translate to: "Row lightly, ho ro . . ." The *ho ro* and the second line are vocables that don't mean anything, like when we sing *fa la la*.

Ist: "Hush."

Loch: lake

M'eudail: "My dear."

Madainn mhath: "Good morning."

Mar sin leat: "Goodbye."

Mòran taing: "Thank you," or "Many thanks."

Obh obh: "Oh dear!"

Och: a noise like a sigh

Plaide: a blanket

Plaideachan: blankets (plural)

Sèis: a wooden bench

Sgian-dubh: Literally translates to "black knife" or "secret knife" and refers to a small knife with the blade on one side, traditionally worn in a boot or sock. In modern day, it is the knife worn in one sock when wearing a kilt.

Slàinte: "Cheers!" Literal translation: Health.

Slighe na Gàidhealtachd an Iar: West Highland Way

Suas leis a' Ghàidhlig: "Up with Gaelic."

Tapadh leibh: "Thank you."

Tha Fionnlagh ag ionnearadh, tha Fionnlagh leis a'bhriogais odhar: A traditional song. The lyrics translate to: "Finlay is spreading manure, Finlay with his dun-colored trousers."

Tha Gàidhlig agad: "I speak Gaelic." Literal translation: I have Gaelic.

Tha mi à Aimearaga: "I am from America."

∽

Scots English (and Some British)

Aye: yes

Bothy: a basic shelter left unlocked and available for use by anyone, typically hunters or hikers

Burn: a creek or small stream

Byre: a shed for animals, either attached to the house or detached

Clarty: muddy, dirty, messy

Close: a narrow passage or alley

Cuppa: a cup of tea

Craic: fun; an enjoyable conversation

Culpable homicide: A criminal verdict given when the defendant has caused the death of another person without the intent to kill. Similar to manslaughter in the United States.

Daunderin: walking

Dinna: don't

Dirk: a long-bladed thrusting dagger

Dram: a small drink of whisky

Eejit: idiot

Fankle: a tangle, a muddle

Feckin' bampot: effing unhinged idiot

Fecking: effing; the "f" word

Flaughter spade: a flat spade used in peat cutting

Fleysome: frightening

Ghillie: A Highland chief's attendant; a servant who attends to one on a hunting or fishing expedition. Literal translation of the Gaelic *gille* (from which *Ghillie* is derived) is "lad."

Glen: valley

Gloaming: twilight

Heid: head

Hogmanay: New Year's Eve

Jockey: an iron rod with an S bend at the top, used to hold kettles and pots with handles over the fire

Kelpie: A water horse. If you ride on its back, it will drag you under and drown you.

Ken: know

Kent: knew

Lad: boy

Lass: girl

Lochan: a small lake

Moor: a tract of open, uncultivated land

Munro: one of the 277 mountains in Scotland that are at least three thousand feet high

Peely-wally: not feeling well, pale

Sair aff: badly off

Sheep fank: a walled or fenced pen for sheep

Spurtle: a wooden stick used for stirring porridge

Strath: a wide river valley

Waulk, waulking: The fulling process; a process in the production of wool cloth that involves soaking the cloth (in urine or water) and then working/beating it to make it fuller and tighter. Historically done by a group of women sitting around a table, grasping the cloth in both hands and pounding it on the table as a "waulking song" is sung.

Wee: little, small

Ye: you

Yin: one

DISCUSSION QUESTIONS

1. Sorcha and Keaka were connected numerous times throughout the story, and sometimes even when one or both didn't notice. Have you ever considered that your own random or coincidental experiences might be something more? Discuss.
2. Both Keaka and Sorcha walk along what is today known as the West Highland Way. What was your favorite location along the path? Would you ever consider walking this long-distance trail? Would you sleep in bed-and-breakfasts, or would you camp? Is there a different region of the world that you would like to explore on foot this way?
3. Colin inherited his love of Scotland from his father, Adam, who, in turn, received the same from his grandmother. Talk about any passions passed down through the generations of your own family.
4. Did you want Keaka and Jorgen to get together? How do you feel about how their relationship was left at the end of the story? Do you think they have a future together?
5. Do you think there is something special in the mother-son relationship or the father-daughter relationship?

Why or why not?

6. This is a story of mothers and sons. How do you think the stories might have been different if Aonghas or Colin had been a daughter?

7. Keaka learned to love hiking and she came to love Scotland, both of which surprised her. Have you ever traveled in a place that changed you in some meaningful way?

8. To Sorcha, "home" was Strathglass and the Scottish Highlands. She felt a visceral connection to the rocks, lochs, trees, people, and animals. To Keaka, "home" is being with the people she loves who also love her back. What is "home" to you?

9. Were you familiar with the Scottish Clearances before reading this story? Do you think the Clearances were a necessary agricultural reform, or do you fall closer to those on the other end of the debate who claim they were an ethnic cleansing? If you were a clan chief at the time, would you have cleared your land of all its people? What other ways might you have found to increase income without the devastating impact to your people?

10. Keaka and Colin discuss how terrible it was for the Scottish people to be displaced by sheep, and how many of them immigrated to America and Australia, where they displaced the Indigenous people there. People today are being displaced all around the world due to wars, famines, and numerous other reasons, yet many countries are tightening their immigration laws. Where do you think people who have lost their homeland should go? If you were a policy maker in your own country, how would you like to see immigration handled?

11. Keaka observes that Americans are into genealogy because the United States is so young and made up of immigrants. Other than Native Americans, the people all

came from somewhere else and they may lack that soul-deep connection to a place or a community that people have in older countries with a long, known history. She says that Americans are "hungry to belong, and we think we'll find that by learning where our people came from." Do you think this is true? Why or why not?

12. Keaka reaches a point where she is heartsick over the cruelties humans perpetuate on one another, and she is quite happy to be walking on a lonely moor, far away from anyone else. Have you ever felt similarly? What are some ideas you have on how we humans can all learn to be kinder to one another?

13. Do you feel more connected to Sorcha or to Keaka? Why?

14. If you were evicted from your home and had no family or friends to help you, what would you do? Where would you go?

15. Sorcha came from a culture that was actively suppressed, and even vilified, by the ruling class. A big part of that culture is the Scottish Gaelic language. Some today think that the language should die away. What do you think, and why? What are some reasons for working to keep Indigenous languages in use? If another government came into power in your country and told you that you had to speak only their language (as the English did in Scotland), would you comply?

16. The *Oxford English Dictionary* defines second sight as "a supposed power by which occurrences in the future or things at a distance are perceived as though they were actually present." Aonghas and Sorcha wonder if she has the ability, and after Colin tells her about the sight, Keaka wonders if that explains her experiences. Do you believe that second sight is possible? Do you think this explains the connection between Sorcha and Keaka? If

not the sight, what do you think explains the women's connection?

17. Sorcha has experienced great loss, which makes her cling tightly to her last remaining child. In her shoes, would you have made the same decision for Aonghas at the end, or would you have done something different? What would you do?
18. Have you ever traveled solo, and did you enjoy it? If you have not traveled solo, do you think you would like to some day? Where would you go?
19. What do you think happens next for Keaka? Where will she be in one year? In five years?
20. What do you think happens next for Sorcha? What do you think her coming years look like?

ACKNOWLEDGMENTS

I often say that I am poorly suited for any job other than writing. This fact makes me eternally grateful to you, my reader, for choosing my books and for encouraging your friends to read them, too. To booksellers, librarians, journalists, book bloggers, Instagrammers, and everyone who works with books, thank you from the bottom of my heart for putting my books into readers hands.

To my writing community—Pat White, Carolynn Estes, Stephanie Christenson, Laurie London, Becky Clark, Carla Crujido—all those encouraging texts and emails, hours writing in coffee shops, walking and talking plot, or brainstorming over lunch have often made the difference in me getting words on the page or not. Thank you! It helps to not feel so alone in what is primarily a solo endeavor.

It is common to see an author thank her agent, but I have so much more to thank mine for with this book. Beth Miller, thank you for being the person to introduce long-distance hiking in Scotland to me! It was your stories and photos from your WHW hike that inspired me to go, and it was you so generously agreeing to my company on the East Highland Way that finally got me out there. I love that we share a passion for Scotland. Thank you so much for all your work in refining this story and finding it a home.

Thank you to the team at Lake Union. To my editors, Melissa Valentine, Carissa Bluestone, and Ali Castleman, thank you for seeing the potential of this story and helping me get it in the hands of readers. To my developmental editor, Charlotte Herscher, thank you for your gentle guidance in making the story stronger. Working with you reminded me how much I love the revision process. To my copyeditor, Rachel Norfleet, thank you for correcting all my errors and misused commas. And thank you for catching all the times I mixed up *further* and *farther*. Many thanks to Jill Schoenhaut, my proofreader, for expertly catching word echoes and the many small details that I would have otherwise missed. To the art department, marketing department, sales team, and everyone else working behind the scenes at Lake Union, it certainly takes a village, and I'm so happy that you are a part of mine. I appreciate each of you!

To my Scottish Gaelic community—*Slighe nan Gàidheal*, Duolingo, and all my Gaelic-speaking friends—thank you for sharing your love of the Gaelic language and culture. To some it may seem like a random interest, but Gaelic has brought so much joy and so many amazing people into my life. Many of you answered my numerous questions about the language, poems, and music, for which I am deeply grateful. Thank you to Barbara Simonds, Seumas Gagne, Mary Ann Kennedy, Stacey Giermann, Aaron Malcomb, Mallie Steele, Penny DeGraff, and anyone else whose name I have forgotten! *Mòran taing, a chàraidean! Suas leis a' Ghàidhlig!*

To Michael Bauer of Akerbeltz Translation, thank you for telling me that the translation I wanted would not work in Gaelic, and for guiding me to Gillebrìde MacMillan for a bespoke poem.

To Gillebrìde Macmillan (Gillebrìde Mac'IlleMhaoil), thank you for your beautiful poem "Air Cnocan na Còinnich (On Conic Hill)," which fit my story perfectly. I look forward to the day when we can meet in person!

Thank you to Katie Schmierbach for answering my long list of questions about being a student at the University of Glasgow. Any errors are my own.

To everyone who has walked or is planning a walk on one of Scotland's trails, including the West Highland Way, thank you for generously sharing your tips on Facebook groups, thank you for your warm greetings and friendship on the trails, and thank you for caring for the trails so that they will endure. Leave only footprints, take only memories. To the West Highland Way Management Group and everyone involved in the expensive and difficult work of maintaining the trail, thank you! I am so grateful for all that you do. On a more personal note, many thanks to the friends who walked Scotland's trails with me: Beth, Iris, Bob, Allie, Alex, Christine, Vikki, Ed, Fred and Buri, Kevin and Bonnie, Chad, Riley, and everyone whose names I forgot. We helped each other through the miles, and I treasure those memories. I would be remiss if I neglected to also thank Thistle Trekking for coordinating each of my Scotland walks. You made our adventures run very smoothly and I am so grateful.

Thank you to my husband, Chad, for being the best dad I could have ever wanted for my boys, and for always supporting my writing goals and my crazy ideas to head off to Scotland and go for a hike. A twenty-mile day isn't that bad, right?

From the deepest part of my heart, thank you to my two boys, Riley and Rowan. You have each taught me so much about life, and I feel truly honored to be your mom. I love you so much.

ABOUT THE AUTHOR

Photo © 2024 Jackie Phairow Photography

Kelli Estes is the *USA Today* bestselling author of *The Girl Who Wrote in Silk*, which has been translated into twelve languages, was the recipient of the Pacific Northwest Writers Association Nancy Pearl Book Award and the Women's Fiction Writers Association STAR Award, and is currently under option for film/TV; and *Today We Go Home*, a nationwide Target Book Club pick. Kelli is passionate about stories that show how history is still relevant to our lives today. Her lifelong love of Scotland has her learning the Scottish Gaelic language and the Scottish fiddle (both badly, but she's working on it). She has walked three of Scotland's long-distance trails (so far) and is currently planning the next. Kelli lives in Washington State with her husband and two sons. For more information, visit www.kelliestes.com.